SPELL OF THE SENSES

Cranwell's eyes strayed to Sarah's lips. And she knew what was going to happen. But her mind was not in control. It was a moment for physical sensation.

There was instant familiarity in his kiss. There was the molding of her body to his as if they had been made to fit into each other's arms. There was the firm warmth of his mouth opened slightly over hers and the surprising strength of his arms crushing her to him. And there was that almost instant surge of heat and passion that blanked her mind to all rational thought and set her to clinging to him and tilting her head and aching to bring him closer, closer.

She did not know how long their embrace lasted. She was jerked back from a timeless world of passionate longing when he pushed her from him and held her away with one hand gripped painfully on her arms.

"God!" he said. "You witch, Sarah. You devil!"

And she had to wonder how this man she loved could both desire and despise her so at the same time. . . .

D1716156

Secrets of the Heart

Mary Balogh

A SIGNET BOOK

To Mildred Jenkins,
my mother,
with all my love

SIGNET
Published by the Penguin Group
Penguin Books USA Inc., 375 Hudson Street,
New York, New York 10014, U.S.A.
Penguin Books Ltd, 27 Wrights Lane,
London W8 5TZ, England
Penguin Books Australia Ltd, Ringwood,
Victoria, Australia
Penguin Books Canada Ltd, 10 Alcorn Avenue,
Toronto, Ontario, Canada M4V 3B2
Penguin Books (N.Z.) Ltd, 182–190 Wairau Road,
Auckland 10, New Zealand

Penguin Books Ltd, Registered Offices:
Harmondsworth, Middlesex, England

Published by Signet, an imprint of Dutton Signet,
a division of Penguin Books USA Inc.

First Printing, April, 1988
11 10 9 8 7 6 5 4 3

 REGISTERED TRADEMARK—MARCA REGISTRADA

Printed in the United States of America

BOOKS ARE AVAILABLE AT QUANTITY DISCOUNTS WHEN USED TO PROMOTE PRODUCTS OR
SERVICES. FOR INFORMATION PLEASE WRITE TO PREMIUM MARKETING DIVISION, PENGUIN
BOOKS USA INC., 375 HUDSON STREET, NEW YORK, NEW YORK 10014.

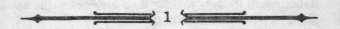

1

THE CITY of Bath during late summer was crowded with visitors from the fashionable world. At nine o'clock in the morning it was already alive with activity. The focal point of it all was the Pump Room, close to the imposing Abbey and next to the baths, the only hot springs in all England. The Pump Room itself was a long, high, elegant room with tall, arched windows stretching down its length, those on one side looking down on the King's Bath, in which many bathers sat immersed to the neck for the sake of their health. Also on that side of the room were vendors selling glasses of the sulfur water, also for the health of the drinkers.

Yet crowded as the room was, it was not full of invalids. This was the fashionable place to be before breakfast, a place where one might promenade and show off one's attire and admire or criticize that of others, where one might see or be seen, gossip or be gossiped about. An orchestra played from an upper gallery, but it is unlikely that many of the strollers paid it much attention.

Two ladies were not walking with the rest. Lady Adelaide Murdoch, an elderly widow, was seated at one end of the room, a glass of water in one hand, a lace handkerchief clutched in the other. The expression of distaste on her face suggested that she was finding her morning drink somewhat disagreeable.

"Bah!" she said to the young lady who stood at her shoulder. "If the Reverend Peabody had not told me himself that the waters would work miracles for my rheumaticks and my digestion, I should say that this was all a clever hoax. Water sellers, bath attendants, subscription collectors: everyone"—the hand that held the linen swept in an arc to encompass the whole of Bath around them—"making their fortunes at the expense of poor unfortunates like me."

"Perhaps when you have finished drinking, ma'am," her companion suggested calmly, "you would like to lean on me and take a turn about the room. I see Colonel Smythe and his lady farther along, and Mrs. Marchmont and her daughter said they would be here this morning. I expect they will arrive soon. You know you enjoy some lively conversation. It will take your mind off the ghastly taste of the water. Really, ma'am, I think you are downright heroic to take two glasses each day."

"Much good it does me, too," Lady Murdoch grumbled, "except to make my pockets lighter and to fill the purses of these thieves." She glared accusingly into her glass, wrinkled her nose in disgust, and sipped grimly at the contents again.

Miss Sarah Fifield gazed around her with some interest. The room was become familiar to her after a week of daily visits, and the people in it were also taking on names and characters. With several she was acquainted. It was easy to make acquaintances in Bath, she found. It was a policy of the masters of ceremony to promote an intermingling of the visitors. Private parties were discouraged, as was a cliquish clinging together of people of high *ton*. Everyone was expected to frequent the public places: the Pump Room, the Upper and Lower Assembly Rooms, and the parks.

Sarah was beginning to feel relaxed; she was almost enjoying herself. And that was certainly an unexpected development. She had not wanted to come to Bath, had shrunk from the prospect in some horror, in fact. She could not remember feeling enjoyment in four years. But she was beginning to feel that after all, her secret would not be found out, that perhaps she could accept the pleasure of these few weeks before retiring to obscurity again. Obscurity was really the only safe way of life for her, the only possible one.

She had lived in obscurity for four years, alone with the exception of Dorothy, her servant since before she had been orphaned. And she had learned contentment, if not happiness there in that little cottage. There she had recovered some of her self-respect, some of her confidence. And she would have been contented to stay there, occupying herself with her needlework, her books, and her garden, consoling herself with her close friendship with the Reverend Clarence and his wife. And she would be living there still if it were not for that fiend Winston Bowen. Thanks to him she had suddenly found herself without money, and she had been forced to seek employment.

She had sent an advertisement to the London papers in an effort to obtain a situation as a governess. She had had a totally unexpected reply from Lady Murdoch, childless widow of a baronet, claiming that she believed herself to be a relative and asking if Sarah was the daughter of David Fifield. A few days after Sarah had written to confirm this fact, Lady Murdoch had arrived on her doorstep, leaning her considerable weight on the shoulder of a liveried footman. She was delighted, she had said, to discover the daughter of her favorite cousin's son.

It had seemed a very distant relationship to Sarah, but Lady Murdoch had insisted on making much of it. She had no one of her own. Not that she was lonely, she had hastened to explain. But sometimes it was provoking to hear her acquaintances boast of their children and grandchildren when she had no one. She realized that Sarah must be in desperate straits if she was prepared to hire herself out as a governess. She wanted Sarah to come and live with her.

"I need a companion, you see, dear cousin," she had said in her strident voice, "and it will be all the better if she is a young relative. Will you come?"

Sarah had hesitated. "Perhaps you would care to

employ me, ma'am?" she had suggested at last. "I really could not be so beholden to you as to do nothing in return for your kindness."

"Employ a relative!" Lady Murdoch had exclaimed, appalled. "Nonsense, cousin. I would prefer to consider you the daughter I never had. Granddaughter would probably be the more appropriate relationship, for I am sure I am old enough to be your grandmama. But forgive an old woman's vanity. It seems such a short time since I was of an age with you. How old are you, cousin?"

"Three-and-twenty, ma'am," Sarah had replied.

"Three-and-twenty!" Lady Murdoch had repeated. "What is your aunt Bowen thinking of to allow you to live alone at that tender age? I understand that you were under your uncle's guardianship after your dear papa passed away?"

Sarah had nodded and held her breath. Had Lady Murdoch also heard of the great scandal? But she had concluded almost immediately that she could not have. She surely would not have come if she had.

The outcome of the visit was that Sarah had packed up her belongings and moved away to Devonshire with Lady Murdoch. She was amazed to think that this distant cousin was prepared to take her in with so little knowledge of what she was like. She judged that Lady Murdoch was far more lonely a person than she would admit.

And Sarah had found herself treated like a daughter from the start. She took her position as companion seriously and would have far preferred to be paid for doing that job, to have been merely an employee. As it was, she had had a new wardrobe and numerous trinkets showered on her, as well as pin money, which she found impossible to refuse.

When Lady Murdoch had announced that they were to go to Bath Spa in late summer, when a large portion of the fashionable world would be present, she was horrified and thought of all sorts of excuses to be left behind. She could not go into society. Her secret would be found out in a day. It was true that she had changed her name, or at least resumed her real name rather than her uncle's name of Bowen, which she had taken on to please him when she moved into his house on the death of her father. But she had done nothing else to cover her tracks. It needed only one person to discover the truth and all of Bath would know in no time at all.

She had agonized over whether to tell Lady Murdoch the whole truth or not. She should have done so at the start. But finally she had decided to take the risk. She had heard that Bath was not quite as fashionable as it had used to be. Most of the late-summer visitors were reputed to be older people. Going to Bath, then, would not be quite like going to London. She would not have dared go there.

But for the first few days she had been terrified. She had expected everyone she passed to turn and point an accusing finger at her, and she had cringed from introductions to acquaintances of Lady Murdoch or to new acquaintances presented by the master of ceremonies of one of the assembly rooms. And miraculously no one seemed to realize that she was different from everyone else. No one had come to order her to leave Bath and all respectable society.

She had been timid, almost ashamed at first, about meeting new people, knowing that she had no right to be in their company. But soon enough she had discovered some exhilaration in being accepted as any normal human being and in being admired. She knew she was beautiful; she knew that her generous figure and masses of red hair were unusually attractive. She had never been proud of these attributes. In fact, they had been directly responsible for her downfall. But suddenly she found it a heady experience to be sought out by the few young and attractive people who were in the city, and to be smiled at indulgently by the older friends her cousin was making.

It was all wrong, of course; she knew that. But she was not intending to make any permanent connections. After a few weeks she would leave behind all these people and never see them again. Surely it could not be wrong to enjoy those few weeks. There had been so little of joy in her life. Her youth had been cut very short. She had been barely nineteen . . .

Thus Sarah looked around the Pump Room with interest.

"Yoo-hoo!" Lady Murdoch called suddenly, making Sarah start with surprise. She winced as she watched her cousin wave her handkerchief in the direction of a gentleman who had just entered the Pump Room.

Several eyes turned in the direction of the two ladies, including those of the gentleman who had been hailed. He smiled, crossed the room, and bowed elegantly before them. He took Lady Murdoch's hand, handkerchief and all, into his own kid-gloved one, and raised it to his lips.

"My dear Lady Murdoch," he said, "you are becoming hardly recognizable. The waters are reputed only to heal infirmities, not to rejuvenate. But I swear you look years younger than when I saw you two days ago."

Lady Murdoch threw back her head and barked with laughter. She appeared quite oblivious of the eyes and quizzing glasses that again turned in her direction.

"Famous!" she said. "You should have been on the stage, Mr. Phelps. I have been telling you so these twenty years, since my dear departed husband first bought those horses from you in London. Both lame! And if I really had lost all the years you always claim, I should be an infant in my mother's arms again."

Mr. Phelps smiled and twirled in his hands the top hat that he had removed from his head. He looked at Sarah. "Ah, the divine Miss Fifield," he said, bowing again. "Still breaking hearts by the score, I do not doubt. Or am I the only one whose invitations to walk and drive you consistently refuse, cruel one?"

Sarah made him a half-curtsy. "Milsom Street is strewn with them, sir," she said. "With broken hearts,

I mean. I am afraid there is little I can do about it. My time and attention are all devoted to the care of Lady Murdoch."

The lady in question crowed with laughter again. "A hit!" she said. "Come, you must admit it, sir. Now, do tell me, is it true that Lord Barton lost three thousand at cards last night? That is what Mrs. Watkins told us as we came in, is it not, cousin? But one never knows with that woman. Three days ago she told us that the Regent himself was planning to come here for a week, and it turned out that there was not a word of truth in the rumor."

"Well, of course, ma'am," Mr. Phelps began, bending his head close to that of his questioner, "I do not gamble myself, you know, but it is said . . ."

Sarah's attention wandered. She found Mr. Phelps amusing. He was a fashionable dandy in his forties, a man who delighted in gossip and in light flirtation. His attentions to her would stop very fast, she guessed, if she once began to take them seriously. She had found that answering his flattery in a flippant manner kept him hovering in her vicinity, pretending to languish after her.

She smiled at the approach of Colonel and Mrs. Smythe, a couple also in early middle age, with whom she and Lady Murdoch had sat at a concert in Sydney Gardens a few days before. With them were the Misses Seymour, two sisters who lived permanently in Bath with their mother, widow of a clergyman. They all stopped and talked with her for a few minutes, but she declined joining them in a stroll about the room, choosing rather to stay with Lady Murdoch. She similarly refused Mr. Gregory Evans, a young and earnest landowner who had been presented to her the day after her arrival and who had singled her out each day since.

Lady Murdoch and Mr. Phelps were still deep in conversation. Sarah looked around her again. It was becoming almost a rarity to see new faces in the Pump Room. The group of people who had just entered

looked unfamiliar, though she could not see their faces
to be sure. They stood with their backs to the room,
looking at the baths below. One of them was an elderly lady, though very different from Lady Murdoch
and many of the others of her generation in the room.
She was slim and held herself ramrod straight and
moved without assistance of cane or human arm. She
was fashionably dressed in lavender walking dress and
dove-gray bonnet. She was in company with a gentleman and two young ladies, one of whom had an arm
resting in the crook of his, though she stood as far
from him as her arm would allow. Both girls looked
very young, judging from the back view Sarah had of
them. The man was of medium height, slender, graceful, and elegant in green coat, biscuit-colored panta-
loons, and black Hessians. Obviously they were people
of fashion.

"Bertha!" Lady Murdoch released the name into
the middle of a confidence that Mr. Phelps was sharing with her. "Bertha Lane. Yoo-hoo! Bertha!"

Sarah cringed and wished for one moment that she
were anywhere but where she was. The handkerchief
was again waving in the air, and Lady Murdoch was
looking directly at the new arrivals who had been
attracting her own attention.

The next moment Sarah was beyond even wishing
she were elsewhere. She was paralyzed, mesmerized,
lifted totally beyond time and place. The whole group
had turned, as indeed had many other promenaders.
But Sarah saw none of them except the man. No one
except George Montagu, Duke of Cranwell. The man
whom, of all others, she had dreaded to see again this
side of the grave.

The Duke of Cranwell had agreed with some reluctance to travel to Bath. His idea of pleasure did not
include the assemblies in the Upper and Lower Rooms,
gatherings in the Pump Room, concerts in the park,
and shopping and gossip expeditions in the crowded

streets. In the summertime, particularly, the prospect was far from appealing.

His idea of comfortable living was to reside at Montagu Hall, his Wiltshire home. The large park offered everything in the way of quiet exercise: lawns and hills and woods stretching in every direction far out of sight of the house. His farms gave ample challenge to his mind and his physical energies. And the house was his pride and joy, the possession that gave his life its chief purpose. In the ten years since he had inherited the title and the estate from his father, he had filled it with art treasures and elegant furnishings. He had remodeled parts of it for more comfortable living. He would have been well content to rusticate there for the rest of his life.

Unfortunately, he reflected, when one had decided to give up one's single status for the advantages of matrimony, one had also to give up one's freedom to do just what one wished with one's life. He was nine-and-twenty and it was high time that he gave up his strong aversion to marriage, well-founded though that aversion might have been. He had no brothers, and his closest male relative was a stranger to him and did not even bear the family name. The title had been in the Montagu family for five generations, and he hated the thought that it might pass to a family of another name if he failed to do something about the matter.

He had not taken great pains to find himself a prospective bride. He could have gone to London for the Season and looked over the crop of young girls newly "out." There he might have looked at his leisure for a lady of beauty and breeding and wit and intelligence and any other qualities that he supposed might be desirable if he gave the matter sufficient thought. But he had decided against such a step. He knew what would happen if he went. Almost every marriageable girl in town would set her cap at him, and it would be very difficult to know the true character of someone chosen under such circumstances.

Cranwell had winced at the thought. It had happened to him once. He had been deceived by a woman, and he had no wish to repeat that experience. He had been four years younger at that time, young and naive enough to believe that when a lady showed interest in him and avowed love for him, it was really him her attention was focused on. It had taken a bitter and painful experience to learn that his dukedom and his wealth and property could be far more attractive inducements than either his person or his character.

When he chose, therefore, he looked for nothing in a bride beyond youth and the apparent ability to breed. And purity, of course. That last was very important and the most difficult of all to be sure of in a stranger. Thus he did not choose a stranger. He chose Lady Hannah Lane, daughter of the Earl of Cavendish. The family lived in neighboring Gloucestershire, and a fast friendship had existed between the earl and the late duke. Cranwell had known Hannah from her infancy and could be reasonably sure of several things about her.

She was seventeen years old and not yet "out." All her life had been spent in the country, either at her father's home or at that of her grandmother. She had been out of the schoolroom for only a few months. She had had a strict and sheltered upbringing. These facts had merely emphasized a natural shyness and timidity of character. Cranwell had discovered during a visit to her father's home that she seemed well-bred and sensible, though she did not have a great deal of conversation. She had some beauty, being small and fragile in build, with honey-colored hair and skin that was almost translucent.

He had offered for her and had been accepted before his return home. The whole transaction had been made between him and Lord Cavendish. He had had only one short interview with Hannah, during which he had made a formal proposal and been accepted by a tongue-tied girl who had not once looked at him.

Cranwell would have been quite content to spend the summer quietly at Montagu Hall until it was time to claim his bride at Christmastime. Not that life at home was as peaceful as it had used to be. His young sister had returned home from school a couple of months before. Fanny had always been a girl of ebullient spirits, but now she seemed positively to bounce with energy. Her schooling was over and she was bursting to taste all that life had to offer. Already she was pestering him for a come-out Season in London the following spring. It gave him quite a jolt to realize suddenly that she and Hannah were of an age. Fanny seemed the merest child. He realized guiltily that he was almost robbing the cradle to have engaged himself to Hannah.

If the presence of Fanny was not enough to rob him of his peace, Cranwell had discovered that the dowager Countess of Cavendish certainly was. She was delighted with the news that her granddaughter was betrothed to the duke, of whom she had always been fond. But she was loudly disturbed by the fact that Hannah had had no come-out. Her son would not hear of postponing the nuptials until the following summer so that his daughter might be taken to London and duly presented at St. James's. There was only one solution, albeit an unsatisfactory one. Hannah must be taken to Bath, where she could at least mingle with society for a few weeks. And if Hannah and the dowager were to go to Bath, Cranwell discovered ruefully, he was to go there too as their escort. And if he was going, then Fanny could not be left behind, even had she wanted to be.

Hence the Duke of Cranwell, who liked nothing better than a quiet life in the country with his farms and his art and his books, found himself by late summer amidst all the bustle and glare of a health spa.

He left the White Hart Inn, where he was staying, at eight o'clock on the morning after their arrival and walked through the Pump Yard, already filling with fashionable men and women on their way to take the waters or seek out gossip. It was no strange matter for him to be up so early. Indeed, he had been sitting in his room reading for upwards of an hour before leaving. But he wondered with inner amusement how the ladies would take to such early rising. Fanny, he knew, rarely put in a public appearance at home until close to noon, and even then she was frequently as cross as a bear until she had breakfasted. Unfortunately, the days at Bath progressed quite strictly to timetable, and the hours of seven to ten in the morning were the fashionable time to take the waters and promenade in the Pump Room.

All three ladies were ready when he arrived in Laura Place, where they had taken lodgings. Lady Cavendish was sitting straight-backed in a chair, looking for all the world as if she had been sitting there for an hour or more already, and Hannah was sitting quietly at her side. Fanny was in a temper, Cranwell could see at a glance, standing at the window of the sitting room glaring out at the sun-bright street.

"I really don't see why we have to be up in the middle of the night, George," she said, rounding on him as he was shown into the room. "Surely no one will be out at this ungodly hour."

"On the contrary," he said. "The Pump Yard was full of people as I passed through it ten minutes ago. I would imagine there is quite a squeeze in the Pump Room already." He bowed to Lady Cavendish and Hannah. "Good morning, ma'am," he said to the former. "Are you still determined to walk this morning? It is not too late for me to go for a carriage. My dear?" He took Hannah's hand and raised it to his lips.

"Take a carriage?" Lady Cavendish said, rising to her feet. "And miss seeing who is who on the street? My dear boy, you will find that I am not yet quite decrepit with age."

"Well," Fanny said, taking her bonnet from the window seat and tying the bow beneath her chin, "what are we waiting for? If we do not leave at once, we may miss all the morning's entertainment."

When they left the narrow three-storied building on

Laura Place, Cranwell took Lady Cavendish on one arm and his betrothed on the other. The latter, he noticed, walked as far distant from him as her arm would allow and proceeded along the pavement with lowered eyes. She had not said a word to him that morning beyond a polite greeting. He wondered suddenly if she were not somewhat in awe of him. The idea irritated him a little, but he supposed that if it were true the fault must lie with him. He must make the effort to find some topic about which they could converse. They must surely have some interest in common.

Fanny tripped along ahead of the others, her parasol twirling about her head. She gazed with animation at the scene around her, apparently having forgotten that humanity was not intended to function at such an ungodly hour of the day. As they passed the Abbey, at which she stared with some awe, having lowered her parasol so that she could look up with more ease, Lady Cavendish joined her, declaring that it was impossible to walk through such a crush three abreast.

Cranwell was not cheered by the sight that met his eyes when they entered the Pump Room. Despite the earliness of the hour, the room was crowded. Some people were clustered around the water vendors; most were strolling or standing in small groups, talking. He sighed inwardly. It was unlikely that he knew many of the room's occupants. He had not ventured far from his home in the previous few years. But undoubtedly Lady Cavendish would know many people; she spent several weeks of each year in both London and Bath. And, of course, they would all be expected to make new acquaintances and to socialize almost constantly. It was an unwritten rule of Bath, he had heard, that one be part of the social life and participate in the many and varied activities that the city offered.

Fanny was exclaiming with enthusiasm as she gazed down at the King's Bath below the window. Lady Cavendish was explaining something to her. Cranwell too stopped and turned to his companion.

"Did you expect such a squeeze, my dear?" he

asked. "I must confess that this all takes me somewhat by surprise."

"Grandmama has told me that we would meet many people here, your grace," she said. Her voice was toneless. She did not look up at him but directed her eyes through the window.

He opened his mouth to continue this unpromising line of conversation.

"Yoo-hoo! Bertha!" a voice called from behind them.

Cranwell had turned before he could stop himself. But then he noticed that many other people had done the same thing. It was not difficult to locate the source of the greeting. A very plump elderly lady sat on a chair not far away, waving a handkerchief in the air. Cranwell was about to turn away and draw his party farther down the room away from such a vulgar display when he realized with some dismay that the handkerchief was waving exactly in their direction. And Lady Cavendish was Bertha, was she not?

He drew Hannah's arm a little more firmly through his own and glanced quickly around to make sure that Fanny was close by. Then he looked back at the elderly person in the chair, who was now smiling and still waving the handkerchief. A gentleman approaching his middle years stood to one side of her and a young lady at her shoulder. Both looked perfectly respectable.

His eyes passed carefully over each of them. But if he had felt dismay at having his party so singled out for public attention, he was struck by a paralyzing horror when his eyes came fully to rest on the face of the young lady. It could not be! was his first reaction. His eyes and his mind were playing tricks on him. But it was. It surely was. There could be no mistaking that golden-red hair, half-hidden though it was beneath her bonnet. No mistaking those arched eyebrows, which always gave her face a look of surprise, and that full, curvaceous figure. It was Sarah, right enough. The one woman in this world whom he had hoped never to set eyes upon again.

* * *

"Well, Adelaide Murdoch, I declare," said Lady Cavendish. "I might have known it without even looking. No one else of my acquaintance could hail a person in such an improper manner and get away with it."

She swept across the floor in the direction of Lady Murdoch, her face beaming, her hands outstretched. "Adelaide, my dear friend," she said, "what a delight it is to see you again. It must be all of five years."

Lady Murdoch reached for Sarah's outstretched arm as a support on which to raise her considerable bulk to her feet. "Bertha," she said, "I knew as soon as I saw you standing over there that there could be no other female of your age who has kept her figure and her health so well. How do you do it?"

Lady Cavendish acknowledged the compliment with a nod. "What are you doing in Bath, Adelaide?" she asked. "Taking the waters? Allow me to present my granddaughter to you. Hannah, my love, meet one of the dearest friends of my youth, Lady Adelaide Murdoch."

Lady Murdoch clasped the hand of the girl who curtsied before her, having handed her empty glass to Mr. Phelps. "Yes," she said, "your grandmama and I have been friends since we were your age, my dear. Ah, and in those days we were both as slim as you, too."

"May I also present Lady Fanny Montagu and her brother, the Duke of Cranwell?" Lady Cavendish continued. "Hannah and his grace are to be wed before Christmas."

Fanny curtsied and Cranwell made his bow.

"The Duke of Cranwell!" Lady Murdoch exclaimed, clasping her hands over her ample bosom and gawking at him. "Well, I declare. Oh, pardon me, your grace. It is not every day one meets someone of such superior rank. I have heard about you, you know. My dear friends the Withersmiths were given a tour of your home last summer when they passed through Wiltshire, and talked of nothing else for weeks afterward. You were from home at the time. Your housekeeper did the honors, I understand."

Cranwell bowed again and murmured some platitude about being sorry that he had missed making the acquaintance of the Withersmiths.

"And my manners have certainly gone begging!" Lady Murdoch exclaimed, gripping more tightly the arm on which she leaned and turning sharp eyes on Sarah. "May I present my cousin and dear companion, Miss Sarah Fifield? And Mr. Marcus Phelps, who was a dear friend of poor Dicky's, Bertha."

Somehow Sarah lived through the introductions and the ten-minute conversation that ensued. But she did not know afterward how she had done it. He looked so familiar standing there, though she had not set eyes on him for four years. The same slight, graceful figure that somehow escaped being either puny or effeminate. The same dark, shining hair and thin, ascetic face with the straight nose and sensitive mouth and deep blue eyes. And that same elusive aura of attractiveness, which owed its existence to no nameable physical feature.

She looked directly at him when her name was mentioned and found that he was looking back with raised eyebrows. He inclined his head in a stiff half-bow and did not look at her again. She could not move. She hardly dared breathe. What would he do now? Lead his party away from her contaminating presence as soon as he decently could and stay as far from her as possible for the remainder of his visit in Bath? It seemed unlikely. Lady Cavendish and Lady Murdoch seemed mutually eager to renew their friendship. Would he expose her publicly as the fraud she was? Perhaps not publicly. George had much to lose himself by doing that. But privately, maybe, when he had his little group of ladies alone? Her acquaintance and doubtless that of Lady Murdoch would be cut quietly. Rumors would begin to circulate in Bath and the nightmare she had dreaded for four years would be reality.

Lady Cavendish was assuring her friend that, yes, indeed, his grace had paid their subscriptions the night before, immediately after their arrival, and yes, they would most certainly be at the Upper Assembly Rooms that night to take tea. Sarah looked at Lady Hannah. She was very young, very pretty. Very innocent. Yes, those qualities would appeal to him. She would be a very suitable bride for the Duke of Cranwell. Sarah felt sick. Four years, after all, did not seem such a long time. Could he really be considering marriage already? Why had she not worked harder during those years to stop loving him? He looked so familiar, yet was so totally unapproachable.

The Duke of Cranwell had often wondered in the years since he saw Sarah last why he had fallen so headlong in love with her. He must have been merely ripe for an infatuation, he had persuaded himself. No female could be as beautiful, as fascinating, and as physically appealing as he had thought her. He had convinced himself that he had never really loved her and that therefore his loss had not been so great. But he had to admit to himself now, having permitted himself one searching look into those green eyes, that he had certainly not underestimated her beauty and physical appeal. She looked appallingly familiar to him, as if it had all happened but yesterday, although if he had tried to recall her face and figure the day before, he could not have done so with any exactness.

As shock receded, anger took its place. How had she dared to come to this place of fashion and decency? And under a different name! How could she stand there calmly supporting the weight of her elderly cousin, who must herself be a respectable person if Hannah's grandmother deigned to recognize a friendship with her? Did Lady Murdoch know? he wondered. Of course, Sarah would contrive some way of avoiding future contact with him and the ladies for whose welfare he was responsible. He must at all costs protect Hannah and Fanny from contamination. He felt the old hatred and was as little able to cope with the emotion as he had ever been.

Finally, to the infinite relief of both Sarah and Cranwell, Mr. Phelps made his bow and announced that he was expected back at his lodgings for breakfast, and his departure set everyone to remembering that they had not yet eaten and that it was high time they did. Lady Cavendish and her party set out to walk back to Laura Place, and Sarah helped Lady Murdoch outside, where the carriage they had ordered for half-past nine waited to return them to their lodgings on Brock Street.

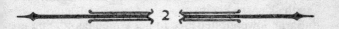 2

LADY MURDOCH declared that they would
do nothing more strenuous than visit the circulating
library after breakfast. A week of almost constant
activity was taking its toll of her energy, and she
wished to be feeling well enough to enjoy the pleasures of the Upper Rooms in the evening, especially as
she had now discovered her old friend and would have
five years' worth of news to catch up on.

"Bertha and I will be quite happy to take tea all
evening, I am sure," she said. "But I feel more than
delighted that we will not have to bore you with our
talk, cousin dear. You are a good girl and have stayed
close beside me day after day, but I know that young
tastes run to brighter pleasures. Tonight you will be
able to join the dancing. Bertha's granddaughter and
Lady Fanny Montagu seemed very proper young ladies and very suitable companions for you. And the
duke is a very gentlemanly sort of man. I am sure he
will be delighted if you join their party."

"Indeed, ma'am," Sarah said in some alarm, "I
have no interest in joining in the dancing. I came here
to be with you. And we have had a delightful time and
made many acquaintances without attending the balls.
I really have no wish to impose my company on his
grace and the young ladies."

"Sarah," Lady Murdoch said, waving in her direction the knife she was using to spread clotted cream on
her scone, "you know I have begun to think of you as
my daughter. And my daughter should be attending
these twice-weekly balls. I have been thinking, in fact,
that I should chaperone you myself. Not that I care to

23

dance, of course, though there was a time when I could have danced from evening to dawn and not paused for breath. Now nothing seems more convenient than that you attend the ball in company with Bertha's party."

Sarah lowered her eyes to her coffee cup. "You are more than kind," she said. "But really, ma'am, I have never danced in public and feel it is far too late to start now."

"Bosh!" Lady Murdoch said, reaching for the jam.

The circulating library was crowded by the time their carriage deposited them outside its doors. Gentlemen read the newspapers; ladies chose novels, some buying, some sitting to read, others taking books away with them on loan. A few people sat quietly writing letters. Several gossiped. It was a crowded but comparatively peaceful place. Sarah relaxed when a hasty glance around the room assured her that there was no one there that they knew with any degree of intimacy. She was feeling too upset by the events of the morning to cope with meeting any casual acquaintance.

While Lady Murdoch sat down with a novel, frequently glancing over its top to check the identity of every new arrival, Sarah bought pen and paper and seated herself at an empty desk to write a letter to Aunt Myrtle. At least, that was what she intended to do. It was such a relief to sit with her back to other people and know that she had perhaps an hour to herself, an hour in which it was unlikely that she would be disturbed. Lady Murdoch would either nod to sleep behind her book or strike up a lengthy conversation with some new arrival.

She was very badly shaken. Indeed, she realized as soon as she had written the first sentence of her letter that neither her hand nor her mind was steady enough to enable her to continue. But she kept her head bent over the paper, the quill pen clutched in her hand. It just seemed too ironic, too unfair. This was her first visit to a public place in four years, indeed ever. And this was the first time in more than four years that she had dared meet new people and enjoy life. And after only one week she had run into him. George. Of all the places that he or she might have gone, they had been fated to converge on the same place. What made it stranger was that unless he had changed in four years, he had never been a man to seek out fashionable pleasure spots.

If his presence in Bath were not enough for her to contend with, there was her knowledge that Winston Bowen was somewhere there too. She had seen his name in the subscription book when Lady Murdoch was paying their dues on their arrival the previous week. She was not as surprised by his presence as by George's. It was almost to be expected that he would be wherever fashionable people gathered in any numbers. It was unlikely that she would see much of him. He probably would not seek her out in such a public setting, and his interests would doubtless keep him away from the places which attracted Lady Murdoch.

Absentmindedly Sarah was dipping her quill in the inkwell and outlining the words that she had already written on the page before her. She could remember the first time she ever saw George Montagu. She had been with Winston, out riding one afternoon. She had always spent a great deal of time with him since she and her brother, Graham, had come to live with her uncle and aunt, Viscount and Viscountess Laing, two years before on the death of their father. Winston was not, strictly speaking, a cousin. He was Uncle Randolph's son by a former marriage. Sarah's mother had been the sister of Aunt Myrtle, who had had the good fortune to make an advantageous marriage. But Winston was kind and had never seemed to mind having her trail around after him, though he was three years older than she. He had been an amiable boy who appeared to take nothing in life very seriously.

She was fourteen when they took this particular ride. It was a hot afternoon and they had stopped for a rest before turning for home again. She was sitting on a hillside, her arms clasped around her raised knees;

Winston was sprawled beside her, a blade of grass between his teeth. But they were not the only riders out that day. A group of four came cantering down the laneway below them, and Winston sat up to watch their approach.

Sarah stayed where she was when he got to his feet and bounded down the slope to hail their neighbors, a twin brother and sister with whom he sometimes associated. While he talked with them, she studied their companions, strangers to her. One was a very young girl who was having some difficulty controlling her pony during the halt. The other was a man. In any other circumstances he might not have drawn her attention. He was not exactly the Prince Charming type around which her youthful dreams were beginning to focus. He looked neither tall nor particularly muscular. His face was not remarkably handsome, nor his smile dazzling. In fact, he did not smile at all.

But looking at him idly, because he was the only real novelty in the scene below her, she was attracted by the grace and apparent ease with which he sat his horse. And she was impressed by the quiet way in which he went to the assistance of the little girl.

"Oh, I can manage him perfectly well myself, George," the child said. "Don't fuss!"

"Not by tugging at the bit and digging in your knees that way, Fan," Sarah heard the man say. "You have to sit him and hold the reins in such a way that he knows you are in charge."

She liked his voice. It was low and calm, with no trace of either impatience or condescension.

After the group rode away, Winston climbed back up the slope and told her that the strangers were the Duke of Cranwell and his sister.

"Lucky dog!" he added. "Finished university a few months ago; succeeded to the title and fabulous wealth two years ago. Off on the Grand Tour next month. Some people have all the good fortune."

"You can't complain, Win," she said soothingly. "You have a good home, and Uncle Randolph is going to send you to Cambridge next year. And he has said that if you do well at your studies he will see about letting you travel Europe. And one day you will have the title. And you do have both a mama and a papa." This last was said somewhat wistfully.

He leaned across and covered one of her hands with his. "Don't get mopey, Sarah," he said. "They love you too, you know, and you have Graham and me for brothers. You like that, don't you?"

She smiled gratefully as he squeezed her hand and jumped to his feet again. For several months after that Sarah's Prince Charming had had a slight, graceful figure, steady, unsmiling eyes, and a calm, low-pitched voice.

It would have been better far if she had not seen the Duke of Cranwell again. Perhaps the other things that had happened would have been a little easier to bear. Perhaps. It would also have been better if she had never set eyes on Winston Bowen. But it was useless to think in such a way. As well to think it would have been better if she had never been born or if her parents had never met. Unfortunately, one had to cope with life as it was presented to one. Really there seemed to be very few free choices.

She had another very good reason for remembering that occasion when she had first seen George. It was only a few days later that Graham had killed Albert Stanfield. The memory could still make her head spin and her stomach churn. Graham was three years younger than she and feebleminded. Mama had died giving birth to him and something must have happened during the birth, because Gray was never normal. As a baby he had been unusually placid, smiling at anyone who bent over his crib, laughing helplessly at any antic that was performed for his amusement. It was only as he grew older that his family became unwillingly aware that this fair-haired, pretty little child was not of normal intelligence.

Sarah was particularly fond of him. And who could

not be? He was a sunny-natured, affectionate child who liked to hang on her arm, stroking her hand lovingly and gazing worshipfully into her face. His mood rarely changed. Only occasionally, when he was teased as a half-wit, did he become agitated. And very rarely, if there was no one around to get rid of the teaser, he would fly into a frustrated rage and throw himself headfirst into a fight, fists clenched and teeth gnashing.

Sarah had not been with him on that particular day. She was helping her aunt plan a dinner party for her uncle's birthday. Graham had gone off to pick wildflowers and was gone for several hours. When he came home, he was very agitated and hid in a corner of his bedchamber, his face pressed to the wall, while Sarah tried to coax from him the reason for his withdrawal. He said nothing, only whimpered for hours.

And then the body of Albert Stanfield, twelve-year-old son of a neighbor's gamekeeper, had been discovered at the foot of a quarry. The boy had fallen thirty feet. His body was cut and bruised, presumably from the jagged stones that protruded from the quarry walls.

"Were you with Albert, Gray?" Sarah asked her brother gently.

"No, Sare," he said. "Gray picked flowers. Pretty flowers."

"Did he slip and fall, Gray?"

"Pretty flowers for Sare," he replied, looking at her with anxious, wary eyes.

"Come, sweetheart," she said, "let me put my arms around you. Did you try to save him, Gray, and you could not? You must not blame yourself."

"Gray don't want to play with that boy no more," he said, coming to nestle within Sarah's arms and gazing earnestly into her eyes. "Nasty boy, Sare."

"Was he?" she said, smoothing back a soft curl from his forehead and kissing his brow. "You don't have to play with him again, sweetheart."

And she had set herself to spend all her time with him for the coming weeks, intent on smoothing away the memories that troubled his dreams and sometimes brought a puzzled frown to his face in the daytime.

Poor Graham had been questioned interminably, it seemed, for several days, but of course it was pointless to try to coax a coherent story from him. He clearly had been present at the time of the accident, but equally clearly he did not know what had happened.

It was Win who finally wormed the truth out of the boy. Gray did not like his cousin; he was frightened of him. But that was understandable. Win was six years older than Graham and a confident, virile young man. The child was overawed. Win's persistent but not unkindly questioning drew from the child an admission that he had hit Albert.

It was officially concluded that Albert had fallen accidentally to his death. There was never any suggestion that foul play was suspected.

But after the funeral, Win took Sarah aside one day and told her the full truth very gently. He had been out walking himself and had been drawn toward the sound of loudly quarreling voices. He had arrived in time to see Graham push Albert over the edge of the quarry. Win had been too late to prevent the disaster.

Why had he said nothing before this? Sarah asked him, wide-eyed with horror.

He directed at her that smile which was very attractive even in those days. "How could I do that to my own cousin?" he asked. "Or to you, Sarah? You know you are like my own sister."

"But if that is what happened, someone should be told," she protested.

"What?" he asked gently. "That Graham is a murderer, Sarah?"

"Murderer!" Her hand crept to her throat. "Don't be absurd, Win. He is a child."

"Child murderers hang in England as well as adults, Sarah," he said, gazing into her eyes.

She shook her head.

His hand covered hers reassuringly. "You and I know Gray is not quite normal," he said. "It would be a terrible injustice for him to swing, Sarah. But it would happen, you know. I am going to keep my mouth shut. You need have no fear. It will be our secret. No one else knows or ever will."

She grasped his hand and pressed it to her lips. "Win," she said. "Oh, my dear Win. How wonderful you are! How will I ever be able to show you my gratitude?"

She had been blind enough over the next few years not even to realize how he made use of their secret. She lent him money that was never repaid, ran errands, was constantly at his beck and call. And she had done it all gladly, worshipfully almost. She had never been conscious of serving him only to buy his silence.

She really had been as fond of Winston as of a brother. And proud, too. He had been an extraordinarily handsome boy as far back as she could remember, with his blond hair, hazel eyes, and white teeth, and with his laughter-filled face. As they both grew older, Sarah had become aware that almost every girl for miles around sighed for one smile from him. And she had become a little conceited about the fact that he was frequently in her company. She had enjoyed feeling envious female eyes on her as they entered church together on a Sunday or walked down the village street together. Foolish, foolish girl.

When she was sixteen and Winston was home from university for the summer, he had started to touch her. She hardly noticed at first. They had always been close. He had often held her hand or lifted her down from fences or tickled her until she was weak with laughter. But these touches were different and made her uncomfortable. He came up behind her once when she was sitting on a stile reading a book and put his arms around her waist. She smiled and put her head back on his shoulder. She expected him to pitch her backward. Instead he held her waist with one arm and explored the contours of both breasts with the other hand.

"Don't, Win," she said, uncomfortable.

"You've grown, Sarah," he said into her ear. And then he did pitch her backward, threatening to drop her on the ground until she shrieked for mercy.

Another time he was lifting her down from the same stile, his hands beneath her arms. And again he touched her breasts, his thumbs this time pressing in on her nipples. She slapped his hands away without stopping to think, and he grinned.

"I think we are losing our angular little Sarah and gaining a shapely woman," he said. "Look at this!" And his hands traced the curve of her waist and the growing fullness of her hips. He gripped her hips tightly suddenly and pulled her lower half against his groin. Then he released her and laughed.

"You really are turning into a woman, Sarah," he said. "I bet that blush reaches right down to your toes."

"Stop it this instant, Winston Bowen," she scolded, "or I shall tell Uncle Randolph."

"No, you won't, Sarah," he said, laughing into her eyes. "You like being touched, don't you?"

It went on like that all summer, small incidents that made her uncomfortable and uneasy yet had not seemed serious enough to make a big fuss over. Winston was an attractive boy, after all, and she was woman enough already, at the age of sixteen, to feel a twinge of excitement over the fact that he had noticed her blossoming womanhood and appeared to appreciate it.

It was the following summer that everything went wrong. He had not been home either at Christmas or at Easter, and she had completely forgotten those small incidents from the previous year. She was delighted to see him, delighted at the prospect of needs having a companion close to her own age again. She was dearly fond of Graham, but he did not satisfy all her needs of friendship. And Winston had grown more attractive than ever, tall and muscular, like a blond god. And he was not one whit less amiable and carefree.

He began on her on their very first ride together. Again it was a hot day, and they had stopped to rest amongst some trees on a hillside several miles from home. She, foolish and naive, stretched out on the ground and spread her hands palm-down on the cool grass, sighing with contentment. Winston was quiet for a while, presumably stretched out beside her. Then she felt his hand on her breast.

"Don't, Win," she said, turning her face to him and laughing in some embarrassment.

"Don't what, Sarah?" he asked with wide-eyed innocence. And he moved the hand deliberately to the other breast.

"Don't do that," she said, flushing. "Please, Win."

"You have lovely breasts, Sarah," he said. "Full and firm." His fingers tightened around the one that rested in his palm.

"Win," she said, laughing again in hot embarrassment. "Please stop it."

"If you say so, Sarah," he said meekly. And he moved his hand away and placed it palm-down on her abdomen. He grinned down into her face as he pushed his fingers down between her legs and tightened his clasp of her.

Sarah pushed him away in a panic and scrambled up onto her knees.

He laughed. "Have I scared you, Sarah?" he asked. "That's more than I ever did with all the ghost stories I told and tricks I played when you were younger. Come and sit down again. You aren't afraid of me, are you? Silly girl. Come on. I didn't mean to frighten you."

She sat, and he stretched out beside her and regaled her with stories of his university days until she was giggling with amusement and forgot the discomfort she had felt a few minutes before.

Even so, she was a little more wary the next time he suggested a ride. She made an excuse not to go. It was several days later that he found her at her favorite haunt, the stile, where she was again reading. He stood beside her, his arms resting on the fence for a while, before suggesting that they go for a walk. She had been sitting and reading for more than an hour and agreed.

The walk took them across the pasture to a clump of bushes at the other side, where he suggested they sit down. She was only slightly uneasy. She sat, her arms around her knees.

He talked for a while, until she was thoroughly relaxed, and then he reached for her hand. She gave it. They had often sat thus in the past. He tickled the palm with one finger until she giggled and would have pulled the hand away. But he turned it palm-up and put it to his mouth, his tongue continuing the tickling movements that his finger had abandoned. And then his mouth moved up her bare arm toward her short puffed sleeve.

She giggled again. "Don't be absurd, Win. You are tickling me." Her giggles stopped cold when he lifted his head and she saw the expression on his face. "Win," she said, "let go of my arm. It is time to be getting back."

"You tease, Sarah!" he said. "You know you don't mean that." And one hand came up to hold her chin as he lowered his mouth to hers.

Sarah froze. She waited for the kiss to stop. She did not like the sensations it created at all. She thought of Winston as a brother. Brothers did not do this with their sisters. And then he opened his mouth over hers and she felt his tongue pushing against her lips. She felt nausea and panic both at the same time and pushed at the hand that still held her chin.

He lifted his head to look at her. "Don't fight," he said. "You are bound to be frightened at first. But don't fight. You will like it if you will just relax."

"I don't like it," she said decisively. "I want to go home, Win."

"No, you don't," he said. "Lie down, Sarah, and relax for a few minutes."

"I don't want to, Win," she said, her voice beginning to shake.

But he would not take no for an answer, and she found that that muscular body, which she had admired for several years, now worked very much to her disadvantage. He took her by the shoulders, laid her back on the grass, and held her there with one hand on her shoulder and one leg thrown across her body. The other hand proceeded to explore her body, his palm pushing and kneading, his fingers prodding and teasing. His mouth was everywhere: on hers, on her throat, on her breasts.

All her struggles were quite in vain. She could not work an arm or a leg free with which to flail at him. Finally, when his hand went under her skirt and began to explore its way up her legs, she stopped fighting and started to cry. And her tears accomplished what her struggles had failed to achieve. He looked at her in surprise and immediately removed his hand from beneath her skirt.

"You are a tender little thing, Sarah," he said affectionately. "Are you still frightened? Most girls love doing this, you know. You are silly, are you not?"

"I don't want to, Win," she said through her sobs. "It isn't right."

"What is so wrong about it?" he asked, smiling down at her tenderly. "We were merely having some fun, Sarah. We have always had fun together, have we not?"

"Not like this," she said. "This isn't right. Aunt Myrtle would not like it."

He laughed and propped himself on one elbow beside her. "It would not be wise to tell her," he said. "Older people tend to forget what it is like to be young. You will learn to like playing, Sarah. The time will come, I guarantee, when you will be begging me to do this to you and more. Silly little girl." And he bent his head and kissed her gently on the cheek.

She accepted the handkerchief he offered her and

dried her eyes and blew her nose on it. "Let me go home, Win," she begged.

"Come on," he said, jumping to his feet and pulling her to hers. "We will go together. Don't cry, Sarah. I wouldn't have hurt you, you know. You didn't think I would hurt you, did you? How could I do that when we have been the best of friends for years? Come on, smile and tell me you are not afraid of me."

She made a poor attempt at a smile. "I am not afraid of you, Win," she said, "but I don't like it when you do those things to me."

He pulled her arm through his, patted her hand, and walked slowly home with her.

"You know, Sarah," he said with an affectionate grin down at her, "you really can be a wild thing when you want, can't you? I didn't realize that you and Gray have that in common. I think you would have killed me back there without realizing what you were doing if I had not restrained you. Silly girl! Just like Gray with that Stanfield boy."

He squeezed her hand and proceeded to talk about other matters. But Sarah's heart felt turned to stone in her breast. Surely that had been a careless remark. Surely it was not a veiled threat. Not from Win! Surely not.

"Have you finished writing your letter, cousin?" Lady Murdoch's voice hissed in a stage whisper from behind Sarah. "This library does not appear to have any interesting novels. And there is absolutely nobody here today. If you need a little longer, dear, I shall sit quietly and wait for you. But really, my rheumaticks are troubling me quite badly. My back aches no matter which way I sit. I have already tried three different chairs to see if I can gain some ease for it."

Sarah looked up with a start and then back to the heavily outlined sentence on the paper in front of her. "Oh, we may leave immediately, ma'am," she said, laying the pen down and hastily folding the paper in two. "I really cannot think of anything to say to my aunt today. Perhaps tomorrow I shall be more in the mood."

"It is perfectly understandable, dear," Lady Murdoch said, still in the stage whisper, "that your head should be too full of the many pleasures in store for you here to enable you to write a duty letter to the viscountess. Maybe after tonight's ball you will have something of more importance to describe." She pursed her lips and nodded knowingly at Sarah.

The rest of the day passed quietly. They returned to their lodgings on Brock Street for dinner. Lady Murdoch decided to forgo the outing that was customary during the afternoon. She preferred to sit at home, she said, and listen to Sarah read to her from the only novel that had seemed at all worth bringing home from the library.

"I am very sensible of the fact that it is an exceedingly dull way for a young lady to spend an afternoon, cousin," she said apologetically, "but I console myself with the reflection that tonight you may be able to do something a little more exciting than sitting and talking with an old lady like me over tea as you would normally feel obliged to do. And really, dear, I am suffering from cruel indigestion. I begin to doubt that those horrid waters are doing any good at all. What do you think?"

Sarah murmured something soothing as she fetched a cushion to prop behind Lady Murdoch's back and a stool for her feet. It seemed to her that the waters would have to perform a miracle indeed to prevent some twinges of indigestion after a meal that had consisted of a large helping of beef and vegetables and two helpings of steamed pudding and custard.

But she said nothing. She picked up the gothic novel from the library and began to read it aloud. Not many minutes passed before the sound of very deep breathing mingled with the tones of her voice. She put down the book quietly when her cousin began to snore and crossed the space between them in order to arrange the cushion more comfortably behind the old lady's head.

She returned to her place and reached for the box in which she kept the purse she was netting in silk. She arranged the work on her lap and bent her head to it. She really was fortunate to have been contacted by Lady Murdoch five weeks before. At first she had been very dubious about going to live with an elderly stranger who was obviously self-indulgent and not a little vulgar. She had expected to be bored at best, to be abused at worst. Yet there had been no answer to her advertisement for employment as a governess, and she was desperately in need of somewhere to go when the lease on her cottage expired. And she could not go back to Aunt Myrtle's, though her aunt was puzzled and hurt by her refusal to do so.

Could she have done anything to avoid the situation with Winston? she wondered. It was easy now to look back and judge herself harshly, to see her young self as a hopeless weakling. It had been harder at the time. Loving as her aunt and uncle were, she had always been conscious of the fact that they were not her parents and that their home was not hers by right. It had been a lonely feeling to know that she had no one of her very own to whom to turn in trouble. Poor Graham had provided her with more than sufficient brotherly love, but of course he was no confidant.

She had thought of going to Aunt Myrtle and explaining her unease over Winston, but it was easier to say she was going to do so than actually to do it. Aunt Myrtle had a very loving nature. She lavished that love on her orphaned niece, but she positively doted on her stepson. There was no one to match him in her eyes; he could do no wrong. And of course she had good reason to feel that way. Winston was a warm and a charming young man. And Aunt Myrtle led a hard life. Uncle Randolph was frequently sick and not likely to get better as time went on. He was consumptive, and though the disease progressed slowly in him, he did become steadily thinner as the years went on, and his spells of fever and coughing became more frequent. Sarah had found that she just could not bring herself to talk to her aunt and add to her troubles.

And then, of course, there was the other reason that had held her back from talking to anyone, the reason she had feared to admit even to herself. Was it possible that Graham could still be charged with murder if the truth of Albert Stanfield's death became known? Could he be imprisoned? Transported? Hanged? Sarah did not know and had no means of finding out without revealing the secret to someone else. But she had always feared the worst. English law could be very cruel. It perhaps would not take into consideration the fact that Gray was not fully responsible for his own behavior and that he was not normally dangerous at all.

She dared not discover the truth. She dared not do anything to offend Win. One word from him in the wrong ear and Gray's very life could be at stake. And he had alluded to the incident again for the first time in more than a year. By accident? She could not be sure.

So she had borne the burden alone. She had not, in fact, been actively unhappy or frightened of Winston. He had still been the brotherly figure whose company had always brightened her days. She still enjoyed talking and laughing with him. But she had steadily avoided being alone with him after the episode in the pasture. She had not even blamed him entirely for what had happened. She must have done something, she had felt, to give him the impression that she would allow such liberties with her person and even enjoy them. There would be no more such incidents, she had assured herself, now that he knew he was wrong.

She had avoided for a whole week being alone with him, but inevitably the time came when she could avoid him no longer. She had been doing an errand in the village for her aunt and was returning home along a country lane, swinging her reticule and singing quietly to herself. She was on foot, from choice, as the

distance was only two miles and the weather cool but
pleasant. Graham, who usually accompanied her on
such journeys, was at home with one of his colds.

She decided suddenly that she would take the shortcut up over the hill to her right and through the woods
to the pasture before her uncle's house. It was not that
she wanted to shorten the distance, but the walk was
so much prettier than that along the lane.

She was at the top of the hill, just about to move
downward again into the trees when she heard a shout
behind her. Winston was below on the lane, and he
was turning and urging his horse up the grassy hillside
toward her. Sarah felt an icy thrill of fear. It was too
late to turn back to the relative safety of the lane. She
had time only to master her panic and try to behave
casually.

"I thought I might meet you," he called cheerfully
when still some distance away. "Why did you not ride
or bring the gig, Sarah?"

"Because I felt like the exercise. And it would not
hurt you to walk sometimes, lazybones," she retorted,
swinging her reticule in an attempt to look quite relaxed.

"I shall have to get revenge for that!" he said with a
grin. And as he reached the top of the hill, he dis-
mounted and moved up beside her.

"Are you not on your way somewhere, Win?" she
asked.

"Certainly," he replied, "and have arrived. I came
to meet you."

"Oh," she said, glancing ahead through the trees,
but knowing very well that the house was well out of
sight.

It was inevitable—she would almost have been surprised if it had not happened—that he would stop
when they were among the trees, tether his horse, and
suggest that they sit down for a while. It was not even
a suggestion, she realized. She had no real choice. He
took her by the arm, not ungently, but she knew she
would not be able to break his clasp. She sat.

She listened to his chatter as he reclined on one

elbow sucking on a blade of grass. But she knew with a hopeless certainty that this was only the preliminary, that soon the touching would start again. She hoped only that he would not go as far as on the last occasion. She would die of mortification if he put his hand beneath her skirt again.

"You are very quiet today, Sarah," he said at last, reaching up and drawing one finger along her jawline.

She smiled. She did not ask to go home. She did not ask him to remove his hand. She sat very still and hoped.

He sat up and drew nearer to her. "You are seventeen, are you not, Sarah?" he said. "A real woman now. And a very pretty one too. I bet all the boys in the village eye you when you walk by, don't they?"

Sarah blushed and looked at her hands, which were clasped around her knees. "I don't know," she said. "I have not looked to see."

He laughed. "Liar!" he teased. "I bet you enjoy the attention, Sarah, even if you pretend not to notice." He reached out his hand and brought it across her breasts, then spread his fingers so that his thumb and one finger pressed inward on her nipples.

She continued to stare at her hands. She did not tell him to stop. "You see?" he said. "You are doing it now. Pretending not to notice. But I can feel your nipples hardening, Sarah. Your body cannot lie, you see."

And it was true, she realized. There was a rush of feeling to her breasts, which seemed to tighten them and which made their tips uncomfortably hard. She continued to stare at her hands.

"Come on, Sarah," he coaxed, moving again until he sat against her. He put an arm around her shoulders. "Lie down with me, and I will make you feel even better than this."

"I don't want to," she said almost in a whisper.

"Yes, you do," he said, kissing her cheek and hugging her closer. "You are just being a silly goose, pretending that you do not want it. Lie down now, Sarah."

She lay down without any assistance or coercion from him. And with her arms at her sides, and her legs stretched out before her, she allowed him to kiss her and fondle her. She did not even protest when he tugged at her skirt and began the exploration of her bare legs again, beyond pressing them more tightly together.

He lifted himself half across her, his hand making circular motions on her calf. "Sarah," he said, "so warm. So soft." His voice, quiet and deep, was hardly recognizable. "Just lie still now. I am going to un- clothe you here."

Finally she reacted. She shook her head. "No," she said, "I don't want you to do that, Win."

He smiled a gentle, dreamy smile that again she hardly recognized as his hand went up over her abdomen to the fastenings of her undergarments. "Sweet little Sarah," he said, "of course you do. Don't be afraid. I won't hurt you. You don't think I would hurt you, do you?"

As he spoke, his hand knowingly undid the fasten- ings at her waist and was dragging the garments free of her body and down her legs.

And belatedly, realizing that this time he had no intention of stopping at merely fondling her, Sarah fought him in a blind panic. Arms and legs, fists, fingernails, teeth: all flailed at him. She cried, shouted, screamed, implored him until his open palm cracked across one cheek and she froze, gazing in horror into his eyes.

He had already dragged her garments free of her legs and pushed her dress up to her waist. "Stop it now, Sarah!" he commanded, though the words were unnecessary now that she lay perfectly still. "Calm down. I am going to take care of you. You aren't afraid that I will take you and abandon you, are you? Or get you with child? Don't worry. I have plenty of knowledge of the ways of the world."

In one mighty effort Sarah brought herself under control. "Let me go, Win," she said in a voice that did not sound quite as cold and steady as she had hoped, "or I shall tell Uncle Randolph and he will turn you off and you will be thrown into prison."

He laughed, a pleasant laugh of genuine amusement. "Dear Sarah," he said, "you look delightful playing the part of the outraged maiden. But you need not be afraid, you know. You are going to enjoy this. Far more than you would enjoy visiting me and Gray in prison. Do you suppose we would be allowed to share a cell? Until Gray's execution, that is."

She had been about to start struggling again. But she lay still then while he laughed and lowered his mouth to hers. She lay still as he brought his full weight down on top of her.

"Just relax now, love," he said, "and it won't hurt. I don't want to hurt you."

She lay still while he dealt with his own clothing. She allowed him to push her legs wide apart with his and to work his hands beneath her. She allowed him to lift her away from the grass. And she lay still, her teeth biting down on both lips, as he pushed very slowly into her.

And he was right. He did not hurt her. She felt as if she was going to be hurt, as if she was being stretched and stretched until she must burst. But then something inside her really did give way and there was no more stretching until he was deeply embedded inside her.

There was no pain. But there was the almost overpowering nausea at being held wide open to his invasion, at knowing that there was nothing left that she held secret from him, at knowing herself violated. During the interminable minutes while he moved in her, rhythmically thrusting and withdrawing, removing from her the last vestiges of personhood, she bit on her lips, concentrating on holding in check the terrible urge to vomit. She feared his hands that could inflict pain, and that part of his body that could impale and degrade without hurting, and she dared not disgrace herself further by being sick.

Finally, when there was nothing of herself left for him to take, he groaned against the side of her face, buried himself deep inside her body, and relaxed. She lay staring at the sky until finally he pulled himself free of her and lifted his body away. He lay on the grass beside her for a while, but finally his hand reached out and took hers.

"You see, Sarah?" he said. "There was nothing to be afraid of, was there?"

She said nothing.

He turned his head to look at her. "Still quiet?" he asked. "Are you sleepy? It is quite natural for you to be so, you know. I am too."

"No," she said tonelessly.

He raised himself on one elbow again and smiled down at her. "You enjoyed it?" he asked.

"No."

"Nonsense!" he said, cupping the side of her face in one hand and turning her to face him. "But of course, it was your first time. You were a little frightened, were you? It will be better next time, Sarah."

And finally she started to cry. "I don't want there to be a next time, Win," she said.

He took her into his arms and cradled her head against his shoulder. "Silly girl," he said tenderly. "I am going to look after you, Sarah. I'll never abandon you. When Papa is gone and I marry, I shall set you up in the dower house and you can always live there, even if you do not remain my mistress for the rest of your life. You don't have to be afraid."

He held her and rocked her until she finished sobbing, and then he dried her eyes with his handkerchief and kissed her eyes and her mouth tenderly.

Sarah jumped as her netting slipped off her lap and fell to the floor with a clatter. The rhythmic snoring across the room from her stopped.

"Oh, goodness," Lady Murdoch said, "I do believe

I missed the end of the chapter, dear. I must have dozed off for a minute. Now I shall have to bore you, poor cousin, by having you read it over again to me. Tomorrow, though. I really think it must be time for tea. I feel quite famished. Why did you not ring for the tray, Sarah? You did not have to wait for an old thing like me to wake up, you know."

"Indeed, ma'am," Sarah said, putting her work away carefully in its box and crossing the room to the bell pull, "I had not realized how late it was. But I am sure the tea is all ready to be brought in. Shall I rearrange your cushion?"

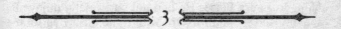

3

THE DUKE of Cranwell sighed and flung aside yet another ruined neckcloth. The third. He turned to his valet, who was hovering in the background, hanging up clothes that had been worn during the afternoon.

"You may take that I-told-you-so look off your face, Peters," he said. "I don't seem to be able to tie even the simplest knot this evening. Come and work one of your masterpieces."

Peters did as he was told. He selected a freshly starched neckcloth and proceeded to arrange it around his employer's neck in perfect and artful folds. "There, your grace," he said finally, eyeing his creation critically from a distance of two feet, head to one side. "I think that should do for an evening appearance." His tone suggested, even if his voice did not state, that anything the duke might have tied on his own certainly would not have done.

"Yes, yes," Cranwell agreed, glancing into the mirror beside him. "I suppose this creation even has some name? It is certainly a work of art."

"A Waterfall, your grace," Peters said with some pride.

"Ah," Cranwell said, "I am sure that there will be scores at the rooms tonight to pay homage to your art, Peters. Come, my coat. I wonder when the fashion began to create garments that cannot be donned without the assistance of one muscular valet or three ordinary ones."

Peters lovingly picked up the pale blue satin evening coat that lay on the bed and proceeded to prove his muscularity.

Ten minutes later, Cranwell was seated in his own comfortable traveling carriage being conveyed the short distance from his hotel, over Pulteney Bridge, and along to Laura Place. He had not particularly enjoyed the day and looked forward with some misgiving to at least four weeks of such dubious pleasures. After breakfast he had escorted the ladies to Milsom Street, where they might visit all the most fashionable shops and see all the most fashionable people. The activity had lasted for several hours. Lady Cavendish had constantly met old acquaintances and stopped to make introductions and to exchange *on-dits*.

They had returned to Laura Place for dinner, and he had expected some reprieve. Surely a lady of Lady Cavendish's years would require a rest after the busy morning, and even the young ladies should be suffering from flagging energies. But all were as eager to venture out again as if they had been abed all morning. So he had accompanied them to Sydney Gardens, where again all the world seemed to be strolling.

Perhaps he would not have found the day such a trial if he had not constantly been fearing that they would meet Sarah and her elderly cousin again. As it happened, they had not set eyes on either of them. But he could feel no relief. Lady Cavendish and her friend had talked of meeting and taking tea at the Upper Rooms that evening. It stood to reason that where Lady Murdoch went Sarah was sure to go as well. That meant that within the next hour he would be in her company again. Worse. Hannah and Fanny would be forced into her company too.

He put his head back against the velvet upholstery of the coach and closed his eyes. Although he had thought of little else during the day, he still did not know what to do about the situation. Unless by some miracle it happened that Lady Murdoch was about to conclude her visit to Bath, the chances seemed good that there would be many meetings between the two old friends and, therefore, between the two groups. It was an intolerable position he found himself in. He

could not be in company with that woman and forced
to treat her with the deference he would afford a lady.
He could not bring himself to converse with her at all.

And there was not even just himself to consider. He
owed it to both his fiancée and his sister to protect
them from such an improper connection. The trouble
was, how was he to do it? He could, of course, insist
on taking Fanny home at once, though his conduct
would seem peculiar, to say the least, if he could offer
no explanation. But that would not solve the problem
of Hannah. He could not take her away with him. The
only other course open to him was to talk privately
with Lady Cavendish and tell her the truth.

All day long he had been wrestling with the possibility, but he had not said a word yet. How could he? At
the time, of course, the whole matter had been appallingly public, but he had never talked about it or about
her to anyone. Few people were likely to make the
connection between the Sarah Bowen of that story and
the Sarah Fifield now in Bath. Making her identity
public now would serve only to bring unbearable embarrassment to himself as well as disgrace to her. And it
was the worst of all times for him to do such a thing.
He had recently become betrothed. He had with him
his very young and shy fiancée. He could not possibly
expose her to all the unpleasantness there would be.

Perhaps Sarah would do something about the matter, Cranwell thought, opening his eyes as the carriage
slowed and realizing that he had already arrived at his
destination. She, after all, must be as dismayed to see
him as he was to see her. Or was she? Perhaps his
presence in Bath mattered not at all to her.

He sighed as his footman opened the carriage door
and put down the steps. He would have to wait and
see what developed during the evening and then make
his decision.

The Upper Assembly Rooms were already crowded
when the duke and his party arrived at half-past seven.
It was a shockingly early hour to have to be out, Lady

Cavendish had explained, but all entertainments finished at eleven o'clock each evening so that the infirm might have a good night's sleep before rising early to take the waters again. This was one of the two evenings each week when there was a public ball. It had already begun. Indeed, the minuet with which it always started was over already, and the dancers were taking refreshments before the country dances began.

Lady Cavendish led the way to the tearoom. Cranwell offered an arm to each of his younger charges and followed her. He could not help noticing the difference between them. Fanny positively glowed. Her gown of white silk, over which she wore a silver netted tunic, glittered under the lights, as did the silver ribbon threaded through her dark curls, but not more than she herself sparkled. He could tell that she was almost bursting from the excitement of making her first appearance at an adult evening function.

Hannah, on the other hand, though she looked very delicate and pretty in her gown of cream striped satin, lacked luster. It was not that she appeared bored exactly, Cranwell decided. It was more as if she did not care whether she was there or not. She certainly did not appear awed by the splendor of the rooms or by the gorgeous attire of the people who crammed them. He supposed he would have to accustom himself to a companion who seemed not given to the extremes of emotion. Perhaps he had become too accustomed to the ebullience of Fanny in the last few months.

Cranwell saw as soon as they entered the crowded room that the moment he had dreaded was upon him. Although it was full, it took but a moment to distinguish Lady Murdoch. The fuchsia color of her satin gown and plumed turban were noticeable enough, but the waving lace handkerchief made her quite unmistakable. And Sarah was seated beside her, a young man and two young ladies standing and talking to her. Cranwell felt his jaw tighten. He still had not decided how such an ineligible connection was to be avoided.

For the moment he must just grit his teeth and hope that he need not stay long before spiriting his charges away to the ballroom.

The two elderly ladies greeted one another as if they had not met for years. It was perfectly obvious that they meant to spend the remainder of the evening in each other's company. Cranwell bowed in the general direction of both Sarah and her cousin. He did not look directly at the former. The people who had been talking to her had left.

"Bertha, I thought you were never coming," Lady Murdoch declared loudly. "I have just been saying to Sarah that I could not understand what could have happened to you. I was hoping to reserve seats for you all, but it has been quite impossible, has it not, cousin dear? But really, it does not matter. You must have Sarah's seat, and the young people, I am sure, will be only too happy to run along to the ballroom without having to be polite and sit with us to take tea."

Cranwell froze.

Sarah stood up immediately. "Please do sit down, my lady," she said to Lady Cavendish. "I shall be quite comfortable standing for a while."

"I keep telling his grace that I am not quite decrepit with age," Lady Cavendish said. "But thank you, dear. It will be easier to have a comfortable coze with Adelaide if I am sitting next to her. Your grace, it seems that you are fated to be the envy of every other gentleman in the ballroom. You have three extremely handsome girls to escort."

"And we would have made two more in our heyday, Bertha, would we not?" Lady Murdoch added, beaming at the young people.

"I should far prefer to stay here," Sarah said. "I see several acquaintances."

"If Miss Fifield would prefer to stay and take tea," Cranwell said simultaneously, "I should be glad to find her a chair."

"Your grace," Lady Murdoch said loudly, "what Bertha and I have to talk about would interest nobody

except two old beings like ourselves. You will not
mind, I am sure, if Sarah joins your party. She has not
danced at all since we came, though there have been
two balls already. And it is high time she did so. She
does not have to stay with me all the time."

Cranwell bowed stiffly. "It would be my pleasure,
ma'am," he muttered. The situation was far more
intolerable than he had expected. But there was no
way out. Sarah was standing stiffly near him, staring at
her cousin, though he did not look directly at her to
note the expression on her face.

"Oh, do let us go to the ballroom, George," Fanny
said, almost jumping up and down on the spot where
she stood. "I can hear the music. Miss Fifield, shall we
walk together? I do so admire your hairdo. Will you
tell me the secret of keeping it piled so high? Of
course, the color of yours helps too. I have always
envied women with red hair. Mine is so nondescript."

She wrinkled her nose and took Sarah's arm. Cranwell
gritted his teeth and laid a hand protectively on Hannah's where it rested on his arm. By God, Fanny
should not even raise her eyes to such a creature, he
thought. Yet she had an arm linked through Sarah's
and was chattering away as if the two had been fast
friends for a lifetime. And Sarah was to be of their
party for the rest of the evening—three hours and
more.

He looked at Sarah for the first time that evening.
She certainly had not lost her looks in the years since
he had seen her last. Her gown of sage-green silk
embroidered with gold thread at the hem was light
and simply designed, but it revealed a figure that
looked even more curvaceous than it had been before.
Her tiny waist and shapely hips were obvious to his
eyes as he walked behind her, despite the loose, high-
waisted style of her gown.

And her crowning glory, her hair, was still sufficient
in itself to draw admiring eyes. "Titian," he had taught
her to call its color. "Red" was too commonplace, and
there was nothing ordinary about the color and texture

of her hair. He had a flashing memory of that hair loose about her shoulders and down her back, his hands buried in its softness. He clamped his teeth even harder together. She might at least, for modesty's sake, have covered her head with a cap or worn plumes. She was not, after all, a young girl in her first bloom.

She walked with her shoulders back and her chin up, but she did not look comfortable. She seemed to be making little response to Fanny's chatter. Perhaps at least there was some trace of decency in her.

The members of the orchestra were tuning their instruments when the four newcomers entered the ballroom, and sets were forming, but the dancing had not begun.

Fanny looked around her with restless excitement. "Oh, I am spellbound!" she cried. "I had no idea so many people could be squeezed into one ballroom. And I thought my gown very special until I came in here. This is my first real ball, Miss Fifield. I shall have to trust to you to instruct me how to go on."

Sarah had no chance to protest. The master of ceremonies was bowing before Cranwell, whom he recognized from his arrival the night before, and asking leave to present the young ladies with partners for the set then forming. It seemed quite true what he had heard, Cranwell thought, that everyone in Bath was almost forced into full participation in each social event. He had solicited the first dance with Hannah, but he was relieved to accept the offer of introductions and partners for Fanny and Sarah. If they could be kept dancing all evening, all the better. He did not want any sort of friendship to be struck up between those two.

Captain James Penny and Mr. John Staple were duly introduced to Fanny and Sarah, and Cranwell felt it safe to lead Hannah into the nearest set. She danced perfectly, he found, mechanically almost, as if she had memorized every step taught by her dancing master. She did not look unhappy. What was it, then, that made her seem a million miles away from him? She

was his betrothed. In four months' time she would be
his wife. Yet he did not know her at all. Was there
anything to get to know? Was she as empty of character as she sometimes seemed?

He felt renewed resentment against Sarah Fifield.
She had occupied all his thoughts today, and he had
totally forgotten that this was the first day in society
that either Hannah or Fanny had spent. Fanny would
do very nicely, of course. She was enjoying every
moment. But Hannah was shy. The day had probably
been an ordeal for her. And he had done almost
nothing to ease her way. He had not used the opportunity to win her friendship. He had virtually ignored
her. He set himself to paying her the attention due his
betrothed for the rest of the evening.

Yet halfway through the figures of the set, which
one could perform quite mechanically once one had
remembered which country dance this was, his resolve
was already forgotten. He was remembering the first
time he saw Sarah. She told him later that she had
seen him once before, the last time he and Fanny had
visited their cousins the Saxtons, but he could not
remember the occasion.

This time Fanny was not with him. She was away at
school. He came reluctantly, only accepting the invitation at all because he had made excuses on so many
other occasions. The twins were to have a house party
this time, seven guests besides himself, all to stay for a
week. He expected seven days of utter boredom. He
could not imagine what could be organized for a whole
week that he would find at all interesting. But he went.

He noticed Sarah immediately. Sarah Bowen she
had been then. No one, of course, could not notice
Sarah with that bright hair and the pretty, elfin face
that appeared to look on the world with quiet surprise
from beneath arched eyebrows. But it was her quietness that made him take a second look. She had always sat in the darkest, remotest corners. When they
rode or walked, she always hung back slightly behind
everyone else. When they entertained one another

indoors with music, she always shook her head quickly when asked if she would play or sing. The others seemed to dismiss her quickly as a girl of no account, but something about her drew him.

He did not think her quietness due to shyness. There was a calm gravity about her and a directness about her eyes that suggested she was quite self-possessed. Was she bored perhaps, so different from the other members of the party that she could find no common ground on which to interact with them? He was a quiet man himself, someone who enjoyed being alone. He decided that he would try to get to know this girl whose looks and figure should have set her firmly at the center of an admiring group.

At first there was no penetrating her silence. When he tried to converse with her, she drew farther into the shadows and answered in monosyllables. When she looked into his eyes, her own were guarded. When he drew back his horse on their rides in order to keep pace with her at the back of the group, she glanced hastily at him, something akin to panic in her eyes. Yet he persisted, perhaps because he found nothing of greater interest with which to fill his days.

And gradually she responded. When they were all out walking one afternoon, they stopped to look at a folly built in the form of a Greek temple and positioned artfully on top of a hill that commanded a view of the valley and their hosts' home beneath.

"I should like to see a real Greek temple," she said wistfully in her low, sweet voice that he had scarcely heard in the three days since he had met her. "Is this very like, do you think?"

"As much like as a toy soldier is to the real thing," he said with a smile. And he felt a totally unfamiliar rush of tenderness when she glanced at him, startled and blushing. He guessed that she had not meant to speak aloud.

He walked beside her, telling her about Greece as he had seen it several years before during his tour abroad. At first she kept her eyes on the ground before her and he did not know if she was listening or not. But after a few minutes she looked up bright-eyed to question him on something he had just said, and he soon knew that she was deeply interested. And knowledgeable. She knew a great deal about Greek mythology and history. He also discovered that she looked ten times more beautiful with her face animated. This was the real Sarah Bowen, he felt. The other, graver manner was a mask she hid behind.

They were still strolling along half an hour later when he looked up to notice that the rest of the group was so far ahead that they were almost at the house.

"Look at that!" he said, laughing. "We have been outpaced and left behind quite shamefully."

Her reaction mystified him. She looked up, startled, and darted looks of dismay and near-panic at the wooded hillside around them. And she clutched her skirt and began almost to run in the direction of the house. When he increased his pace to match hers and reached for her elbow to help her over the rocky slope ahead, she snatched her arm away and increased her speed still further.

"Don't, please!" she said in a voice that he could only describe as frightened.

He concluded that she must have had such a strict and sheltered upbringing that she was almost incapable of mingling comfortably with new acquaintances. He was not offended. And he continued to seek her company.

And gradually, through the remaining four days of the house party, her reserve broke down to the extent that she often smiled at him with animation while they talked, and sometimes looked up at him and smiled with real pleasure when he came into a room. He had found his breath catching in his throat at such moments. He had never known a more beautiful girl. They talked endlessly. It was hard now to remember what they had found to talk about; Cranwell did not usually find it easy to hold a sustained conversation with anyone, man or woman. He could remember talking about books—he was surprised by the range and extent of her reading. And they talked about art and music. He told her all about his travels and his home, a subject that he did not normally broach with anyone. It was too precious a part of his life to be the subject of light conversation. And she listened, wide-eyed and flushed with wonder. They became friends. Almost.

Almost. Yet there was something unknowable about her. Sometimes when they were deep in conversation she would suddenly begin to fidget and glance about her, ill-at-ease, especially if the rest of the group was not very close by. At such times she would not meet his eyes. And she would never let him touch her. Not that he would have presumed to behave with any familiarity. But more than once he offered his arm to lead her into the dining room. Each time she acted as if she had not noticed the offer. If it had happened once, perhaps he might have believed that it really was so. But every time?

And she had a strange reaction to her own beauty. Although her quietness had set her a little apart from the group as a whole, she nevertheless had her fair share of compliments, about her hair or about a dress she wore. Each time she disclaimed the compliment. Some females did so artfully. By denying that they had the attribute commented upon, they forced the speaker to redouble his flattering remarks. But Sarah Bowen seemed alarmed, even frightened, by the compliments. She convinced him almost that she did not want to believe them true.

She was a strange girl. Yet he found when he was back home again, alone in the place where he most loved to be, that he could not forget her. She had a beauty that set her apart from the ordinary. And he had seen flashes of a vibrant, intelligent, and well-informed mind that was closely in tune with his own. It did not take him many days to realize that finally, without his at all knowing that it was happening, he had fallen in love. He spent the whole of the winter scheming to meet her again, and wondering if they had been acquainted long enough for him to call on her uncle without further ado and ask permission to pay his addresses.

He had been very foolish to allow his feelings to overcome his judgment, Cranwell thought now. Even at the time he had realized that there was something mysterious about Sarah Bowen, some part of her that he was not even close to knowing. He had certainly not suspected that she had spotted him for a fool from the start and had set out very carefully and cleverly to trap for herself a title and a fortune. He had not suspected that she lacked a heart.

And now it looked very much as if she was up to her old tricks again. That poor fool she was dancing with was making sheep's eyes at her and was probably enormously impressed with her grave modesty. She danced with lowered eyes. But she was easily the loveliest female in the room and was drawing the eyes of the other gentlemen in her set, if he was not mistaken.

Sarah was feeling extremely uncomfortable. She had hoped beyond anything that she could convince Lady Murdoch that she really did prefer to sit and drink tea rather than to dance. It was quite intolerable to have her cousin scheming to throw her into company with the very people in Bath she most wished to avoid. But she might have known it would be hopeless. Lady Murdoch seemed quite determined to treat this visit to Bath as basically a pleasure trip for her adopted daughter. And this evening Sarah had been able to put up almost no fight at all. It would have been absurd to have insisted on staying with the two friends when they so obviously wished to be left *tête-à-tête*. And there was no chair for her anyway. And then Lady Fanny had caught her arm and drawn her in the direction of the ballroom as if the matter had been all settled.

She was horribly embarrassed and very much aware

of George and his fiancée walking behind her and his sister all the way to the ballroom. What must he be thinking? She had not dared look at him in the tearoom, but she had felt his disapproval. The few words he had spoken had suggested his own eagerness that she remain with Lady Murdoch. And how could it be otherwise? He must be feeling horror indeed to be watching her walking along, his sister's arm linked through hers, the younger girl chattering away brightly to her. He must long to bound forward and snatch them away from each other.

It was almost a relief to find that the master of ceremonies was determined to find partners for all comers to the ballroom. The timidity she would normally have felt at attending her first ball—if Lady Fanny only knew!—was completely swallowed up by her desire to move away from her present company. She went through the introduction to Mr. John Staple with all the calm aplomb of one used to such social niceties and allowed herself to be drawn into a set across the room with a feeling of deep relief. If she could only keep her distance for the rest of the evening. Three interminable hours! Surely by the time this set was over she would have spotted some other acquaintance with whom to converse between dances.

Mr. Staple, she found, was a personable young man. He was tall and fresh-faced, with unruly brown hair and unusually high shirt points half-covering his cheeks. And he made an effort to please during those minutes when they danced together. Sarah tried to respond, though she kept her eyes lowered to the floor. She had a dreadful feeling of being an impostor. She felt conspicuous, exposed, as if everyone was looking at her and realizing that she had no business being there. And the man who could really expose her for what she was was even then in the ballroom, dancing with his fiancée. She dared not look up even once, for fear of encountering his accusing glance. She hated what she was feeling. For a few days she had learned almost to relax in company. Now the old fears and sense of unworthiness were back.

Mr. Staple was also a very correct young man, she discovered when the dance drew to an end. Sarah told him that he could leave her close to the orchestra, where they had finished the dance, but he would not hear of doing so. Nothing would do but for him to deliver her safely to the party with whom she had arrived. And again she found herself standing with the silent figures of the Duke of Cranwell and his betrothed and the excited person of Lady Fanny.

"Miss Fifield," that young lady began as soon as Sarah took up her position beside her, "did you have a pleasant partner? I do declare I do not know how he succeeds in turning his head with those shirt points, but he seems gentlemanly enough. Did you take note of my partner? Do you not just adore a man in regimentals? He hardly needs to be handsome or witty; the uniform is enough. Captain Penny said that he will engage to dance one more set with me later in the evening." She giggled.

"I think we will not lack for partners," Sarah said quietly to her. "Here comes the master of ceremonies again."

And indeed he was advancing in company with two other gentlemen. Fanny, affecting not to notice their approach, turned and chattered brightly to Sarah. But before they could be interrupted by the master of ceremonies himself, Sarah found that someone on her other side had laid a hand on her shoulder.

"Well, upon my word," a pleasant masculine voice said before she could turn, "if it isn't Sarah. And looking quite breathtakingly lovely, as usual. What are you doing in Bath?"

She turned, not at all surprised. "Hello, Win," she said. "I had the advantage of you. I read in the subscription book last week that you were here. I am here with Lady Murdoch."

"Murdoch," he repeated, eyebrows raised. "Am I supposed to know her?"

"No," she said quietly. "I have been living with her for the last month. She is a relative of my father's."

"Really?" he said, a frown marring his handsome features for a moment. "You are not reduced to being a poor relation, are you, Sarah?"

She flushed and turned away from him and realized immediately the extreme awkwardness of her situation. Lady Fanny was standing a mere few feet away, looking interested. The Duke of Cranwell and Lady Hannah were beyond her. The master of ceremonies and the two gentlemen with him had disappeared, possibly on seeing Winston accost her. What was she to do now?

Winston solved her dilemma, though not necessarily to her liking. He eyed Fanny with open appreciation and smiled down at Sarah. "May I beg the honor of being presented?" he asked.

Sarah closed her eyes for a moment, realizing the enormity of what he asked. She drew a steadying breath. "Lady Fanny," she said, "may I present Viscount Laing, my step-cousin? Winston, Lady Fanny Montagu."

Fanny was gazing with heightened color at the extremely handsome young man who was smiling and bowing elegantly before her. She curtsied. But Cranwell, seeing what was afoot, had grasped her by the elbow and was looking inquiringly at Sarah. She met his eyes and felt her stomach turn over inside her.

"Your grace," she said, "may I present Viscount Laing to you? Winston, his grace, the Duke of Cranwell." She felt utter misery and despair. Could fate have played her a more cruel hand?

Cranwell bowed coolly. Winston smiled.

"Ah," he said, "we have already made each other's acquaintance, Cranwell. Many years ago on a country road when you were visiting the Saxton twins. Your cousins, I believe? And you were present too, Lady Fanny, though you were a mere child at the time. I could not know then that you would one day become such a dazzling beauty."

Fanny's face was scarlet. Lady Hannah was behind Cranwell, and he made no move to bring her forward.

"May I have the honor of leading you into this set, ma'am?" Winston asked, bowing again and making full eye contact with Fanny. He looked politely at Cranwell. "By your leave, your grace?"

Cranwell inclined his head, and Fanny laid her hand in Winston's and was led away. Sarah closed her eyes again. When she opened them a few moments later, it was to find Cranwell staring into them, his own eyes hard and cold. He said nothing, but she could not look away.

"Your grace," the hearty voice of the master of ceremonies said from behind Sarah, "here is a set lacking one pair. Would you bring your partner, and we will be ready to begin? I have taken the liberty of introducing Mr. Sheldon Parke to Lady Hannah Lane."

Cranwell looked sharply behind him to find that indeed Hannah had disappeared, and back again into the wide eyes of a petrified Sarah. "May I have the honor, ma'am?" he asked in a voice so cold that she scarcely recognized it as his. He held out a hand.

It was as she had always thought. There was very little freedom of choice in one's life. Sarah looked down in dismay at the hand held out for hers. Even now it looked familiar: slim, long-fingered, fragile almost, if one did not know that its palm was callused from working on his farms. She placed her own hand in it and closed her eyes yet again. His fingers closed around hers. Warm. Surprisingly strong. George's hand. Sarah opened her eyes and allowed herself to be led toward the set indicated.

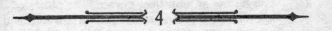

4

IT WAS a terrible ordeal. In many country dances, one was separated from one's partner through much of the pattern. This was not one of those dances. For fully twenty minutes they moved side by side, their hands almost constantly clasped. Sometimes they had to join both hands and twirl together down the set. It seemed that the music played on interminably.

Not once did they exchange either a word or a glance. Sarah kept her eyes fixed ahead of her or, if Cranwell was before her, on his hands. She remembered his hands well: slim, expressive hands, which he used with unconscious elegance when he talked. She had forgotten the ring, though she recalled now that he had always worn it. It was made of heavy silver in a design of entwined bands. She expected him to speak. She expected him to command her to leave Bath, to threaten to expose her to society there, to vent his fury at the way she had foisted herself on his company and that of his sister and fiancée. But he said nothing. She did not know if he looked at her at all.

When the music finally drew to an end, Cranwell offered Sarah his arm and escorted her back to the place where Hannah already stood and where Winston was also bringing Fanny. He bowed without a word or a look and turned to his betrothed.

"I am so enjoying myself," Fanny said to the group in general, releasing Winston's arm but smiling gaily into his face. "Lord Laing has been teasing me mercilessly about this being my first ball and my behaving for all the world like a schoolgirl all agog at a birthday treat. But I positively refuse to have my spirits dampened. So there, sir." She tapped Winston sharply on the arm with her fan.

He laughed and bowed, his hazel eyes dancing at her. "You do me an injustice, ma'am," he protested. "I merely remarked that your enthusiasm is refreshing at a time when the fashion is to appear bored with every entertainment."

"Lord Laing is going to dance with me again later," Fanny said brightly, looking across at her brother. "Soon I shall have no free dances left, George."

Winston meanwhile had turned to Sarah. "I hope you have a free set left," he said, smiling into her eyes. "The next one?"

"Yes, I should be delighted," she said, taking his arm without further ado and drawing him away from the others. This was one way, at least, to keep both him and herself away from Cranwell for a while.

"Do you really want to dance, Sarah?" he asked. "Or shall we see if we can squeeze into the tearoom?"

"Tea would be welcome," she agreed.

By chance, although the tearoom was still crowded, two ladies were just leaving a small table in one corner of the room. Winston led his companion there. Sarah glanced across to where Lady Murdoch and Lady Cavendish were still tête-à-tête, but they had not seen her.

"What is this about living with someone other than us, Sarah?" Winston asked, leaning his arms on the table and looking closely at her.

"It is true," she said. "I have accepted a home with Lady Murdoch. She is very kind to me and, as you see, I am not being treated as a servant. You need not start pitying me, Win."

"Pitying you?" he said. "Why should I pity you, Sarah? I have offered you a better life many times. I am not sure that this is not better, anyway, than that cottage in the back of beyond, where you insisted on living for years."

"Freedom and independence mean nothing to you, do they, Win?" she said. "Not for females, anyway."

"I really cannot see how you could have considered

yourself freer in that life you led than you would have been with me," he said. "You would have seen something of the world by now and had plenty of trinkets and clothes."

"There is no point in reopening that argument," Sarah said, leaning back a little from the table so that a cup of tea could be set at the place before her.

He chuckled suddenly and reached over to touch her hand. "How came you to be in company with Cranwell?" he asked. "I must confess that I had not planned to enter the ballroom tonight. I was on my way to the card room. But when I spotted you, I stopped for a second look. Then when I saw Cranwell beside you, I was so intrigued that I voluntarily gave up an evening of gaming to find out the meaning of it."

"We were forced into each other's company," Sarah said warily. "Lady Murdoch and Lady Cavendish, who is the grandmother of his betrothed, are old friends. They are sitting across the room together now."

Winston glanced in the direction of her nod. When he looked back, he was grinning. "I say," he said, "is old Cranwell about to tie the knot? He certainly won't be delighted to have you around if he is, will he? Have you met the poor female? And does she know, my love?"

"I don't think so," Sarah said with a hot flush. "But it is possible that soon several people will put two and two together, especially if you become generally known as my cousin. I would prefer to change the subject, Win. Have you had any luck at the tables?"

"You know me," he said. "I have a great deal of luck. But I can never seem to stop playing until I have lost more than I won." He shrugged philosophically. "You aren't still wearing the willow for Cranwell, are you, Sarah? I never could understand the attraction in the first place. The fellow isn't exactly a Romeo, is he? He is well-enough-looking, I suppose. But a woman like you can do much better than that. And he is generally known as a thoroughly dry old stick, you know. He has rank and pots of money, of course, but you would have been bored silly in a month. You were well out of that, you know."

Sarah stared stonily into her cup. "That is all old history, Win," she said. "It is really not at all worth talking about."

"You are looking quite stunning, you know, Sarah," he said after a short silence. "You grow more beautiful as time goes by. Those were good times we had together before you left home, were they not?"

Sarah said nothing.

"Well," he said at last abruptly, "we had better get back to the ballroom, Sarah. I promised that chit another dance. She is quite a fetching little thing, isn't she? It might be amusing to pursue the acquaintance. And is Cranwell's betrothed with them too? I really must get a glimpse at the maiden who has replaced you in his heart."

"Win," she said, her voice low but urgent, "leave them alone. Please. Nothing can be gained by stirring up any sort of trouble in that direction."

"Trouble?" he said with a soft laugh, his eyes caressing her face and lingering on her mouth. "Silly girl, Sarah. Always so suspicious. Do you think I mean mischief? You always seem to expect the worst of me."

Sarah declined to return to the ballroom with him. She accepted his escort across the room to her cousin. Lady Murdoch and her friend probably would not welcome her company, but as far as that was concerned, she was caught between the devil and the deep blue sea. Cranwell would not welcome her return either. She might as well follow her own inclination.

Lady Murdoch was not at all chagrined to have her tête-à-tête interrupted when she was presented to Winston, who was at his most charming. She smiled and nodded knowingly at Sarah. When Winston finally bowed and took his leave, she patted Sarah's hand and smiled at her kindly.

"I am sorry you are too tired to dance anymore, cousin," she said, "but I am delighted to know that you have enjoyed yourself so far. What a very handsome young man. And your cousin, you said? He likes you, Sarah, I can tell. Ah, Bertha, the time was when we would never have admitted tiredness on the floor if there were such handsome young bucks to dance with, would we?"

"Pardon me, ma'am," Sarah said, "I have no wish to interrupt your conversation. Please do not mind me. I shall sit here and look around. There is so much of interest to see."

Lady Murdoch patted her hand again and turned back to her old friend. "Do you remember that Mr. Hancock, Bertha? Not a groat to his name, and a reputation that should have sent us into the vapors. But so very handsome. We were all in love with him."

"You might have been, Adelaide," Lady Cavendish retorted, "but I had more of an eye to a secure future. Can't even remember the man."

In the ballroom Fanny, with heightened color and bright eyes, begged her brother to partner her in the next set. Cranwell was surprised. He would have expected to be the last person she would want to dance with. However, when Hannah had been led onto the floor by someone else, he found that his sister did not want to dance but was eager to talk. She drew him to some empty chairs at the side of the ballroom.

"George," she said, her flush deepening, "Lord Laing said he had met us when we were staying with the Saxtons. I cannot remember him, but that is beside the point."

Cranwell glanced at her warily.

"He must be a relation of . . . of . . ." she said, tongue-tied for once in her life.

"Yes," he said abruptly, "a cousin by marriage. He is son of the late Viscount Laing, grandson of the Earl of Newberry." He held his breath.

"Miss Fifield is his cousin too," Fanny said.

"So she is."

"George." She looked into his face, her own flaming. "Miss Fifield's given name is Sarah too."

"So it is."

"Is it . . . ? Is she . . . ? George?"

"Yes," he said curtly. "When I knew her, Miss Fifield went by the name of Bowen."

Her eyes were as wide as saucers. Her mouth formed an O, but no sound came out. "George," she said finally, "what are you going to do?"

"Nothing, I think," he said. "I have been concerned about you and Hannah. It is not at all proper for you to be in her company. But now that you know, both you and I can make an effort to stay away from her as much as possible."

"Are you going to tell Lady Cavendish?" Fanny asked.

"No," he said. "I really do not want any public scandal here, Fan, especially with Hannah present. It was hard enough to live with the first time. I survived it only because I buried myself at Montagu Hall, I believe."

"I can hardly believe it," Fanny said. "Miss Fifield seems such a refined person. And I certainly envy her beauty. I was hoping that perhaps we could be friends."

"Well, now you know that is impossible," her brother said sharply.

"You never did tell me exactly what happened," she said, looking hopefully across at him.

"And I am not about to do so now," he said firmly. "That is ancient history, Fan, and you are still only seventeen years old."

"But how am I to become adult if everyone treats me as a child?" she asked reasonably.

He patted her hand. "I have brought you to a subscription ball in Bath tonight," he said. "Is that treating you like a child, Fan?"

She pulled a face at him. "All the same, George," she said, "Miss Fifield fascinates me. I really want to get to know what is so very bad about her."

"Stay away from her," her brother warned, seriously alarmed. Fanny could be deucedly stubborn once she got an idea in her head.

She smiled at him. "And how do you feel seeing her again, George? It must have been quite a shock to be presented to her this morning as to a stranger."

"Let us drop the topic, shall we?" Cranwell said. He really was not sure if a problem had been solved or if a worse one had been created.

"Do you think Lady Cavendish will realize the truth if she meets Lord Laing?" Fanny asked. "It does not take much intelligence to make the connection between their names, after all."

Cranwell had been dreading the same possibility. Fortunately, Fanny did not wait for him to answer.

"Do you like Lord Laing?" she asked. "I do not believe I have ever in my life seen a more handsome man. Have you, George? When I was at school, I always used to picture Apollo as being just like him. That smile could melt the hardest heart. His eyes crinkle at the corners when he smiles. Have you noticed, George?"

He let her babble on, though normally he would have reprimanded her for speaking so freely of a new acquaintance. Scandal and gossip could so easily burst around him. It merely needed someone in addition to Fanny to realize that there might be a connection between Sarah Fifield, Winston Bowen's cousin, and Sarah Bowen, also his cousin. He could not decide whether to wait and see what happened or to rush immediately back to his hotel to start packing his bags.

Sarah glanced around the tearoom, determined to let the two friends forget her presence. She was almost glad to find that none of her particular acquaintances was present. She felt so uneasy that she was almost sorry she had not returned to the ballroom with Winston. Was he really going to claim that other dance with Lady Fanny? And was he going to try to wangle an introduction to Lady Hannah? Those actions in themselves would be bad enough. But she could not trust Winston to be satisfied with that. He would probably take great delight in beginning a flirtation with

the sister of the Duke of Cranwell. And Winston
could be most persistent when he wished to be, as she
knew well to her cost.

He would always be the plague of her life, she
supposed. Yet sometimes it was hard even for her to
realize how villainous he was. She could never expect
a stranger to detect his true nature. He seemed so
completely unaware of his own villainy. Life was a
game to him. He could not seem to take it seriously,
and therefore he seemed incapable of understanding
that other people might do so.

She did not think he had ever really believed that
she did not desire his lovemaking. She had thought at
one time that it was personal conceit that made him
refuse to believe. He just could not imagine any female resisting his undoubted male beauty and charm,
she had thought. And doubtless there was some truth
in that theory. But there was more than that. Life for
Winston was to be lived and enjoyed. Making love
was enjoyable. Everyone must feel the same way. It
was an almost naive outlook on life. It was strange
that such naiveté could cause such destruction.

That summer during which he had taken her virginity had continued on into September until he returned
for his final year at Cambridge. And that one occasion
when he had ravished her had not satisfied him. For
him it had been a beginning. Despite her tears and her
denials, he had firmly believed that she must have
enjoyed the experience, and he had assumed that the
affair would continue, to the mutual satisfaction of
both.

She had done her best to avoid him, never to allow
herself to be alone with him. She had kept Graham at
her side wherever she went. Tall and thin now, he had
never lost his fair, curly baby hair and his look of
bright, happy innocence. He was contented as long as
he could be close to his beloved "Sare," picking flowers for her and frequently holding to her arm and
stroking her hand.

But despite it all, Winston had maneuvered matters

in such a way that twice he caught her alone again, both times when he had misled her into thinking that he was away from home. Both times, the indignity of the first encounter was repeated. Both times she cried, protested, pleaded, fought. And both times he laughed at her—cheerfully, not maliciously, as if he thought she played a game merely. And both times, when his desire demanded an end to the amusement of physically restraining her, he gently reminded her of the nonphysical hold he had over her. Her panicked, nauseated mind was dragged back to Graham, to the gentle, innocent child who had once been goaded into terrible violence. And in the end she would submit quietly to the inevitable, her head turned to one side, her eyes closed, her will fighting a battle with her stomach to hold in check the nausea she felt.

And she had begun to hate herself. Surely there must be something she could do to put an end to this intolerable situation. If only she were a strong, decisive person, she would have found a way. She told herself this over and over again until her mind was weary. But she could never find the solution. If she told Aunt Myrtle and Uncle Randolph, they might come to her aid. They might also turn Graham off or—worse—feel it their duty to report him to the authorities. If she told the vicar, he might expose her to public scorn as a fallen woman and he also might feel it his duty to turn Graham over to the law. And who else was there to talk to? If she killed Win—the idea did occur to her!—she herself would hang, and heaven knew what would happen to her brother then.

But the fact that she said nothing, that she knew even as she fought and pleaded with Win that she would eventually lie meekly beneath him and allow him his will, made her appear utterly weak in her own eyes. Worse than weak. Degraded. Unclean. She *was* a fallen woman. A woman's virtue was worth more than life itself, she had been taught. Surely she would be able to respect herself more if she did kill Win. But she did not kill him. She merely avoided him whenever she could. And she scrubbed and scrubbed herself after each encounter until her flesh felt red and raw. But she never felt clean. She felt spoiled, ugly. Only the sight of Graham's happy, vacant expression kept her sane, she was convinced.

The summer had finally come to its interminable end. On the day before he returned to university, Winston had had to be contented with a farewell in the morning room, he and Sarah seated side by side at one end of the room while Graham was stretched out happily on the floor at the other, drawing one of his laborious pictures of a forest with hundreds of individual trees.

"This has been a summer to remember, Sarah," Win said. "It is going to seem a long time until next year."

She said nothing.

"I do believe you have spoiled me for other women, you know," he said. "Do you know that your very presence inflames me, Sarah? I do believe I am in love with you."

She allowed him to take her hand, though her arm stiffened.

"We won't be together for a whole year," he said. "Tell me you will miss me."

"Win," she said at last, turning and looking into his eyes, "I feel nothing but enormous relief at our parting. You are a truly despicable and evil human being!"

He smiled slowly. "You are still frightened, aren't you, afraid that I will not care for you or that I will tire of you? You are trying to harden your heart so that you will not be hurt. You really need not fear, you know. I shall take as good care of you as if you were my wife. I almost wish I could marry you, Sarah, but you know that I can't. When Father dies, I shall be Viscount Laing and perhaps the Earl of Newberry too, unless Grandpapa survives him. The old man must be seventy already. I owe it to my position to marry someone of consequence. And besides, you know that money passes through my hands like water. Father has enough, and Grandpapa is an old moneybags, but I still think it prudent to marry someone who can bring me a lot of blunt. You have no dowry, Sarah. It's a deuced shame, but there it is. I'll never love a wife as I do you, though. You do believe that, don't you?"

"No," she said, "if you did, you would not, *could* not, use me so ill!"

"*Ill?*" he said. "When there has been no one but you for me all summer, Sarah? You are a strange girl. But quite adorable."

Sarah's eyes were still roaming the tearoom, though she saw nothing with any consciousness until she became aware of the figures of Cranwell, Hannah, and Fanny crossing the room toward the table at which she sat. She lowered her eyes and reached out a slightly trembling hand for her teacup.

"Lady Cavendish," Fanny said in a bright and breathless voice. She was slightly ahead of the other two. "What superb fun we have had. Hannah has danced every set, and only two of them with George. I have hardly sat down since we were in the carriage coming here. I have had a different partner for each set, except that Captain Penny and Lord Laing danced with me twice."

Lady Cavendish smiled up at the girl. "None of what you have said has surprised me in the least," she said. "You are both remarkably pretty and fashionable young ladies, and it is only natural that the young men would be sensible enough to make the most of you. And have you enjoyed yourself too, Hannah, my love?"

"I have, Grandmama," the girl said gravely. "Indeed, the master of ceremonies would not let any of us miss the dancing. He was obliging enough to introduce us to several gentlemen."

"And George was forced to dance all evening too," Fanny said with a giggle. "I never thought to see that."

"Miss Fifield presented Lord Laing to us," Lady Cavendish said. "A very presentable young man."

Fanny darted her a bright-eyed look. "He danced with Hannah too," she said. "He says that he will be in the Pump Room tomorrow morning and will be honored to pay his respects to us there."

"Very right and proper," Lady Cavendish said with an approving nod. "And if we are to make a timely appearance ourselves in the morning, young ladies, I think it is time we set out for home."

Cranwell bowed and announced his intention of calling for his carriage immediately. He turned to Lady Murdoch and asked if he might summon her conveyance too.

"Such a wonderful young man, to be sure," Lady Murdoch said as Cranwell made his way across the room on his double errand. "How very fortunate that your son was able to net him for your dear granddaughter, Bertha. A duke, too! I hope I might do as well by you, Sarah dear. Indeed, you are lovely enough to ensnare even a duke of the royal blood."

"Miss Fifield," Fanny said, glancing hastily at the doorway to see if her brother was yet returning, "will you be in the Pump Room tomorrow morning?"

"Yes," Sarah said hesitantly, "I believe so. Lady Murdoch drinks the waters each morning."

"We will see you there?" Fanny asked. "I am persuaded that you must have many acquaintances here already. I should be happy to walk with you and perhaps meet some of them."

"Sarah will be delighted, my dear," Lady Murdoch declared loudly. "She has made some very eligible acquaintances, but she seems to feel obliged to stay with me in the Pump Room. I cannot walk about much, you know, because of my rheumaticks. Not but what I am helpless, mind you. But I am not as spry as I used to be. Tomorrow morning I shall positively insist that she take a turn about the room with you, Lady Fanny."

The girl smiled rather guiltily at Sarah and glanced

toward the doorway again to see her brother approaching.

It was a relief to know that the evening was over, Sarah thought as they made their way out to the waiting carriages. Not that there was any reason to relax entirely. It was highly probable that the following days would bring her frequently into company with George and his party.

But even the ordeal of this evening was not quite over. Cranwell handed his companions into his own traveling coach and then turned to do the like for Lady Murdoch. Sarah watched him, supporting with patience the weight of her cousin. She waited quietly for him to turn away when Lady Murdoch was safely seated inside. She was not prepared for him to turn to her and offer his hand for her support.

She hesitated and he looked up at her in some surprise. Their eyes met and held for an uncomfortable moment. Sarah felt incapable of any motion at all.

"Miss Fifield?" he asked, his tone all cool politeness.

It would have been so easy to place her hand in his and climb into the carriage. It would have been over in a moment. She had held his hand for a much longer period in the ballroom. Instead, she continued to stare at him and shook her head almost imperceptibly. She could not. She could not so force herself upon him, unwilling as he must be to so much as look at her.

He remained in the same attitude for a few seconds, hand outstretched. Then his jaw set noticeably and his eyes hardened. He made her a stiff bow and turned away.

"Good night, ma'am," he said.

Sarah clambered unceremoniously into the carriage and drew as far as she could into the corner opposite that taken by her cousin. Fortunately, Lady Murdoch was occupied by a fit of yawning, and Sarah was left to her own thoughts.

How stupid. Stupid! Why had she had to so draw attention to herself? What, in heaven's name, would he think of her?

If only she had never met him. She would not have
done so if she had had her way. She had not wanted to
attend the house party of the Saxton twins. She had
never associated much with them, as they were more
of an age with Winston. They had invited her that
time only because someone else had let them down at
the last minute and they had needed to make up
numbers. Not that she had been offended by that. It
was just that she had been horrified at the thought of
joining for a week a group of people from the best
society. She did not belong with them. But Aunt Myrtle had been delighted for her and persuaded her that
it was high time she went about more and met new
people. She had lost her natural ebullience of spirits in
the last little while, her aunt had said.

She had hardened herself against regret and self-pity
for the first few days. She did her best to remain aloof,
to avoid contaminating the other guests with her less-
than-respectable person. And she would have been
moderately contented just to sit and look—to look at
the Duke of Cranwell, who appeared every bit as
attractive to her as he had on that first glimpse she had
had of him several years before.

He seemed to her to be everything a man should be.
He could hardly have been more unlike Winston. He
was barely above medium height, and slim. His face
was narrow, though his features set it above the commonplace. He rarely smiled, yet his blue eyes were
kindly and his mouth sensitive. His hair was as dark as
Winston's was blond. He rarely talked, but when he
did, he had something sensible and interesting to say.
He had an air of elegance and refinement that she had
not met in a man before. She fell instantly and deeply
in love with him during the first day.

Yet it was a love that held no hope or even desire of
fulfillment. The Duke of Cranwell was as far above
her as the stars above the earth. She was contented to
worship from afar.

When he tried to talk to her, she cringed away from
him. She had no business even to be in the same room

as he. He must not talk to her. He did not know what she was. But it happened anyway. He befriended her, she supposed because he felt sorry for her. She was drawn in almost without realizing that it was happening. She loved to listen to him talk—about his travels, about books, about his home. His words opened up for her a world beyond her dreams, a world that was, of course, shut permanently to her.

She was afraid of him sometimes. Not so much afraid of him, perhaps, as afraid of herself. She was an evil woman, one who excited ugly passions in men. She was terrified that she might have this effect on the duke. She could not bear it if he tried to touch her as Winston did. She studiously avoided his touch and avoided being alone with him. If he once touched her, she was convinced, he would know that she was not as she should be, and he would want to use her for what she was.

But she loved him passionately. And for the last four days she allowed herself to relax into his friendship. She was warmed by the kindness and regard in his eyes when they met hers. She was excited by the fact that he so often singled her out and talked to her about his private world as he did with no one else. She watched his hands, sensitive and expressive, his face, refined yet alight with a warmth of character, and his blue eyes, smiling deeply into hers. And she felt an ache and a yearning that she did not fully understand. He made her feel human again so that for hours at a time she forgot that she was a spoiled and degraded creature, unworthy even to raise her eyes to the man she gazed at with such adoration.

She was wretched indeed when those last four days were at an end and she had to return to Aunt Myrtle and Uncle Randolph—and to Graham. Until she saw him again, she felt a resentment toward him that she had never known before. Why should she have suffered so much for a boy who did not even realize that he needed protection? Why was the world she had briefly glimpsed in these days with the Duke of Cranwell so permanently closed to her? Why must her own self-respect, even her very life, be so utterly destroyed?

Then, of course, she had descended from her uncle's carriage before his door, and Graham had come running in his characteristic ungainly manner, his arms outstretched, his face alight with welcome, his excited laughter almost a sob. And she had hugged his thin body to her for a whole minute, rubbed her cheek against his soft hair, and known that she would die for him before she would allow him to be taken away to prison or an institution for the insane.

There was nothing left in life but to keep Gray happy and wait in dread for the return of Winston. But she was still thankful for those four days. They would be something to remember; the Duke of Cranwell would be someone to dream of for the rest of her life, a symbol of all that might have been.

The carriage was already pulling up before the house in Brock Street, Sarah saw with a start. It really was hardly worth riding to and from the Upper Rooms, but of course Lady Murdoch was incapable of walking any great distance. She smiled cheerfully across the carriage at her cousin, who was busy collecting her belongings around her.

"You must be very tired, ma'am," she said. "It has been a busy day."

"Well, my legs are aching and my back is somewhat sore," Lady Murdoch agreed, "but what can an old woman like me expect? You have had a pleasant day, anyway, cousin, and that is the important thing. I really think you have taken the fancy of Bertha's two little girls, and it can certainly do you no harm to be seen in the company of a duke and his party. And Lord Laing, my love! You never told me you had such a handsome and charming cousin. I shouldn't wonder if he is sweet on you too. You mark my words. I can always tell these things. He would be such a good catch for you, dear, a viscount and heir to an earldom."

*   *   *

The Duke of Cranwell was returning in his carriage to the White Hart Inn, having seen the ladies safe inside their lodgings on Laura Place. It had certainly been an eventful first day in Bath. Lady Cavendish was feeling quite at home. She had met a large number of acquaintances during the course of the day, and she seemed particularly pleased to have met her old friend Lady Murdoch again. Cranwell felt some amusement at the latter lady. His first impression that she was a loud, vulgar creature had been modified somewhat. She was both those things, and yet there was a kindliness and friendliness in her manner that made one tend to forget the less desirable aspects of her character. "Eccentric" was perhaps a kinder word to describe her than "vulgar."

He could wish that Fanny had not learned the truth about Sarah's identity. Perhaps, though, in a way her knowledge would make it easier for him to shield her from the undesirable connection. But Fanny was not always a predictable girl. Most sisters would shrink with some horror from any further contact with such a person, but Fanny was not most sisters. It was just possible that she would pursue the acquaintance just to satisfy the curiosity she had expressed to him. All that business aside, though, he was at least pleased to have observed during the day that his sister had behaved with decorum, though she had not seemed at all shy at the new scenes and fashionable people.

Hannah was becoming more of an enigma to him with every moment he spent in her company. In one way he was satisfied. She had behaved throughout the day with perfect propriety. There were in her manner none of the silly airs of many a seventeen-year-old let loose in society for the first time. She had behaved in a manner suited to his fiancée and future duchess. Yet her quietness defied label. It did not seem like shyness. It did not even seem like boredom. He sighed. He must pay her more attention.

For himself the day had been far from satisfactory. The problem with Sarah had grown as the day progressed. It seemed too terrible a coincidence that both she and Winston Bowen should be in Bath at the same time as he.

He had found himself growing more and more furious with her as the night progressed. She had hardly raised her eyes all evening, had neither looked at him nor spoken while they danced. She had refused his assistance into her cousin's carriage. He had wanted to grab her shoulders and squeeze until he hurt her and shake her until her teeth rattled. He had wanted to shake free the mask, to see her throw back her head, thrust out that magnificent bosom of hers, and laugh at him. That was what she must be doing inside, what she must always have been doing. How foolish of him ever to have believed that someone with her beauty could feel any real attraction to him. She surely could never have loved him, even if she had not already been hardened against all finer feelings.

He hated her with a passion. It would be so much easier to bear if she would just show herself in her true colors. But she had been such a picture of quiet decorum tonight. Almost a caricature of Hannah. He hated her. He wanted the satisfaction of having his hands around her throat. He wanted . . .

Cranwell shook his head sharply. His forehead was damp with perspiration. He must not allow this to happen. Not again. It was quite unreasonable. The woman was nothing to him now. And if she really had learned some modesty, if she really did choose to conduct herself with quiet dignity, then all the better for her. He must learn to forget her when she was not present and to ignore her when she was. And he must keep Fanny away from her as much as he could without a total breach of good manners.

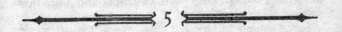

5

THE FOLLOWING morning found a large segment of Bath society at the Pump Room again. Those who were brave enough or sick enough were bathing in the King's Bath. Lady Murdoch was standing at the window, leaning heavily on Sarah's arm. She had been declaring for several days that she too would bathe if only she did not have to look so freakish to do so.

"You know, cousin," she said now, "I am not as slender as I used to be in my youth, and I really cannot see myself looking to advantage dressed in one of those jackets and petticoats of brown linen that all the ladies wear down there. And have you noticed how many of them fix handkerchiefs to their straw bonnets? I should be the laughingstock."

"It seems that the handkerchiefs are necessary for wiping their faces," Sarah said. "You can see even from here that the water is hot. The steam is constantly rising. Besides, ma'am, they are all sitting up to their necks in water. I do not see that you would be conspicuous. From here it is impossible to tell who is who."

"Do you think so?" Lady Murdoch asked dubiously. "But I would have to be helped into the water and out again, dear, and I should be in full view then."

"Perhaps you should try the Queen's Bath, ma'am," Sarah suggested. "It is far more private, I believe, and for ladies only."

"What?" Lady Murdoch cried. "And miss all the activity here? Besides, what is an old woman like me doing worrying about what people will say? I am long past the age of vanity." She laughed loudly, turning a few heads. "Tomorrow, perhaps, dear. This morning I have promised to meet Bertha. Maybe I will just drink the waters today. They must be helping my digestion somewhat, don't you think?"

Sarah smiled and led her employer slowly to a chair at one end of the room before procuring for her a glass of the mineral waters. It was the same story every day. Today, though, she had really hoped that Lady Murdoch would choose to try the more private bath. Then the ordeal of the meeting with the other party would be at least postponed.

While she waited at Lady Murdoch's shoulder, though, it was not the duke and his group who first accosted them. Mr. John Staple came to pay his respects and had to be presented to Lady Murdoch. He appeared as thoroughly respectable as he had the previous evening, Sarah found. He must be younger than she, she was convinced. He was a fresh-faced young man with impeccable manners and a slight stammer when he tried to make conversation.

"Are you taking the waters, ma'am?" he asked Lady Murdoch. "M-my father came here to bathe last year and all through the w-winter his gout was not nearly so troublesome as usual."

"I merely have some slight digestive problems," Lady Murdoch said. "I just drink, you know. But I might try bathing sometime. I suffer from the rheumaticks." She laughed heartily. "It comes with age, young man."

Mr. Staple looked disconcerted for a moment. "I was reading in the Bath *Chronicle* yesterday," he said, "the advertisement for Scot's Pills. Did you see it, ma'am? They are now improved, you know. They are reputed to cure most maladies: the headache, giddiness, deafness, ulcers, gout, and rheumaticks, as well as numerous others. It is amazing what modern medicine can accomplish."

Lady Murdoch launched into a conversation on one of her favorite topics: her health. Sarah looked up to

see Winston strolling toward them, smiling with pleasure. Physically he really did put all other men into the
shade, she had to admit. His tall, muscular figure
showed to great advantage in his skintight cream pan-
taloons and gold-tasseled Hessians, in his blue, close-
fitting jacket and crisp white cravat and neckcloth. His
blond hair was like a halo around his head. She marveled that such a handsome body should hold such an
ugly spirit.

"Ah, Sarah," he said, taking her hand and bowing
over it, "last night I would have said that green was
most certainly your color. Now I have to admit that
that particular shade of blue becomes you to perfection."

"Good morning, Win," she said coolly. "I did not
know that you were in the habit of taking the waters."

"And neither am I," he said, "but how could I resist
the pleasure of meeting you and Lady Murdoch again.
Ma'am?" He bowed and smiled at Lady Murdoch,
who had paused in her conversation with Mr. Staple.

Lady Cavendish and Lady Fanny had entered the
Pump Room, Sarah saw during what must have been
her hundredth glance in the direction of the entry.
Lady Hannah and George were close behind. Lady
Murdoch noticed them at the same moment.

"Yoo-hoo!" she yelled, raising her glass and nodding and smiling until she had attracted their attention.

Sarah's eyes met those of Cranwell across the room,
and she looked down in some confusion. She could
not stop herself from remembering her very stupid
behavior of the evening before, when she had refused
his perfectly civil offer to hand her into the carriage.

"Win," she said, turning to him and speaking quickly,
"would you care to take me for a turn about the
room?"

He smiled dazzlingly. "I could think of nothing more
delightful," he said. "Let us only first pay our respects
to the new arrivals, Sarah."

She had hoped to avoid the meeting. But of course
it would have appeared ill-mannered in the extreme to

move off at that moment. She smiled and curtsied to
Lady Cavendish, nodded vaguely in the direction of
the two girls and Cranwell. Winston was at his charming best.

"Ma'am," he said, turning to Lady Murdoch last,
"may I borrow your cousin for a few minutes for a
turn about the room?"

She nodded graciously. "Sarah does not need my
permission to enjoy herself," she said. "I am always
telling her to run along and find some amusement
suited to her age. Old persons like me are not much
company for young folk, you know."

"Well, Sarah," Winston said when they had moved
away from the group, "and to what do I owe this
unexpected preference? Are you avoiding Cranwell or
choosing me?" He smiled down at her, his eyes crinkled at the corners.

"I merely felt like walking," she said. "Lady Murdoch
is unable to walk very far, and I sometimes get tired of
standing."

"I would hardly call this walking," Winston said.
"This is the merest strolling, Sarah, and the room is
deuced crowded. If you really wish to walk, I should
be delighted to take you out to Beechen Cliff. Have
you been there yet? There is a magnificent view of the
city from the top, so I have heard."

Sarah smiled. "You know I would not do that,
Win," she said.

He looked searchingly down at her. "There was a
time when you would have come anywhere with me,"
he said. "I still treasure those memories. And I still
cannot really understand why you will not allow us to
recapture those times. It could be good, Sarah. We
were good together. I have never been able to find
anyone to take your place, you know."

"Win," she said, "you delude yourself. I thought
you had finally accepted the fact that I am no longer
your victim and never will be again."

"You can't blame me for trying," he said, grinning
at her and covering her hand with his for a moment.

"That Cranwell has a great deal to answer for. Everything was fine between us until you fancied yourself in love with him, or with respectability, or whatever the attraction was. I must confess that my self-esteem has never quite recovered from the indignity of your having preferred him to me. He is not even remarkably handsome, is he?"

"Not as handsome as you, Win," Sarah admitted.

"There, you have had the compliment you were fishing for."

"No," he said, "but do you really find him attractive, Sarah?" He glanced the length of the room to where Cranwell was still standing close to Lady Murdoch's chair.

"It really does not matter whether I do or not," she said shortly. "But you must understand, Win, why I find it embarrassing to be forced into his presence like this. He could make things very uncomfortable for me here if he chose to do so. One word whispered in Bath spreads throughout the city in a mere few minutes. He could ruin my reputation. So could you, for that matter."

"Why would either of us want to do that?" he said. "You are really far too sensitive, Sarah. I always did tell you that. The man looks too haughty for his own good, though. Shall I flirt with his sister and see how he reacts?"

"No!" she said sharply. "For heaven's sake, Win, leave her alone. I would much prefer to see you go back to your cards. I am sure that is where your heart really belongs."

He grinned. "You know, Sarah," he said, "I do not believe I can resist the temptation. If she weren't such a pretty and vivacious little thing, I wouldn't think it such a famous notion, perhaps. But she is something out of the ordinary way, is she not?"

"No, Win," she said. "Please don't."

The words rang an echo in her ears. She had said those words to Winston many times, and always the pleadings seemed rather to urge him on than to make

him comply. Sarah felt a terrible dread as their slow
progress around the room took them nearer and nearer
to their group again.

"One can really see the most extraordinary display
of fashions in a walk around," he said gaily to the
others as he approached, Sarah still on his arm. "I
have two arms and one is entirely free. Lady Fanny,
would you care to take it and join us in another turn
around the room?"

Fanny blushed and smiled brightly, first at Winston
and then at Sarah. "I would be delighted, sir," she
said, taking the proffered arm and turning to her brother
only as an afterthought. "May I, George?"

Cranwell bowed stiffly. "A good idea," he said.
"Hannah and I will join you."

Sarah kept grimly to her place on Winston's left-
hand side. She listened to the flow of charming compliments to his new companion and his humorous
comments on the other strollers, which soon had Lady
Fanny in peals of laughter. His eyes were bright and
twinkling, Sarah noticed in one brief glance, and his
smile at its most beguiling. And she was constantly
aware of George and Lady Hannah walking behind
them.

They were stopped before they reached the end of
the room by Captain Penny, looking as dashing in his
uniform as he had the evening before. He bowed to
Fanny and asked her how she did. She introduced him
to her present companions and to her brother and
Hannah.

"Would you care to join us?" Winston asked after a
few minutes of inconsequential chatter. "We are engaged in the exertion of circumnavigating the room,
and we are, as you see, an uneven number. I have
been fortunate enough until now to have a lady on
each arm. But I shall condescend to relinquish Miss
Fifield into your charge, Penny, and I shall amuse
Lady Fanny."

While the captain bowed politely and offered Sarah
his arm, Fanny smiled brightly into Winston's laughing

eyes and walked off with him. What was it about Winston, Sarah wondered, that seemed to enable him always to have his own way without any apparent exertion? It had always been so. He was in a very public place, of course, with two other couples of his group only a few paces behind him, but even so he was very obviously making the most of these few minutes of near-privacy to charm Lady Fanny into what might easily develop into an infatuation. He had always been irresistible to most females, she had noticed through the years, except herself. And even she, foolish girl, had been proud to be seen with him when she was much younger.

When they again came to that part of the room where Lady Murdoch and Lady Cavendish were both seated, it was to find that Mr. Staple had taken his leave, and Mr. Phelps and the Misses Seymour had joined them. The following few minutes were taken up with the several introductions that had to be made.

"Lady Fanny and I have conceived a famous notion for this afternoon," Winston said, including the whole group in his charming smile. "Why not take advantage of the summery weather, we have decided, take a drive out to Beechen Cliff, and then climb to the top? The view from there is one not to be missed, I have heard."

"Oh, do let's," Fanny said, her arm still resting on Winston's. "I do so feel like a brisk walk. Yesterday and this morning we have merely strolled."

"Bless me," Lady Murdoch said, "I do not believe I could climb even a molehill, Lord Laing." She laughed loudly. "But that need be no impediment to the outing. I have no wish to spoil the pleasures of you young people, who have so much energy to use up. I shall drive out there with you and merely sit in the carriage when you begin to climb. I am sure that by then I shall be quite glad of a quiet read or even a little sleep."

"There really will be no need of either," Lady Cavendish assured her. "I am not yet in my dotage, Adelaide, and I am sure I could keep up with the young people if I wished. But in the circumstances I shall stay in the carriage with you. We might even take a short stroll, you know. We do not have to go right to the top."

"A splendid idea," her friend said, beaming. "Of course, if you are not going to the top either, Bertha, there will be no close chaperonage for the young people. But I really do not think they need to be watched all the time. We shall observe the proprieties by pacing back and forth halfway up the hill."

Winston and Fanny exchanged triumphant smiles.

"That seems to be settled then," Cranwell said in a tone that defied interpretation. "Hannah, do you feel up to the exercise?"

"If you wish to go, your grace, and if Grandmama agrees," the girl replied dutifully.

"Splendid. Miss Seymour? Miss Stella? And Captain Penny? Phelps?"

Cranwell received a bow of acceptance from both gentlemen and a smiling nod from the ladies. Sarah noticed that her own approval was not solicited. Then, of course, she was not seen as a free agent. Where Lady Murdoch went, she would be expected to go too. No invitation was necessary.

She wished suddenly that she were free. She had no wish to continue this situation: George, his fiancée, his sister, Winston, and herself all in company together, Winston determined to flirt with Lady Fanny and create mischief.

"Miss Fifield," Mr. Phelps said, making her an elegant bow, "may one hope that you too will make one of the party?"

"I shall certainly come," she replied in some confusion. "But I shall not be climbing to the top, sir. I shall stay with Lady Murdoch to lend my arm when she walks."

"Nonsense, cousin!" that lady declared loudly. "You must accompany the young people. Sometimes, Sarah dear, you behave just as if you were an old maid already. If I need assistance, I shall lean on Bertha. She is strong. There was a time, you know, when both of us would have tripped to the top of any hill you could name and not even have been out of breath when we arrived."

Lady Cavendish nodded and smiled graciously at Sarah. "Yes, Miss Fifield, you really must run along," she said. "It does not do Adelaide good to have someone catering to her every wish, you know. She likes to play the invalid if she has a sympathetic audience. She always did."

"Well," Lady Murdoch said, looking as if she were not quite sure whether to be offended or to bellow with laughter. She finally did the latter.

"I am so glad that you will be coming too, Miss Fifield," Lady Fanny said, smiling brightly at her. She carefully avoided meeting her brother's eyes.

The outing had been Winston's suggestion, but it was Cranwell who was left to make the arrangements. Before the various members of the group went their separate ways to breakfast, he had agreed to order the carriages to pick up the ladies at their various lodging places. The Misses Seymour were to share a hired carriage with Lady Murdoch and Sarah. Lady Cavendish and her two charges were to ride in Cranwell's own carriage. The gentlemen were to ride.

Sarah was furious. Winston knew that she wished to stay as far away from the Duke of Cranwell as possible. Indeed, he knew that it was positively dangerous for her to be much in his presence, especially with Winston himself present too. He knew that she did not covet his own company and that he could only cause her further embarrassment and pain by beginning a flirtation with George's sister. Yet he had almost single-handedly ensured that all her wishes were ignored. Why did he enjoy confounding her? To deliberately set out to make her miserable?

All through a short shopping trip to Cheap Street after breakfast she fumed.

Perhaps the only time Winston had not caused her

pain was unconscious on his part. She had dreaded his return the summer after he had ravished her, the summer after she had fallen in love with the Duke of Cranwell. But he had not come. He had acquired a taste for more lively social activities and pursued his pleasure in Brighton and Bath. He had returned home for only a few days before beginning his tour of Europe and she had managed to escape his attentions.

Sarah shook herself free of her thoughts when Lady Murdoch suggested that they make their way to Mr. Gill the pastry cook's for a jelly or a tart.

"I really think, cousin, that as well as healing my digestive problems, the waters give me an appetite," she said. "We had breakfast less than two hours ago and I am quite famished already."

Sarah thought of the beefsteak, liver, and kidneys that had formed part of Lady Murdoch's breakfast and turned in the direction of Mr. Gill's.

The Duke of Cranwell did his part to organize the carriage ride and walk for the afternoon. They were to leave immediately after luncheon, but that meal was eaten so late in Bath that they would be fortunate to make a start before half-past three. He found it difficult to adjust to the hours of the city. He was accustomed to rising and breakfasting early and to having luncheon at noon.

He had declined meeting the ladies again after breakfast. They planned a shopping trip. Fanny had declared emphatically that she was already tired of wearing the bonnets she had brought with her and intended to find a milliner's shop that sold something more fashionable. He had given his permission and was prepared to pay the bills, but he refused to punish himself further by accompanying her.

He spent the time instead wandering alone. His steps inevitably led him to the Abbey. He stood in the Pump Yard for many minutes looking up at it, totally oblivious of the fashionable crowd that strolled by. It amazed him that the Abbey could be at the heart of all activity in the city, a mere stone's throw from the Pump Room, in fact, and yet be almost ignored by the people who crowded past it. Most seemed completely unaware of it. His eyes roamed over the intricately carved stonework, the Gothic doors with their pointed arches. He decided to go inside.

There too, surrounded by cold silence, he marveled at the magnificence around him. The church was surprisingly light, its Gothic windows huge. It amazed him how the stonemasons of a previous age could have known how to construct the building in such a way that the massive weight of the walls and roof did not collapse around the large windows. He gazed in wonder at the stained-glass windows, each telling its own intricate story, each gloriously lit by the sun outside.

He sat down, feeling very small and insignificant. Yet for the first time since leaving home he felt at ease, happy almost. He would sit here until he felt thoroughly calm again and able to cope with the day ahead. He felt very much out of control. He did not like the turn affairs had taken. Yet there seemed almost nothing he could do to put matters right. Although he was Hannah's intended husband and Fanny's guardian, all of them were basically Lady Cavendish's guests during their stay in Bath, even himself. She had suggested the visit and he felt obliged to fall in with whatever activities she favored. He did not feel that he could assert his will and dictate to her where they went and—more important—with whom they would associate.

There was only one thing he could do to change the situation and that was to talk to Lady Cavendish and explain matters to her. Surely then she would break this association with her old friend. But he could not do so. He could not be sure that the information would remain confidential. And despite all, he found that he could not knowingly expose Sarah again to public censure and even rejection. She would have to leave Bath and would never again be able to show herself in any public setting. He could not do that to her.

There was no reason why he should feel that way, of course. She should not be there. She should have imposed such restrictions on her own behavior. And certainly it was not right that she should force herself on such an unsuspecting innocent as Hannah. He had every right to force her into more decorous behavior, he more than anyone. He was the one she had most hurt. But he could not do so. Revenge had seemed sweet to him once, but had brought no real satisfaction. It held out no real lures for him now. He had loved her once. And though that love had died a cruel death a long time before, he could still remember. And memory held him inactive.

He had almost invited himself to stay with the Saxtons a year after he met Sarah. They had asked him during the spring when he met them in London, but he was almost sure that they had not expected him to accept. But he went just in order to see her again. Perhaps when he saw her, he thought, he would find that he had been loving a dream all those months. He rode over to her uncle's house to call on her the day after his arrival.

At first he thought that he should not have come. She seemed not at all delighted to see him. He spent a whole hour conversing with her uncle and aunt without once hearing her voice. And the following day, when he returned and asked her aunt if he might be permitted to walk in the park with her niece, Sarah almost visibly cringed away from him into the large wing chair in which she sat, and said that she thought it would rain. Her aunt almost had to force her to fetch a shawl and a bonnet.

But he remembered how long it had taken the year before to break through her reserve, and he persisted. And on the third such walk he finally drew some response from her. He was describing a performance of *The Merchant of Venice* he had seen in London the previous spring, with Edmund Kean as Shylock.

"It must be wonderful actually to see a play performed on the stage," she said, looking up at him for a moment with such a look of bright-eyed yearning on her face that he clasped his hands behind his back and resisted the urge to take her face between his hands and promise her that he would spend the rest of his days showering her with the good things of life.

Gradually she warmed to him again, though for a while longer he carried the burden of their conversations. Yet, although he was normally a quiet man, he did not mind talking to her. She was so obviously interested, and the questions she asked and the comments she made showed that she did have the knowledge to understand what he talked about. She came alive during those conversations, and her beauty became vibrant and dazzling. They walked out almost every afternoon for more than a week, though she would never go beyond sight of the house. They always walked side by side, not touching. She would never accept the offer of his arm.

It was on the tenth day after his arrival that he talked with her uncle before taking her out. There was no objection to his paying his addresses to Sarah. Viscount Laing explained that she had no personal fortune. There was no dowry, though her uncle had decided that he would make a money settlement on her either on her marriage or on his death. No one else knew of this.

They were standing leaning on a fence watching a group of sheep grazing in a meadow when he spoke.

"Miss Bowen," he said, "I think I must have made my intentions clear by calling on you every day for more than a week now. I would be greatly honored if you will consent to be my wife."

Her reaction took him completely by surprise. She jerked around to face him, her cheeks suffused with color. "No," she said in a voice that shook with some emotion that sounded very like fear. "Do not say such things. Please don't."

"Have I taken you by surprise?" he asked gently. "I

am sorry. We have built a friendship in the last few days to match that we shared last year. I thought that perhaps you were not indifferent to me."

She was shaking her head from side to side. "No," she said. "No, you must not say these things. You cannot wish to m-marry me."

"But I do," he said. "I love you."

She gazed with wide, dismayed eyes into his before turning away with a moan and stumbling along the fence line.

"Miss Bowen," he said, alarmed and not a little hurt. He followed her and caught eventually at her arm. "Please, don't upset yourself. If I have spoken out of turn, I am sorry. Truly. If you have no feeling for me, no wish to receive my addresses, I shall say no more. If my company is abhorrent to you, I shall leave immediately and trouble you no more. But please, don't upset yourself."

She snatched away her arm but stood still again, her face in her hands. "I cannot," she said. "I cannot marry you, your grace. I am sensible of the great honor you have done me, but I cannot." Her voice was low, miserable.

"I see," he said quietly. He intended to turn away and leave her there, but the unhappiness in her voice held him. "Are your feelings engaged elsewhere?"

"No!" she said vehemently, pulling her hands away from her face and looking up at him with wide eyes. And then, more quietly, "No, there is no one else."

"Have you no affection for me?" he asked hesitantly. "Have my visits in the last days been unwelcome?"

He watched the tears well into her eyes as she shook her head slowly.

"What is it, then?" he asked, reaching out a hand to brush away the one tear that had spilled down over her cheek. "Is it your brother?" He glanced sympathetically at her black dress. "Have I spoken too soon? Should I have waited? You loved him dearly, did you not?"

She pulled back slightly from his hand, but she continued to look at him with those unhappy eyes. 'I have lived for your visits," she whispered. She did not mention her dead brother.

He frowned in incomprehension.

"You must go away," she said.

But he sensed her pain. "What is it?" he asked.

"I do love you," she said. "Oh, I do love you."

"But you will send me away?"

She put her hands over her face again and shook her head. He put his own hand loosely around one of her wrists and stroked the back of her hand with his thumb. It was the first touch of his that she had not resisted. And a few moments later she was within the loose circle of his arms, her head on his shoulder.

"Do you truly wish to marry me?" she asked finally, raising her head and looking into his face. "I mean really and truly?" She sounded almost as if she were hoping that he would say no.

He smiled. "It is the dearest wish of my heart," he said.

"Then marry me," she said fiercely. "But soon. I do not care that I am in mourning. Oh, please, marry me soon and take me away from here."

He had been surprised. She spoke almost as if her aunt and uncle were tyrants whom she could not wait to escape. Yet he thought them quite unusually fond of her.

"That is my wish," he said. "I have no interest in an elaborate wedding. I want you in my home and in my arms."

"Do you?" she asked him passionately. "Oh, do you truly?"

"I also want to kiss you at this very moment," he said with a smile. He was feeling very exultant, very happy. "May I, Sarah?"

The fear was back in her eyes, but she lifted her chin, inviting his kiss. It was very sweet. He tried to show her the depth of his love without frightening her with the passion he was controlling. Instead of catch-

ing her to him and kissing her deeply as he wanted to
do, he held her gently and kissed her softly on the lips.
Rigid and shrinking as she was at first, she finally
relaxed against him and put her arms around his neck.
Her lips softened beneath his own. And when he lifted
his head and looked into her eyes, he saw that they
were shining with tears and with love.

Cranwell was looking unseeingly ahead to the altar
of Bath Abbey. He had thought it was love. And was
he to believe now that it had all been artifice, an
elaborate trick to intrigue him and lure him into marrying her? That was the interpretation of events he
had accepted during those months of blinding hurt
four years before. And he had never had reason to
think back and reassess his judgment. He would never
know, perhaps. She had always been something of an
enigma to him and there was no point now in trying to
understand what motivated Sarah Fifield.

"By Jove, it *is* Cranwell!" a hushed voice behind
him said. "How are you, my old friend? I ain't inter-
rupting anything, am I? Prayers or anything?"

"Josh!" Cranwell said, jumping to his feet and clasping a tall, thin young man by the hand. "Of all the
good fortune. I have been here almost two days and
not clapped eyes on a familiar face yet." Except Sarah's, he thought with a jolt.

"Hardly surprising," the Honorable Joshua Stonewall said with a grin. "You must be quite a hermit,
Cran. Ain't seen you since Greece. Was it five years
ago? Or longer? I follow the crowds around every
Season, but rumor has it that you stay at Montagu
Hall all year round and actually work on your farms.
You always were something of an eccentric, but really,
there are limits, old fellow. You ain't grown since five
years ago, eh?" He grinned.

Cranwell smiled back. "And you haven't gained an
ounce in that time, either, Josh. Your brow is wider,
though."

His friend passed a hand ruefully over his receding
hairline. Wiry dark curls stood like a tarnished halo

around the back of his head. "It ain't fair that wigs are out of fashion, is it?" he said cheerfully. "I'll be hard put to it to find a female willing to shackle herself to this bare dome. Should have married years ago when I had a full crop."

"Let's go and find the coffeehouse on North Parade," Cranwell said. "We can reminisce about Oxford days, and you can tell me what you have been doing since. Apart from traveling, of course. Perhaps you would care to join a party of my acquaintances this afternoon on a ride out to Beechen Cliff and a climb to the top. City dogs like you usually need the exercise."

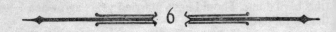

THE DRIVE out to Beechen Cliff was not a long one. They soon left behind them the noise and glare of Bath, though soon enough they had climbed the hill far enough to see the yellow-white buildings spread below them.

Sarah was glad that the Misses Seymour were of the party. They were sensible, well-bred young women with whom she felt comfortable. Miss Seymour was a few years older than she, Miss Stella a year or two younger. Both had been brought up in modest circumstances in a country parsonage. They reminded her of the Clarences, the vicar and his wife with whom she had been friendly in the past four years. These sisters would not condemn her or shun her company even if they knew the truth about her, she felt certain.

With the Clarences she had been able to hold her head high again and put the past behind her. She had confided her story to them, and they had assured her that she would be no more condemned than was the poor adulteress in the Bible whom Jesus had refused to judge, telling her to go and sin no more. Even less so, in fact, the vicar had told her. Being ravished could hardly be counted a sin. The only real wrong she had committed was not telling the Duke of Cranwell the truth that he had every right to know.

Cranwell finally decided to halt the conveyances and leave the horses in charge of the groom who had ridden on the box of his own carriage with the coachman. They would walk the rest of the way to the top, he announced.

Lady Murdoch was all good-natured compliance.

"This is a most delightful spot," she declared. "I can be well content to spend a few hours here."

She insisted on being handed down from the carriage immediately and called upon Lady Cavendish in the other carriage to do likewise.

"I am sure the traffic along here is not heavy, Bertha," she said. "Let me take your arm and we shall walk along for a little way. It is best not to try to climb higher, you know, for then the young people out of politeness would feel obliged to slow down to our rate of walking, and we should altogether spoil their enjoyment. Not but what we could have outpaced them in our heyday, eh, Bertha?"

The two friends were soon strolling in leisurely fashion along the road by which they had come, the heavy figure of Lady Murdoch leaning on the arm of her slim, upright companion.

"Lady Fanny." Winston was bowing and smiling and offering his arm to her. "Shall we lead the way to the top and leave behind the stragglers?"

She linked her arm through his and they began the climb. Sarah's hope of spending the time with the Misses Seymour was dashed when Mr. Phelps claimed her instead.

"Finally, Miss Fifield," he said, "I may solicit with some confidence the company of the fairest lady in Bath. His grace will walk with his betrothed, you see, and Mr. Stonewall and the captain are taking charge of the Misses Seymour. That does seem to leave you and me as obvious companions."

"Your logic is irrefutable, sir," Sarah replied, and resigned herself to an afternoon of matching wits with Mr. Phelps. He was not an unpleasant companion. He obviously was a man of some intelligence, which he used in her case to flatter outrageously. She enjoyed keeping up the repartee, refusing to allow him the last word.

They reached the top of the slope only a little behind Winston and Fanny. The others were quite a distance behind. The two sisters and their escorts, she noticed, were in a group talking animatedly. Cranwell and Hannah made frequent stops, during which he could be seen to fan her face with his handkerchief. She seemed to be having some difficulty reaching the top.

"Oh," Fanny said, stretching wide her arms as if to embrace the city below, "it truly is a splendid sight and well worth the climb. I am so glad you suggested it, Lord Laing."

Winston bowed graciously. "How could I resist an outing that was almost bound to bring an even greater sparkle to your eyes and roses to your cheeks?" he said with one of his charming smiles.

"And how could I resist the hope that a stiff climb would encourage Miss Fifield to lean more heavily on my arm?" Mr. Phelps added.

"I protest, sir," she said. "You are the one who is short of breath."

"Alas, ma'am," he said, "you have too much of youth to enable me to realize my hope."

"Miss Fifield," Fanny said, her sparkling eyes regarding her new acquaintance, "shall you and I walk farther around the hill and see the view from a different point?"

But four of the stragglers had by this time reached the top of the hill, and Captain Penny immediately directed his attention to Fanny and suggested the same walk as she had wanted to take with Sarah. She shrugged at that lady, linked her arm through the captain's, and set off with him into the breeze at the summit.

Hannah was leaning heavily on Cranwell's arm, the color high in her cheeks when they joined the others a few moments later.

"I fear I am not used to such exercise," she panted, looking apologetically around the group.

"I can see that Lady Hannah is in need of a rest," Winston said. "I guarantee that the view will quite take your breath away, ma'am, once you have got it back again and had a chance to take a second look.

There is a group of stones over there that were created by nature as seats for weary climbers, I am convinced. May I lead you there?"

He was at his most charming. Sarah recognized the gentleness of manner that was meant to lull a female into believing his motives to be quite selfless. She felt instant alarm. Was he not even to be contented with flirting with Lady Fanny? Must he use his charm on George's betrothed as well?

Hannah looked up at him with gratitude and immediately transferred her arm from Cranwell's to Winston's. He led her away in the direction of the large flat stones.

Miss Seymour was eyeing a copse of trees just below the summit to the left and declaring that it would make quite a delightful setting for a watercolor. Her sister agreed.

"But just imagine, ma'am," Mr. Phelps said. "You would have to carry all your painting paraphernalia up here. Unless, of course"—he bowed elegantly—"you would accept the services of a humble admirer."

"Shall we walk that way and see if it really would suit?" Mr. Stonewall suggested amiably. "Can't say I'm an authority on the picturesque m'self."

He and Miss Seymour led the way toward the copse with Mr. Phelps and Stella following.

The Duke of Cranwell and Sarah were left alone, both standing rigid with dismay in the spot where the group had shielded them from each other's company but a few moments before.

Each was to think afterward that the solution was easy. Sarah could quite easily have followed Winston and Hannah, claiming fatigue. Cranwell could as easily have offered to take her there and then wandered away as if to admire the view alone. But it is always easy to think of the right thing to do too late. In the event, they both just stood where they were.

The silence lengthened to the point of further embarrassment.

"Do you admire the view, your grace?" she asked

finally, closing her eyes with dismay at the utter inanity of her question.

He did not answer. He stood silent a moment longer, then turned his head to look at her. He looked very grim.

"What are you doing here, Sarah?" he asked coldly. "You must know that your appearance in public is quite improper."

She flushed. "Yes, I do know," she said.

"Then why?"

She hesitated. It did not occur to her to tell him that it was none of his business what she did. "I had no choice," she said. "Lady Murdoch decided to come here for the sake of her health."

"And what is that to you?" he said. "Could you not have told your cousin that you chose not to come?"

"No, I could not do that," she said.

"Why not?" His tone was harsh. "Could you not resist the opportunity for pleasure?"

Sarah flushed again. "I have been living with Lady Murdoch only one month," she said. "I could not have asked so soon for the special favor of being left behind."

"Are you so beholden to her?" he said sharply.

"I depend entirely on her generosity," she said. "Dependents have no choice where they go, your grace."

He looked at her closely, his eyes narrowed. "Is there such need?" he asked. "Do you have no money of your own left?"

"No," she said.

"I thought I had provided well enough for you," he said. "You should have been able to live in modest comfort for a lifetime. You must have been very extravagant."

She lowered her eyes. "As you say," she said.

There was silence between them for a while as she kept her eyes lowered to the ground and he looked searchingly at her.

"Why did you not apply to me if you were destitute?" he asked abruptly at last.

She looked up at him startled, her eyes wide. "I would have died sooner," she said.

"Why?" he asked quietly. "You were my wife."

"I was," she said vehemently. "*Was*, George. You divorced me. I did not even want to accept the money you settled on me, but Uncle Randolph said I must. Do you think I would ever again make myself beholden to you? I would rather beg and starve."

"I would have thought you could think of another alternative," he said.

She looked at him wide-eyed, unable to believe that he meant what she thought he meant. But he was sneering, an expression she had never seen on his face before. She clenched her hands into fists, but she could not prevent herself from trembling or her voice from shaking.

"No," she said, "I could not."

Captain Penny and Fanny were strolling back toward them again, though still some distance away. Cranwell looked hastily toward them.

"Listen to me, Sarah," he said. "You know that it is quite unacceptable for a woman to appear in society when she has once been involved in the scandal of divorce. No one would receive you if the truth were known. It is even more unspeakable for a whore to mingle with respectable people."

Sarah was turned to stone. Her hands were still in hard and painful fists at her sides.

"You need not fear that I will expose either of those unsavory truths about you," he continued. "I could not bear to have people know your identity and realize my connection with such a creature. I will keep my mouth shut if you behave with suitable decorum while we are thrown into company here. You will stay as far away from my sister and my fiancée as you possibly can. And the oftener you are out of my sight, the happier I shall be. Do I make myself understood?"

"Ye-e-e . . ." Her voice was shaking so much that

she could not even get the word out. "Yes, your grace," she said finally, and turned and began to stumble down the hillside in the direction of the carriages.

The Duke of Cranwell stood looking after her. He felt almost immediate shame. Even after four years she still had the power to bring out the worst in him. Hatred, spite, the desire to hurt: they were all emotions that he had thought foreign to his nature. He had said to her what needed to be said, and he could not feel sorry for that. But had he really needed to call her a whore? It was a word that normally would not pass his lips. Yet he had used it just a minute before to describe Sarah, his former wife. Why had he allowed himself such a vulgarity? He knew the answer, of course. The word had arisen from his bitter desire to hurt her, the woman who had hurt him almost beyond endurance.

He watched her stumble and fall onto one knee lower down the hill. Instinct made him start forward as if to rush to her assistance. But he held himself in check and watched her pick herself up and proceed more slowly.

"George, I am so glad you consented to bring us here," Fanny called as she and Captain Penny came closer. Her cheeks were still flushed with color and her eyes bright. "The air is most exhilarating."

Cranwell eyed her and her companion. They both looked immensely pleased with themselves. He approved of her companionship with such a man. The captain was the younger son of a baronet of good repute, he had learned, an ambitious young man who had risen with unusual speed in the army to his present rank. He had won commendation for bravery in Spain, from whose wars his regiment had but recently returned.

Cranwell was not quite so sure about Winston Bowen, who had also singled his sister out for some attention. He did not need to investigate that young man's credentials. He had been Viscount Laing since the death of his father less than a year before, and he was heir to an earldom. He believed Laing's estate to be a prosperous one.

He turned to watch Winston walk toward him with Hannah on his arm. His head was bent to her and he was smiling encouragement. He had reduced his own stride to match hers. He seemed to be a man of considerable charm and gentleness of manner in addition to occasional gaiety. There was, in fact, only one objection to him, and that was his connection with Sarah. They had grown up almost like brother and sister, the viscountess had once told him. That might possibly mean that if he and Fanny did form a connection, Fanny would frequently move in the same circles as Sarah. But to be fair, Cranwell decided, he could hardly object to the suitor merely on those grounds.

"Where did Miss Fifield go?" Hannah asked when Winston had returned her to Cranwell's side. "Did she go back to the carriages alone?"

"Yes," he replied. "She did not want to wait. She is concerned about Lady Murdoch's health, I believe." And now he was telling lies to add to his other sins.

"That is a pity," Hannah said, and blushed. "I wished to speak to her."

Cranwell looked his inquiry at her.

"Grandmama has invited several of her acquaintances to tea tomorrow," she said, "and I wanted to invite Miss Fifield. I like her," she added lamely.

"I shall go on ahead," Winston said with a smile and a bow, "and make sure that she does not go riding off before you descend the hill, Lady Hannah. You may speak to her before she leaves."

"Oh, thank you, Lord Laing," Hannah said with a grateful smile.

Sarah descended the hill more slowly after she had fallen. Her knee was scraped, she was sure, and her ankle hurt when she put her weight on it, but she was glad of the pain because it had brought her to her senses. It would not do at all to arrive in the presence of the two older ladies in panicked flight, sobbing hysterically.

She tried desperately to bring herself under control. He had called her a whore. She put her hands over her ears and shook her head from side to side as if the action could shake the word from her mind. A whore! And it was not the first time. He had called her that once before. And she had not then denied it. She had felt almost as if it were true. She had allowed herself to be taken on three separate occasions. She had not fought as fiercely as she might because of the blackmail. And she had never been able to tell anyone of the blackmail even after Graham was dead and could no longer be harmed. In the years since, she had recovered somewhat from her feelings of degradation and convinced herself that she was not to blame for what had happened. But George had called her a whore again. And she felt as wretched and as soiled as she had ever felt.

She had partly forgotten that, fault or no fault, she was still a fallen woman. Nothing could restore virginity and innocence, once lost. The past would always be with her, making it forever impossible for her to hold up her head in decent society. She had partially forgotten during the four quiet years she had lived in her cottage, minding her own business and trying to make amends for her scarlet past by doing good works. And now she was totally forgetting the careful and kindly reassurances of the Reverend Clarence.

George was right. She had done him a terrible injustice four years before, and she owed it to him to stay out of his life.

She could equate herself with Winston. He had wronged her terribly while claiming to love her. She had done exactly the same to George. If she had truly loved him, she would have had the strength of will to resist his courtship. She had tried, of course. When he came to the house day after day, she had tried to show indifference, even coldness to him. She had begged Aunt Myrtle to tell him she had the headache or simply that she did not choose to walk with him. But Aunt Myrtle had been puzzled. He was such a pleasant and influential man, a duke. He was obviously very interested in Sarah. Surely she could not reject him so ruthlessly.

And she had given in. Aunt Myrtle had never actually ordered her to accept George's invitations. In her heart of hearts she had wanted to go. Life had held so much of misery in the year since she had seen him last. There had been the constant fear of Winston's return in the summer. And there had been the numbing grief of Graham's death early in the autumn. She had not even been alarmed by his cold, since he had very frequently caught chills. It was only when his fever rose and he became delirious that she had agreed with Aunt Myrtle that the doctor must be sent for. He had seemed a little better on the third day of the fever. He had known her. She had held one of his hands. With his other hand he had stroked hers and smiled sleepily.

"Pretty hair," he had said. "Pretty dress, Sare."

And then he had become delirious again. Two hours later he was dead.

It had taken her two weeks to come out of her stupor and realize that Gray was really gone. It took several more for her to realize that now she was also free of Win when he should return from Europe. He could no longer harm her brother.

She was free, but not free to walk with the Duke of Cranwell. Never free to be with him and accept his attentions. But she *had* walked out with him. And all too soon she had found herself unable to conceal the interest she felt in what he had to say to her, and unable to resist the powerful attraction she felt for him. She had come to live for his visits. And she had felt herself come alive again under his regard, as she had the previous year.

She knew that he was about to offer for her. Unbelievable as it seemed, she sensed his growing love for her. And it was perfectly clear to both her and Aunt Myrtle what he was discussing with Uncle Randolph the afternoon he asked to talk with him privately. And she tried hard to steel herself for the ordeal ahead. There was no doubt whatsoever in her mind that she would refuse him. She had to. There was no choice in the matter.

But what had happened? Her resolve had crumbled in the space of a few minutes and she was almost begging him to marry her, to marry her soon, before Winston could return from Europe and stop her and before even a decent time of mourning could be observed. And when he took her into his arms, the last vestiges of common sense disappeared. For the first time she was being held by a man whose closeness did not make her flesh creep and her stomach heave. She was terrified that his kiss would bring back all her horror of physical intimacy. At the same time, she almost hoped that it would do so. Then perhaps she would have the strength to put a stop to this madness.

But it was not so. Being kissed by George was the most wonderful experience of her life. He was a great deal smaller than Winston, only a few inches taller than she, and slender. She did not have the feeling that her head was about to be snapped off her neck or the sensation of being swallowed completely in his embrace. And there was no feeling in the kiss that he wanted to devour her body, that it was only that for which he panted. It was a shared experience, a kiss they exchanged equally, an embrace in which they demonstrated their love of each other without the medium of words. He held her closely but lovingly. She could break away at any time. She put her arms around his neck in a gesture of free surrender and reveled in the feel of his lips on hers, his warm breath against her cheek.

It was not quite like that, of course. At the time, she did not analyze her feelings. She did not even think consciously. But she knew that she had found the meaning of her own life. She had reached a safe haven. She loved him.

And so she had sinned. She had given in to temptation and done something far worse than any of those unspeakable acts she had performed with Winston. She had married George Montagu. She, a fallen woman, degraded, unclean, had played a terrible trick on the man she loved most in the world. She had married him.

She had meant to tell him, of course. He accepted an invitation to stay at Uncle Randolph's and moved there the day after his proposal. He stayed for almost two weeks. Then he went home for two weeks in order to settle some affairs before coming back to marry her in the village church. He decided to tell no one until after the ceremony, though the Saxtons must have guessed some of the truth. He did not want anyone trying to persuade him to have a grander wedding, and he did not wish to appear disrespectful to her dead brother. She persuaded her uncle and aunt to maintain a similar silence. They were to be the sole witnesses at the wedding.

She meant to tell him during those two weeks. Several times as they strolled outside or sat together in the salon or music room she felt her heart thump uncomfortably and her breath shorten as she prepared to begin her confession. But the moment never seemed right. Always she put it off until a more suitable time. After he went home, she planned to write to him. It would be easier to tell him in a letter, and easier for him to reject her. Every day she wrote, and every day the letter was torn up because it did not seem just right. She would tell him when he returned the day before the wedding, she decided. He would spend some hours at the house, though he was to stay the night at the local inn. But she was not able to do so.

Apart from this terrible inability to tell George what he most needed to know, Sarah found the days with him enchanted ones. She lost all traces of shyness and talked and talked with him, reestablishing and deepening the friendship that had grown the year before. Unknown to her, she became again the beautiful, vibrant, and interesting girl she really was.

She relaxed in his presence, no longer alarmed if they were left alone in a room, no longer concerned that they walk within sight and sound of the house. She no longer cringed away from being touched. She loved to link her arm through his and rest her shoulder only just below the level of his. She loved holding hands with him, as she did sometimes when they walked, and feeling the slim strength of his fingers. She sometimes touched the calluses on his palm, and kissed them once.

He laughed. "Will you be offended to marry a laborer, love?" he asked.

Her heart was in her eyes as she smiled back. "I shall be proud, George," she said, "to know that I am not wedding a soft aristocrat who does not know the meaning of work."

She loved the touch of his body and his mouth on hers. And she marveled that she felt no shrinking, only a yearning for more, a longing to give herself fully as the ultimate gift to him. He did not kiss her frequently, and when he did so, he pulled away again as soon as passion threatened to replace affection. He smiled at her once and touched his forehead to hers.

"I am sorry, love," he said. "I would not have you think that my desire is stronger than my love. I shall always try to treat you with the reverence I feel even after we are wed. You are so beautiful, Sarah. I can scarcely believe you love someone as ordinary as I."

She felt worshiped. And she learned to accept her own basic worthiness again. She must not be as evil as she had thought if George loved her. He taught her not to be afraid of her own beauty. For so long she had considered herself ugly and dirty. He once traced the features of her face with his fingers, admiring the smoothness of her complexion, the unusual green of her eyes, the high arching of her eyebrows. He teased her about these, declaring that she constantly looked surprised. And he taught her to value the one feature she had always hated because it made her so conspicuous: her hair.

"I hate red hair," she said once in the salon, when he sat beside her, his hand resting gently on her curls. "Everyone has to comment on it and assume that I must have a bad temper."

"Not red, love," he said, smiling tenderly into her eyes. "Titian. There is a world of difference. You have the most lovely hair in the world." He bent his head and kissed the curl that he held.

And all the time, while she gloried in his love and in her newfound sense of worth, she carried the burden of her secret, the knowledge that she must talk to him and watch his look of love turn to one of revulsion. She was convinced that she would lose him once he knew the truth. And she did not tell him. She married him.

Sarah's slow steps had carried her down to the level of the horses and carriages. She stumbled along, trying to look calm and cheerful as she reached the carriage from which the sound of voices was coming.

"Why, Miss Fifield," Lady Cavendish said as Sarah drew level with the open door, "are you back already? I declare Adelaide and I have been talking so much that it seems a mere few minutes since you left. But are you alone?"

"I came ahead of the others," Sarah said hastily, "to make sure that Lady Murdoch is not too fatigued."

"Gracious, I am not at all fatigued, cousin," Lady Murdoch said, leaning forward and looking closely at Sarah, "except that my back aches and the rheumaticks in my legs prevented me from walking far. But has something happened to upset you, dear?"

"Oh no, really," Sarah said. "I merely stumbled coming down the hill and hurt my leg slightly."

Lady Murdoch threw up her hands in alarm and insisted that Sarah climb into the carriage and put her foot up on the seat. She examined the leg herself, despite Sarah's assurance that really she was scarcely hurt at all.

"My dear cousin," she said, "your ankle is badly swollen. I marvel that you were able to walk at all on it. It is most unfortunate that one of the gentlemen was not with you to carry you to the carriage. I am sure it has not done you good at all to have your weight on the ankle. And your knee, my dear! The skin has been completely scraped away. We shall have to summon a doctor immediately on our return."

"Please do not fret, ma'am," Sarah said, and burst into tears.

"My poor Miss Fifield," Lady Cavendish said, "I do feel for you. It looks as if you will not be able to participate in any of the pleasures of Bath for at least a couple of days, and that is a very disappointing prospect for a young lady. But we will not desert you, my dear. If you cannot leave your lodgings, then Hannah and I will visit you there. And I daresay Fanny and his grace will come too. And I wouldn't be surprised if your cousin doesn't call on you as well. He seems fond of you. You will have so much company that in a few days' time you will be glad to go out merely to have some peace and quiet."

Sarah tried to laugh through her tears. "I am sorry," she said. "How missish of me to cry merely because I have had a little fall. But I beg you, ma'am, not to curtail your own activities merely on my account. I shall be quite contented to spend a few days at home with a book and my netting and embroidery, if indeed my ankle is badly sprained."

Winston arrived at that point and was all solicitous concern when he heard about the fall. He jumped into the carriage, knelt on the floor, and felt Sarah's ankle.

"It really does feel swollen," he said. "But there is no cause for serious alarm, Sarah. You would not have been able to walk on it at all if it were broken. Merely a slight sprain, we will hope."

Sarah itched to slap him. Even through the throbbing of her ankle and the misery of her feelings, she was well aware that under cover of her long muslin skirt Winston's hand had reached higher than her ankle and was unobtrusively caressing her leg. And getting away with it. How could she protest and slap him in the present company? She finally got rid of his hand by wincing and pushing at his arm as if his touch had hurt her injury.

Hannah was the next to appear at the doorway of the carriage, a few minutes after Winston had alighted.

"Oh, Miss Fifield," she said, "I am so glad you have not left yet. I was afraid you would have set off for Bath again because Miss Seymour and Stella were ahead of us. And I did want to make sure that you will be coming to Laura Place tomorrow afternoon to take tea with Grandmama. I am sure she has asked Lady Murdoch, but I was afraid that she might have assumed you would consider yourself invited too without actually mentioning it to you. Will you come?"

"Miss Fifield has had a fall and has sprained her ankle," Lady Cavendish explained as Sarah gazed at the girl in embarrassment.

"Oh, I am so sorry," Hannah said. "How very dreadful for you. Your grace," she called to Cranwell, who had stayed out of sight, "do come and see poor Miss Fifield. She has hurt her ankle."

Sarah thought she would die of humiliation when Cranwell joined his fiancée and looked in at her.

"Can you put the foot to the ground, ma'am?" he asked. "Do you need a physician?"

Sarah could not look at him. She shrank into the corner of the carriage.

"My first task will be to send for one, your grace," Lady Murdoch said. "I inquired after the most reputable doctor in Bath as soon as I arrived. I shall doubtless have need of his services before our stay is over. I suffer badly, you know, from the rheumaticks and indigestion. I have always had the most delicate stomach. I am quite a martyr to the migraines as well, though I suffer those more in the winter when I can go outside less often to take the air. But I am very thankful now that I did have the forethought to think of a doctor, though it might have seemed unnecessary when the waters have such miraculous healing powers. Now you will be able to avail yourself of his services, dear cousin, without the delay of having first to find out who is a real doctor and who is a quack in the place."

Cranwell nodded. "Miss Fifield must ride home with her foot up on the seat," he said. "She must not aggravate the injury. Lady Cavendish, will you take Miss Seymour up in your carriage? Miss Stella can sit beside Lady Murdoch, perhaps."

Sarah thought the afternoon would never be over. She was very thankful when the carriage finally moved off, even though the bumping did not help ease the throbbing in her ankle. Stella was quiet and sensible and talked of other matters once she had made polite inquiries about Sarah's fall. Lady Murdoch fussed and pulled her vinaigrette out of her reticule, not to restore the senses of the patient, but to calm her own ruffled nerves. But Sarah found her cousin's distress for her injury strangely touching. It was almost like having a mother to worry over her.

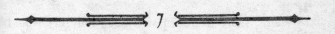

7

IF SARAH had expected the next few days to be quiet ones, she was soon to be disillusioned. The doctor called at Brock Street less than an hour after Captain Penny had volunteered to ride to summon him. He bathed the cut knee and bandaged it, and he poked and prodded at her ankle until she had to bite her bottom lip to prevent herself from screaming out loud. It was sprained, he gave as his verdict. She must keep it from the ground for at least two days, at which time he would call again to see if the swelling had gone down at all.

It was strange to feel relief at such a painful injury. But that is exactly what Sarah felt. It gave her the excuse she needed to avoid accompanying Lady Murdoch around Bath. It gave her a relatively easy way of obeying her former husband's instructions. It was not a total answer to her problems, of course. If she were lucky and the swelling in her ankle persisted, she could hope to remain at home for a week at the outside. Once she was fit again, it would be hard to refuse to go out. Lady Murdoch was so kind, and so anxious to give her all the opportunities to mingle with society that she would wish for her own daughter. It was hard to disappoint such kindness.

Lady Murdoch was determined to stay at home during the evening following the accident. She even offered to read to Sarah from the same book that had put her to sleep the previous day. But Sarah knew that Lady Cavendish had invited them both to join her party at the theater, and she pressed her cousin not to forgo the outing on her account.

"Indeed, ma'am," she said with utter truth, "I shall not mind at all being alone. I shall almost welcome some solitude after the busy days we have enjoyed so far."

"Well," Lady Murdoch said doubtfully, "I would gladly give up my own pleasure for the sake of keeping you company, cousin. Not but what the company of an old woman like myself is a trifle dull for a young person, of course. How can a young lady like you enjoy listening to me talk about my indigestion and my migraines? Though as for that, the waters have been doing me so much good that I have not felt above one twinge in my stomach all day, and I have not had a single headache in a week. For which, my dear, I should touch wood and hope for it to continue so that I do not have to hold you back from enjoying yourself once your ankle has healed. Are you sure you will not mind if I go to the theater?"

Sarah smiled. "The draft the doctor gave me has made me quite drowsy, ma'am," she said, "and has eased the throbbing in my foot. I should not be surprised if I am fast asleep in a half-hour's time. And then you would have wasted your evening on an insensible audience."

"And my prattling might keep you awake," Lady Murdoch agreed. "Not but what it might put you to sleep, too. I know I do prattle on just too long sometimes."

A half-hour later, Cranwell's carriage came for Lady Murdoch and she left, still apologizing and justifying her decision to go out and leave Sarah alone.

Sarah put her head back against the cushions of the sofa on which she reclined, her foot stretched out in front of her and elevated on another cushion. She closed her eyes and smiled. Lady Murdoch really was a dear. For all her loudness and preoccupation with her own health, and for all her tendency to talk a great deal about nothing, she had one of the kindest hearts Sarah had ever encountered. She spoke and behaved constantly as if it were Sarah who had conveyed the great favor in coming to live with her.

She really had not deserved to find such a haven. She did not feel as if she had ever quite atoned for the great sin she had committed. Probably she never could atone for it. The Reverend Clarence had assured her that she was forgiven and that she must look to the present and future instead of dwelling on a past that could not be altered. She had been comforted by such advice, and for a few years she had started life again and gained some satisfaction from the works of charity she had been able to perform under the direction of the vicar and his wife.

But now that life seemed unreal. How could she have convinced herself that the past no longer mattered? It mattered a great deal when she saw George. It remained indelibly with her when she saw Winston. Her sin was still with her. She was still a woman who had allowed her virtue to be taken, whatever her motive had been, and she was still a woman who had had the weakness of character to keep the truth about herself from the man she had married. She was still someone who would be shunned with revulsion if the truth of her identity became known. And it could become known at any moment. At any time she might find out what it was like to be looked upon by many people as a scarlet woman.

She had married George, as planned, in the village church, with only Uncle Randolph and Aunt Myrtle as witnesses. But she had not craved crowds. She wanted only George and the air of unreality that had surrounded her and him since she had agreed to marry him. He looked very splendid in white satin knee breeches, waistcoat and shirt, pale blue brocaded silk coat. He looked every inch the aristocrat, not tall or obviously handsome like Winston, but elegant and very attractive in that way she had never been able to define.

They returned to dine with her uncle and aunt before leaving on their wedding journey to the south

coast and the Continent. They sat on the seat of the
carriage opposite the older couple, and George drew
her arm through his and conversed with her uncle and
aunt. Even then, only minutes after they had become
husband and wife, he was meticulously correct in his
behavior. She could feel the tight muscles of his arm
holding hers against his side, but he would not show
any more open sign of affection, which might perhaps
have embarrassed her uncle and aunt.

Sarah was so happy that her feelings would not
show themselves at all. She sat serious and almost
dumb beside her husband throughout the journey and
the luncheon that followed it, but she knew from the
looks that George gave her, looks with fire smoldering
somewhere below the surface, that her heart must be
in her own eyes too. Even then she believed that the
jewel of their love was hers to keep forever.

Aunt Myrtle jolted her back to reality. She followed
Sarah to her room when the latter retired there to
change into her lavender traveling clothes, half-
mourning in deference to Graham. She waited until
the maid had finished dressing her and touching up
Sarah's hair. But as soon as the maid left the room,
Aunt Myrtle smiled at her and began very gently to
prepare her for what she might expect in the night
ahead. And suddenly it was there in the forefront of
Sarah's mind again: the deception that she was perpe-
trating. She had married George a few hours before,
and she had still not told him.

Was it too late? she wondered. Would he somehow
forgive her if she told him now, before they even left
on their wedding journey? If she withheld the truth
from him, would he know it for himself that night?
There was the merest chance that he would not. Perhaps he had not had a great deal to do with women
himself. Yet even as the thought flashed into her mind,
she despised herself for wanting to continue the deception. Somehow, before night came, she would have to
tell him. Oh, why had she not done so the day before,
a few weeks before? It would have been so much

easier then, before they were linked by any legal and spiritual ties.

They were to spend the night at an inn that George knew, and which he considered suitable accommodation for his bride. She was very quiet on the journey. They were traveling in his well-sprung traveling coach, his coat of arms on the door. She reminded herself with mingled wonder and panic that she was now the Duchess of Cranwell. Her husband moved closer to her on the seat and took her hand in his.

"Nothing to say, love?" he asked her gently. "Are you afraid?"

"Yes. Very," she said.

But he did not comprehend her meaning, of course. He put one arm around her shoulders and drew her closer. "You need not be, you know," he said. "I am not a monster, Sarah, and I love you very dearly. You love me too, do you not?"

She nodded, buried her face against his shoulder, and started to cry.

"Sarah!" he said in some distress. "What is this? Are you so very frightened? And is it tonight that is causing your terror? You may rest easy, my love. I would not force you. If you would prefer that we be merely friends still until you become more accustomed to me, I shall be patient. I want it to be a good experience when we finally come together."

She moaned against his shoulder. "George . . ." she said. "George?"

"Yes, what is it, love?" he asked, shrugging his shoulder so that he could look into her tearstained face.

She was going to tell him. She would have told him if he had not looked at her. But his face was so full of tenderness and gentleness that she could not bear to watch its expression change.

"Nothing," she said. "I am just being a silly goose." She reached for her reticule and fumbled around in it for a handkerchief.

"Here, use mine," he said. And he took her into his

arms again while she dried her eyes and blew her nose. And he kissed her reddened eyes very gently one at a time, her nose and her flushed cheeks, and her lips. When she did not resist, he kissed her mouth more deeply, parting his own lips over hers and pulling her closer when her mouth too opened.

"Sarah," he said a few minutes later, "I love you and I want you. But you must always stop me if I move too fast for you. Now or tonight or any other time. Do you understand, love? You must never be frightened of me. I shall never force you to do more than you wish to do."

She hid her face against his shoulder again and twined her arm around his neck. And she did not tell him.

She suffered agonies later that night when waiting for her husband to come to her. It was a large inn. They had a bedroom each and a parlor between the two rooms. He kissed her after they had dined, late, before a cheerful log fire in the parlor, and told her that he would come to her later. And she undressed herself, having declined the services of a maid, put on the silk-and-lace nightgown that Aunt Myrtle had made for her for this occasion, removed the pins from her hair and brushed it out until it crackled and lay in a shining mass along her back, and tried to bring her thumping heart under control.

She almost cried again when George entered the room after tapping lightly at her door. He wore an ivory-colored dressing gown over his nightshirt. She almost sent him away, as he had given her leave to do. But she did not. She stood and stared mutely at him.

He crossed the room to her and put his hands lightly on her shoulders. "You look beautiful, Sarah," he said, his blue eyes looking searchingly into hers. "Your hair is breathtaking. It is a shame that you cannot always wear it like that. Will you always wear it so for me, love, and never dream of covering it with a nightcap?"

She smiled stiffly. "My titian hair?" she said.

"Yes," he said, "your titian hair, my beautiful Sarah." He touched his forehead to hers and twined his hands in the heavy silken masses of her hair.

And then he kissed her. It was different from his other kisses. Even in the coach that afternoon, there had been restraint in his embrace. In this one, she was able to feel his passion held only on a very thin thread of control.

She wanted to push at his chest, to run in panic from the room. She wanted to sink to her knees and beg and plead with him not to hate her when he knew. She wanted to break free of him and run from the inn so that she could find air to breathe again. Instead, she put her arms around him and allowed her body to rest against his. She parted her lips as she had done that afternoon so that she could feel his kiss more closely. She picked up the heat of his body and ignited into a flame of passion. Conscious thought receded. Pure physical sensation took over.

She did not know how long they stood thus in an embrace that neither seemed willing to end. But finally he stooped and lifted her into his arms, arms that were amazingly strong for a man who was little taller than she. He carried her to the bed and laid her down on the white sheet. He stood there looking down at her, his eyes smoldering with passion, removing his dressing gown. And then he snuffed the candles. In the darkness she was aware that he stripped off his nightshirt before joining her on the bed.

Sarah reached up her arms to him. Every part of her body throbbed with longing for him. It did not occur to her to fear what she had found so nauseating with another man. She forgot Winston; she forgot the secret that he must soon discover. She offered George eager lips, an aroused body, her whole self.

He kissed her passionately: her lips, her eyes, her cheeks, her throat, her open mouth again. His hands sought and fondled her breasts, traced the curve of her waist and hips. And finally he reached down and grasped the hem of her nightgown. His hands moved warmly up the whole length of her body as he stripped the garment from her and dropped it over the side of the bed.

"Sarah," he murmured over and over again. "My beautiful Sarah. My wife."

And she too was whispering to him: his name, endearments, words of love and passion—she did not know what. Their hands worshiped each other. And her body hummed with heat and passion until she thought that she could stand it no longer.

And then he was gazing down into her eyes, dimly visible in the light from the innyard below, wordlessly asking if she was ready. She looked back through passion-heavy eyes, longing and aching to feel him in her, to give him the most precious gift she had to give, herself. He lifted himself on top of her, murmuring soothing words, feathering kisses on her face and neck as she parted her legs to receive him. Then he gathered her to him with tender hands and pushed into her.

His hands tightened as he held deep within her, motionless. His whole body tensed. But Sarah, beyond thought and endurance, lifted her hips against him, her body urging deeper intimacy. And, still clasping her tightly, he withdrew and drove into her with a powerful thrust that was repeated again and again with anything but gentle force until her taut body could resist the agony of unfulfillment no longer but shuddered into violent release. He tensed deep inside her and relaxed his weight on her at almost the same moment.

He lifted himself away from her almost immediately and lay beside her on his back, not touching her. She forgot all anxiety. She knew only that she had had her womanhood restored to her, that she had been made a wife by the man whom she loved above everything else in life. She was not ready to be apart from him yet. She rolled over onto her side and stretched an arm across his bare chest.

"George. My love," she said, wonder and trembling in her voice.

He did not reply. He was staring at the ceiling, she could see in the light that came through the window.

After a minute during which her heart turned to stone inside her, he pushed aside the blankets, climbed out of the bed, pulled on his dressing gown, and crossed to the window. He stood there silently for several minutes, staring down toward the source of the light.

"George?" she said finally. She was not able to stand the suspense.

There was a pause before he answered. "You were not a virgin?" he said. It was a question.

She gripped the bedclothes tightly. "No," she said in a voice that shook only slightly.

"What?"

"No, George."

He turned to look at her, though she was not able to see his face in the darkness with the light behind him.

"What happened?" he asked again. "I have a right to know, Sarah. You are my wife, and you were no virgin when you came to me."

His voice was still quiet, gentle almost, but she was consumed with terror. "Please," she said, reaching out a shaking hand in his direction. "George, I—"

"Did it happen just once?" he asked. "Tell me."

"No," she said in a whisper.

"No?"

"No, George," she said. And then in a voice that blurted unnaturally loud, "Not just once."

He moved a step farther into the room. "How many times, then?" he asked. His voice was tense.

"I . . . I . . ." she stuttered, utterly miserable, utterly without the ability to think or speak sensibly.

There was a silence. "You do not know?" he prompted at last.

"It was more than once," she said.

"You did not keep count," he said. "A pity. I should have liked to hear an exact number."

"George . . ." she said.

"I think perhaps you had better be silent, madam," he said. And she could have sworn that it was a stranger who stood there, his back still to the window so that she could see nothing of him except a dark outline.

He stood there for what seemed like interminable minutes. And she sat there, the bedclothes still clutched in cold fists, her mind screaming at her to start talking, to tell him the whole story, to convince him that it had not been of her own choosing, that she had been blackmailed and ravished. She said nothing.

"You are a whore," he said at last, incredulity in his voice. And he laughed harshly. "I have married a whore. I congratulate you, madam. You thought to retire from a demanding profession and made sure that you chose a permanent protector whose pockets are not likely to run dry. I do not doubt that you know how rich I am."

She was able to respond in no other way than to shake her head from side to side and look at him imploringly. But perhaps in the darkness he did not even see her.

"God!" he said at last, apparently losing control for the first time. He passed a hand over his face and head. "God! What a fool! And I imagined that you could love me. What could a beautiful creature like you see in someone like me to love? What a romantic fool to believe in such miracles. God! To be fooled by a whore."

And finally sound came from her. She wailed against the blankets that she pressed to her mouth. "George . . ." she said. "George . . ."

"I cannot think," he had wearily. "God, Sarah, I cannot think."

And finally he turned abruptly toward the door and left her alone, his nightshirt lying abandoned on the floor beside the bed.

She did not move for several hours. She sat holding the blankets to her mouth, unaware that her bare skin was cold against the night air. She was unable to think for most of that time, did not want to think. But with the coming of dawn came the knowledge that she would have to fight to keep her marriage. She would have to do what she should have done weeks ago and go to him and tell him the whole story. He would be angry, hurt. Their love would perhaps never be the same again. But surely he would at least have to admit that she was not that horrible thing he had called her. He would understand about Gray. Surely. He had a sister, whom he loved.

She rose and washed and dressed herself. She brushed and dressed her hair carefully. And then she took a deep breath and crossed the parlor to knock on his door. She tried the handle timidly after the third knock and found that the door was not locked. It did not need to be. There was nothing and nobody inside except the inn furniture.

She hugged herself against panic for a half-hour until a knock at the outer door sent her hurtling to open it. Her husband's wooden-faced coachman announced that he was at her service to convey her to her uncle's house as soon as it was her pleasure to leave.

She packed her things with trembling hands, trying not to think, trying to convince herself that George would be waiting for her in the carriage. Somehow she would convince him that she was not as bad as he had thought the night before. Somehow she would convince him not to take her back to Uncle Randolph's.

But when the footman handed her into the crested carriage, she found it empty. And she was not consulted by the coachman as to the destination she desired. By early afternoon she was being helped down outside the front door of her uncle's home.

Sarah was roused from a waking nightmare by a knocking at the outside door. She pulled herself more upright on the sofa and frowned. It was too early for the play to be finished, surely. But who would be calling at such an hour?

The housekeeper knocked lightly on the door of the salon and came inside, closing the door behind her. She was frowning in some disapproval.

"There is a Lord Laing to see you, Miss Fifield," she said. "I told him that you were indisposed and that her ladyship is from home, but he said that he knows all that and has come to see how you do. Shall I let him in, miss?"

Sarah sighed. 'Yes, Mrs. Bergland," she said, "I shall see him."

"Will you be wanting me to stay, miss?" Mrs. Bergland asked.

"No, it is quite all right," Sarah assured her. "Lord Laing is my cousin. He is naturally concerned about my accident. He was with us this afternoon, you see."

The housekeeper went away and a few moments later opened the door again to usher Winston in. He handed a black cloak, a top hat, and a cane to her and smiled at Sarah. He really was looking quite devastatingly handsome, she thought dispassionately. He was dressed all in silver silk and black velvet, a stunning choice of colors with his blond hair and his very masculine figure.

"Win?" she said. "To what do I owe this great honor? I would have thought you would be deep into a card game by now."

He grinned. "The card games that are allowed in this place were designed for old ladies," he said. "Low stakes. No excitement. And the games that are not allowed I cannot afford to get into at the moment. My pockets are sadly to let."

"I was not aware that that usually stopped you," she remarked.

"Sarah," he said, "you are developing quite a sharp tongue. You need not worry about me, you know. I shall come about. I always do."

"Yes," she said, "I remember one of those occasions well."

He made a gesture of surrender. "I didn't come here to talk about my financial position," he said. "I was worried about you, Sarah. I was at the theater, and there were your so-called cousin and all her cronies sitting together with not a sign of you. I waited on them during the interval only to discover that indeed your injury was serious enough to confine you to your lodgings. I missed the second half of the play in order to call and try to cheer you up." He smiled and seated himself on the sofa close to her shoulder.

"That is kind of you, Win," she said, "but I really was not feeling lonely, you know. I was quite glad of some quiet time to myself."

"Poor Sarah," he said, smiling warmly into her eyes and placing one hand on her shoulder. "Does it hurt very much, your ankle?"

"Not at the moment," she said. "The doctor has given me a draft to ease the throbbing."

"Ah," he said, "you will be feeling drowsy then?" The back of his forefinger stroked lightly along the skin of her neck above the high neckline of her dress.

"Not that drowsy!" Sarah said, pulling away from his hand.

"Sarah," he said, his face hovering above hers, "will you never stop fighting me? You know you are living on the edge of a cliff here, do you not? Bath society would not tolerate your presence if they knew you were a divorced woman. And the secret of your true identity is really not a very safe secret, is it?"

"Are you threatening me, Win?" Sarah asked, staring coldly back at him.

His eyes widened. "Threatening you?" he said. "Whatever do you mean? I am merely trying to get you to face reality, Sarah. If you have come here husband-hunting, you might as well forget your plans. Even if you can keep your secret long enough to get someone to offer for you, he is bound to find out before the marriage. To me none of these things matter. Only you. I have never fully recovered from losing you. I would take you back in a moment, Sarah. And once you are my mistress again, you do not have to worry about what anyone says. You will be under my protection. And I would protect you. You are very precious to me."

Sarah looked into the handsome face so close to her own and marveled afresh at how such beauty and such apparent sincerity could hide an almost frightening lack of moral awareness. Winston seemed totally unable to identify with the feelings of other people. Were his own feelings so shallow that he did not know that such things existed?

"Win," she said steadily, "I told you a long time ago that our affair was over. Forever. You took full advantage of me when I was a very young and green girl and did not know how to fight you. And my life will forever be in ruins as a result of that. But even a fallen woman, you know, can have some remnants of self-respect. I am old enough now to choose, and I choose to belong to no man."

He shook his head. "You always were a tender and silly girl, Sarah," he said. "What is all this about a fallen woman? There is nothing so dreadful about becoming a man's mistress when you do not have the connections or the fortune to expect a husband."

She stared stonily at him.

"Oh, I know," he said. "You have the old complaint, I suppose. You did attract a husband and a pretty impressive one too, if one considers only his title and wealth. But that could not have been foreseen, Sarah. You are very beautiful, of course, and even a man of Cranwell's consequence can sometimes lose his heart to beauty. And of course, I was blamed because the man objected to being handed damaged goods. I'm sorry. There, does that make you feel better, Sarah? I'm sorry."

"No, not at all better, Win," she said.

"Come back to me, Sarah," he said suddenly with some urgency. "God, I want you. You are so beautiful." He put a hand on each of her shoulders and leaned over her.

"Don't come any closer, Win," she said calmly, "or I shall slap you very hard."

"You don't mean it, Sarah," he coaxed, his eyes straying to her lips. "Let me remind you of what it used to be like."

"Go away, Win," she said.

"I could marry you, you know," he said. "There is the faintest possibility. Is Lady Murdoch the old moneybags she looks to be?"

Sarah stiffened.

"She is very fond of you," Winston said. "It seems altogether possible that she will make you her heir, Sarah, if you play your cards right."

Sarah put up her hands and pushed at his chest with such furious energy that he let go of her and sat upright. "Win," she said, "there is not the smallest possibility that I will ever marry you. Not the slightest. You have taken my virtue. You have destroyed my marriage. You have taken the little money I had. That is all, Win. I have done with giving to you."

He stood up and looked down at her, his head on one side. "You may change your mind yet," he said, and he smiled slowly at her. "If your secret suddenly becomes known, you will be very glad to come to me. There will be no other choice for you, will there? And I won't reject you. I shall welcome you with open arms. We were made to be together, Sarah, and we *will* be together. Believe me."

"Oh!" Sarah said, pulling herself upright on the sofa and wincing with the sudden pain. "You are threatening me. Either I become your mistress or you drop a suggestion into someone's ear. Am I right?"

He smiled until his eyes crinkled at the corners. "Now, Sarah," he said gently, "would I do a thing like that?" He kissed two fingers and leaned over to place them against her lips. "Good night. I shall call tomorrow, perhaps, to see how you do."

Sarah resisted the urge to snatch the pillow from beneath her foot and throw it at his head as he left the room unhurriedly.

The effects of the draft were wearing off, she thought wearily as she leaned back again and closed her eyes.

Her head was beginning to thump and her foot was
throbbing so persistently that her whole body felt like
a giant and painful pulse. Thank heaven the day was
finally over, she thought. What a disaster it had been!
In a moment she would ring for Mrs. Bergland and
beg her help up the stairs. Then she would take the
draft that the doctor had left for the night and put
herself into merciful sleep.

Another ring at the doorbell brought her back to
the present again. This time it doubtless was Lady
Murdoch returned from the theater. Well, perhaps it
would help to sit and listen to an account of the
evening's events for a few minutes before retiring.
Perhaps it would help her mind to relax. She smiled
and prepared to hide her pain as she heard the strident
voice of her cousin approach the salon.

But when Lady Murdoch entered the room, Sarah's
smile faded. Behind her was the Duke of Cranwell.

"Yes," Lady Murdoch said, "I thought she would
still be up. I said so, did I not?"

Sarah stared, mesmerized, into the serious blue eyes
of her former husband.

"Sarah, my love," Lady Murdoch said, "I was telling Bertha that I had left you reclining in the salon,
and it suddenly occurred to me that it would be painful for you to climb the stairs to bed. Mrs. Bergland
would help you, of course, as would I, my dear, if my
rheumaticks would not make me so unreliable as a
support. But hopping along even with support, you
know, can jar an injury quite nastily. His grace very
kindly insisted on conveying me back here in his own
carriage after taking Bertha and the girls home, and I
have taken the liberty of asking him to come in and
carry you up to your room." She beamed down on her
young charge.

Sarah was cold with horror. Somehow her eyes had
become locked with George's. The idea was unthinkable. Even if he were a mere acquaintance, it would
be most improper for him to carry her upstairs to her
bedchamber. Only Lady Murdoch could have suggested

such a thing without a thought to propriety. But
George . . . !

"I . . . I . . ." she said. "I had planned to sit up with
you for a while, ma'am. And really, my leg is not
nearly so painful now. And I am far too heavy for his
grace to carry upstairs."

"Oh," Lady Murdoch said, "I am too weary to sit
up and talk tonight, dear. Not but what there is not a
great deal to tell you. Such an entertaining play, Sarah.
And so much else besides to look at."

"I think I can contrive to carry you to your bed
without dropping you, Miss Fifield," Cranwell said,
his eyes still locked on hers.

He had carried her to her bed on a previous occasion! Sarah shook her head, panic rising in her, but he
was approaching her with purposeful strides.

"Put your arm around my neck, ma'am," he said.

She found herself complying, and tightened her grip
when he slipped one arm under her knees and one
beneath her arms and lifted her off the sofa. She
closed her eyes.

And again she was surprised by the strength of the
man who held her. He strode up the stairs just as if he
bore no burden at all. Neither spoke until he reached
the top. She was achingly aware of him, made faint by
her love for him. She was almost overpowered by the
need to put her other arm around his neck and hide
her face against him. She wanted to beg and plead for
. . . What?

"You will have to tell me which is your room,"
Cranwell said, his voice quite toneless.

"It is around to the left," she said, her jaws so tense
that the words would hardly form themselves.

When they reached the room, he paused and she
turned the doorknob with her free hand. The candles
had already been lit and the bedclothes turned down,
Sarah saw at a glance. Her face burned at the intimacy
of the setting. She had expected that Lady Murdoch
would follow them up the stairs, but she had not.

Cranwell crossed to the bed and set her down gently. She waited tensely for him to leave.

He looked down at her, his face expressionless. "You are in pain," he said. A statement.

"Just a little," she admitted.

"Do you have anything to lessen it?" he asked.

"Yes," she said. "The doctor left a draft."

He nodded and half-turned to leave. But he turned back again. "I should not have said what I said this afternoon," he said, his face and voice still without expression. "I wish you would accept my apologies."

Sarah looked back at him numbly. "You spoke only the truth," she whispered.

He frowned and shook his head slightly. "I spoke to wound," he said. "There can be no excuse for that."

He looked at her a moment longer, the frown still creasing his brow. Then he turned abruptly.

"Good night, Sarah," he said.

She was in tears before he closed the door quietly behind him. Sarah! Surely this must now be the end of the day. There could not be any more. She would not be able to endure any more.

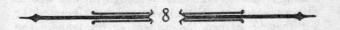

8

THE DUKE of Cranwell was riding in the hills outside Bath with his friend Joshua Stonewall very early the following morning. It felt good to be away from city streets and crowds of people. With Josh he could relax and talk if he wished or be silent if he preferred. That was the mark of true friendship, he felt. He had never done so much talking and so much listening as he had been forced into in the last three days. When one was in society it was necessary constantly to maintain a conversation, even when there was nothing to say. And he was so tired of it all. He longed to be at home in his own company again.

Josh had suggested the ride when they were both at the theater the previous evening, though he had been planning one anyway. Sitting idle in his inn room until it was time to fetch the ladies to the Pump Room was something he could not do day after day. He must have some exercise and some space around him. He liked Bath; it must be one of the most beautiful cities in all of England. But he would never be able to live in a large center. He felt hemmed in. He felt as if his identity was being sapped by the demands of society around him. He was becoming less an individual than an anonymous member of the British aristocracy.

He had noticed that fact particularly the evening before. At the theater people had bowed and curtsied to him wherever he turned. And it had taken him a while to realize that he was being paid more deference than most of the people around him. Clearly it was his title that had drawn attention. In the course of two days news had circulated that there was a duke in

residence at Bath. Thus he was treated as if he were
someone of particular importance.

It was quite comical, really. He felt like a rather
ordinary person. At home, although he was treated
with a respect that he took very much for granted, he
felt that he earned the esteem of his tenants and
neighbors. He worked as hard as any of them did,
doing as much manual labor as they as well as much
paperwork and managerial duties. He never felt as if
he was deferred to merely because of his superior
rank. His dukedom meant very little to him as such,
though he admitted freely to himself that he enjoyed
the benefits that it had brought him, in particular his
home. Montagu Hall and its vast estates were very
dear to him.

"Do you spend much time at home, Josh?" he asked
his friend curiously, reining back his horse so that they
rode abreast.

"At Oakland?" Joshua asked. "Not more than I
have to. M'mother lives there, of course, and I have to
pay a duty call twice a year or so. Why?"

"Don't you have the urge to live on your land,"
Cranwell asked, "and to get to know how it works?
Don't you ever feel that you want to get right into the
land and make it work for you?"

"Good Lord, no!" Joshua said emphatically. "What
do I pay a bailiff and laborers for?"

"You spend all your time, then, moving from one
fashionable spot to another?" Cranwell said.

"Why have money if one can't enjoy it?" his friend
asked. "I go hunting and shooting in season, spend
part of the year in London, parts in Brighton or Bath
or Tunbridge. I even went to Harrogate last year. All
that way because I heard the delectable Miss Weston
would be there. She was, and her betrothal was announced two days after my arrival!"

Cranwell laughed. "I shall have to have you come to
me at some time," he said. "I shall teach you to get
down on your knees and take up a fistful of good
black soil. Your life is too frivolous, Josh."

His friend laughed too. "And yours too mundane for me," he said.

Cranwell drew his horse slightly ahead again. How strange it was sometimes to find how different other people could be from oneself. His life would seem so rootless, so pointless if he lived as Josh did. He really did wish he could go home, or at least that a term of one week or perhaps two could be put on their visit. Unfortunately, Lady Cavendish appeared to be more intent on staying at least a month. And Fanny would doubtless do her part to see that that time would be extended.

She was doing very well in her debut in society. They had been here only two days, and already she had gathered a small court of admirers as well as a group of young lady acquaintances. Last evening Captain Penny, Winston Bowen, and two or three other gentlemen with whom she had danced at the ball had come to pay their respects to her, and she had detained each of them with her bright chatter. He was aware that her position as his sister probably accounted for some of the notice that was being taken of her. But despite that fact, she was a very pretty girl. He had not particularly noticed before, but now he could see her with new eyes. She was almost as tall as he and very slender. Her cheeks were always flushed pink and her eyes sparkling with zest for life. Her hair was the feature that she hated because it was no decided color. But its high gloss prevented it from ever being labeled mousy.

He did not want Fanny to attach herself too soon to one man. He had already resigned himself to spending the following spring in London so that he could introduce both his wife and his sister to the *ton* during the Season and see them properly presented at court. There Fanny could look around her in more leisurely fashion for a husband. Even then she would be but eighteen. But even so, it was gratifying to see her gaining practice at mingling with people of her own class and making some connections that could be reestablished in London.

Cranwell thoroughly approved of her friendship with Penny. He was a silent young man but perfectly respectable. In fact, if Fanny were to choose a husband soon, she could hardly do better than to pick such a man. His reticence would balance her exuberance, yet it did not denote weakness, Cranwell guessed. The man was, after all, a military hero.

Bowen too seemed to be a perfectly acceptable suitor. Cranwell had watched him carefully the day before and approved of his gaiety and charm. He had looked for irresponsibility in the one and lack of sincerity in the other, but there had been no signs of either. During yesterday's walk, Bowen had climbed the hill with Fanny, but he had not monopolized her company, as was most proper. At the top he had shown concern and kindness to Hannah by perceiving her tiredness. The evening before he had conversed with the whole party amiably during one interval but had not hung around them to make his stay an unwelcome length. In fact, Cranwell had not even seen him again during the rest of the evening.

He had not missed noticing, either, the attention Bowen paid Sarah. He was her cousin and, of course, must know the scandal of her past. Yet he did not shun her. He stood by her. Cranwell could admire his loyalty.

Bowen was the only person with whom he had seen Hannah conversing the previous evening. The man seemed to have the gift that he himself did not have: the knack of conversing easily with all kinds of people and getting them to respond.

Cranwell was becoming downright troubled about Hannah. She had not enjoyed the play, though she had dutifully claimed to do so when asked by her grandmother on the journey home. And she had not responded to any of his overtures at conversation. He really had tried. He had had no distractions that evening, but for once had been free to devote his whole attention to his fiancée. But it had been hopeless. She had rarely responded with more than a monosyllable to even his most careful questions.

Had he made a mistake in engaging himself to her so precipitately? he wondered. It was true that he would hate to have a prattling wife, but could not a silent one be almost equally provoking? When he had chosen, he had considered only his own satisfaction and comfort. It had not entered his mind that his chosen bride might also have ideas of what constituted happiness. Perhaps Hannah had an active aversion to him. Perhaps she had been given no choice in the question of his proposal. Maybe she had been forced in some way into accepting. It was a humbling thought.

He did not know whether he should bring the matter into the open and ask her outright, or whether it was better to leave matters as they were. After all, even if she freely admitted to him that she did not wish to be his wife, there was little they could do about the matter. Only she could break the engagement, and if she did so, she would be in deep trouble with her father if it was true that he had forced her into it in the first place.

Cranwell sighed. Life could be so complicated when one became involved with another person.

"Should we turn back, Cran?" Joshua asked from behind him. "We will have to do so now if we are to attend the Pump Room this morning. I should hate the thought of missing a whole morning's gossip."

Cranwell laughed. "And I should hate to face my ladies if I fail to arrive in Laura Place in time to escort them," he said, turning his horse's head in the direction of Bath again.

"You certainly have a handsome trio," Joshua said. "It don't seem fair, Cran, that you never make an effort to go into society, yet when you do appear, you are surrounded by all the most handsome females. Lady Cavendish is always held to be the most striking of the ladies above forty. And Lady Hannah is lovely. It shouldn't be allowed, my friend, that you can rob the schoolroom before any other male has a chance to put in a bid."

"Josh," Cranwell said dryly, "you have had chances

galore these past ten years. I can remember the time
when any one of half a dozen very eligible young
ladies would have taken you at the drop of a hat. But
you were always too much afraid that if you got leg-
shackled you would have to stop your eyes from
roving."

"Ah, very true," Joshua sighed. "And it becomes
harder as the years go by, my friend. The ladies become lovelier, I would swear. Take Lady Fanny, for
example. Pure English rose, Cran. And have you noticed that young cousin of Lady Murdoch's? Or have
your eyes been too taken with your betrothed? Pure
loveliness, Cran. A body to die for. And that hair! Do
you think an introduction yesterday afternoon is enough
of an acquaintance to enable me to call on her while
she is confined to her lodgings? A deuced inconve-
nient accident, that."

There was a noticeable pause in the conversation. "I
think you are a better judge than I, Josh, of what is
correct social behavior and what is not," Cranwell
said.

"Come with me," Joshua suggested. "You are better acquainted than I. This afternoon?"

"I think not," Cranwell said hastily. "I am not much
in the way of paying calls on strange ladies, Josh."

His friend sighed with exaggerated frustration. "I
may be doomed to wait until she is able to go abroad
again," he said. "The delectable Miss Fifield! Ain't
she Viscount Laing's cousin or something like that? I
see I shall have to cultivate his friendship. Perhaps I
shall have better luck with him than with you, Cran."

They rode on in silence again.

Cranwell was still furious with himself about the
evening before. It had been horrifying enough to find
himself trapped into going into Lady Murdoch's lodgings with her in order to carry Sarah up to her room.
He could not imagine any other lady of his acquaintance even dreaming of making such a request. But
there had been no way he could avoid the task, short
of being extremely rude himself. But why could he not
have performed the task in silence and left again?

But no! He had had to look at her before picking
her up. He had had to look and notice the pale, drawn
expression on her face, which somehow only succeeded
in making her look even more beautiful than usual.
He had had to give himself time to realize that she was
in pain. And he had felt a sympathy for her, a quite
unreasonable desire to comfort her. Instead of picking
her up and carrying her upstairs with his mind fixed
firmly on his farms or his coming marriage or some
equally safe topic, he had held her and allowed memory to wash over him. Just thus she had felt on their
wedding night when he had carried her to their bed to
make love to her: surprisingly light, warm and soft
against him. Just so she had smelled, a light fragrance
that appeared to come from her hair. Just so she had
twined her arm around his neck.

By the time he had deposited her on her bed, he
had almost allowed himself to forget what she was.
For one mad moment he had wanted to follow her
down onto the bed, to cradle her head against his
shoulder, and to soothe away the pain. He had resisted. Thank God, he had resisted! But even then he
had not been content to walk away. He had turned
back, quite unaware that he was about to do so, and
apologized for calling her a whore. And he had meant
it. He should not have meant it. He must never soften
his heart to that woman. But he had done so.

What had she said? She had said that he had spoken
only the truth. She had made no attempt to deny his
charges. She never had, in fact, once he had confronted her with the truth. Of course, by that time she
had already lived the great lie. But he must give her
credit for that one thing: she had never denied the
truth once he knew it. She had never tried to justify
herself.

He had never lived through such a terrible night as
his wedding night. He shuddered at the memory now.
May God protect him from having to live through
anything as horrifying ever again. He had loved her
totally, as perhaps only a solitary person can love once

his heart is given. And he had trusted her utterly. It had never even entered his head that perhaps she was not the pure, quiet young innocent she appeared to be. His shock on discovering that she was not a virgin had destroyed in an instant all his determined efforts to be gentle with her and to show by his every movement and every touch that he loved and worshiped her. He had completed the act of love in a blind and bewildered fury.

And she had not denied any of it. She could have lied and said it had happened only once, a youthful indiscretion, perhaps. He probably would have believed her and forgiven her. He probably would have grown to love her again almost as much as he had before. But she had clearly implied that she had lain with men more times than she could count. She had not denied his charge that she was a whore.

He hated even to remember the night and the two days that followed this discovery. He had ridden around the countryside, eating and sleeping at inns, he supposed, though he could never recall any of them. He had tried to assimilate his new knowledge, had tried to adjust to this new picture of Sarah. His wife! He had finally faced the numbing reality that he was married to a whore, and he had asked himself honestly if anything could possibly be made of the situation. An annulment was out of the question. He had consummated the marriage. The prospect of divorce and all the publicity that would be involved in such a rare occurrence were not to be contemplated.

Three days after his wedding, Cranwell returned to her uncle's house. He knew that he must face Sarah, talk to her now that the passion had gone, see what could be worked out between them. He hated to remember.

Her aunt was bewildered, her uncle closer to anger. It was obvious that they did not know the truth of why he had sent her back. She was outside somewhere, they told him, where she had been all day and every day since her return. He found her sitting on a stile quite close to the house, but out of sight of its windows. She was sitting with hunched shoulders and was staring ahead of her.

"Sarah," he said when he was no more than eight feet behind her.

Her back stiffened but she did not turn around. "Go away!" she said.

"Sarah, we must talk," he persisted.

"There is nothing to say," she said. "You must go away."

"Sarah." He walked up beside her and rested his arms along the fence. "There must be more to say. I must know more. I cannot believe . . . I cannot, Sarah."

"Why?" she asked, and she turned to look at him half-defiantly, half-coquettishly. "Do you not think I am pretty enough to attract lovers, your grace? I do assure you there are other men who would disagree with you."

He frowned. He felt some revulsion. "Talk to me," he said. "Let us have done with this barrier between us, Sarah. We are husband and wife. Let us talk."

She looked ahead of her again. "I am bad," she said. "I have been since I was very young. I first lay with a man when I was but seventeen. And I have done so numerous times since. You see those hills and those trees?" She pointed ahead to the hills that rose in the distance. "They have been my bed so many times that I have lost count. I am bad. You have married an evil woman, your grace, a whore, as you yourself said. And I married you because I wanted a different life. You were right." She shrugged and turned to smile at him.

The smile seemed grotesque to him. It was like a caricature of his Sarah who was before him. He felt that he was seeing her for the first time.

"Perhaps you would like to go up into the hills with me now," she said, that smile still on her face, her eyebrows arched inquiringly, her eyes on his.

He put his head down on the fence between his hands. "Oh God, Sarah," he said, "I could not have been so mistaken. Could I?"

"You should have known," she said in a careless sort of drawl that he hardly recognized as her voice. "You must be a dreadful innocent."

"God, what are we to do?" he asked.

She did not answer. When he lifted his head again it was to find her staring stonily ahead of her.

"Do you have any feeling for me, Sarah?" he asked, dreading the answer. "Do you have any love for me at all?"

She laughed, a light flirtatious sound that made him grit his teeth. "What do you think, your grace?" she said. "What do you think?"

His mind flashed back to his courtship of her, to the friendship they had seemed to share, to their wedding, to the consummation of their marriage. Could this unfeeling coquette possibly be the same woman as the one he had loved with such passion and such tenderness? Surely only some unusually fiendish woman could act such a part so convincingly. She had played the part of young innocence without a flaw. He felt a deep revulsion for her, a fear almost.

He turned away from her and left her uncle's house without further delay. And this time there was no indecision left. He would not, could not go through life shackled to such evil. Even divorce was preferable. He had to be free of her. He would never know a moment of peace until she was no longer a part of him. He rode straight to London to consult his lawyer, whom he had not seen in five years, on the validity of his case against his wife.

He had not seen her since, though he had weakened enough when the deed was accomplished to instruct his lawyer to settle on her enough money to allow her to live independently of her relatives and of her former profession if she so chose. His lawyer had advised against such a move, but he had done it anyway.

Josh was quite right, though. Sarah was even more beautiful now than she had been when he had loved her. Her body had a woman's maturity now. Her face had the beauty of one who has experienced something of life. And her hair was still her crowning glory. Her titian hair. Damn!

Lady Cavendish had invited several friends and acquaintances to call on her for tea after luncheon. She and the girls, therefore, were contented to stroll in Sydney Gardens for a mere hour after breakfast before returning to Laura Place to rest and to prepare themselves for the exertion of entertaining.

Cranwell was quite delighted to have still more free time before the inevitable visit to the Upper Assembly Rooms again in the evening. It was to be a ball night again. He went to the coffee shop on North Parade that he had visited the day before with Josh. It was a place for men only, a gathering ground for relaxation and conversation more than for the drinking of coffee. He joined a group of new acquaintances for a while and spent an interesting half-hour solving with them all the problems of Europe and the spreading power of Bonaparte.

He was joined there by Winston Bowen, who seemed delighted to see him, and was soon drawn a little apart from the main group, which had now moved on into solving all of Britain's trading problems.

"All alone, Cranwell?" Winston asked.

"Yes," the other answered with a rueful smile. "There is a tea party this afternoon, you know. Strictly ladies' business. I have escaped."

"Ah," said Winston, "and were your sister and your betrothed bent on escaping also?"

Cranwell looked his enquiry.

"They were arriving to call on Sarah as I was leaving a short time ago," Winston said. "Very kind of them, in my opinion. Lady Murdoch had already left, but Sarah is still unable to put her foot to the ground."

Cranwell frowned. "Indeed?" he said.

"But they are charming ladies," Winston said. "Your fiancée does credit to your taste, Cranwell, and your sister to your influence."

Cranwell inclined his head and then looked curi-

ously at his companion. "You, of course, know of my
connection with Miss Fifield," he said.

Winston smiled. "You need not fear that I shall say
anything to anyone else," he said. "Sarah is my cousin
and as dear to me as a sister. I would do everything in
my power to protect her reputation. You are not thinking of causing any trouble, are you, Cranwell?"

The duke looked at him levelly across the width of
the table. "Miss Fifield is no longer any connection of
mine," he said. "Her affairs are none of my concern."
He winced inwardly at his unfortunate choice of words.

Winston smiled again. "I wanted to be sure," he
said. "I value your acquaintance, Cranwell, and that
of Lady Hannah and your sister. But I should have to
forgo the pleasure of continuing the connection if you
meant my cousin any harm." His eyes looked with a
steady sincerity into those of the other man.

He left soon afterward, leaving Cranwell slightly
apart from the group, whose conversation had become
loudly argumentative. He had just discovered a new
dimension to the character of the gay and charming
Lord Laing. The man had a depth of character that he
had not suspected. He undoubtedly enjoyed the social
life of Bath, and he seemed to like the company of
Fanny, yet he would give it all up out of loyalty to
Sarah if he had to. He had made that perfectly clear.
Cranwell was in no doubt that Bowen had been warning him in a very tactful manner that if he intended to
make trouble for Sarah, he would have her cousin to
contend with. And Bowen would be no mean adversary. He had a powerful and athletic physique.

Cranwell absently turned his coffee cup in its saucer.
The woman might not be worth such devotion; in fact,
she undoubtedly was not worth it. But he must still
admire such loyalty. Such a man would be a thoroughly desirable husband for his sister. He certainly
did not want her to make her choice in any hurry, but
if it should happen that she became attached to him
and he to her, then he himself would be foolish indeed
not to encourage the match.

And why did he feel strangely comforted to know that Sarah had someone of steady character to stand by her? She was not entirely alone.

He frowned suddenly and pushed his chair from the table. He raised a hand and gestured a farewell to the men around him. He left the shop deep in uneasy thought. Fanny and Hannah had gone to call on Sarah? And just on the day when he had been relieved to know that there would be no awkward meetings with her.

Why had they done such a thing? They were supposed to be at Laura Place with Lady Cavendish entertaining all the callers who were expected. He could imagine how it might have come about. Lady Murdoch would have arrived and announced that Sarah was unable to come as she must still rest her sprained ankle. And Fanny, probably, would feel sorry for her, at home alone, and would announce her intention of going to Brock Street. Hannah would go along to keep her company. Of course, the idea might have been Hannah's. She was the one the afternoon before who had wanted to make sure that Sarah was given a personal invitation to tea.

Under any circumstances he would have been annoyed at such an occurrence. Under the particular circumstances he was furious. Fanny knew the truth. She knew that it was improper to consort with Sarah, and she knew that it was against his express wishes. Yet she had deliberately and behind his back sought out that woman. And she had seemingly done nothing to guard Hannah against such impropriety. He would certainly have something to say to her when he saw her later.

And why had Sarah let them in? It would have been very easy for her to have them denied entrance. She could have pleaded indisposition. He had commanded her the day before to stay away from both girls. Was she deliberately defying him? Was she courting the friendship of his sister and his fiancée merely to provoke him? Was she deliberately flaunting her knowledge that he would not expose her true identity to anyone? There must be some way he could remove her more permanently from his own sphere and that of those who were dear to him.

He had commanded her! He came to an abrupt stop in the middle of a busy Cheap Street and almost laughed aloud. What right did he have to command Miss Sarah Fifield to do anything? He had forfeited the right to have any control over her actions when he had divorced her four years ago. He was behaving for all the world as if she were still his wife.

Was she still in as much pain today as she had been the night before? he wondered. He must ask Hannah later. If she was, perhaps he should suggest to Lady Murdoch that another physician be consulted. Was the present one sure that a bone had not been broken? It must be set properly immediately if such were the case, before permanent damage was done.

Cranwell stopped again, as abruptly as before, and right in the middle of the road he was crossing. He must be taking leave of his senses. What concern of his was Sarah's sprained ankle?

An angry carter shouted abuse at the Duke of Cranwell as he turned his team to avoid an accident and almost collided with a gig coming in the opposite direction.

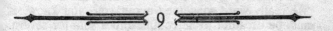

9

IN BROCK Street Fanny was pouring the tea that Mrs. Bergland had just brought into the salon. She insisted on doing so, explaining that it would be extremely awkward for Sarah to pour while propped on one elbow.

"And I have poured for George since I was a mere child," Fanny explained. "He has been my guardian since I was very young, and he always insisted that I was the lady of the house."

"That is most kind of you," Sarah said, "though I am sure it would do no real harm to swing my legs to the floor during your visit. My ankle really does feel very much better."

"Oh, you must not do that, Miss Fifield," Hannah said anxiously. "Papa always says that people do not look after their injuries properly and suffer all sorts of ailments later in life, like rheumatism. My friend Donald caught his hand beneath a horse's hoof two years ago and hurt it. He would not see a physician. But he has never been able to straighten out one of his fingers since. Papa says he must have broken the finger."

"Yes," Fanny agreed, "you really must behave yourself, Miss Fifield, and keep your foot up or Lady Murdoch will find out and tell Hannah's grandmama, and then she will say we are a bad influence on you and forbid us to go about alone again."

Sarah smiled. "Have you been using me as an excuse to go out unchaperoned?" she asked.

The two girls exchanged a look, and both giggled. "Grandmama's guests were almost all elderly ladies,"

Hannah said. "It will doubtless be a most tedious afternoon. We far preferred to come to see you, Miss Fifield."

"Of course," Fanny added with wide, innocent eyes, "we really were concerned about you, you know. It must be dreadful to be confined to a sofa for several days when you are in a place like Bath. Is it not heavenly, even if there are not very many young peole here? But you will miss the ball tonight. How will you possibly stand it!"

Sarah took the cup that Hannah had carried over to her and settled into a more comfortable position. She really was enjoying the visit of the two girls, even though she knew she should not be doing so. They were so refreshingly young and eager. Even Hannah, she was surprised to notice, was not the silent, shy girl she had seemed to be when in George's company. She chattered quite freely about her home, her horse, her dog, and her childhood playmates Donald Ferris and his sister Iris. She seemed much more today the seventeen-year-old child that she was.

Fanny was every bit as exuberant as she had seemed on previous meetings. She regaled the other two with stories of mischief from school. Sarah suspected that many of the stories were grossly exaggerated versions of the truth, but she laughed anyway. Fanny also asked many questions.

"Miss Fifield," she said with the lack of tact that only a very young person could show, "you are much older than Hannah and I, are you not? What have you been doing since you left the schoolroom? Why are you not married?"

Sarah gave the girl a searching look and received a blush in return. So the girl did know. She replaced her cup carefully in its saucer.

"I lived in a small village for several years," she said, "very quietly. I tended my house and garden, and helped the vicar with some of his parish work. And I have been living with Lady Murdoch for several weeks now."

"Oh," Fanny said, "did you not find life dreadfully dull?"

Sarah smiled. "No," she said, "I was happy. I do not believe I was intended for a gay social life. I like life in the country. It seems more real."

"You are just like George," Fanny said, and had the grace to blush hotly as the words escaped her.

"I can sympathize with you, Miss Fifield," Hannah said, "but did you live entirely alone?"

"I had one faithful servant," Sarah said.

"I do not believe I could live happily without some animals," Hannah said. "I do so miss my horse and my dog. Dear Argus! And a few close friends are very important too, are they not?" She looked wistful.

"What are your interests, Miss Fifield?" Fanny asked. "You must have many if you have spent so much time alone."

"I like to walk a great deal," Sarah said. "That is one reason why I prefer the countryside. Indoors I read almost anything I can lay my hands on. I particularly enjoy works of history. And of course I do all types of needlework and such. I am netting a purse at present, but I am afraid that today I am being lazy and idle."

Fanny made a face. "Embroidery is about the limit of my accomplishments," she said. "And I would not even do that if George did not insist that I must have at least one ladylike activity. I cannot play the pianoforte because I have ten thumbs, and my voice has been compared—by my dear brother—with a rusty saw. I shall have to make a brilliant match with a wealthy old man who will dote on my youth and not mind my lack of talents."

"Oh, you have a great talent that I envy enormously," Hannah said, leaning forward in her chair and looking earnestly at her future sister-in-law. "You find it so easy to talk to other people and to hold their interest, Fanny. I can never think of anything to say. That is a great talent, you know."

Fanny shrugged. "I never think about it," she said. "My mouth opens and words come out."

The other two laughed, and Hannah rose to take Sarah's cup over to Fanny to be refilled.

"Lord Laing is your cousin," Fanny said, looking back to Sarah. "Did you grow up together?"

Sarah flushed. "After my father died, yes," she said. "My uncle and aunt gave me and my brother a home."

"Was he always so handsome?" Fanny asked. "Hannah and I think he is without a doubt the most gorgeous man we have ever seen. He even puts Captain Penny in the shade, though the captain has all the advantages of his regimental uniform."

Both girls giggled.

"Yes," Sarah said, "Winston was always extremely good-looking, even as a boy."

"I wonder you were not hopelessly in love with him," Fanny said. "I would have been if he were my cousin and living in the same house."

"Cousins seem more like brothers under such circumstances," Sarah said quietly.

"Anyway," Hannah added, "love really has very little to do with looks."

"Well," Fanny said, "I mean to set my cap at Lord Laing while we are here. But you must not tell him, of course, Miss Fifield."

"Have you ever been in love, Miss Fifield?" Hannah asked.

Sarah darted a look at Fanny and found the girl watching her with heightened color.

"I suppose so," she said hesitantly. "Yes. Once."

"Oh," Hannah said, her eyes wide with sympathy. "How you must have suffered. It hurts to be separated from someone you love, does it not? At least, I would think it must hurt."

Sarah smiled briefly, and her cup clattered clumsily in her saucer as she set it down.

"Yes, indeed," she said. "But how serious we

are becoming. Are you to attend the ball this evening?"

"Oh, yes," Fanny said. "And I have already had my hand solicited for four dances. Of course, one of those is with that droll character Mr. Phelps. Maybe he is the wealthy old man I should ensnare into wedlock. Is he wealthy, do you think?"

The visit continued for a whole hour. Finally Hannah got reluctantly to her feet and looked at Fanny.

"We really have taken up too much of your time, Miss Fifield," she said. "Perhaps you were planning to have a sleep this afternoon. But it has been so lovely to talk with you. I hope your ankle will be better soon so that we can meet again during the days and the evenings. I am so glad that Grandmama knows Lady Murdoch. We might not have met you otherwise."

"I have enjoyed this afternoon far more than I would have liked the tea party," Fanny said. "You are so much different, Miss Fifield, from what I . . . You are different from what I would expect a red-haired lady to be. One expects bad temper, I suppose," she ended lamely.

The room seemed very quiet after they had left. Sarah sat listening to a bird chirping outside the window for several minutes. She should not have enjoyed the visit. She should not have allowed it to continue for so long. She should have frozen them out long ago. She could not feel guilty for having given them admittance. She had had no choice. Winston had been in the hallway when they were admitted, and he had brought them into the room himself.

She had wanted to obey George on this one issue. And even had he not given the command, her own sense of propriety made her wish to avoid contact with these two particular girls. But she had enjoyed their visit and had encouraged it to continue for a whole hour.

It was only now that she realized how starved she had been of friends in her own age range. She had

never had women friends, except Mrs. Clarence, who
was much older than she. And she liked these two
girls. It had struck her several times during the afternoon that Fanny had been her sister-in-law for a brief
time and might still be so if circumstances had only
been different. She would have liked to have such a
sister.

And she liked Hannah, though she had not expected to do so. The thought of the girl—or any other—
with George, sharing his thoughts, his dreams, his
bed, was one that she did not care to dwell on. And
she did not think the woman existed who was good
enough for him. No one else would ever know him or
understand him as she had done for a brief time. But
Hannah was a sweet and a likable girl. She was certainly not insipid, as she had perhaps appeared to be
at first.

What was really disturbing was the fact that both
girls seemed to like her. Sarah could not understand
why that was. She had made no particular effort to
appear agreeable to them. And if she thought about
the matter, it seemed strange to her that anyone could
like her. Their feelings certainly complicated matters.
It might not be enough when she was sufficiently well
to go out again to try to keep her distance from them.
What if they actively sought her out? How could she
avoid the meetings without being downright rude? What
would George think? Do?

For the first time Sarah began to think that perhaps
she should make plans for leaving Lady Murdoch after
all. Should she write again to the London papers and
try to obtain a position as a governess or even as a
companion? How could she do so, though? Such a
move would hurt Lady Murdoch terribly. Sarah knew
that she was already very important to the old lady's
happiness. Should she just disappear and hope that
later she could find some employment? She wanted to
put the whole idea from her mind, but she was aware
that she must be prepared for some such move. At any

time some circumstance might force her to leave the life in which she had just been starting to feel secure.

There was another problem too, Sarah thought, suddenly remembering Fanny's announcement that she was going to set her cap at Winston. How disastrous that would be. Especially as Winston had set out to woo her. The girl's heart would be very vulnerable, and Winston seemed to have a gift for winning female hearts. He would marry her too, doubtless. She must be a very wealthy girl, and wealth was the one criterion by which Winston would choose a bride.

But Sarah could not allow it to happen. Winston would be a terrible husband. He would surely neglect the girl for other women, and he would squander her money on gambling until there was nothing left. Perhaps he would be no worse than a thousand other husbands, but Fanny was George's sister. She could not allow it to happen. And Winston was unprincipled, he had no moral sense at all. He was totally insensitive to other people's feelings, yet equally unaware of his own insensitivity.

Yet how was she to prevent such a marriage from taking place? And did she have the right, anyway? But she knew that her uneasiness over the possibility would make it that much harder for her to leave Bath. She might be dooming the young and exuberant Fanny to a life of misery with a handsome fiend if she did.

And she was undoubtedly dooming herself to a great deal of unwanted attention if she stayed, again by Winston. He had come earlier in the afternoon, so soon after Lady Murdoch left that it seemed almost as if he must have been lying in wait outside. Of course, she was stupid to have been surprised. Although she had given him no encouragement the evening before, she should have known by now that Winston did not need encouragement.

He had come to inquire after her health, of course. And he seated himself beside her on the sofa as he

had done the evening before. But he quickly moved
on to other topics.

"I really am concerned about you, you know, Sarah,"
he said, all serious sincerity. "I hate to think of you
alone here, no one to keep you company."

"Like you, Win?" she asked with a fleeting smile.
"I had Lady Murdoch's company all morning. She
refused to go out and leave me alone. I am not lonely."

"But the company of an elderly lady cannot be very
stimulating," he said, his face moving imperceptibly
closer to hers. "I shall stay with you for a while,
anyway, Sarah."

"That is most kind of you, Win," she said. "If you
get up and ring for Mrs. Bergland, she will bring you
some refreshments, I am sure."

"I need none," he said. "You are refreshment enough
for me." And he put his arm across her body and laid
it on the sofa along her side so that his hand rested
against her breast.

"Take your hand away, Win," she said calmly. "You
know that I will not allow that."

He sighed. "Are you never going to admit that you
need me, Sarah?" he asked. "If it is Cranwell you are
hankering after, you must have realized by now that
the situation is hopeless. He will be married to that
mousy little chit by Christmas."

"Take your hand away, Win," she repeated.

"Sarah." His face loomed over hers and his elbow
moved in closer against her hip. "Don't keep fighting
me. You know that you need me. I do not believe that
you feel nothing at all. Let me kiss you."

"I warn you, Win," Sarah said, "that if you come
one inch closer I shall scream. I know that only Mrs.
Bergland will hear, but you may find the situation
embarrassing, nonetheless. Let me go now."

He sat up, removed his arm, and grinned at her.
"You certainly like to play hard to get, Sarah, don't
you?" he said. "Perhaps that is why I have never tired
of you. Most females cling and whine as soon as they

sense that I am tiring of them. You never did admit that you wanted me, did you?"

"No, I never did," she agreed.

He stood up suddenly and walked over to the window to stare down on the street. "Old Lady Murdoch must have plenty of blunt if she can afford lodgings on this street," he said. "Why, you are almost on the Crescent, Sarah."

She did not deign to answer.

"What has she said about her will?" he continued. "She must have given the matter some thought. Has she said anything, Sarah?"

"If she had," Sarah replied, "I would not be likely to confide in you, Win."

He turned to face her, a smile on his face. "You really have developed quite a tongue," he said. "Will you come away with me, Sarah? I would leave with you now if you were willing to go. We could travel around together until there are enough people in London to make it worth going there. I could rent a nice little house for you there. It would be far better than living here with a vulgar old lady, waiting for someone to realize who you are."

"You must be very much in debt here if you are prepared to leave," Sarah said.

"Now, Sarah," he scolded, "I was thinking of your welfare. Actually, I am quite content to stay here. I have prospects. The Montagu girl, for example."

Sarah looked sharply up at him, to find him grinning.

"Are you jealous?" he asked. "She is a very fetching little thing, you know. I would find it most amusing to engage her affections."

"You would not do so," she said.

He raised his eyebrows. "Why ever not?" he asked. "I imagine I must be considered quite a matrimonial catch since inheriting the title. And there is another on the way as soon as grandpapa decides to give up the ghost. I do not believe that her brother would object to such a match."

His eyes were laughing at her.

"Win, please," she said, realizing the hopelessness of pleading even as she began, "leave the girl alone. You have caused enough trouble in that family already."

He laughed outright. "I have caused trouble?" he said. "I was not the one who foolishly thought to get away with marrying the Duke of Cranwell, my girl. You belonged to me. You were fortunate that I was not a great deal more angry than I was, Sarah. Your face might not still be as pretty as it ever was. No, I have caused no trouble to that family. And I have no intention of causing any now. My intentions are entirely honorable."

"Why are you telling me this, Win?" she asked suspiciously. "Are you not afraid that I will tell the whole to his grace?"

"No." He laughed. "I hardly think you are likely to reopen that topic with him, my dear. And it seems very unlikely that he would believe you anyway. I imagine he has a lowish opinion of your morals. No, you will say nothing, Sarah. Of course, if you really find the prospect of my marrying the delectable Fanny so unpalatable, you can always run away with me now and take me away from her sphere."

"Oh," she said, anger flaring, "is that what this has been all about? My compliance in return for your leaving Lady Fanny alone. Is that it, Win?"

He laughed again. "Sarah, you always paint me in the blackest colors, do you not?" he said. "The situation is as I say. I want you. I want to go away with you now and spend the rest of the summer and autumn with you alone, making love to you whenever I feel the urge. That is what I want. I love you, as I have told you numerous times over the last years. If I cannot have what I want, then I shall seek the next best thing, which happens to be Lady Fanny Montagu. Of course, I shall have to offer her marriage. Either way, Sarah, I shall continue to want you. And I think that eventually you will admit to yourself that you want me too."

"You had better leave, Win," she had said wearily. "I need to rest."

He had come across the room to stand over her. His face had been serious once more. "Think about it, Sarah," he had said. "If you become my mistress again now, you may not have to share me with a wife for a long time. Perhaps never if Lady Murdoch does what she ought to do. We might even be able to marry in the future. Think about it."

Before she realized his intention, he leaned down over her and kissed her firmly on the mouth. She was still shuddering and rubbing her mouth with the back of one hand when a knock came at the door and Mrs. Bergland could be heard crossing the hall to open it. Winston went out into the hallway too, and a minute later he ushered in Fanny and Hannah. He was his most charming self for the few minutes he remained before taking his leave.

Lady Murdoch was full of enthusiasm for her afternoon spent at Laura Place. But what seemed to gratify her most of all was the fact that Sarah had not had to spend a solitary afternoon after all.

"How kind it was of those girls to call on you, Sarah dear, was it not," she said, "when they might have stayed and been entertained by all the visitors who called? Not but what it would have been unpleasant for them to be here. I am sure you entertained them just as well here as they would have been there. And it is only right that they should cultivate your friendship, you being as good as my daughter, you know."

Sarah dutifully agreed that indeed it had been most kind.

"Lady Cavendish is most taken with you too," Lady Murdoch continued. "She would have called on you herself this afternoon, she said, if it would not have appeared most strange for all the hostesses to disappear from the tea party at once. But you must admit, my dear, that such a move would not have been the most decorous behavior."

Sarah most certainly agreed.

"Lady Hannah was telling his grace what a pleasant afternoon she and Lady Fanny had here," the older lady went on. "I am sure he must be gratified, dear, for that young lady does appear to be very shy and does not make friends easily."

"Oh," Sarah said casually, "was he there?"

"He came just before the young ladies returned from here," Lady Murdoch said. "I am sure Bertha was well satisfied to have a duke present in her drawing room when most of her guests were still there."

"Yes," Sarah agreed.

"He did not stay long, though," Lady Murdoch continued. "He had to take his sister to make some forgotten purchases, though I am not at all sure that any shops would still have been open. Not that I know for sure, of course, being as we always make our purchases in the morning and have never had to discover if the shops stay open late or not. I daresay they are still open if his grace thought of taking his sister shopping. He should know. Though as for that, he is no more from Bath than we are, and indeed has been here for only a few days. Is it two or three?"

Sarah's mind had wandered. Why the sudden shopping trip? Was Fanny to receive a lecture and orders never to visit her again? There seemed to be little doubt that Fanny knew who Sarah was. The girl was not practiced in deceit. She had given away her knowledge more than once during her visit. Perhaps George was hoping to have more success with his sister than with his former wife.

Sarah was not far wrong in her surmise. Cranwell had brought his coach with him to Laura Place, and as soon as he could courteously leave Lady Cavendish's party, he reminded Fanny of the gloves she had promised to help him choose. There had been no such promise, of course, but he credited Fanny with enough presence of mind to know that he wished to talk privately with her. He was quite correct.

The coachman was given instructions to drive for one hour in whatever direction he chose. Cranwell drew the velvet curtains across the windows and had no idea where the coach was actually taken.

"I recognize all the signs, George," Fanny said cheerfully. "I gather I am in for a thundering scold."

He settled into one corner of the carriage and regarded her steadily. "Then you must know on what grounds too," he said.

"Oh," she said, "I suppose it is because I visited Miss Fifield this afternoon."

"Why did you do so, Fan?" he asked.

"I am intrigued by the fact that she was my sister-in-law," Fanny said, looking her brother straight in the eye. "I wish to get to know her."

"You know that such a wish is most improper," he said.

"Why?" Fanny had a disconcerting way of turning aggressor when she was being scolded. Cranwell always dreaded their not-infrequent confrontations. "Just because she is a divorced woman, George? You are a divorced man, but no one ever suggests that it is improper to associate with you."

"I am afraid that is just the way our society works," Cranwell said.

"Well, it just does not seem fair to me," Fanny said.

Cranwell sighed. "Fan," he said, "we have had similar arguments to this one numerous times recently. You are a woman now, and you must learn to live with the fact that life is not always fair. It is only children who expect it to be so."

Fanny's jaw tightened. "So," she said, "the only reason I am to avoid Miss Fifield is that she is divorced?"

"There is also the fact that she is *my* divorced wife," her brother added. "That makes your association with her doubly imprudent, Fan."

"Give me another reason," she said. "You would never tell me what happened, George. You always used to say that I was too young to understand. Well, you just said that I am a woman now. Tell me what happened. Perhaps then I shall see good reason to do as you say."

"I am still your guardian," Cranwell said, his face setting into hard lines. "I do not have to give reasons for you to do as I say."

"Nonsense," Fanny said. "We are not living in the Middle Ages. And what will you do to me anyway if I disobey you? You gave up spanking me when I was twelve years old."

"I prefer not to live by threats," her brother replied. "Please do as I say, Fan, just because I am your brother and your guardian."

"Oh," she complained, "it is not fair. When you get serious and reasonable like this, George, it is so hard to resist you. Your manner is designed to put me so much in the wrong. But I must resist you on this. I met Miss Fifield this afternoon and I liked her greatly. She has a dignity and a maturity that I admire. And until she started to live with Lady Murdoch a mere few weeks ago, she lived quietly in the country, reading and walking and doing needlework. At least, that is what she said, and I see no reason to disbelieve her. What did she do that was so heinous?"

Cranwell swallowed and stared at the empty seat across from him. "I cannot discuss it," he said. "I can only say that it was something I could not forgive and felt that I ought not to forgive."

Fanny was silent for a while. "I am sorry, George," she said, "but even for you I cannot judge another person harshly without having observed for myself or been given proof that I should do so."

"I see." Cranwell's voice was tight and cold. "You will not avoid her, then?"

"No," Fanny said. Her voice was small and not at all triumphant. "I cannot, George. I am sorry. You loved her once, did you not? I think you must have, for I remember how unhappy you were for a long time afterward. There must have been something to love, or I do not believe that you would have felt as you did."

They rode side by side in silence for long minutes, both unhappy and unyielding. Cranwell spoke first.

"You took Hannah there too," he said. "That I find hard to forgive."

"It was her idea to go," Fanny said. "What was I to do? Tell her?"

"My God!" he said passionately. "Think about it, Fan. My divorced wife and my intended wife in a room together, becoming friends."

"I cannot be expected to do anything to prevent that," Fanny said. "Hannah is a person in her own right. I am not even any older than she is, to be giving her advice."

"You are right," he said abruptly. "It seems that I have been inactive for several days hoping that other people would solve the problem for me. Sarah has let me down. You have let me down. It is time I did something myself."

Fanny waited to be told what it was he planned to do. She sat looking at him expectantly for several minutes. But she waited in vain. The Duke of Cranwell propped one foot on the seat opposite, rested an elbow on his knee and his chin in his hand, and withdrew into deep thought.

She was clearly more dangerous than he had realized. She was weaving her spell around Fanny and Hannah just as skillfully as she had manipulated him years ago. Hannah had been more talkative for a few minutes after returning from the visit to her than he had ever known her to be. And the talk had been all admiration for Sarah. And Sarah had convinced Fanny that she had lived an exemplary life in the last several years. Fanny was growing to like her even though she had every reason not to do so. A night before, Sarah had even drawn sympathy from him for a few unguarded moments.

Why? Why would she wish to ingratiate herself with his connections? Was it merely that she took fiendish glee in upsetting his life? Was she trying to wreak some sort of vengeance for the unpleasant publicity he had caused her through the divorce? He would probably never know the answer. People of such devious minds as Sarah's totally eluded his understanding. And it was very easy to be deceived by such people. That was what made them so dangerous.

He would have to do something to remove Sarah Fifield far from his presence and that of his sister and his fiancée. And he must act soon. No more hesitancy and halfhearted hopes that the problem would solve itself.

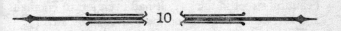

10

SARAH WAS very glad late the following afternoon to be visited by the doctor again and told that she would be able to start walking on her foot the next day, provided she rested it frequently.

"No dancing, young lady," he said, "for at least a week."

She had almost welcomed the injury for the excuse it gave her to stay away from those people she wanted to avoid. But circumstances had not worked that way. She saw almost as much company from the sofa in the salon as she did when she was free to go abroad all day long.

Even that day she had had hardly a moment to herself. Lady Murdoch had gone to take the waters and meet acquaintances in the Pump Room before breakfast. Sarah had risen later than usual because she was not going herself. But even at that early hour she had been called upon by the Misses Seymour and Mrs. Smythe, whom she had met early in her stay at Bath. All three claimed to have missed her company in the last day and a half. They had stayed with her until Lady Murdoch's return.

As on the day before, Lady Murdoch had insisted on remaining home after breakfast to keep Sarah company. But scarcely an hour had passed before Mrs. Bergland was ushering into the salon George and his party and Mr. Stonewall. Sarah had been deeply embarrassed. Both George and Lady Fanny had been subdued; she guessed that the poor girl had been lectured after her visit of the day before. Lady Cavendish, after sitting for five minutes, had borne Lady

161

Murdoch away to stroll on the Crescent, explaining
that one could not stay in Bath without at least once
walking with all the most fashionable set on the most
beautiful street in the city. It had been left to Hannah
and Mr. Stonewall to keep the conversation alive.

Hannah did not speak as freely as she had done the
previous day, either. Sarah did not know if it was the
presence of George that inhibited her or if perhaps she
also had been alerted to the truth. The latter seemed
unlikely, though. Surely the girl would be far more
embarrassed than she was if she realized that she was
talking to her fiancé's former wife.

Sarah was greatly beholden to Mr. Stonewall, who
took the chair closest to the sofa and proceeded to
monopolize the conversation, entertaining her and all
of them with his endless supply of amusing *on-dits*
concerning the fashionable set in London and Brighton. She was all the more grateful to him because he
scarcely knew her. They had been no more than introduced on the afternoon of her fall.

Even though Mr. Stonewall ensured that there were
no lengthy pauses in the conversation, it seemed an
age until the opening of the front door heralded the
return of the two older ladies and the imminent departure of all the guests.

And even that had not been the end of the company. Winston called after dinner. Fortunately, Lady
Murdoch was tired after her walk and decided not to
go to the Sydney Gardens as she had earlier planned
to do. If Winston was surprised to find her there, he
certainly did not show it. After inquiring solicitously
after his cousin's health, he proceeded to charm the
older lady as only he knew how. She rhapsodized
about him for long minutes after his departure.

"He clearly likes you, Sarah," she said, not for the
first time. "I can always tell, believe me. I think he
admires Lady Fanny too. He walks with her in the
Pump Room each morning, and she told us that he
danced with her twice at the ball last night. But I still
think he has a preference for you, dear. Mark my

words. And that is as it should be. You are his cousin, and you are a remarkably lovely young lady. In fact, you two would make an extraordinarily handsome couple." She winked and nodded.

Sarah bent her head over her netting. "We are more like brother and sister than anything else," she said.

"Oho!" Lady Murdoch said with a knowing laugh. "That can very quickly change, my dear. He will be offering for you before we leave Bath, I should not be surprised."

Sarah said nothing.

"And you need not hesitate to accept him," her cousin continued. "It has occurred to me, Sarah, that perhaps you would discourage him because you cannot bring him a dowry. Though as to that, I do not suppose that young man would be so mercenary. He would be getting a beautiful and an accomplished wife, and I am sure he is wealthy enough in his own right. But you are not to worry, anyway. I shall see to it that you have a handsome dowry, my dear. Not that that will be all, of course. You must never think that I would leave my dear Sarah, whom I think of as a daughter, unprovided for. I saw my lawyer before we even came here, and he is drawing up a new will for me. I say no more, my love, but I will say that you are to think of yourself as my chief heir."

"Oh!" The exclamation came out as a sort of wail from Sarah. "Please, ma'am, you must not. I am in no way worthy. I have done absolutely nothing to earn such a mark of distinction."

"There you are very wrong, my dear," Lady Murdoch said with much head-nodding and winking. "You have made an old woman extremely happy. Can you imagine how left out I would feel now, Bertha with her granddaughter and her other charge to boast of and fuss over and me with no one? As it is, my love, I feel I have every advantage, for you are easily the most handsome young lady in Bath. And, of course, dear, just your company in the last weeks has brought me enormous pleasure. It is my dearest wish to see you well settled. Then I may have grandchildren to boast of. Or near enough to grandchildren, anyway."

Sarah's eyes were swimming in tears. "I am so undeserving," she said. "If you only knew! Oh, I do love you, Lady Murdoch. You have the kindest heart!"

"Well," that lady said, embarrassed for once, "I have the money with which to be kind, my dear. Some people do not. And I do hate to have you call me 'Lady Murdoch,' as if there were no close connection between us whatsoever. I cannot ask you to call me 'Mama,' for you must have fond memories of your real mama, though I understand you were a mere infant when she passed on. You must call me 'Cousin Adelaide.' Let me hear it."

"I should be honored to do so," Sarah had said, "Cousin Adelaide."

Altogether, then, the two and a half days she had been forced to spend indoors had proved eventful and emotional ones. Sarah welcomed the chance to go out-of-doors. Perhaps there she would have more freedom to avoid unwelcome companions.

She did not go to the Pump Room on the following morning, having agreed to accompany Lady Murdoch to the Crescent after breakfast. It was just around the corner from Brock Street and was not a particularly lengthy street, though breathtakingly picturesque, with its smoothly curved crescent of tall, attached buildings, its wide cobbled street, and the park sloping away in front of it to the busier part of the city below. She had walked there only once before, but Lady Murdoch had been greatly impressed the day before with all the fashionable crowds that strolled there and were willing to stop to talk.

During breakfast, Sarah was sorry that she had made such definite plans earlier. Lady Murdoch, of course, had divulged these plans to what must have been a large gathering of acquaintances in the Pump Room, with the result that everyone she was most wishing to avoid was coming too. She had no objections whatsoever to hearing that Mr. Stonewall and Captain Penny were coming to the lodgings on Brock Street to accompany them, but she could certainly have lived without the additional presence of the Duke of Cranwell, Lady Cavendish, Fanny, Hannah, and Winston. And she wondered with some puzzlement and anger why George had allowed this excursion to happen and yesterday's visit. Could he not have prevented both?

Cranwell could not have prevented the first meeting. Josh had maneuvered yesterday's visit by commenting innocently when they had all met on Milsom Street after breakfast that poor Miss Fifield must be feeling very restless, having been confined to her lodgings for almost two whole days. It had taken no more than that hint to set Lady Cavendish to suggesting that they all go right then to visit the poor young lady. She would quite welcome the chance to take her friend from the house for an hour. Poor Adelaide was too concerned for the welfare of her young cousin to go about much herself. What could he have done? Especially as Hannah's face had glowed at the suggestion, and she had smiled up at him—a rare occurrence—and asked him if they could really go.

But this morning's arrangement to walk on the Crescent with the ladies from Brock Street had, surprisingly, been his own suggestion. It was time to put his plan into action. He was not sure that the morning would offer the opportunity to put it into effect, but he must try. It was tempting to procrastinate, but it was becoming increasingly obvious to him that his own party and Lady Murdoch were becoming inseparable. There seemed no chance that the novelty of a renewed acquaintance would wear thin with the two older ladies. They seemed all set to spend their time in Bath together.

It was quite a gay party that set out for the Crescent from the house on Brock Street. Cranwell had Hannah on his arm, Josh had quickly stepped forward to beg Sarah's company, Captain Penny had claimed Fanny with no less alacrity, and Winston Bowen, quite un-

abashed, declared that the greatest honor was his in
having a lady for each arm. He led the way between
Lady Cavendish and Lady Murdoch. The latter was
loudly proclaiming that they would draw all eyes, as
they had captured the most handsome young blade in
Bath.

Cranwell did not rush his plan. He waited until they
had all strolled up and down the Crescent, stopping
frequently to talk to acquaintances. After a half-hour
their party was quite widely dispersed along the street,
he and Hannah talking with Mr. John Staple and his
sister, Sarah and Josh talking with two ladies, a Mrs.
and Miss Marchmont, he seemed to remember from
an introduction a few days before. He waited until the
two groups came together again.

"It is a beautiful day for a stroll," he said conversationally, drawing Hannah to a halt and smiling at
Sarah and Josh.

"It is amazing what stories one can pick up during a
morning's walk," Joshua agreed, "is it not, Miss Fifield?
Mrs. Marchmont had a few shockers for us."

Cranwell smiled and looked closely at Sarah. "How
is your ankle feeling, ma'am?" he asked.

She looked at him for the first time, surprise raising
those arched eyebrows even higher.

"Really quite well, I thank you, your grace," she
said. "It is only now beginning to ache slightly."

He had not expected his task to be quite so easy.
"Ah," he said, "I had feared as much. It is very easy
to overdo things when one is recovering from such an
injury. It is quite obligatory, I believe, to stroll for a
whole hour here. But I am sure that under the circumstances even the highest sticklers will excuse you." He
smiled warmly. "Josh, may I entrust Lady Hannah to
your care for the next half-hour while I accompany
Miss Fifield home?"

Her eyebrows had almost disappeared under her
hair, Cranwell noted with fascination. The expression
beneath those eyebrows was one of mingled alarm and
incredulity.

"Eh?" Joshua said. "I can take Miss Fifield home, Cran. You needn't trouble yourself."

"Ah, but I know how you thrive on such scenes, my friend," Cranwell said with a smile. "Miss Fifield, will you take my arm?"

She obeyed him without hesitation. She looked dazed. He had been afraid that she might express a preference for Josh's company, and then his plan would have had to wait for another occasion. They turned in the direction of Brock Street, and he explained his purpose to Lady Murdoch, who was just then coming up with her two companions.

"But you must not rush home, ma'am," he said graciously. "I shall take care of Miss Fifield and stay to converse with her until you arrive. There is really no hurry at all."

He waited until they had turned out of the crowded Crescent and onto Brock Street.

"I wish to talk to you, Sarah," he said quietly.

"Oh?" she said. "What about?" Her voice was breathless.

"I think we should wait for the privacy of your lodgings," he said. "It is no light conversation that I plan."

"I did not think it was, your grace," she said.

She felt very familiar beside him. She had a way of laying her hand along the inside of his arm in what he had always thought an unconsciously provocative manner. Now he knew it to be the gesture of a practiced coquette, but it nevertheless had the effect of making him very aware of the shapely figure at his side. Even without looking directly at her he was aware of the glorious red of her hair beneath the poke of her bonnet and felt a stirring of the old desire to feel that hair over his hands. He could not now understand how he could ever have imagined her innocent. The woman positively exuded sexuality. He gritted his teeth. He had been the one with all the innocence.

She led the way into the house past the housekeeper and into the salon. She motioned him to a chair as she removed her shawl and bonnet and laid them down close to the door. He shook his head, putting his hat and cane beside her things.

"You had better take the weight off your foot," he said. "Your ankle has not swollen again, has it?"

"I think not, your grace," she said stiffly, seating herself on the sofa where she had reclined on his two previous visits.

He crossed the room to fetch a small footstool and placed it in front of her.

"Rest your foot on this," he said, and he knelt on the floor in front of her and took her foot in his hand as she lifted it.

She pulled sharply away, but he tightened his grip on her ankle.

"There is really no need to panic, ma'am," he said, looking up at her with one raised eyebrow. "I am merely checking to see if there is any swelling."

He pressed gently around her ankle and set her foot down on the stool.

"I think there is no further damage done," he said. "But if I were you, I should not do any more walking today."

"Your grace," she said, "you did not bring me back here so that you could play at being physician. You wished to talk to me?"

He straightened up. She was right. Why did he always have this tendency to put off an evil moment?

"You must leave here, Sarah," he said abruptly. "There is no other solution."

She looked down at the hands in her lap. "I have already told you," she said, "that I am not free to come and go as I wish. I must do what Lady Murdoch decides."

"You must see," he said, "that the situation is impossible. Every day, several times every day, you are in company with my sister and with my betrothed. It will not do."

"You think I have not tried to do as you asked?" she said, looking up at him with a flash of some spirit.

"I have no wish to be in your company either. Do you think I like to be reminded of the past any more than you do, George? Do you think I have done anything in the last two days or so to seek out anyone's company? Yet I saw you twice, and the girls twice. And this morning I did nothing to plan this walk."

He watched the color rise in her cheeks and along her throat. He watched her green eyes flash.

"I think the fault is not all yours," he admitted. "For some reason, Hannah has taken to you. And Fanny is fascinated by you. She knows who you are, of course. Sarah, I cannot allow it. Hannah is to be my wife. She is a young and innocent girl."

He watched the green eyes brighten before she put her head down sharply. With tears?

"Do you think I have not thought of leaving?" she asked, her voice subdued again. "It would take time for me to find employment. And I would hurt Lady Murdoch dreadfully if I left to be a governess. She has been kind to me, and I know that she has come to rely on my company."

"She obviously knows nothing about you," he said. "Do you not think you will hurt her worse if you stay with her until she finds out the truth? These things have a tendency not to remain hidden forever, you know."

She lowered her head even further so that all he could see was the thick curls on top of her head.

"I am sorry," she said. "I have no choice."

"Yes, you do," he said. He took a deep breath and fixed his eyes on that titian hair. "I do not know exactly what you have been doing for the last four years, Sarah. Fanny says you were living in a cottage somewhere and were happy. I do not know if that is the truth. But were you happy enough to go back if you could?"

"I cannot," she said, looking up at him again. Yes, there were definitely tears in her eyes. He steeled himself to resist the power of her acting skills. "You know I cannot."

"Yes, you can," he said. "I will pay your way back. I will give you three times as much as I settled on you after our divorce. That should cover your expensive style of living. But you must leave within the next few days."

She kicked the stool aside and jumped to her feet. Her cheeks were flaming. "Don't!" she said. "Don't treat me like dirt. Oh, I know I deserve to be despised, but you demean yourself to be so cruel. Don't insult me so." She buried her face in her hands.

"Sarah," he said, "don't. Please don't cry. I did not mean to insult you. I have no right any longer. I merely have a problem, and I cannot think of any other way to solve it. I must send you away. Can you not see? I have the welfare of two young girls to consider, not just my own comfort."

She said nothing. He guessed that she was making an effort not to sob aloud. Damn! She was such a good actress that he could never be sure that she really was acting. He always felt guilty, afraid that he was doing her some terrible injustice. Was she merely holding out for more money?

"Don't cry, Sarah," he said, uncomfortable. He walked closer to her, reached out a hand, and tentatively covered one of hers over her face. "Stop now. I wish you no harm, believe me. Sarah?" He twined his fingers around hers and stroked the back of her hand with his thumb.

She tried to pull away, but in the effort a sob finally escaped her. Oh, damn! Hell and damnation! He caught her by the shoulders almost as if he wanted to punish her and yanked her against him. He put a hand on the back of her head and held her face against his neckcloth.

"Hush now," he said. "Hush." Without conscious thought he was rocking her in his arms. "Don't cry anymore. Stop now and we will talk about it. We do not have a great deal of time, Sarah."

She gulped and pushed away from him. She groped around in the pocket of her dress for a handkerchief.

He pulled one out of his own pocket and put it into her hand.

"Here," he said, "use mine. You never seem to have a handkerchief when you need one, do you?" And then he could have bitten his tongue out. What in heaven's name had sent his mind back to his carriage on their wedding day?

"I shall have it laundered and returned to you," she muttered after drying her eyes and blowing her nose. She sat down on the sofa again.

"Well," he said after a short pause, "you tell me, Sarah. What is to be done?"

"I do not know," she said. "I wish I did. Why do you not go away?"

"I hardly think that is to the point," he said, angry for some reason that she would so glibly suggest that he inconvenience himself. "Do you not realize, Sarah, that even without my presence here you are living on a volcano? A secret like yours is very difficult to keep, you know."

"I suppose you do have that other alternative," she said. "You can get rid of me very fast if you choose to do so, your grace."

"I think you know I would not do that," he said.

"Why not?" she asked, looking up at him with anger in her eyes again. "You did it once before, did you not? You dragged me through the mud once. I wonder that you hesitate to do so again."

"After what you told me," he said, "after the contempt you showed me, did you really expect me to remain married to you?"

"I thought perhaps you were a gentleman in every sense of the word," she said. "I was mistaken."

He stood and stared at her incredulously. "And it was on that assumption you gambled?" he asked. "I have often wondered why you allowed the marriage to take place when I was bound to discover your secret very soon afterward. You thought that once caught, I would remain in your net for a lifetime, did you? A perfect gentleman I may not be, Sarah, but neither am I an utter fool."

They glared at each other silently, both breathing rather fast. But this was solving nothing, he thought, and the others might return to the house at any moment.

"Sarah," he said, forcing himself to look away and speak reasonably again, "I have offered you a certain sum of money. If it is not enough, I shall increase my offer. And if you find it offensive to be bought off, think of it this way. We have a common problem. We can solve it together, me by\ paying a certain sum of money, you by making a journey and another way of life. We both make an effort, and together we solve a problem. Please, will you accept?"

She lifted her chin and looked into his eyes. "I found it humiliating the first time, George," she said, "to take your money when you did not want my person. But at that time, too, there was an insoluble problem. With the scandal fresh on everyone's mind, I was doing terrible harm to my aunt and uncle by living in their home. So I took the money. After four years I lost it in a manner that I choose not to discuss with you. But I will not take anything more from you, even though this situation is equally as bad as the other one. I would die rather, or suffer all the humiliation of being exposed here for what I am."

God! Why did she seem so righteous? Why did he suddenly feel so much in the wrong? His temper snapped.

"Perhaps you would accept the money if I called upon you to render suitable services," he said through his teeth, advancing menacingly on her.

She shot to her feet. "How dare you!" she spat out. "Of all the filthy—"

Her hand was raised to strike at him when they both became aware of the outside door opening and several voices approaching.

She sat down abruptly and grabbed for a box beside her, which she tipped onto her lap. A heap of tangled silk threads and numerous needles fell out. Cranwell crossed the room with rapid strides and was looking out of the window, hands clasped behind his back, when the door opened and the whole of the outside world seemed to spill inside.

Sarah insisted that Lady Murdoch not change her plans to go to the Lower Rooms that evening, though she would not go herself. She explained that she wished to be wise about her ankle and to rest it after the morning's walk so that she might have an outing the next day. When she was alone, she took the precaution of retiring to her room with a book. She left instructions with Mrs. Bergland that she was not to be disturbed under any conditions. She could not imagine who might visit her at such a time, but she had learned from the experience of the previous few days that in Bath any hour seemed suitable for visitors.

She had brought a book upstairs with her, but she looked at it with some incredulity as she sat on the edge of her bed. Had she really imagined that she might read? She had so much on her mind that she already felt as if her head were spinning on her shoulders.

He really did hate her. She did not know why she should be surprised at that. Even the real facts would justify his feelings, but she had seen to it that the facts were magnified and distorted. She was not quite sure why she had done so. Heaven knew, she had loved him and had wanted his love in return more than she had ever wanted anything else in her life. There had been so much of suffering and degradation in her past that she had longed with all her being for the refinement, the courtliness, the deep affection that life with George had seemed to offer.

Perhaps it was her deep love and respect for him that had finally made her act as she had. When he had left her and sent her back to Uncle Randolph, she had been numb with grief and horror for the first day, wanting only the chance to talk to him again, to explain as she had been unable to do when he had confronted her. But by the second day the old humiliation had taken control of her again. She had convinced herself that he was right: she was evil, no better than a whore. By right, she was Winston's mistress, not George's wife.

And she had blamed herself bitterly for what she had done. She should never have allowed even a friendship to develop between the Duke of Cranwell and herself. She should certainly not have encouraged his visits or his growing attachment to her. And she should have refused his proposal in no uncertain terms. There should have been no question of acceptance.

The fact that she had married him, had involved him in her own shame, became to her the worst sin she had committed. And it had seemed to be one that she could never atone for. She had ruined the life of the man she loved most in all the world. Her silence in allowing the marriage to proceed had been worse than the active sins she had committed with Winston.

She had not expected to see George again. She had thought he would stay away from her forever afterward and pretend that she did not exist. And she had felt no resentment against him. She had only grieved that she had destroyed his freedom and his ability to find happiness with another wife. When she had seen him ride up to her uncle's house, she had quickly hidden herself in the grounds, taking refuge on the stile that had always been one of her favorite spots. And she had quickly planned what she should say and do if he came to seek her out.

She was totally unprepared for his words and his manner. She had expected him to come to accuse and to preach. She had not expected his reasonable, almost humble attempt to come to some sort of explanation and understanding. She was not prepared for his forgiveness. He did not openly offer that forgiveness, but she sensed that she could win him back. He was prepared to listen, to sympathize, and to pardon.

And she completely took fright. She could not accept his forgiveness; she did not deserve it. She would

never be able to look into his eyes again, knowing that
he knew, knowing that he must be suffering agonies of
remorse for having been deceived into marrying her.
She could not trap him into a life like that, a life in
which honor would hold him close to her when inclination must make him wish to be anywhere but near her.
She had dealt him the greatest injustice of all by
marrying him. Now she must do all in her power to
give him some measure of freedom, at least.

And so she did something she had never done in her
life, something that she did not know she could do.
She acted a part, the part of a heartless, cynical coquette. She quite deliberately tauted him until she saw
his look of pain and gentleness turn to one of disgust.
And she watched him go, her chin up, a malevolent
smile on her lips. And she crumpled up against the
stile afterward and cried until she had no energy left to
continue.

She had still not expected him to divorce her. Truth
to tell, she scarcely knew what divorce was. And even
when Uncle Randolph had called her into his study to
read the letter from George's lawyer, she had not
really comprehended. The marriage was to be ended;
she had understood that. But she had not realized that
the whole matter must go before Parliament, that everything must be dragged into the open. Uncle Randolph had called his own man of business down from
London, and he had explained matters to both of
them.

She might have fought the action, the lawyer had
advised her. The Duke of Cranwell would have difficulty winning his case unless he could prove that at
least one of her indiscretions—that was the euphe-
mism the man had used—had been committed after
the wedding.

She might have fought. What had she done? She
had coolly looked the lawyer in the eye, with Uncle
Randolph sitting there listening, and told him that in
that case there was no point in fighting the case. She
had been indiscreet—she had emphasized the word—at

least once since her marriage. And she had smiled at the man until he had lowered his eyes to the papers he shuffled in his hands, obviously embarrassed. She had done the only thing in her power to atone for her chief sin. George wanted to be completely free of her. She had made it possible for him to be so.

And she wondered now why he hated her so.

And he wanted her to go away. He wanted never to see her again. He was willing to pay a small fortune to achieve his wish. And she had refused, had become angry at the insult. She did not have the right ever to be angry with George, ever to refuse him anything reasonable. And his request was reasonable, was it not? She found the present situation intolerable. What must it be for him?

Oh, but she could not accede to his wishes. She had thought that she had already sunk to the greatest depths of degradation possible. And to take money from George again so that she could set up an independent life would be further humiliation. He would be keeping her. She could not allow that.

But what, then?

There seemed to be no answer, though Sarah racked her brains and thought in endless circles until the sound of Lady Murdoch's voice in the hallway below set her to blowing out the candles on her dresser and undressing quickly in the dark.

She would think of something tomorrow.

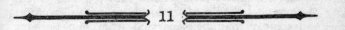

11

IT WAS the next day that Sarah realized that she must decide on some immediate course of action. She could delay no longer.

Lady Murdoch had been so busy in the previous few days that she had given far less thought than usual to eating. It was to this fact that Sarah attributed the improvement in her digestion. But Lady Murdoch swore that it was the magic of the waters at work. She continued to go to the Pump Room each morning to drink her pint of torture. Sarah accompanied her the morning after her walk on the Crescent.

She was greeted like a long-lost friend by people she had considered mere acquaintances. Mr. Phelps declared that though the sky had been blue and totally free of clouds, the sun had not shone since she had injured herself. Mr. John Staple came to ask her earnestly if she had taken the advice he had offered Lady Murdoch the day before and tried Scot's Improved Pills.

"It is true that they are intended mainly to cleanse the body," he explained, "but they are also reputed to comfort the nerves, and I am sure your nerves must have suffered from so nasty an accident."

The Misses Seymour came to tell her that she had missed a gathering at Colonel Smythe's the afternoon before, when they had discussed the news of Lord Wellesley's successes against the French troops in Spain. Colonel Smythe was chafing to go there himself to help in the rout. And Mrs. Smythe declared that if he went, she would go too.

"I do think it brave of her," the elder Miss Seymour

177

said. "I have heard that there are some wives in Spain, but conditions are said to be far from comfortable. And I am sure there is a great deal of danger."

"But if I had a husband in the army," Stella added, "I am sure I should prefer to put up with discomfort and danger than be separated from him perhaps forever."

And Hannah came across the room to where Sarah stood beside Lady Murdoch, bringing Cranwell with her. She was smiling warmly.

"I am so pleased to see you, Miss Fifield," she said. "Yesterday I feared that perhaps you had ventured out too soon and would be forced to stay at home for a few more days."

"I really am feeling quite fit," Sarah assured her, carefully avoiding Cranwell's eyes.

"We are to have breakfast in Sydney Gardens today," the girl continued, "and walk there afterward. Grandmama said that the weather is just too lovely for us to have to go inside merely to eat. Will you come too?"

"I think it likely that we will return to Brock Street," Sarah said. "Mrs. Bergland will be expecting us."

"But someone can be sent to let her know that you will not be returning," Hannah said. "Oh, do come. Your grace, do persuade Miss Fifield to come with us."

Sarah was never to know how Cranwell would have responded. At that moment Lady Murdoch turned to them.

"Sarah dear," she said, "Bertha has kindly invited us to breakfast with her in Sydney Gardens this morning. Is not that a splendid idea? Perhaps I shall recover some of my appetite in the open air, dear. I have quite lost it lately. Mr. Staple has been obliging enough to offer to call at Brock Street to tell Mrs. Bergland not to expect us until dinnertime."

"There! You see?" Hannah said triumphantly.

So here they were again, Sarah thought. There was no avoiding the association. She was almost glad to see Winston approaching, smiling with friendly charm at the whole group. She must have been regarding him with unusual warmth, she realized afterward; he looked at her appreciatively and almost immediately asked her if she would take a turn around the room with him. She took his arm without hesitation.

"Ah, Sarah," he said as soon as they were out of earshot, "how you put every other female into the shade. You look particularly dazzling this morning. Is it the primrose color of that very fetching gown? Or is it that very absurd little bonnet, which allows only a teasing glimpse of your hair?"

"How long are you planning to stay in Bath?" Sarah asked conversationally.

"What?" he said. "Trying to get rid of me, Sarah? I plan to stay as long as you do. And how long is that?"

She sighed. "You know there is no point in this line of conversation, Win," she said. "We might as well change the subject. What have you heard about Aunt Myrtle? She seemed somewhat oppressed by loneliness the last time I had a letter from her, but that was a few weeks ago."

Winston shrugged. "She is finding the adjustment hard," he said. "She was so used to doing everything for father before he died."

"Poor Aunt Myrtle," Sarah said. "She deserves some happiness now."

'Well, you did not help matters much," Winston said. "You know how upset she was when you were involved in such scandal. And you made no attempt to deny anything, Sarah. In fact, you even made matters worse by lying about committing adultery, though to this day I cannot imagine why you did so unless it was to protect my name. After all, I could hardly have been lying with you when I was in Italy at the time. However it was, you hurt your aunt and perhaps precipitated father's death."

"Oh, don't say that, Win," she said, looking up at him in distress. "I . . . Don't say that."

"Well, it was all very silly, was it not? Why did you have to marry Cranwell in the first place? You could not have really wanted him, Sarah. I am not unduly conceited, but I don't think you could have been very satisfied with him after being with me. And you were courting disaster trying to deceive someone quite as high in the instep as Cranwell. If you had not become ambitious but just waited for me to come home, everything would have been all right and Mother and Father would not have had to suffer so much. Mother is very fond of you, you know."

Sarah blinked her eyes fast. She must not show distress in such a public setting. "I stayed away from them," she said. "I tried to atone."

"But you have not made any effort to make things up to me," he said. "You have consistently rejected me ever since that time. You even threatened me on that first occasion I went to see you in your cottage, Sarah. Said you would go to that vicar friend of yours if I did not go away. As if I was about to ravish you or something! When are you going to realize that your future lies with me? I am not the one who abandoned you and publicly humiliated you."

"Let the matter rest, Win," Sarah said. They were approaching Cranwell and Hannah, Captain Penny and Fanny, who were strolling toward them.

"For now, perhaps, Sarah," he said, smiling down at her with a warm earnestness that she imagined was as much for the benefit of the approaching audience as for her. "But I want you and I shall not give up. Not ever."

Somehow Sarah found herself walking for the remainder of the promenade around the Pump Room with Captain Penny. Winston was smiling at Fanny and bending his head close to hers to talk and listen. She was glowing up at him.

Sydney Gardens were designed to entertain all comers. One could enjoy merely wandering over the lawns and along the walks. One could enjoy the labyrinth, the grottoes, the Chinese bridges, the manmade waterfalls. And each day there was a public breakfast. At night there were frequently concerts and fireworks displays. But now it was early morning, and the park sparkled in the sunshine. The Misses Seymour, Captain Penny, and Winston had been persuaded to join the party.

Sarah again had to endure the company of those she wished to avoid. Fanny sat next to her at breakfast and talked to her almost exclusively. Hannah asked her to take a stroll afterward while the others were still sitting at the table. And when Sarah rose to her feet, unable to think of a reasonable excuse, the girl linked an arm through hers and began to walk in the direction of a waterfall without looking for the company of anyone else.

"I am so happy that you are better again, Miss Fifield," the girl said. "I find it easy to talk to you. I do not know why that is so. Do you find that some people are easier to talk to than others? Maybe not. You have a poise that I envy. I hope you do not find it dull to be with me. I did not think of that." She looked at Sarah in some dismay.

"No," Sarah said, uncomfortable despite her smile, "of course I do not find you dull."

"Thank you," Hannah said. "I do find all this most bewildering, you know. This time last year I was still with my governess. Papa never would send me away to school. Not that I was sorry. I would have hated to go away. I am very attached to my home, you see. Have you ever had pets, Miss Fifield? If so, maybe you will understand how desperately I miss Argus. And my horse, too, but not quite as much."

"I never had a special pet," Sarah said, "but I think I can sympathize."

"And then there are Iris and Donald," Hannah continued. "They are our neighbors, you know. They are not very rich or particularly important, Papa says. But I had not thought of that until recently."

"You miss them too?" Sarah asked.

"Oh, yes," Hannah said. "I had not thought I would

ever leave home. Silly isn't it? Of course girls must leave home. They must marry and go to live with their husbands. It does not seem quite fair, does it?"

The girl's manner was bright and nervous, Sarah noticed. She was usually so quiet, almost lusterless.

Sarah could not resist the question. "Do you not wish to marry his grace?" she asked.

"Oh," Hannah said, turning to give her a bright smile, "you are not to think that. He is a very important man, you know, and it is a quite dazzling match for me. And he is kind. He is very patient with me and never scolds or preaches as Papa frequently does."

"But you do not love him?" Sarah was hardly aware of the fact that she held her breath.

"Papa says love has nothing to do with marriage," the girl said, again with that bright, empty smile. "Love is something one outgrows, he says. One marries for security and position. I shall be a duchess. That is much better than being merely . . . Well, one has to marry. It does not do to become an old maid."

"I hope you will be happy," Sarah said carefully. "I think the duke is a kind man."

"Oh, yes," Hannah agreed, "he is. He was married before, you know."

"Was he?" said Sarah.

"Yes. He divorced her. I do not know why. Papa would not tell me. But it must have been for something dreadful. She must have been a very bad woman, I think."

"Yes, she must," Sarah agreed.

"But it does make me a little afraid," the girl confided. "If he could dismiss one wife, would he do it again? I hope I shall be able to please him."

"Oh, Hannah," said Sarah, startled into familiarity with her companion, "of course you will. You are sweet and very innocent. You must not even think you will offend him. His first wife was more evil than you could even imagine. The fault was not his at all."

Hannah's eyes had grown as round as saucers. "You know what happened?" she said.

"I heard some rumors," Sarah said evasively. "It is not worth even talking about. Just look at the rainbow in the spray from the waterfall. Is it not spectacular?"

Hannah's attention was diverted for a few minutes. When she spoke again, it was of Fanny.

"She likes Lord Laing," the girl said confidentially, "and I am quite sure he has a preference for her. Would it not be splendid, Miss Fifield, if he offered for her? Then you and I would have some slight connection through marriage."

Sarah controlled the shock she was feeling. "I think your conclusion must be precipitate," she said placidly. "They scarcely know each other. Such a connection as they enjoy is quite natural in a place like this, you know."

"Oh, but he has expressed his regard for her in the warmest terms," Hannah said earnestly. She giggled suddenly. "He even kissed her at the last ball, Miss Fifield. Fanny said that she scolded him severely, but he smiled, she said, and declared in the most speaking manner that his intentions are entirely honorable. Fanny pretends to think nothing of it, but I know she is in hourly expectation of his speaking to his grace."

Sarah could scarcely hide her dismay. "And does she mean to have him?" she asked.

"Oh, I am sure she will," Hannah said. "She is quite in love with him, even if she will not admit it. He is so handsome and charming and amiable. He seems quite too good to be true, in fact. You were fortunate to grow up in his company."

"Yes," Sarah said, her brain humming. "And how would her brother receive a proposal, do you think?"

"He speaks of Lord Laing in the warmest terms," the girl replied. "I do not believe he will make any objection. Quite the contrary."

As they were strolling back to the tables where most of the others still sat, Sarah could see that Winston had again singled out Fanny and taken her to look at a nearby flowerbed. He was clearly using the full force of his charm on her. Sarah's unease was compounded

when the two walked back and Winston addressed
Cranwell.

"I look forward to that ride to Beacon Hill this
afternoon," he said. "The weather is perfect for such
an outing."

"Yes, indeed," Cranwell said. "My sister, Lady Hannah, and I will be glad of the exercise. We are all
more used to the countryside than to the city. You will
meet us at Laura Place after luncheon, Bowen?"

"Indeed," Winston said, smiling warmly at Fanny.
"I would not miss being one of the party for worlds. It
will be a great honor to accompany Lady Fanny."

When Sarah dared glance their way, it was to find
George giving Winston a measured but unsuspicious
look, and Fanny looking very pleased with the world.
Captain Penny, she fancied, was annoyed but was
talking determinedly to the younger Miss Seymour.
Winston, of course, was looking sincerely charmed.
But he turned around quite deliberately, met Sarah's
eyes, and raised his eyebrows in a look of unmistakable challenge.

Yes, Sarah thought as she helped Lady Murdoch
into the carriage that had been brought to convey
them to the bookseller's on Milsom Street, she had to
make some sort of active decision. She could not bear
this situation much longer, yet there seemed no hope
that the pattern of their days would change of its own
accord for perhaps several weeks. She could no longer
sit back and hope that the problems would go away.
She was going to have to do something.

This fact was reinforced most painfully during the
evening. She was at the Upper Rooms taking tea with
Lady Murdoch. Mrs. Marchmont and her daughter
and Mr. Phelps sat with them. Sarah was feeling a
little more relaxed than she had for several days, as
Lady Cavendish and her party had been invited to a
private dinner.

But there was to be no respite. Winston joined their
table and conversed amiably with the whole group
until the opportunity came to draw Sarah a little apart.

"Have you been to Beacon Hill?" he asked. "It is a very pleasant area for a ride, Sarah. Perhaps you and I could go there one morning."

"You are wasting your breath, Win," she said. "You know I would not agree to anything so improper."

He grinned. "We could invite other people to come too," he said, "just to satisfy your very correct mind. You used not to be such a prude, Sarah."

She did not reply but tried to return her attention to the conversation of the others at the table.

"I think Fanny would come again," Winston said. "She is quite a bruising rider. She has obviously had much practice."

"Fanny?" said Sarah sharply, looking back at him. "Do you speak so familiarly when you are with her, Win? And in her brother's hearing?"

He smiled into her eyes. "I believe I might soon do so without raising a single eyebrow," he said.

Sarah could not resist the bait. "What do you mean?" she asked.

"I believe I might not be rejected out of hand if I decided to pay the young lady my addresses soon," Winston said.

"You would not!" Sarah said. "Oh, you would not, Win. Just because she is very wealthy?"

"Hush, Sarah," he said, lowering his own voice and leaning closer to her. "You would not believe that I have a *tendre* for the girl? No, perhaps not. But really, I do not find the prospect of being leg-shackled to her entirely displeasing. She might make an interesting armful. And if I cannot have the woman I want, then I must make do with the next-best one."

"You are unspeakable!" Sarah hissed under her breath. "You would not really marry her. You are merely trying to goad me into agreeing to go away with you. Why would you think you will succeed? Why would you think I care?"

"Ah, but I know you do care," he said, still smiling at her with gentle warmth. "For some reason—pride, I suppose—you do care what Cranwell thinks about you.

And you are afraid that I will disgrace you further in his eyes by mistreating his sister. You are quite wrong, you know. If I marry the chit, she will find me a most indulgent husband."

"You would not," Sarah said weakly.

Winston smoothed the lace of his shirt cuffs over the backs of his hand. "It is a little soon," he said. "I have known the lady for only a few days although I have perhaps . . . ah . . . hinted to both brother and sister that my intentions are serious. And not been discouraged by either, Sarah! I believe I must wait at least . . . er . . . a week? After that I think I will be ready to make my declaration."

The challenge was unmistakable.

Winston turned back to the group and joined in the conversation as smoothly as if he had not missed a word. Sarah was left to confer with her own thoughts until Mrs. Marchmont asked her opinion of the new milliner on Milsom Street.

That night, alone in her room at last, Sarah sat before her dresser brushing out her long hair slowly. She was in no hurry. Although the hour was late for Bath and she was clad in her nightgown and had already drunk her bedtime chocolate, she had no intention of going to bed yet. She knew that it would be impossible to sleep. Her brain was racing as if it were trying to reject all the unwelcome information with which it was being asked to cope. She must somehow sort everything out and decide on some course of action before trying to sleep.

Some points were clear. One was that if she stayed in Bath and allowed life to continue as it was, she would be daily in the company of George, Hannah, and Fanny. And more than that. Hannah considered her to be a friend. The girl was shy. Sarah guessed that she was the sort of person who had few friends, but who held fast to those she had. And Hannah liked her. Fanny, too, although she apparently knew the truth, seemed to wish to extend their acquaintance.

Was she willing for these things to happen? That was one of the questions with which she had to grapple. She did not believe that she would actively corrupt either girl by being connected with them. But the truth remained that she was a fallen woman, one whose honor and reputation were permanently tainted, one whom no respectable person would receive if she were known. It was not fair to either girl to remain in their company if there was any way she could contrive not to do so.

And certainly it was undesirable to be in George's company every day. Even if she did not love him, it would be painful to be reminded of all that had happened in the past. As it was, she did love him, as deeply and as passionately as she had from the start. She would not even try to hide the fact from her own heart. She had wronged him terribly in the past. And while she could do nothing to change what was over and done with, she could perhaps do something about the present. It must be ten times worse for him to have to face her every day than it was for her to face him. Sarah's face burned with shame as she thought again of what she had deliberately made him believe four years before. As if the truth had not been bad enough!

She must do something, then, to remove herself from daily contact with all three. The problem was, what? There was still the idea of applying for a position, but that would take far too long. The need to leave soon had become quite urgent. And then, too, there were Lady Murdoch's feelings to be considered.

Even all that was not the end of her problems. There was Winston too, and his threat to offer for Fanny if Sarah did not go away with him. He certainly knew best how to have his way. There was no particular reason why she should be concerned about the welfare of Lady Fanny Montagu, but she was. And Winston knew that she was. The girl was George's sister, and she loved George. Somehow it seemed to be her responsibility to save Fanny from what could only be a disastrous marriage.

And if Hannah were to be believed, Fanny would be quite receptive to Win's addresses. It was to be expected, of course, Sarah had to admit if she looked at the matter objectively. Fanny was in society for the first time and she had been singled out by surely the most handsome and charming man in all of Bath. What girl would not be flattered by such attention?

But would George allow it? Would he not refuse to allow his sister to be swept into matrimony so soon? But then, why should he? Winston must seem perfectly eligible to him, and short courtships were not frowned upon by the *ton*, provided the match was respectable. Then, with his own marriage pending, it might seem convenient to have Fanny removed to a different household. And both Hannah and Win believed that George would support the match.

She must do something to prevent the marriage. Tell George the whole truth? Impossible. She would not be believed, and she did not think she would have the courage at this late date to face him with her story. Lure Win away? She was not sure, of course, that even if she did agree to go away with him, Winston would leave Fanny alone. It was quite within the bounds of possibility that he would contrive to satisfy both of his desires. He wanted her person, but there was nothing else to be hoped for from her. She had no money, and Winston was always chronically in need of that. Fanny, on the other hand, was undoubtedly a very wealthy young lady. She would appear an extremely desirable bride to Winston. He might marry Fanny even if Sarah became his mistress.

The brush paused in its slow journey through Sarah's hair. She realized in some horror where her thoughts were leading her. She was not seriously considering resuming her affair with Winston, was she? The prospect was entirely unthinkable. She had decided quite finally after her divorce from George that no other man would ever possess her. In her heart, she would remain his faithful and obedient wife. And least of all Winston Bowen. She would never allow him to so much as touch her ever again, she had decided.

And was she now to go back on that decision, resume of her own free will the degradation of her former existence? She did not believe she could allow Winston those intimacies again and remain sane. The very thought made her stomach churn and her palms grow cold and clammy.

Could she do it for the sake of her love of George? She gave a short and bitter laugh, which sounded startlingly loud in the quiet of her room. What an irony! Her love of one man was threatening to send her into an illicit affair with another man who repelled her. Her sense of honor was forcing her to consider giving up the shreds of her reputation and decency.

And it might all be in vain. She might take him away, give up her own damaged virtue, even her own sense of personhood, merely to find that she was mistress to the husband of the girl for whom she had made the sacrifice.

She could not do it.

She must do it!

There was, of course, another alternative, one that would make the future safe for the family that had been hers for a short time. It was a definite choice, but it would involve her in deeper degradation than anything else she had considered.

Sarah closed her eyes and replaced the brush on the dresser. Could she?

She had to.

She wanted to vomit.

Perhaps something else would occur to her before morning.

The Duke of Cranwell was also in his bedchamber, clad in nightshirt and dressing gown. He too was still up, pacing back and forth in the narrow confines of his room. He had dismissed Peters half an hour before.

He did not normally consider himself an indecisive man. For many years he had borne the responsibility of running enormous estates almost single-handedly. He employed both a bailiff and a secretary, but his was the hand that was firmly in control. And he had made a success of his lands. They were prosperous and progressive. There was not a tenant or laborer on his land who was in want or who had a grievance that had not been heard and redressed where possible. He was a man who expected respect from both his peers and his subordinates simply because he felt he had earned it.

Yet now, taken out of his milieu by the demands of his betrothal, he suddenly felt very much out of control of his destiny. And he was not happy with himself. He was allowing life to happen around him and making no effort to shape it according to what he knew to be desirable and right. He had agreed to accompany Hannah to Bath because he had considered it right to be seen with her in public and to give her a chance to be seen in society before their nuptials. And he had decided to bring Fanny with him because it was time that she too began to take her rightful place as an adult in society. The plan had seemed sensible and thoroughly respectable.

And then everything had collapsed around him. Sarah was in Bath too. And if that were not bad enough, she was in company with one of Lady Cavendish's closest friends. And for almost a week now he had stood weakly in the background, totally inactive, as she had wormed her way into the affections of Hannah and Fanny. Now matters had reached a point at which both girls considered her to be a friend, even though Fanny knew who she was.

Perhaps it seemed a little unfair to put the blame for the developing friendships entirely on Sarah. It seemed as if it was the two girls who were pressing the acquaintance. If he did not know Sarah, he would not think to blame her at all, perhaps. But he did know her of old. He knew that she had a consummate skill in getting what she wanted while seeming to do nothing at all to gain her own ends. She had lured him into marriage by seeming almost to discourage him. Now she had lured the girls into friendship by exactly the same tactics.

It really was an uncanny gift that she had. She must be the most devilish person he had ever known in his life. Cranwell paused at the foot of the bed and rested one hand on a sturdy post. He swore satisfyingly into the silence of the room. Even on him, who knew her better than anyone, she was working some of the old magic. When they were in company together, he could not rid himself of his awareness of her. And it was not just the awareness of hatred and discomfort. He was aware of her vivid beauty and of the vibrance that he sensed in her, though she kept it very much in restraint as she had when he first knew her. No other woman had ever made him as aware of his own bodily needs. In unguarded moments he could even now find himself looking at her and wanting her.

Cranwell swore more viciously, and his knuckles turned white against the bedpost.

There was no point at all in waiting around hoping that Miss Sarah Fifield would do the noble thing and leave Bath. There was no point even in offering her more money to do so. For some reason she seemed more interested in staying and tormenting him than in acquiring for herself independence and a modest fortune. Unless, of course, she was holding out for a much larger amount. It seemed entirely likely that her design was to wreak some sort of vengeance for the ugly publicity he had caused her during their divorce.

He could not rely on Sarah, then, to leave. There was only one alternative. He must leave Bath, and both Fanny and Hannah must leave with him. He did not know how this was to be accomplished when they had arrived barely a week before. Lady Cavendish fully intended to remain for at least four weeks. But he must think of something, some reason for leaving that would be acceptable to the ladies.

God, but he had loved her! He doubted that he would have ever divorced her if he had not loved her so much. His pain at finding out the truth about her had been so unbearable that he had been able to think of nothing else to do but rid his life of her, sever all ties with her, as if he had expected to be able to erase her from his heart.

Even so, despite all the pain, which had robbed him of his ability to think clearly and reasonably, he did not think that he would have carried through the divorce plans just on the evidence he had collected. He might have been weak enough despite it all to have forgiven her, to have tried to patch up their marriage somehow. The saner part of his mind could not bear the thought of completely destroying her reputation through the publicity of divorce.

He had visited her uncle's lawyer, against the advice of his own, to try to persuade the man to talk to her, to see what might be arranged. He had pointed out to the lawyer what that individual surely knew already, that his case against his wife must be very shaky if only her premarital behavior was in question. He had urged the lawyer to explain this to Sarah. He had been offering her a way out. He had expected her to break down and protest that her life was now blameless. He had hoped that he could go to her and win from her a commitment to their marriage, a renunciation of her past.

He had loved her enough. He would have forgiven her.

Her uncle's lawyer had reported in almost cruel detail what had happened during his interview with the duchess. She had freely admitted adultery. She had laughed in his face as she confessed.

And he had been blind with grief, anger, humiliation, shock—every nameable painful emotion, in fact. He had hardened his heart and continued with the divorce, which she had now made relatively easy for him.

His own pain had made it impossible for him at the

time to ask himself why this woman who had gone to such lengths to trap him into marriage had seemed to go to almost equal lengths after the marriage to release herself from its bonds. He had never asked himself that question until now, in fact. And there was no point whatsoever in teasing his mind with it. He would never understand such a devious mind as Sarah Fifield's. It was too purely devilish.

Tomorrow he would think of a plan to get away from this city, which he was beginning to hate more each minute. Away from Sarah.

12

IT WAS the evening of the following day before Sarah had any opportunity to put her plan into operation. Lady Murdoch woke in the morning with one of her migraine headaches and declined even to go to the Pump Room for her morning drink of the sulfur waters. She kept to her bed in a darkened bedroom, declaring that she would stay there all day, as she was quite determined to be well enough to attend the concert and fireworks display in Sydney Gardens that evening.

Sarah found herself with an unexpectedly free day. Not that it was entirely free. She did undertake to run a few errands for her cousin, including a visit to the circulating library to try to find a book that would not put Lady Murdoch to sleep every time she opened its cover. She made the journey soon after a fairly early breakfast in the hope of avoiding anyone she knew. She did not entirely succeed, but she did not meet anyone she particularly wished to avoid.

It was an ordeal of a day nonetheless. She almost wished that the headache would persist and they would not be able to attend the evening's entertainment. But she felt guilty for even allowing such a thought. The headache was very clearly not an imaginary ailment.

Anyway, she thought with an attempt at being sensible, if she did not have the opportunity to act this evening, she would have to face the same unpleasantness tomorrow. She felt sick at the thought of what lay ahead, but since it had to be done, she might as well do it before the day ended. She did not wish to have quite such a sleepless night of agonized indecision as she had had the night before.

And indeed, by the middle of the afternoon Lady Murdoch had ventured from her room to the salon and was taking tea and even halfheartedly thumbing through the book Sarah had chosen. She would be quite well enough to go out that evening, she told Sarah.

"And it is only right that I should be well enough," she said, "for you have missed a whole day of enjoyment, Sarah dear. There was really no need for you to stay at home, for I am sure that Bertha or Mrs. Smythe or Mrs. Marchmont would have been only too happy to have you join them in whatever they had planned. But I know you well already. You are too kind to me. I am quite becoming spoiled, I do declare."

The words did nothing to make Sarah feel better about the evening ahead. She smiled.

"It really is no sacrifice to stay at home, Cousin Adelaide," she said. "I have enjoyed a quiet read."

A hired carriage arrived early in the evening to take them across the river to Sydney Gardens, which looked quite enchanted lit by lanterns, Sarah thought. If only she could relax and enjoy the evening. Normally she would have loved nothing more than to sit and listen to an orchestra play in surroundings of such beauty. And she would have looked forward to the fireworks for Lady Murdoch's sake.

But these were not normal circumstances. They sat and waited for the concert to begin. And they waited for the arrival of Lady Cavendish and her party, Lady Murdoch with eagerness, Sarah with dread. Though whether she dreaded more their coming or the possibility that they would not come, she would have been hard put to it to decide.

She was not to be held long in suspense. A mere few minutes after their own arrival, as she exchanged pleasantries with Mr. Joshua Stonewall, who had come across to them and asked leave to sit beside her, Lady Murdoch stirred at her side.

"Yoo-hoo!" she yelled suddenly, waving the kid gloves that she had removed a few minutes before. "Over here, Bertha."

Mr. Stonewall jumped to his feet to greet the ladies and there was a great deal of bustling as they all found seats. Sarah felt her heart begin to thump so uncomfortably that she was finding it hard to breathe. Cranwell seated himself several seats away from her. Lady Murdoch, Lady Cavendish, Fanny, and Captain Penny sat between her and him. She tried to concentrate on what Mr. Stonewall was saying to her.

"Can't understand why I ain't seen you before, Miss Fifield," he said. "I move around quite a bit and thought I knew everybody who is somebody."

Sarah smiled. "Perhaps I am not somebody very special," she said.

Mr. Stonewall gave her an incredulous look. "I assure you, ma'am," he said fervently, "there ain't the man living who would forget you once he had set eyes on you."

Sarah's attention was fully caught. She looked at the tall, thin young man beside her with full awareness. She was always taken by surprise when any man showed interest in her person. But there was something in Mr. Stonewall's tone that suggested more than mere repartee or gallantry.

"It is my red hair, sir," she said lightly. "It is the curse of my existence."

The concert began soon afterward and Sarah was able to withdraw into her own thoughts again. However, she was constantly aware of the man who fidgeted and frequently yawned beside her. She could certainly do without the complication of having another man developing a *tendre* for her. Of course, if her plan worked, she would not have to worry about that.

Eventually the music drew to an end for the interval before the second half of the concert. Joshua turned to Sarah and suggested that they take a walk along the lantern-lit paths. She rose to her feet.

"Come along, Cran," Joshua called. "You were quizzing me just a few days ago about not having enough exercise. Will you and Lady Hannah join us for a stroll?"

Fanny turned eagerly to Captain Penny. "Shall we walk too?" she asked. "I feel quite cramped from sitting still for so long."

Lady Murdoch loudly urged the young people to go walking and enjoy the evening air.

Amid the bustle and confusion Sarah moved close to Cranwell. "I wish to speak to you," she said in a low voice without raising her eyes to his.

She did not know if he had heard or not. He turned to offer his arm to Hannah and moved off along the path without a word. They walked for several minutes, past a waterfall, across a Chinese bridge, until the sound of music came quite distinctly from behind them. Fanny wrinkled her nose and looked up at the captain.

"Let us walk for a little while longer," she said. "We can hear the music quite clearly from here."

"Better, in fact, Lady Fanny," Joshua said, turning to her with a grin. "Here on one's feet one can perhaps remain awake to listen."

"It really is beautiful here," Hannah said. "It is quiet. One can almost imagine that one is in the countryside."

"Am I the only honest music lover in this whole group?" Cranwell asked, amusement in his voice. "But, ah, no. I distinctly recall Miss Fifield saying that she loves to listen to music too. Josh, change partners with me, will you, old fellow? We two music lovers will walk back to rejoin the concert. Miss Fifield?"

"I say!" Joshua began to protest. But he shrugged, smiled gallantly at Hannah, and took her arm. "Come, ma'am," he said, "let us see if we can outdistance that noise, shall we?"

Cranwell said nothing until they were completely out of earshot of the rest of the group. He turned out of the main path onto a narrower, more winding one that received its light only from the main thoroughfare.

"Well?" he said finally. "You wished to speak to me?"

"Yes," she said, breathing deeply in an attempt to control the thumping of her heart. "Two days ago you offered to pay me to leave Lady Murdoch and Bath and to return to my former way of life. Three times the sum you gave me after our divorce was the amount you named, I believe?"

Cranwell looked at her briefly. "That is correct," he said.

Sarah smiled ahead of her. Quite unconsciously she was assuming the coquettish manner she had used on a previous occasion, when he had come to speak with her a few days after their marriage.

"I have given the matter some thought," she said, "and I have decided that the sum is too small."

"Indeed?" he said coldly.

"I find that my life is very comfortable at present," she said. "It is much to my liking. If I am to give it up, you will have to make it worth my while."

"Well, Sarah," he said briskly, "and what is your price?"

"Twice what you have offered me," she said without hesitation.

He was silent for a long while. They strolled along the deserted pathway, her arm still linked through his.

"And what do I receive in return?" he asked finally.

"I shall leave Bath within three or four days," she said, "and I shall make quite sure that our paths do not cross ever again."

"I see," he said, and there was another pause.

"If you really wish to be rid of me," Sarah said, glancing sidelong at him, the provocative smile still on her lips, "you will consider my price a bargain."

"Yes," he said, "I do. I shall send my man to Brock Street with a draft on my bank tomorrow morning. Will that be acceptable to you?"

"Entirely," she said. "Here. I shall leave my glove with you. You may send the draft to me under cover of returning my lost possession."

He took the white kid glove and thrust it into his pocket. He did not offer his arm to her again, and she made no move to look for his support. They walked on side by side in a heavy silence. But almost by unspoken consent their footsteps lagged as they approached the bend in the path that would take them in the direction of the main path again.

Cranwell stopped finally and turned to face her. "Sarah," he said softly, "what will you do?"

"Gracious!" she said with a brittle laugh. "That is none of your concern, your grace. You have ensured that I will not be a pauper, at least."

"Use the money wisely," he said earnestly. "Don't go back to your old way of life. Please!"

"And what is that?" she asked, looking into his eyes, the smile falling away from her.

He shrugged. "Men," he said. "I don't know what you do, Sarah. I don't know what it is in your character that has kept you from a respectable way of life. Perhaps the death of your parents when you were young set you to looking for love in the wrong places. Perhaps your brother's death unsettled your emotions. But there are depths to your character that could so easily make you into a completely different person."

"How do you know?" she said, and laughed. "You really know nothing at all about me, your grace."

"I do know," he said decisively. "I loved you once."

She laughed again. "You loved the girl you thought I was," she said. "A young innocent who did not exist."

"Sarah," he said, and his hand reached out to brush a strand of hair from her face, "please assure me that you will not go back to being whatever it was that you were."

"A whore?" she said, pulling back from his hand.

He stared at her. "You see," he said, "I have just realized that I am in some way responsible for you. You seem to be living with some respectability under the influence of Lady Murdoch. With my money perhaps you will be free to be tempted by the lure of the past again."

"You are not in any way responsible for me,

George," Sarah said vehemently. "Not in any way. I am no longer your wife."

He looked at her and nodded slowly. "Yes," he said. "Sometimes I forget that. The money will be yours tomorrow to do with as you wish."

"We must return," Sarah said, "before the others come back and wonder what has become of us."

"Yes," he said.

But they still stood and looked at each other. And each was aware that this was probably the last time they would ever be alone together. They would never talk to each other again. In a few days' time she would be gone.

Cranwell held out a hand to her. "I do not hate you, Sarah," he said, "and I cannot wish you ill. Let us not part bitter enemies. I wish for you a happy life."

Sarah took a deep breath and put her hand in his. She watched his slim fingers close around hers. "I wish you a happy marriage, George," she said, "happier than the first. I am sorry for . . . I am sorry," she ended lamely.

He lifted her hand to his lips but did not take his eyes from hers. "I am too, Sarah," he said.

His eyes strayed to her lips. And she knew what was going to happen. Her mind was fully aware of the emotionally charged atmosphere that had destroyed their common sense. But her mind was not in control of the moment at all. It was a moment for physical sensation.

There was instant familiarity in his kiss. There was the comfortable molding of her body to his, as if they had been made to fit into each other's arms. There was the distinctive smell of some cologne, which she had forgotten until this moment. There was the firm warmth of his mouth open slightly over hers and the surprising strength of his arms crushing her to him. And there was that almost instant surge of heat and passion that blanked her mind to all rational thought and set her to clinging to him and tilting her head and aching to bring him closer, closer.

She did not afterward know how long their embrace lasted. She was jerked back to reality from an unknown, timeless world of passionate longing when he pushed her from him and held her away with one hand gripped painfully on each of her arms.

"God!" he said. "You witch, Sarah. You devil! What is it you do to me?"

She swallowed painfully and fought the tears that were lurking very near the surface. "Take me back, George," she said. "I want to go back to Cousin Adelaide."

He too was visibly fighting for control. "Please accept my apologies," he said. "I have insulted you, and I am without excuse. Forgive me, please."

He turned abruptly and began to walk rapidly along the path. But when Sarah hurried along at his side, he slowed his pace again, took her arm, and drew it through his.

"I really am sorry," he said, not turning his head to look at her again. "Damned sorry for everything. I wish you and I had never met, Sarah. It would have been so much better for both of us if we had not. God, I wish we had not met."

Sarah said nothing.

"Will you mind if I do not accompany you to the shops, Cousin Adelaide?" Sarah asked the following morning during breakfast. "Winston asked me in the Pump Room if he might call on me later."

Lady Murdoch looked up sharply from spreading jam on a scone. "Did he indeed?" she said, smiling broadly. "And did he say what he wished to see you about, dear?"

"No, he did not," Sarah said.

"Well, depend upon it," the older lady said, pointing the jam-covered knife across the table, "he is going to propose to you, Sarah. I have known it all along. Did I not say days ago that Lord Laing was sweet on you? Well, I declare. I shall certainly have something to tell Bertha."

Sarah blushed. "Please, cousin," she said, "say nothing this morning. Indeed, I do not know what Winston wishes to say to me. Perhaps he has some news from home."

Lady Murdoch nodded knowingly. "If that were so, he would not have asked for a private meeting, you may depend on it," she said shrewdly.

"I suppose not," Sarah said, blushing still.

Lady Murdoch bit into her scone, having piled clotted cream on top of the jam. "Oh," she said, her mouth full, "I can scarcely wait for this evening, Sarah. By then I shall surely have the most wonderful news for Bertha. Such a handsome couple!"

Sarah felt guilty an hour later when she stood on the pavement outside the house waving to Lady Murdoch as her carriage drew away from the curb. She had had to say that Win had asked to call on her. Even Cousin Adelaide would have thought her most improper if she knew that it was Sarah who had asked Win to call on her.

She went inside the house again and into the salon, where she waited in some agitation. It was impossible to settle to any task. She wished he would come soon. She was still moving with the momentum that had carried her through the previous evening and the night, during which she had slept surprisingly well. She was holding her mind as blank as possible. When she had accomplished everything she had planned, then she would stop to think. And to feel. She dared not feel yet. That conversation. That kiss! No, she dared not think.

Fortunately, she did not have long to wait for Winston. She heard his cheerful voice in the hallway a few moments after the knock on the door and breathed a sigh of relief. She might have known that Winston's curiosity would make him prompt. She stood in front of the fireplace, facing the door.

Mrs. Bergland announced the guest and closed the door behind him. He stood there for a moment looking appreciatively at her spring-green sarcenet gown, which set off to perfection the shining red of her hair.

"Well, Sarah," he said, "you are looking quite beautiful, as usual. And to what do I owe the pleasure of this invitation?" He smiled warmly and crossed the room to stand a little way in front of her.

Sarah had to tip her head back to look up at him. He really was extremely handsome. There was not a detectable flaw in his whole appearance. Light from the window was catching his blond hair and making a halo of it. His hazel eyes were smiling into hers.

"Do you still wish me to go away with you, Win?" she asked.

His eyes lit up. "You know I do," he said. "There has always been only you, Sarah. You know that."

"Very well," she said, "I am ready to do as you wish."

He moved forward and reached for her. But Sarah held up a hand. She was not smiling.

"There is one condition, Win," she said.

"Name it," he said. "I could not deny you anything, Sarah."

"You must marry me," she said.

Winston's arms dropped to his sides again. He regarded her with his head tilted to one side. "Now, Sarah," he said, "you know that I would like nothing better. You know, too, that I cannot do so. I must marry for money."

"Then marry me for money," she said. "I think you will agree I have a handsome dowry. It should be sufficient to pay your debts here and allow us to establish ourselves somewhere other than Bath." She took Cranwell's bank draft from the mantelpiece behind her and put it into Winston's hands.

"The old lady?" he asked with widened eyes. Then he looked down at the paper and whistled. "Cranwell," he said. "How did you get this out of him, Sarah? It is a fortune!"

"Yes," she said. "You might say it is a wedding gift, Win. It is mine. He gave it quite freely. And it can be

yours if you will take me away from here and marry
me. You may also be interested to know that Lady
Murdoch plans to make me the chief beneficiary of
her will."

Winston looked up from the bank draft, folded it
deliberately, and put it into his pocket. "Well, Sarah,"
he said softly, smiling into her eyes, "so now your
behavior for the last several years becomes understandable. You really did want marriage, did you?
And you have very cleverly gone about making it
possible for me to offer for you. I was never sure until
now that you cared at all."

Sarah smiled, her hands clenched into hard fists
behind her back. "Well, what do you say, Win?" she
asked.

"What can I say?" he said, closing the small distance between them and placing his hands on her
waist. "I had better make this matter formal and official. Will you do me the great honor of becoming my
wife?"

"Yes," Sarah said.

He stood looking down at her for a while, his smile
slowly spreading until his whole face was alight. "I had
almost run out of patience, you know," he said. "It
has been a long wait, Sarah. And we have a great deal
of lost time to make up for. I have almost forgotten
what it feels like to have you. But I have never found
any female with whom I liked it more."

Sarah swallowed hard and stood very still. She did
not look away from him.

"And you are so much more beautiful than you
were then," he said, his hands moving up to cup her
breasts. He looked down at them. "You were a girl
then, Sarah. You are a woman now."

She took a deep breath and braced herself as she
watched his face come closer. Finally she closed her
eyes and held her mouth steady beneath the soft moist-
ness of his. She imposed relaxation on her body as his
hands pressed her against the length of him and proceeded to roam and explore. She even parted her own

lips eventually under the persistent probing of his tongue and allowed it entrance. And she gazed resolutely at the ceiling when his head forced her own back so that his mouth might trace a hot trail along her throat.

"Sarah," he said against her mouth again. "I cannot stand the restraints. Will that old housekeeper stay out until summoned? Can we lie down? Let me touch you. It will not take long."

Then at last she pushed against his shoulders. "No, Win," she said. "This time I want everything to be as it should be. After we are married, I will be yours. You may have me then whenever you want. It will be your right. But not until then."

"Tease!" he said. "You always were a tease, Sarah, inflaming me to the point of madness and then pretending reluctance so that I almost had to force you. Very well. I shall be patient. But not for long, mind. I want you in my bed very soon."

"Yes," she said. "I want it to be soon too, Win. I want us to leave here within the next few days."

"There is no particular hurry now," he said. "With this"—he tapped the pocket in which he had deposited the bank draft—"I shall be able to hold off the worst of my creditors here. But if I must take you away before you will allow me to possess you again, then go we must." He smiled cheerfully and kissed her slowly on the lips again.

"I think you should go now, Win," Sarah said. "I have much to do. I have to pack my trunks and break the news to Lady Murdoch. She will be very pleased, by the way."

"I shall charm her out of her mind," Winston said with a grin. "She must be convinced that that change in her will should be made without further delay."

"Yes," Sarah said. "Come this evening, Win, to escort us to the Upper Rooms. It will be a suitable occasion on which to announce our betrothal to our acquaintances."

"It will be my pleasure," he said. "Until tonight then, Sarah. One more kiss?"

Sarah held up her mouth to him once more. No, she could not do this, her mind was screeching at her. There must be some other way. Somehow, before the day appointed for their wedding, she would think of something else.

The Duke of Cranwell was seated at dinner in Laura Place. They had all finished eating, but it was not a formal meal. The ladies had not left him to his port. They were all drinking tea at the table instead of having adjourned to the drawing room to do so.

"I really would have liked to stay here longer, George," Fanny was saying. "I am just getting used to having so much to do each day and so many different people to meet."

"But it will be lovely to be in the countryside again," Hannah said. She looked anxiously at Cranwell. "And you did say, your grace, that you would send for Argus?"

"Yes, indeed, my dear," he said. "One more dog at Montagu Hall will scarcely make any difference at all."

"But it will to me," she assured him.

"Well, your grace," Lady Cavendish said, "I was fully looking forward to a four-week stay in Bath. It is my yearly habit. But I must admit that it is a most splendid idea to adjourn to Montagu Hall for a formal betrothal party."

"Yes," Fanny agreed, "that idea has my thorough approval, George. Sometimes I wonder why we need to live in such a spacious mansion, since other people rarely see it. You hardly ever entertain even for dinner. But there should be quite a houseful for once if you invite all our relatives and all Hannah's. All the ones within reasonable traveling distance, of course."

"I have been thinking ever since we arrived here that perhaps I should have organized something more formal to mark our betrothal," Cranwell said. "But I am not sorry we came. It has been a good experience for Fanny and Hannah, I believe, to see something of society here. But when I first spoke of this yesterday afternoon, I had decided that the house party would be more the thing."

"Very right and proper," Lady Cavendish said, "and we still have almost a week to enjoy Bath. Shall we stroll along by the river for a while before resting in preparation for this evening?"

It was an hour later before Cranwell was free to walk back to the White Hart. It was tempting to wander around the streets of the city, in the fresh air, but it was so hard to avoid meeting acquaintances here, and really he was in no mood for making polite conversation. He would order a light tea to be sent to his private parlor and spend a couple of hours with a book before getting ready to go to yet another ball at the Upper Rooms. How could people come here year after year and spend several weeks doing the same things day after day? The monotony was beginning to tell on his nerves.

He would be glad to get away next week, though now, of course, there was not the necessity to do so that there had seemed to be yesterday when he had made the suggestion. Sarah would be gone within a few days, if her promise was to be relied upon. After that, he would no longer have to dread going out-of-doors and taking Hannah and Fanny about with him. But he was not sorry that he had spoken up before Sarah had had a chance to talk to him. It was as well for them both to be away from here. There were many memories that were best forgotten as soon as possible.

He was still burning with shame from the night before. What, in heaven's name, had possessed him? If he had had any doubts about her in the past few days; if he had begun to suspect that perhaps she had changed her way of life and was trying to put the past behind her, last night must have completely disabused him. She had quite coolly blackmailed him, extorting from him an enormous sum in return for her removal from Bath. He was a very wealthy man; yet what he had given her would make a noticeable dent in his fortune. And she had taken it without a qualm after having already squandered the not-inconsiderable sum he had given her a mere four years before.

And even apart from the blackmail there had been her manner as she spoke to him. He had never had a whore, but Sarah's manner the night before fit perfectly the way he imagined that such a woman would behave. She had been brightly flirtatious while robbing him of a small fortune. And she had laughed at him when he had tried to plead with her to change her way of life. With the promise of the sum she had asked for already given, she had coolly told him that her life was none of his concern.

He had been disgusted with her, horrified, repelled. And what had he done? He had kissed her! He did not know what madness had possessed him. There she had stood, the woman of loose morals whom he had married and divorced, and all he had seen was Sarah, the beautiful, cultured, vibrant girl he had wanted to spend his life with. And he had kissed her and held her to him. He had wanted to take her into his own body. He had wanted to hold her safe from all the evil that threatened her.

Damn! He had loved her all over again for those few mad minutes.

Cranwell entered the inn and climbed the stairs to his rooms without pausing to speak to anyone. He entered the parlor, threw down his hat and cane, and rang for Peters to send for tea. He sat down in front of the fire that was burning in the hearth and stared into the flames. He did not pick up a book.

It was certainly a good thing that she was leaving. He wished it could be sooner than in a few days' time. This morning there had been all the awkwardness and embarrassment again of trying to avoid her in the Pump Room. Tonight, doubtless, she would be at the rooms, and the two elderly ladies would take for granted that she would join him and the two girls in the ballroom while they took tea. And tomorrow the same thing would happen all over again.

He wondered sometimes if he had any moral fiber at all. Why was it he could be attracted so powerfully to a woman like her? He could perhaps be excused for his early attraction. She was, after all, an excellent actress. He did not believe that even the most worldly-wise cynic would have seen through her mask before he married her. But why had he wanted so desperately to forgive her and return to her after that? And why did he now find his mind absorbed with her when he was here with his new fiancée four months before his wedding? Why had he kissed her?

Perhaps he really was not worthy of Hannah. She was young and very innocent. She deserved better than a man of weak will and low tastes. Yet it was too late to think that way now. He was as good as married to her already. He must just make sure that once Sarah was gone, and once he had left Bath, he put this shameful episode in his life completely behind him. There was a house party to host at Montagu Hall, an activity he would not normally relish. But now he would almost welcome the necessity to be constantly busy and constantly in company.

He would have to purge his mind of Sarah Fifield before he made Hannah his bride. He must be able to offer her a whole and unsullied heart.

What was Sarah going to do? he wondered. He wished there was some way he could have insisted that she use that money wisely. As it was, she had enough to set herself up in some style and entertain any number of people. He shuddered, though, at the thought of the type of visitor she was likely to attract. Once her identity became known, as it surely must sooner or later, there would be only one type of man who would frequent any home of hers. And for only one reason, too.

Cranwell swore into the flames at which he stared. When he thought of other men touching her, making love to his Sarah, he was ready to do dreadful violence. The trouble was, there was nothing and no one on whom to wreak that violence. If he were at home already, he could go out onto his land and find some hard manual work with which to punish himself. As he had done many times in the previous four years.

But her life was her own business, of course. She had been quite right about that the night before. If she chose to spend her youth in promiscuous pleasures, then there was nothing he could do to stop her. He must put her from his mind.

He wondered again fleetingly why she had practiced such deception to trap him into marriage, only to be so openly honest with him afterward that he had divorced her. Had she been so repulsed by him that she could think only of being free of the marriage? Had she not expected him to react so decisively? Had she hoped to live in style for the rest of her life, the Duchess of Cranwell, without the necessity of living with him?

He closed his eyes and shook his head wearily. Sarah Fifield was like some disease raging through his mind and body. He could not shake off the thought of her. He put his head back against the rest of the worn leather chair and kept it there. He kept his eyes shut. He willed sleep to bring him merciful unconsciousness for an hour at least.

13

Sarah SAT on her bed, the contents of a wooden box spread before her. She was sorting through her belongings, deciding what should go with her when she left Bath with Winston and what could more conveniently be left behind. So far she had not accomplished a great deal. Everything she had with her was useful enough or precious enough to be kept. This box contained the most precious of her possessions, though nothing would have brought a large sum at a sale or a pawn shop. Most of it was jewelry that had been her mother's. It was not expensive; Papa had never had money to lavish on ornaments. But it was invaluable to Sarah—the only mementos she had of her mother.

She sighed and piled everything back inside the box again. She should be going to bed. It was not very late, it was true, but mornings began early in Bath. But she did not feel tired. She had too much to think of. In a few days' time she would be starting a new way of life yet again, one of her own free choosing. She was to be Win's wife, the Viscountess Laing.

Sarah shuddered. She would belong to Win, be his possession. She would have to allow him to touch her and lie with her whenever he wished. It would be like it had been during that nightmare summer of her youth, only worse. There would be no end to this. She would lose all rights to her own life and her own body. And she was entering this marriage of her own free will.

She shivered at the memory of Winston's kiss that morning. Every nerve in her body had shrunk from contact with him. And she had been very quickly

reminded of the feeling of nausea that had been a
part of the ordeal of being with him.

She knew that a large number of people would
consider her fortunate indeed to be betrothed to Winston. Lady Murdoch earlier that afternoon had been
ecstatic. She had hugged and kissed Sarah several
times and sung both her praises and Winston's. She
had found the time between her return home from
shopping and her departure for the assembly rooms
endless. She longed to be able to break the news to
Lady Cavendish.

And then during the evening, with a smiling and
charming Win at her side, her arm linked through his,
Sarah had received the congratulations of almost all
the acquaintances she had made in Bath. Lady Cavendish had been delighted. It had been painful for Sarah
to await the reactions of George and Fanny, but she
had held her head high. She wished no one but herself
to know the misery, even horror, she was feeling.
Hannah was the first person after Lady Cavendish to
speak to her. She had even hugged Sarah, her color
heightened.

"I am very pleased for you, Miss Fifield," she had
said. "I am sure you will be very happy. But I could
near die of mortification when I recall how I spoke to
you of Lord Laing in Sydney Gardens. I really had no
idea that he was your beau. Please forgive me. And I
am very sorry that you are planning to leave before we
do. Perhaps it will be a long time before we meet
again."

And she had turned to Win, smiled shyly, and held
out a hand to him. "I do wish you happy, Lord Laing.
I know you are fortunate to have Miss Fifield for a
bride."

Fanny had been flushed and bright-eyed when she
approached the couple. She was with Captain Penny.
Sarah had not really been able to tell from her manner
if she was severely disappointed at Winston's defec-
tion or merely somewhat embarrassed. But she had

given Sarah a hard look as the captain was talking to Winston.

"I wish there had been more time to get to know you, Miss Fifield," she had said. "I must confess you intrigue me."

They were words that still rang in Sarah's mind. She did not know if they should be taken at their face value or if the girl had been somehow insulting her.

George had come to speak to them, though Sarah had not expected him to do so. He had been unsmiling, his face a blank mask. It was impossible to tell what his reaction to their announcement had been. But he had behaved with perfect propriety, shaking hands with Winston and taking her hand in his and carrying it to his lips for the most fleeting of moments. He had wished them well.

Winston had loved every moment of the evening. He had basked in the attention that was directed his way. He had danced with Sarah twice and had watched her throughout with possessive eyes and with almost open desire. He had danced with Hannah and with Fanny and with several other ladies, all of whom had appeared thoroughly flattered by the attention. The consensus seemed to be that Sarah was the most fortunate lady in the company.

Lady Murdoch had been disappointed to know that they planned to leave Bath within a few days and to marry as soon as possible. She had hoped to stay for their full term, enjoying the social pleasures of the city. She openly admitted that she wished to enjoy her new status as adopted mother of the prospective bride. She had hoped they would marry from her home in Devonshire. Winston had answered her protests. He must take Sarah to see his stepmother, he had said. She must be informed of the coming event, which had always been the dearest wish of her heart. The marriage must take place at his home. Lady Murdoch had melted at the love and concern "dear Lord Laing" showed for his stepmother.

It all seemed very unreal. Despite the events of the day, Sarah could not quite believe that in two days' time she would be leaving, probably to go home, and that a few days after that she would be marrying Winston. A week from now the deed would probably be accomplished, she told herself. There would be no going back. Of course, there was no withdrawing now, either. Her promise was given; the matter had been made very public. And, more important, there was her promise to George and her commitment to protect Fanny from an amoral fortune hunter.

Sarah prepared to get into bed. She looked at the sheets and blankets neatly folded back. And she shuddered again. Within a week even the privacy to climb alone into a bed at night would be denied her. She wondered how long Winston would remain faithful to her. He undoubtedly felt a real passion for her. It had lasted for many years; perhaps it would last as many more. But the time would inevitably come when he would turn elsewhere for gratification of his appetites. She must hope that once he knew he could have her whenever he wanted, his desire for her would wane. It was a horrifying realization to know that one was not even married yet but already looking forward eagerly to the time when one's husband would turn his attention to mistresses.

It seemed very likely that when she was married, her true identity as the divorced wife of the Duke of Cranwell would become public. And doubtless there would be a fresh scandal. She would be ostracized, gossiped about. But she was past caring about such matters. The misery and degradation of being married to Winston would outweigh any embarrassment that public censure could bring her.

Sarah snuffed the candles and climbed into the high bed. She pulled the blankets up over her ears and curled up on her side. The silk sheets felt cold to her chilled flesh. She closed her eyes, and the unsmiling, aristocratic, sensitive face of the Duke of Cranwell

was there before her. George. She should not think of
him. She must not think of him.

She could feel his arms around her, his body pressed
to hers, his mouth on hers. So very right. Her husband's embrace. Her body responded again as it had
the evening before in Sydney Gardens. She ached
again, as she had then, for a deeper intimacy, not only
for the touch of his flesh against her own but also for
the sound of his voice speaking words of love, binding
her to him in a bond closer than the merely physical.
There was an ache in her throat, the prelude to tears.
Of course, she would never hear those words, never
feel that touch, never even see him again after two
more days.

He had loved her once. He had said that himself.
Once. Not now. Not ever again. And she had done
everything in her power from their wedding night on
to set the distance between them wider and wider. He
clearly believed what she had set out to convince him
of, that she was beyond redemption. He had begged
her to use his money to set herself up in a respectable
way of life. And she had laughed at him. She had
asked for and received an exorbitant sum of money,
and then she had led him to believe that she would
spend that money to lure more men. She really did not
know how he felt about her impending marriage to
Win.

Her own mind swept back to that marriage. She
suddenly realized the appalling reality of what she was
doing. She hated Win. It would be hard to imagine a
more satanic man—a man who could appear such an
angel in looks and disposition, but one who was capa-
ble of achieving anything he wanted by the most ruth-
less methods. He had won her submission in the cruelest
manner possible, using a handicapped child as a weapon.

And she still was not free of him. In fact, she was
more surely in his clutches now than she had ever
been. She was to be his wife. His wife! Sarah bur-
rowed further under the bedclothes as if by doing so

she might block the realization from her mind. And how had it come about? Had she been wholly free to make her decision? Or had he somehow maneuvered matters? He had an uncanny ability to know her weaknesses. How could he have known so surely that Fanny Montagu's future was important to her? How could he have known that she would run away with him rather than see him marry Fanny? She had not known it herself. Was it perhaps that she was willing, even eager, to do something dramatic to atone for the suffering she had caused George? Even though no one but her would ever know? Strange! Win must have known too that she would not go to George telling tales. He must know her better than she knew herself.

And it was no longer the much-loved body of George that she could feel against hers, but Winston's, tall and strong, crushing the life out of her. She could feel his wet mouth open over hers. She shuddered and pulled the blankets over her head.

The Duke of Cranwell and Joshua Stonewall were standing together in the Pump Room the following morning, having withdrawn a little from the cluster of ladies gathered around the seated figure of Lady Murdoch.

"You really are the life-saver, Cran," Joshua was assuring his friend. "Bath would be dashed boring if I had to stay here much longer. Each year there seem to be fewer people of any interest. And I have always had a hankering to see Montagu Hall. It is reputed to be one of the more impressive homes in the south."

"It is to be mainly a family affair," Cranwell said, "but I decided to ask you to come too, Josh. It has been good to discover you again. We should not have let our friendship lapse."

"If you were not such an infernal hermit, we would not have done so," Joshua said. "What do you think of this betrothal, Cran?"

"Miss Fifield's?" Cranwell asked. "Why? What is there to think? They make a handsome couple."

"I find it deuced depressing," Joshua said, singling that lady out of the group with his eyes and regarding her gloomily. "I was just working m'self up to begin a major campaign on m' own behalf. Delectable lady, Cran."

"Beautiful, yes," Cranwell agreed.

"Ah, that hair!" his friend sighed. "But more than that, Cran. There is something about her. Character. She is no piece of tinsel."

Cranwell did not answer but absently watched as Winston Bowen, who had joined the ladies a few minutes before, began to stroll around the room, Fanny on one arm and Hannah on the other.

"I think I shall persuade the lady to walk with me," Joshua said. "It may be my last chance. Excuse me, Cran."

Cranwell watched as Joshua talked with the older ladies for a minute or two and then bowed to Sarah and began to walk with her. Character! If Josh only knew. The man was dazzled merely by her beauty and made the assumption that there must be character behind it. And she was beautiful. The pale cream of her gown this morning and the brown-trimmed straw bonnet threw her hair into vivid relief. Yes, she was surely the loveliest woman he had ever known.

He was still in shock from the evening before. She was to marry Bowen. The fact hammered at his consciousness as it had since Lady Murdoch had loudly made the announcement of their betrothal in the tea-room of the assembly rooms. They were to leave together within the next day or two and marry almost immediately. Had that been in her plans all along? he wondered. Was that why she had wanted the money? Was it important to her that she bring some sort of dowry to the marriage? He did not see why. Viscount Laing was prosperous enough, as far as he knew.

Or had she been taken by surprise? Had Bowen asked her to marry him after she had made her decision to leave? Perhaps he had proposed only because he knew she was leaving and wished to offer her his protection. He had already made it plain to Cranwell that he felt a deep affection for his cousin. It seemed quite likely that he was marrying her to protect her from herself. It certainly seemed to have been a sudden decision. Bowen had appeared to be interested in Fanny.

Cranwell watched him again from across the room, his head bent to one side, listening to something Fanny was saying. He had to admire the man, but it seemed to be just too much of a sacrifice to give up one's own freedom for the rest of one's life merely for the sake of saving someone else. What was most admirable, perhaps, was the fact that one would not know from looking at Bowen that he was sacrificing his own happiness. He had the gift of cheerfulness as well as charm.

Of course, perhaps he really had a fondness for Sarah strong enough to compensate somewhat for the sacrifice. But could it compensate entirely for the knowledge he would always have of the type of wife he had married? He would never be able to trust her. Cranwell wondered what her aunt would think of the match.

And what did he himself think of the marriage? How did he feel about Winston Bowen marrying Sarah, living with her, making love to her? How did it feel to know that someone else would possess his wife? But of course, an unknown number of equally unknown men had already done so.

"Your grace?"

Cranwell came to himself with a start and realized that it was the second time Lady Cavendish had called him. He walked over to where she was standing straight-backed beside the seated figure of her friend.

"I have been telling Adelaide about what we talked of this morning," she said, "and she has accepted. As I pointed out to you earlier, your grace, she will be alone again once Miss Fifield leaves for the viscount's home. And what is there to enjoy in Bath when one is alone? And why go home alone when one has a chance to join a house party?"

Cranwell bowed in the direction of Lady Murdoch. "I am delighted, ma'am," he said, "that you have agreed to visit Montagu Hall. I know that Lady Cavendish will be very happy to have your company, as will my sister and I."

"It is a place I have always wished to see," Lady Murdoch declared loudly, "especially since the Withersmiths visited last year and came home so full of its praises. But of course, your grace, it will be so much more impressive to visit as your guest. I am quite overwhelmed and quite speechless. My only disappointment is that this comes at a time when dear Sarah is leaving me for a while. I would have loved nothing more than to bring her to visit you too, for she has had very little pleasure in her life. Living in a drab little cottage she was when I found her, with no one for company except a single servant. However, of course, now she has a wonderful future ahead with Lord Laing. Such a handsome couple! But I wish this house party might have come first, Bertha."

"Nothing is written in stone, you know," Lady Cavendish said sagely. "Perhaps for such an occasion, Adelaide, both Miss Fifield and Lord Laing would postpone their nuptials and join the party. I am sure his grace would be only too delighted to have them as guests." She looked inquiringly at a dismayed Cranwell.

He bowed. "I certainly regret that Miss Fifield will not be with you, ma'am," he said to Lady Murdoch. "But I understand that Lord Laing is anxious to take her home to visit his stepmother as soon as possible. It would be selfish of me to try to persuade him to change his mind."

Lady Murdoch was sitting forward in her chair, a look of eager excitement on her face. "But it may be possible for them to do both," she said. "I have already thought that instead of sending a maid with Sarah during the journey, perhaps I should go myself. A maid is hardly chaperone enough. And besides, I think it only fitting that I meet the aunt with whom my Sarah spent much of her youth. Now, if I go with them, then we could all come along to Montagu Hall next week."

Cranwell stood speechless, his hands clasped behind his back. He had that feeling of being out of control again. There must be all sorts of decisive things he could say at this moment that would squash forever the plan that was being formed by the two elderly ladies. There must be. But he could not think of one of them. He could almost have panicked had he not remembered that neither Sarah nor Bowen was likely to give the suggestion even a moment's consideration.

"Here is Lord Laing quite close now with the your dear girls," Lady Murdoch was saying. "Yoo-hoo! Lord Laing!"

Winston smiled and bowed to the lady on each side of him. "Thank you for the pleasure," he said to them. "I must have been the envy of every gentleman in the room." He turned and smiled at Lady Murdoch. "I may be of service to you, ma'am?"

"The most wonderful thing, Lord Laing," she said. "His grace has most generously invited you and dear Sarah to Montagu Hall next week to help his family and Lady Hannah's celebrate their betrothal. I have been invited too. Now, I know what your objection will be, for you young people are ever impatient to put your plans into effect. You are impatient to take Sarah to your dear stepmother, and that is as it should be. But you can do that and still go to Montagu Hall next week. It will mean putting off your own nuptials for perhaps another week, but it will give us all a splendid opportunity to celebrate your betrothal too. And you would certainly be doing me a favor, for I feel I must accompany you to your home as a chaperone for dear Sarah, you see, and I shall need company in my journey to his grace's home."

Winston continued to smile throughout this long speech. He looked across at Cranwell and bowed. "This is most generous of you, your grace," he said.

"And it is very difficult to disappoint other people's plans, even though my own impatience to make Miss Fifield my wife is a strong inducement."

"Oh," Hannah cried, her face aglow, "what a marvelous idea. Lord Laing, will you come? And persuade Miss Fifield to come too? I should love it of all things."

Fanny darted a look at her brother, and a look of sheer devilment came into her eyes. "George wishes it. Hannah wishes it. And clearly Lady Murdoch and Lady Cavendish wish it. Lord Laing, you must come. I shall help you persuade Miss Fifield."

Winston laughed and looked around at the group, his eyes dancing. "It seems I have little choice," he said. "I do not know quite how I am to break the news to my betrothed that the date of our wedding may have to be postponed for a few days, but I am sure that the occasion merits such a delay. I shall see what I can do with Sarah."

Lady Murdoch chuckled. "You are the person to persuade her, Lord Laing," she said. "What female could resist your persuasions, especially when she became betrothed to you less than a day ago?"

He bowed and turned, as they all did, to watch Sarah and Joshua Stonewall slowly strolling toward them along the length of the long windows that lined one side of the room. They were deep in conversation, apparently unaware of the attention focused on them.

Sarah looked up as she and Mr. Stonewall approached again the place where she had left Lady Murdoch. She had been very aware earlier of George standing a little apart from the group. She wondered if he was still there. To her embarrassment, her eyes met his immediately, but before she could look hastily away, she became aware that the whole group appeared to be watching her.

"I had no idea that life in the capital could be so full of intrigue," she said in response to what Mr. Stonewall had been saying. "It looks, sir, as if everyone is waiting for us. It must be time for breakfast."

"'Pon my word, ma'am," Joshua said, "if it is, your company has certainly made time fly past."

"Sarah dear," Lady Murdoch called shrilly without waiting for the pair to reach her, "Lord Laing has something to say to you. And you must consider carefully, dear. Do not say no without even giving the matter thought, though I know your first reaction will be to say no. But think what it will mean to his grace and Lady Hannah. And think what pleasure you will be giving me, dear. Surely putting off your wedding for a few days will be a small price to pay for such a favor. Not that it will be all a favor to others. I am sure you will enjoy yourself immensely once you have had a chance to think about the matter."

Sarah stared blankly at her Cousin Adelaide and then looked inquiringly at Winston. He smiled and reached for her hand.

"His grace has arranged a house party at Montagu Hall for next week," he said. "To celebrate his betrothal. It is to be mainly a family affair, but he has been gracious enough to invite you and Lady Murdoch, and me in my new role as your betrothed. I have provisionally accepted, my love."

Sarah felt that she must have stepped into some dream. "You have what?" she asked blankly.

"Lady Murdoch had already accepted the invitation," Winston said gently, smiling into her eyes. "And she had also kindly agreed to accompany us to my home in two days' time. It would seem only fair, Sarah, to go with her to Montagu Hall next week. The holiday will give us a chance to celebrate our own betrothal amongst our new friends. And our wedding need be delayed by only a week. We have a lifetime ahead of us; surely a few days will not be the end of the world."

Sarah glanced hastily at Cranwell. He was looking steadily and coldly back at her.

"It will be impossible, Win," she said, "much as I

appreciate the kindness of the invitation. There will be much to do in preparation for our wedding, and I am sure Aunt Myrtle will wish to help me with my trousseau. We really will have to say no."

"We all have our hearts set on your being there," Fanny said. "I have been looking forward to showing you Montagu Hall, Miss Fifield. I know you will love it. Do please say yes."

Fanny's eyes, Sarah saw, when she glanced at her in dismay, were twinkling with merriment. That girl definitely had the devil in her.

"I think I can understand how you feel, Miss Fifield," Hannah said more quietly. "It is hard to change plans once your heart is set on something. But I too wish you would reconsider. Both you and Lord Laing would add something to our party. I would like you to meet Argus. His grace has sent for him. He will come, I expect, with Mama and Papa."

Winston squeezed Sarah's hand, which he had linked through his arm, and grinned down at her. "It seems we have no choice, my love," he said. "How can we be selfish enough to disappoint so many people?"

Sarah opened her mouth to protest, then shut it again. What was there to be said? Any more denials under the present circumstances would be offensive. She darted another look at Cranwell. His position and expression had not changed. But his face was almost as pale as his shirt. He said nothing.

Sarah smiled warmly around at the group. "I firmly believe that there is some conspiracy afoot here," she said. "I do thank you most warmly, your grace, for your invitation. But it is so sudden. Perhaps Win and I can talk it over together today and give you our answer later?" She beamed at Cranwell.

He bowed stiffly. "Certainly. I understand, ma'am," he said.

Fanny clapped her hands. "I know that our case has been won," she said. "When people say that they will see, they invariably mean yes. Lord Laing, you just wait until you see the forests and hills that we ride in.

One may ride all day and never cross the same trail twice or leave George's land."

"I shall look forward to having such a charming guide," Winston said.

"I say, Cran," Joshua said, "you are making this house-party business sound more and more interesting by the minute."

Lady Cavendish announced at that moment that it was breakfasttime and that, speaking for herself, she was ravenously hungry. The members of the group began to go their separate ways, having agreed to meet again in the evening at the Lower Rooms to take tea.

Winston went back to Brock Street to breakfast with the ladies and to accompany them on a shopping trip afterward. Lady Murdoch was not in the mood for walking a great distance. When they entered a book-seller's shop, she was quite content to sit with some newspapers and to keep her eyes open for acquaintances with whom to exchange gossip. There were still several people who had not been at the rooms the previous evening to be told of the betrothal.

Sarah made an excuse to take Winston away from the shop, having promised to be back to accompany Lady Murdoch home in one hour's time. She took his arm determinedly as soon as they were out of the shop.

"Now, Sarah," he said pleasantly, "where is it you wish to go? To a milliner's? to a haberdasher's?"

"I want to walk," she said, "as far away from crowds as we can, Win. We have something to discuss."

"You are not referring to this Montagu Hall business, are you?" he asked in some surprise. "I thought that was all settled."

"It is by no means settled," she said. "You know that our going there is absolutely out of the question, Win."

"Why is that?" he asked. "Are you so anxious for our wedding, love? We need delay for only a few days, you know. In fact, I am sure that once we get home and to Montagu Hall, we can quite easily arrange to anticipate the wedding somewhat. Will that please you? I am every bit as impatient as you on that matter, you know."

"That is not what I am talking about," she said crossly, "and you know it, Win. I cannot go to George's home. Can you not see how out of the question it is? His home, Win! I am his divorced wife."

He grinned. "I can imagine it might be a little sickening to see what you have missed," he said. "I have heard that the Hall is quite magnificent. But don't let it worry you, Sarah. Remember that Cranwell came with the house. Would the house have been worth the sacrifice?"

"You do not get the point at all, do you?" Sarah said, looking up at him incredulously. "Do you not see what a terribly embarrassing predicament we would be putting his grace in? Not to mention me."

"Yet he is the one who issued the invitation," Winston said.

"Oh, bosh!" she replied. "He had as much freedom of choice this morning as I had. Of course he does not wish us to go. Nothing could be farther from his mind."

"Well, I say we go," he said.

"Win," she said, "it is impossible. The matter is not even open for discussion. Do you realize how I got that money? Do you think his grace made me a gift of it out of the kindness of his heart? I made an agreement with him. The money in exchange for my disappearance from his life."

Winston stopped walking and faced her on the pavement. He was grinning broadly. His eyes were positively dancing with merriment. "No!" he said. "I always knew the man was insufferably high in the instep, Sarah, but I did not dream he could be such a dry old stick. Does he find it so hard to face the memory of the big mistake he made? He really is not too intelligent, though, is he? Why would he part with the money when you are still here? What is to say that you will keep the bargain?"

"My word," she said, glaring at him.

He laughed again, took her arm, and resumed their walk through some of the quieter residential streets of the city. "Sarah, Sarah," he said, "sometimes you talk as if you were still a schoolgirl. Such high ideals, my love. We will torment him, that is what we will do. We will go to his house party and you must flirt with him and with that Stonewall fellow who fancies you, and I shall flirt with that sprightly sister of his and the little mouse of a fiancée. We will drive him mad."

"We will do nothing of the kind, Win," Sarah said, fury bringing a deep flush to her cheeks. "We will do as we planned yesterday, or I shall take the money and return it to his grace. I shall tell the whole truth to Lady Murdoch, and she will take me back to Devonshire. Then I shall be able to keep my promise."

"What money?" Winston asked innocently.

"The bank draft," she said.

"Your signature was on it, love," Winston said, bending his head close to hers so that the brim of his hat touched the poke of her bonnet.

Sarah stopped and jerked her arm away from his. "What have you done?" she asked, horror in her eyes. "Have you cashed the draft already?"

"But I thought that was the idea," he said, smiling more gently, almost apologetically at her. "Did you not intend that I pay my debts here, Sarah? They are paid. The rest of the money is safe. Do not worry."

"Give it back to me, Win," Sarah said, but she felt a sinking feeling inside. "I shall return what is left."

"Come, Sarah," he said. His smile was now warm and tender. "I am to be your husband very soon. You will be completely under my protection. I shall manage our money. You need not worry. I shall always look after you."

She stared at him numbly. "It seems that the Duke of Cranwell and I are a pair of fools," she said.

He raised his eyebrows. "Are you afraid that I will

cheat you, Sarah?" he asked. "Why will you always believe the worst of me? I have always remained loyal to you, have I not? Even through the years when you refused to have anything to do with me."

"You have always been at the root of my troubles, Win," Sarah said bitterly. "If it were not for you my marriage would have worked. If it were not for you, I could have kept my independence. But as soon as Uncle Randolph died, you took the money I had entrusted to his care and used it to pay your gambling debts. You swore you would repay it, but I knew the truth of the matter. You took all I had. And now I have a chance again to do something at least half-decent and leave alone a man I have wronged. And yet again you have stolen the money."

"Harsh words, Sarah," he said. "Are we not getting somewhat carried away here? All we are talking about is postponing our wedding for a week while we attend this house party to please other people. I am not crying off, you know. And this business of flirting was not a serious suggestion. Sometimes I like to joke. You should have some sense of humor, Sarah."

"I will not go," Sarah said. "I will stay with Aunt Myrtle next week."

"Then I must go alone," Winston said, the old grin back on his face. "I find the prospect of those rides with Fanny quite irresistible. Quiet hills and woods, Sarah."

Her hand tightened on his arm. Fury had clenched her jaw by the time she turned to him. "That is blackmail, Win," she said through her teeth. "Blackmail pure and simple. Do you think I would let you go alone to torment that poor innocent young girl?"

His eyes widened and he grinned deliberately down at her mouth. "No," he said, "I did not think for a moment that you would allow it, Sarah. You will have to come to protect what is your own, will you not?"

She nodded, still almost rigid with fury. "Oh yes," she said, "I will come, Win. You always get your way, do you not?"

Winston glanced hastily around to make sure that the street was deserted. Then he bent and kissed her indignant lips.

"I like having my way with you, Sarah," he said. "And do not try to pretend that you do not like it too. On second thought, though, keep on pretending, love. You are quite irresistibly adorable when you are angry."

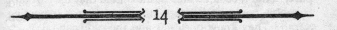

14

THE DUKE of Cranwell was riding down from the rolling hills to the east of his home. It was a shortcut he frequently took when coming from his bailiff's cottage. It was also his favorite approach to Montagu Hall. He could see it mapped clearly below him, the square classical building constructed around a central courtyard, the lawns to the east dotted with ancient oak and beech trees and sloping to the narrow meandering river, which never seemed quite important enough for the imposing Palladian bridge that spanned it.

To the north of the house were the formal gardens—a stone pond with a fountain surrounded by carefully planned flower gardens, box hedges, and gravel walks. Beyond them was the great stone archway with its wrought-iron gates, which formed the main entrance to the house. He could never look upon the scene without feeling a rush of wonder and a humble pride that it was all his, including the land for as far as the eye could see in every direction. How could anyone own such treasures and still feel the necessity of looking for pleasure elsewhere?

He urged his horse forward again. He really should not delay. At any time now guests were going to be arriving through that archway. The Earl and Countess of Cavendish, Hannah's parents, had arrived the day before, so that he already felt as if he had a houseful. Lady Cavendish and Hannah, of course, had come from Bath with him two days before. But there were still two sets of uncles and aunts and numerous cousins from Hannah's family to arrive today, as well as his

own Uncle Justin with his family. He had not invited
the Saxtons and still felt guilty at the omission. They
would feel slighted if they ever learned of the house
party. And it seemed almost inevitable that they would.
But how could he invite them when he was expecting
Sarah? They knew both her and the old scandal.

And that reminded him of what he had been trying
to keep in the back of his mind for a whole week.
Josh, Winston Bowen, and Captain Penny, those other
friends from Bath, he could quite look forward to
seeing again. But Sarah! He felt impotently furious
just to think what a dupe she had made of him. He
was the foolish one, of course, to think that he could
trust a woman who experience had taught him was
untrustworthy. He should never have handed her the
money just like that, with only her word to guarantee
that she would keep her part of the bargain. He should
have insisted on sending the bank draft to some distant destination, giving her only enough money with
which to travel to that place and feed herself along the
way.

What a fool she was making of him. Not only had
she failed to take herself out of his life, but she had
even contrived to be a guest at a very private house
party in Montagu Hall. And she would probably arrive
decked out in finery purchased with his money.

Cranwell turned his horse in the direction of the
stables to the west of the house. Perhaps he was not
being strictly fair. He had been present when the
invitation to his home was first mentioned to her. And
she had not wanted to accept. She had seemed to be
as intent on finding some excuse as he had been. He
had been completely overwhelmed by the two older
ladies and even by Hannah and Fanny. Could he entirely blame Sarah for doing no better?

Then, too, she had had the added inducement of
Bowen's obvious eagerness to accept. How could she
go against the will of the man who had become her
fiancé only the day before? Cranwell frowned. When
he thought about it, he could blame Bowen for the

way things had turned out every bit as much as he blamed Fanny. Both knew of the former connection between him and Sarah. Both should have realized just what an embarrassment it would be for them to be thrown thus together.

But really, he thought, swinging himself from the saddle in the cobbled courtyard of the stables and proceeding to remove the saddle himself, Sarah should have thought of some excuse. When she had been alone with Bowen, she should have explained quite clearly to him why she did not wish to accept the invitation. After all, it was not as if he did not know the situation. And he seemed to be fond enough of her. Surely he would have given in to her wishes without argument if she had just made it clear to him that it would be painful to her to go to Montagu Hall. Obviously she had made no such plea. Once she had had time to think about the matter, she had decided that she wished to go after all.

But why? Did she enjoy taunting him? Did she perhaps remember his behavior in Sydney Gardens and hope to arouse his desire again to such a degree that he would make a fool of himself afresh? Did she hope to bribe more money from him in return for a promise to go away early? Did she feel a curiosity to see the home that had very nearly been hers? He could not fathom the reason. And he did not know why he tried. He had realized many times that he would never understand the devious mind that occupied the very lovely head of Sarah Fifield.

Cranwell turned his horse over to a groom who had appeared from the stable block on hearing his master's entry. He strode toward the house. He must bathe and change his clothes as quickly as possible so that he would be ready for the earliest arrivals. It would be strange to have Montagu Hall occupied by a large number of people.

Sarah was beginning to feel very nervous. They were in the beautiful green countryside of Wiltshire already. Lady Murdoch had declared several times that they must be almost at Montagu Hall. Around each bend in the road she expected to see it. And at each bend, when the house did not come into sight, she felt a great churning relief. How would she ever be able to face George? She felt an embarrassment and a humiliation that made her feel physically sick.

Ever since they had left Bath she had hoped that by some miracle the plan would change and she would not be forced to attend this house party. She had hoped that once at home, Win would not want to leave again so soon.

And when they had reached home, her hopes had soared. She had been afraid that her aunt would be horrified by the betrothal. But she was not. She seemed actively delighted. She had warmly welcomed Lady Murdoch, who had been clearly gratified by her reception.

And Sarah had renewed her efforts to show affection to Winston. She had smiled warmly at him whenever their eyes met, and she had always chosen a chair close to his when she entered a room after him. On one occasion, when they were strolling outside, slightly behind Aunt Myrtle and Lady Murdoch, she had sighed and told him how she wished that nothing stood between them and an early wedding. But all she had got for her pains that time was a quick caress across her breasts and a promise that he would come to her that night when it was safe. She had had to assure him again that she wished to keep such intimacies for their wedding night.

All her hopes had failed. Aunt Myrtle, in fact, had seemed to be her worst enemy. She had assured Sarah that preparing a trousseau and a small celebration for their intimate friends on the wedding day would take a great deal of time. She would find it all easier to do if she was alone. The party to Montagu Hall would, therefore, suit her perfectly. She had been somewhat dubious, it was true, when she first heard that the invitation came from the Duke of Cranwell. But Sarah, not wishing her aunt to suspect her distress, had assured her that there was no cause for embarrassment. Each was now betrothed to someone else.

And Lady Murdoch, of course, was not to be distracted from the promised delight. She was very impressed to be on friendly terms with a duke. And to be invited to spend a week in his home was the pinnacle of ambition for her, especially when that invitation included her adopted daughter. Then, of course, there was Lady Cavendish. She kept remembering items of news from the previous five years that she had completely forgotten about when the two were in Bath.

Here she was then, Sarah thought in despair, on her way to Montagu Hall, about to arrive there, in fact. Lady Murdoch sat across from her and had talked almost without pause throughout the long day's journey. Winston sat beside her, his shoulder and arm and one thigh pressed rather unnecessarily against hers. The seats of the coach were narrow, but not as narrow as he pretended. She made no move to pull away from him. There was no point. Soon now she would be married to him. She must accustom herself to his touch. She could not go through a lifetime cringing away from her husband.

Yet again as the coach swung around a sharp bend in the road, Sarah looked anxiously out of the window to see if the house were close. And this time her stomach lurched even more painfully. Only a little ahead of them was a massive stone archway with open gates leading onto a graveled driveway. She could not see beyond the wall, but surely this must be it. Only some grand mansion could be hidden behind such magnificence, she was sure.

"We are here! Sarah, dear, we are here," Lady Murdoch cried, the poke of her bonnet pressed against the window of the coach. "Just look at that statue on horseback at the top of the arch. Now, I wonder whoever could have lifted it up there."

The coach slowly negotiated the sharp turn through

the archway and into the courtyard. The ornamental gardens stretched before them and, beyond them, the house.

"Well," Winston said with a whistle, "I always knew Cranwell was rich. But if this is what he owns, he must be wealthy indeed."

"Just look at that structure over there," Lady Murdoch said, pointing to the left. "It looks like a temple. A bridge, is it?"

The coach had followed the graveled pathway around the gardens to the forecourt before the impressive Gothic doorway that formed the north entrance to the house. Liveried footmen waited there, one coming forward immediately to put down the steps and help the travelers down. Lady Murdoch made a great bustle and to-do about descending. Sarah closed her eyes briefly as Winston vaulted out ahead of her, and took a deep breath. She could never remember feeling quite so embarrassed in her life.

Winston helped her to the ground, but she was almost instantly aware that Cranwell had come from the house and was bowing over Lady Murdoch's hand.

". . . wonderful, wonderful house," she was saying. "I do not wonder the Withersmiths spoke of little else when they returned from their travels. It is so kind of you to invite us here, your grace."

"It is my pleasure, I assure you, ma'am," he replied, and turned to Sarah and Winston.

"Did you have a good journey?" he asked, shaking Winston's hand. "You must be very tired after such a distance. Do come inside. There is tea in the drawing room—or something stronger if you prefer."

He looked at last at Sarah. "Miss Fifield," he said. "You will wish to freshen up before taking tea. Come. I shall have you shown to your room."

He was unsmiling, she saw when she dared look into his face, but he was looking steadily at her and directing her to the doorway as he held his arm for Lady Murdoch's support. Her heart turned over. After a week away from him, she was newly aware of the aristocratic elegance of the man, of his attractiveness, which was very different from the obvious sexuality of Win. And now she saw him for the first time in his own proper milieu. She had seen only the outside of one part of the house, but already she knew that the property suited him to perfection. This was where he belonged. And this was where, under different circumstances, she might have belonged too.

A pointless thought, she told herself as she took Winston's arm and smiled up at him. He grinned back and raised his eyebrows in the direction of George's back. He appeared to be finding this formal welcome amusing.

Cranwell was up early the following morning and out riding before breakfast. He was eager to look at his crops, as he did every morning. They were almost ready for harvesting now. Another few days would bring the grain to full fruition. It would irk him to know that his laborers would have to begin the task without him this year. Most of his time would be taken up with the entertainment of his guests for the following week.

Benjamin Fairlie, one of Hannah's cousins, rode with him. He was not the only guest who had expressed a determination to ride with Cranwell that morning. His cousin Samuel and Josh had also been determined to get up early. But that resolve had been made the evening before. This morning the house had seemed deserted except for the servants and Benjamin, who assured him that he always rose early except when incarcerated at Cambridge.

"Why get up early, or get up at all," he had asked Cranwell, "when one knows that there is nothing to do all day but attend lectures and study books?"

Hannah's cousin was a talkative young man, but Cranwell found after a half-hour of diligent listening that it was sufficient to pay only half of one's attention to the conversation in order to make the correct responses in the right places. With the other half of his mind he could enjoy the late-summer sunshine with its suggestion of an autumn nip in the air, and assess the state of his crops.

And think. The day before had really not been as bad as he had anticipated. Only Josh had arrived later than Sarah. The house was bustling with noise and activity by the time she came, with the result that there had been no awkward intimacy. Apart from the formal greeting that he had felt obliged to extend on her arrival, he had been forced to exchange hardly a word with her for the rest of the day. And he had made sure that she was seated far from him at the dinner table.

On one point he felt relief. No one had seemed to notice any significance about her name or the fact that she was betrothed to a cousin by the name of Bowen. He had been afraid that his own uncle or aunt might make the connection, or even one of their four children, though the oldest was only twenty years old. But all six had politely acknowledged the introductions without a flicker of suspicion. And the same thing had happened with Hannah's relatives. It seemed little short of a miracle to Cranwell.

On another matter he felt less pleased. Both Fanny and Hannah had been openly pleased at Sarah's arrival and had greeted her like a long-lost friend. Hannah, in fact, had hung about her all evening in the drawing room, drinking tea when Sarah did, crossing to the pianoforte when Sarah did, and bending over a pile of music with her to pick out something suitable to play. And even when Sarah had refused to play herself and Hannah had complied, the latter had asked her new friend to stay and turn the pages for her. The situation had been very awkward for him. Under the circumstances, he had wished to be close to his betrothed for much of the evening. But how could he be so when being close to her meant also being close to Sarah?

He had been right on one point. She had worn a particularly handsome gown during the evening, clearly a new purchase. Its jonquil color had looked startlingly vivid with her bright hair. The jaconet fabric had seemed very expensive. And she had certainly attracted attention. Josh had almost fallen over himself to lead her in to dinner and sit next to her. He had reached her side only a moment before Allan Wright, another of Hannah's cousins, had arrived on the same errand. Wright had led in Barbara Tenby, Cranwell's own cousin, but he had been careful to seat himself to Sarah's left, with Barbara on his other side. Benjamin had been making sheep's eyes at her too during the evening, even though he was considerably younger than she.

Bowen had behaved with perfect propriety, Cranwell had noticed with satisfaction. He had not hung around his fiancée's skirts all evening, but had conversed with the utmost charm with all the aunts and with Lady Cavendish and Lady Murdoch, all of whom seemed to dote on him. And when he had finally joined Sarah and Hannah at the pianoforte and Sarah had wandered away, he had stayed with the greatest good humor to turn pages for Hannah and even to join her in the singing of a duet. A very well-bred young man, Cranwell concluded. It was a pity that his early attentions to Fanny had been mere gallantry.

"And sheep are very wasteful of land," Benjamin was saying at his side. "I keep telling Papa that if he would just sell the flock and enclose the land, he could more than double the amount of corn he plants. Our land would be far more profitable, and moreover, we would have work for far more laborers, and the drain of manpower to the factories would be eased. But it is very difficult to fight against tradition, you know. Papa is very much a traditionalist."

"Quite," Cranwell said. "And there is something to be said for custom, you know. Change that comes too fast often proves to have been unwise."

His thoughts returned home. He had promised to take his guests on a tour of the house later in the morning. It was years since he had personally shown off its treasures to anyone. His housekeeper had instructions to show the state apartments and the cloisters to the occasional summer traveler who came to ask for a tour, but on such occasions he deliberately kept well out of the way. The visitors were told merely that he was from home. On rare occasions he came face-to-face with these visitors, but he always escaped after an exchange of bows and the barest civilities.

He was not looking forward to the morning. In his experience, people were interested in the general splendor of his mansion but quickly lost that interest as soon as one tried to explain details to them. His treasures were too precious to him to be treated as mere spectacles. However, Lady Murdoch had been very loud in her entreaties that he give the tour, and Hannah's two aunts and one uncle had been almost equally eager. He hoped that everyone would not want to come. He hoped that Sarah would stay away.

For her part, Sarah had been carefully planning her day since she had got up early enough to see George and young Mr. Fairlie ride off to the west. They had said the night before that they were going to inspect the fields. A few of the other gentlemen had planned to join the ride, but there were unmistakably only two riders this morning.

She was safe for at least an hour or two, she estimated. And she sat down at the dressing table to brush the tangles from her long hair before washing with the warm water in the water jug, which a maid must have brought quite recently. She would go down as soon as possible and have breakfast early, she decided. Then she would try to slip outside before anyone else was about, or at least before George returned from his ride. She would find somewhere secluded to walk, perhaps up in the hills she had seen to the east of the house the previous day. And she would stay out until she judged it time for luncheon. The glorious weather would make her absence seem quite natural. And she would miss the guided tour of the house that George had promised the evening before.

Sarah got up and began a hasty toilet without ringing for the maid who she had been assured was assigned to care for her. Her hair she twisted into a simple knot high on the back of her head. She pulled on a plain blue calico dress and laid a gray wool cloak and straw bonnet on her bed ready to be put on as soon as she had finished breakfast.

She could not resist one last look around her room before leaving it. She was as enchanted now as she had been the afternoon before, when the late sun had been slanting bright rays through the window and across the bed. If she did not know better, she would have felt that it must have been handpicked for her. The Chinese wallpaper was covered with brightly painted birds and flowers so that she felt as if she were in a garden. The bed was surmounted by a dome from which hung green-and-silver silk hangings looped against the four bedposts. The carpet too was green. She had fallen in love with the room as soon as she saw it the previous day.

When she descended to the breakfast room, Sarah found that she was indeed the first to arrive, although the sideboard was already covered with an appetizing array of hot foods. Unfortunately for her, though, she did not long remain alone. Both Captain Penny and Winston joined her there before she had eaten more than a few mouthfuls.

Captain Penny bowed and wished her a cheerful good morning.

"Good morning, my love," Winston greeted her, taking her hand and lifting it to his lips. "How do you always contrive to look so fresh and lovely even early in the day?"

Sarah did not try to answer so unanswerable a question. "Good morning, Win, Captain Penny," she said. "I was beginning to fear that I would have to eat breakfast in lone state."

"Why so early, Sarah?" Winston asked. "I thought

you would have stayed abed until midmorning, at least, like the other ladies."

"I am planning to take a walk," she said cheerfully. "This weather is too lovely to be missed."

Winston raised his eyebrows and smiled. "You are not going to miss the tour of the house, are you?" he asked. "I thought you were keen on all this old stuff, Sarah."

She shook her head. "Perhaps another time," she said.

"In that case," Winston said, seating himself beside her and putting his heaped plate down on the table, "I shall walk too, love. There seem to be endless miles to explore around here. Perhaps we should eat as quickly as possible and leave before anyone else gets up. We may be hopelessly delayed if someone else decides to join us." His thigh, as if by accident, made contact with Sarah's beneath the table.

"I hear that this house is particularly splendid," Captain Penny said. "The present duke has spent years, I have heard, acquiring new treasures and renewing and reorganizing what was already here. And it is quite a privilege to be given a guided tour. Apparently those visitors who dare to knock at the door are shown certain designated apartments by the housekeeper. But his grace is the man who knows everything there is to know about the building and its contents. I should hate to see you miss such a treat, Miss Fifield."

"Miss it!" The words were spoken by Joshua Stonewall, who had just entered the breakfast room. "Who is going to be such a philistine as to miss the show? Miss Fifield? Quite out of the question. Can't allow it. Laing, order your betrothed to join the viewing party. Whatever else she had planned for this morning can wait." He grinned and crossed the room to the sideboard.

"How can I fight such opposition?" Sarah said lightly. "It seems that I am to be subjected to this guided tour after all."

"Take my advice, Laing," Joshua said, beginning

systematically to heap his plate with a sample of everything before him. "When you want females to do a certain thing, be firm about it. They invariably fall into line." He chuckled at his own humor.

Sarah ate on, her appetite suddenly lost. For a few moments she had felt utterly caught between the devil and the deep blue sea. If she stayed, she would have to follow George around, listening to his voice, viewing the house that might have been hers. If she went walking, she would have to fend off the advances of Winston, and in the secluded setting of Montagu Hall and its grounds, she would almost certainly lose. She had been forced to choose the lesser of two evils. But an evil it was nonetheless. Lord and Lady Wright and Lady Murdoch entered the breakfast room together at that moment and the conversation became lively and general.

"You have been put in the Chinese bedroom, have you not?" Hannah asked Sarah half an hour later, when the latter was still in the breakfast room, drinking a second cup of coffee. Winston had left with Captain Penny to find the billiard room.

"Yes," Sarah said, "and it is quite lovely."

"May I come up with you and see it?" Hannah asked. "Fanny has been meaning to show it to me for days, but always something has prevented her from doing so. She says it is the loveliest room in the house."

"I would not be surprised if she is right," Sarah agreed, pushing back her chair and getting to her feet. "Shall we go now?"

The girl looked around her with obvious pleasure when they got upstairs. "Oh yes," she said, "it is quite different from any of the other rooms. How pretty it is."

She sat down on the bed and absently played with the large button at the top of Sarah's cloak.

"Do you like this house?" she asked. "Of course, you have not seen much of it yet. His grace took

Grandmama and me all over it the day after we arrived. I find it rather oppressive. It is lovely, of course, but it is really not my idea of a home."

"The architecture is magnificent," Sarah said. "I love the classical lines. They are so simple yet so elegant. And it appears to be made for the setting."

"Rather the setting was made for it," Hannah said. "That man they call Capability Brown planned the grounds as far back as the hills, I believe. His grace says that everything was carefully laid out so that one sees a picturesque scene from any angle or distance from the house."

Sarah smiled. "I am looking forward to seeing the state apartments," she said. "Shall we go down?"

Hannah made no immediate move to get up from the bed. "It is all very well to admire the building as a visitor," she said, leaning forward and looking at Sarah with wide eyes. "But can you imagine being mistress here, Miss Fifield? I shall be overwhelmed. I shall not be able to manage at all."

"You are nervous," Sarah said. "But you have been brought up in a large house. I am sure you will find that you will be far better able to cope than you expect."

"Oh, but I shan't," Hannah said, her face tense. "I feel like the merest child here, Miss Fifield. And he scares me. He is always so correct and so serious. And he seems so old. I am terrified when I realize that I shall belong here in just a few months' time."

Sarah bit her lip. "I do sympathize with you," she said. "You are very young to be faced with such responsibility. But I am sure that his grace is not as formidable as you think. He is a kind man, Hannah. He will have patience with you and will not expect the impossible."

"Oh," the girl said, jumping to her feet and crossing the room hastily to look out of the window, "I am terrible, am I not? I should not burden you with my worries. And I should not murmur a complaint now that I am betrothed to his grace. I should keep it all to myself. Do please forgive me."

Sarah busied herself putting away the cloak and bonnet she had laid out earlier. "Don't apologize," she said. "Sometimes one needs another person in whom to confide. I know how it is to feel all alone. I wish you would feel free to talk to me whenever you wish. You may be assured that what you say will go no further." She spoke with the utmost reluctance.

"Oh," Hannah said, turning, her eyes bright, "you do understand. I knew you would. I sensed that about you. Is not that silly?"

"Not at all," Sarah said with a weary smile. "What do you want of life, Hannah?"

The girl shrugged. "Nothing grand," she said. "Pomp and ceremony scare me. I never know what to say or do. I always feel most comfortable at home and with my friends."

"The ones you mentioned to me in Bath?" Sarah asked.

"Did I?" Hannah said. "Donald and Iris Ferris. I grew up with them. I never expected to be parted from them. That was very silly of me. They are so easy to talk to." She sighed.

"Perhaps other people will be too, if you give them a chance," Sarah said encouragingly. "You find me easy to talk to, after all."

"Oh yes," the girl said. "And Lord Laing. How fortunate you are, Miss Fifield, to be betrothed to him. He is always friendly and always smiling. I can talk to him too. I was telling him about Donald and Iris last night, and he said that it sounded as if I have a close relationship with Donald like he had with you. He understands, you see. The connection has had a happy ending for you, though, has it not?" She sounded wistful.

Sarah did not know what else to say. She felt desperately sorry for Hannah, and she could understand perfectly how the girl must feel with no one in whom to confide. She had been too long in the same predicament herself not to sympathize. But how could she become the intimate confidante of George's fiancée? It was an impossibly embarrassing situation. And how could Hannah be unhappy when she was engaged to marry George!

"Would you like to come to the stables and see Argus?" Hannah asked, brightening visibly. "He has to stay there. His grace said I might bring him into the house even though none of his dogs are allowed in. But Papa said no, and Grandmama backed him up. She says that dogs make her sneeze."

"Yes," Sarah said, "let us go."

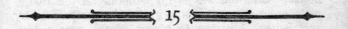

15

THE DUKE of Cranwell led his visitors along the upper cloisters of his home. They had been built, he explained, during the first three years of his dukedom as an easier form of access to the upstairs rooms. They had been constructed around all four sides of the central courtyard, with the result that this area had been considerably reduced. But the convenience of the new closed-in corridors and the beauty of their Gothic architecture more than compensated for the loss, he said.

The whole party dutifully looked up to the delicately arched ceiling and windows. They looked at the cedar and walnut chests that lined the walls and the marble busts dating back to ancient Roman days that Cranwell himself had gathered during his travels. And they viewed the dinner service of Meissen china displayed in a glass-fronted case. The two-hundred-and-fifty-piece set was used only on state occasions, their host explained.

Throughout it all, Sarah hung in the background, embarrassed. It was all very beautiful, she knew, and she wished that she were free to look and appreciate. But she could not. She suffered agonies from having to look at George and listen to him on his favorite topic, the one that he had talked about so much with her during their courtship. And she suffered untold humiliation in wondering what he must think of her for joining the group like this. It was not as if everyone had come. His own uncle and aunt and two of their children already knew the house. Lady Cavendish and Hannah had been shown around a few days before. Fanny had declined to come. Two of Hannah's cousins had gone riding.

"You see here one of the greatest treasures of the house," Cranwell was saying, stopping at one of the pictures on the wall. "It is a winter scene painted by Jan Brueghel in the first part of the seventeenth century."

Everyone looked.

"How delightfully pretty!" Lady Murdoch declared. "Look at all the dear little children playing. Not but what it is lacking in some color. I must admit I prefer something a little brighter, your grace."

Cranwell inclined his head in acknowledgment of her opinion. "You will prefer some of the portraits and ceilings in the state rooms, ma'am," he said. "I shall be taking you there directly."

Sarah moved closer to the picture as the group dispersed. It had been one of his favorites as a boy. She could vividly remember his saying so. Oh, and she could see why. There were children skating on a frozen pond, all in an individual dynamic position. There were other figures moving along the snowy streets, some driving carts, others carrying burdens on their heads. Others merely gossiped in groups or watched the skaters. And one could almost feel the crisp cold. The buildings glowed with their snow-covered roofs. The crooked and bare trees shivered toward the sky. The sky itself was weighted down with unshed snow. And it had been painted two hundred years before!

"Are you coming, Miss Fifield?" a quiet voice said at her shoulder.

Sarah turned with a start and gazed blankly into the blue eyes of her host. Then she noticed with embarrassment that they were alone. The sound of voices came from an open doorway nearby.

"Oh," she said foolishly, "yes. I was looking at the picture. It is very pretty."

What an inane statement, she thought with dismay as she heard the words come out of her mouth.

She walked through the doorway ahead of Cranwell

and felt her breath catch in her throat. They were in
one of the state rooms, the smaller of two drawing
rooms, he explained to an admiring audience. Sarah's
eyes traveled up the pine-paneled walls, painted white
with a carved cornice of gold leaf, to the arched ceiling
above. It was covered with richly colored painted figures. She could hear Lady Murdoch exclaiming appreciatively from across the room. The scene was the
birth of Venus, Cranwell was explaining. The paintings on the walls were all portraits of his mother's
family, the Tenbys, he told them. He had spent many
years finding them and persuading the owners to sell
to him.

Sarah lagged behind again as the whole chattering
group moved through the high double doors, flanked
by massive pillars, into the larger state room, twice the
size of the one they had just exited. In his own lifetime, Cranwell explained, it had been used only rarely,
and as a ballroom. When there was dancing, of course,
the Persian rug that covered all but the outer rim of
the floor was rolled up.

As a child he had always loved to watch a long line
of footmen undertake the difficult task of rolling it up
neatly, he had told Sarah a long time before.

The ballroom was similar in design and decoration
to the smaller drawing room. Sarah found her eyes
feasting on the portraits of the Montagu family, which
dominated the walls. These were all his ancestors. Was
there any family resemblance? she wondered. While
the rest of the party exclaimed over each wonder
pointed out to them by their host, she turned her
attention to the largest painting of all, a Van Dyck,
which almost covered the width of the room along the
south wall.

It was a picture of an earlier duke and duchess and
their large family. The fashions and the hairstyles were
very different from today's. Quite magnificent, in fact.
How would she feel in those voluminous silk skirts and
sleeves, and with the massed cluster of ringlets around
her head? How would George look with the curled

shoulder-length hair of his ancestor and the pointed beard and curled mustache? He would look very handsome, she decided, and smiled.

"It is the pride and joy of the house," Cranwell said from close behind her. "Do you like it?"

"It would be just too inadequate to say that it is lovely or magnificent," Sarah said, her eyes still on the painting. "Can you imagine that once this canvas was blank and the painter planned and executed this! How did he know where to start?"

"What I always like best about the picture," Cranwell said, "is the cluster of little cherub angels in the top corner. Apparently they were the children of the duke and duchess who died in infancy."

Sarah chuckled. "What a charming idea," she said. "I wonder if it pained the parents to look at them painted here."

"They had a large enough family without them," Cranwell said. "Four sons and three daughters."

"And two dogs," Sarah added, pointing to a pair of greyhounds sniffing at the clothes of one of the sons. "Oh!" She laughed outright. "This one looks like you, George. Look. If you take away those long curls, he has your face exactly."

"My height, too," Cranwell said ruefully, pointing to the difference between the son in question and his taller brother. "Come and see this picture, Sarah. It has always been my favorite painting in the house. But I rarely point it out to visitors because it is so small. I find that most people prefer what is more obviously magnificent to the eye. But you will appreciate it."

He took her to a comparatively small canvas on an adjoining wall, set in a circular frame. It was another Van Dyck, a charming portrait of three young children, grand and formal in their state garments. A brown-and-white spaniel sat docilely at the feet of the eldest.

"These are the grandchildren of the duke in the large portrait," Cranwell explained. "This one is my ancestor—the boy with the dog."

"Oh, it is charming," Sarah said. "Just look at how well the painter has captured the delicacy of the lace at the boy's collar and the hems of the girls' dresses. And the rosettes on the boy's shoes! And how he has caught the chubby, fresh complexions of childhood." She laughed. "I can remember your telling me about this picture, George. You said that when you were very young you liked the spaniel best."

"I always loved the lopsided look the brown patch over one ear and one eye gives him," Cranwell agreed. "I desperately wanted one like him."

They both laughed and turned to each other to share their amusement. They were very close. Blue eyes smiled into green—for perhaps five seconds. Then both flushed painfully and turned away in confusion. The rest of the group sounded quite faint in the distance. They must have been two rooms farther on already.

"I must join Cousin Adelaide," Sarah muttered, hardly knowing what she was saying. "She may need my support."

"I am sorry, ma'am," he said at the same time. "I am keeping you from the rest of the house and neglecting my other guests."

Sarah turned toward the doorway leading through to an anteroom, and would have hurried away without another glance at her host. But he detained her suddenly with a hand on her wrist.

"Sarah," he said, "what have you been doing since . . . ? What have you been doing for the last four years?"

The words were impulsively spoken. But Sarah's mind was in too distraught a state to notice their impertinence. She did not think to tell him that it was no concern of his what she had been doing.

"I left Uncle Randolph's," she said. "Not that he turned me off. In fact, he was very upset that I should leave. But I could not involve him and Aunt Myrtle in my shame. I rented a cottage in a village ten miles away and lived there until Cousin Adelaide found me."

"Alone?" he asked.

"Dorothy came with me," she said. "My maid."

"What did you do?" he persisted. "How did you live?"

She smiled fleetingly. "I was happy," she said. "Contented, at least. I tended my garden and did a great deal of needlework. And I read and read. I was fortunate enough to make friends with the vicar and his wife. And he had a wonderful library, inherited from some family member. I helped them a little with parish visiting."

"Did they know who you were?" Cranwell asked, frowning.

"No," she said. "They were far removed from high society and all its scandals. But I told them all about myself. They were my friends anyway." She tilted her chin and looked at him almost defiantly, her eyes glistening with unusual brightness.

He said nothing. He still held her wrist tightly. Sarah's eyes dropped to his hand, slim, well-manicured, strong despite its elegance. The curious silver ring was twisted to the inside of his finger. She smiled nervously down at his hand.

"It is not what you expected to hear, is it?" she said. "Of course, perhaps you do not believe me." She looked determinedly back into his eyes. "But it does not matter to me what you believe. With the Reverend Clarence and his wife I learned to live with myself. That is all that matters."

Cranwell still said nothing. But he looked intently back at her and retained still his vise-like grip of her wrist.

"Oh, I believe you," he said at last. "Both Fanny and Lady Murdoch have told me something similar."

He looked down at his hand on her wrist, almost as if he did not know it was there. He frowned and released his hold on her.

"There are the state bedrooms and the library still

to show," he said. "I hope my guests have not given up waiting for me. Are you coming, Sarah?"

"No," she said. "If you will show me the way back to the living apartments, I shall return there. I feel a little faint."

He led the way silently through the anteroom and out onto the upper landing of the grand curved staircase that was the official entryway to the state rooms.

"If you turn to your left at the foot of the stairs," Cranwell said, "you will find yourself out in the lower cloister."

"Thank you," Sarah said, and moved hurriedly to the staircase.

"Sarah," he said abruptly, "are you all right?"

"Oh yes," she assured him without looking back. "I merely need some fresh air."

And she fled down the stairs and through the doorway to the left at the bottom until she could no longer feel his eyes following her.

Cranwell stood and stared at the staircase long after Sarah had disappeared from view. He leaned his arms on the oak banister. His guests, whose voices had now faded beyond hearing, were forgotten.

He felt bereft, almost as if he were only now losing her for the first time. A few minutes before, she had been vibrant, interested, absorbed in his world. In his mind he had been back in the time before their marriage, the time after he had overcome her reticence and had shared his inner life with her. He had been almost unaware of her as a separate entity. As then, he had talked to her without conscious thought, almost as if she were another part of his being. And she had responded in kind. He had to believe that she had been as forgetful as he of the bitter years between now and the time when they had talked and shared their thoughts and grown to love each other.

And now she was gone. She was the other Sarah again, the one whose existence he had not even suspected until their wedding night. She was the one with whom he must forever feel uncomfortable, whom he must always treat with suspicion and hostility. The one from whom he must protect his sister and his betrothed.

But was she really the other Sarah? And did that other woman exist with any more reality than the one he had known in those days of courtship? Who was the real Sarah? Since his marriage and divorce he had looked back on those early days with bitterness and assumed that everything she had said and done had been a calculated part of a plan to trap him. Had he been quite fair to those memories? She had not been acting this morning. He would wager his life on it. She had been genuinely interested in his paintings, and her memories had been tender ones of what he had said about himself as a child.

Would he ever understand her? And did it really matter now if he never did? Yes, he decided immediately, it did matter. Very much. However much he must hate her, he must also admit to himself that Sarah had been a very important person in his life. Perhaps the most important. She had been his first love. And his only love. He was marrying Hannah for other reasons.

Cranwell frowned suddenly. What an enigma she was! She had spent the four years since their divorce living with one servant in a cottage in a village that apparently had little contact with the fashionable world. Gardening, doing her needlework, reading. And visiting the sick and poor. Her only friends a vicar and his wife. Learning to live with herself, she had said. A vicar, no less! Yes, her life had been different indeed from what he had imagined.

She must have reformed her life very soon after their marriage. There had been the adultery—how many times repeated, he did not know. But she must have succeeded in putting it all behind her. Had he acted too hastily? If he had given her a little time, would she have returned to him? Was it possible that they might have been able to patch up their marriage and have learned to live together? To love again?

Cranwell swallowed convulsively. The thought did not bear contemplating. They might have had four years together. By now they might have been happy, the past merely a bad memory. They might have had children.

She had left her uncle's house voluntarily, she had said, to avoid forcing him and her aunt to share in her shame. Had she felt it, then, that shame? How much had he made her suffer? Until he began his divorce action against her, presumably only he and the men with whom she had erred had been aware of her indiscretions. His actions had informed the gossip-hungry society of a nation that Sarah Montagu, Duchess of Cranwell, was no better than a whore. How had it felt to be so regarded by everyone who looked at her? And had it been fair to force her through that when deceit and corruption raged beneath the surface of so much of the seemingly respectable society of which he was part? He had not been a virgin himself on his wedding night.

For the first time Cranwell faced his own part in the events of four years before with some unease. Of one thing he was sure before he turned from the staircase and went in search of any of his guests who might still linger in the state rooms. He must no longer treat Sarah Fifield as if she had some sort of deadly infectious disease. Whatever she might have been in the past, she had obviously taken great pains to turn away from her errors and reshape her life. The least he could do was treat her with proper courtesy.

He turned and looked back through the open doorways of the anteroom and the ballroom. How lovely she would look dancing in there, her hair bright, her face alive with color and animation. He could almost picture her. His duchess!

His jaw set suddenly as he clamped his teeth together. He turned abruptly away and strode in the direction of the state dining room.

Sarah hurried along the lower cloister until she came

to the stairway leading up to the bedrooms. She felt
pursued, though she knew that she was long out of
sight of Cranwell. She went up to her bedroom, intending to stay there until she had had time to com-
pose herself. But two chambermaids were cleaning her
room, and she left again clutching a shawl that did not
even match her dress, after muttering an excuse about
having come for a wrap before going outside. She
went down the stairs again and along to the morning
room, but she could hear voices coming from inside.
She threw the shawl over her shoulders and turned to
the main doors, which a liveried footman opened for
her. A minute later her thin slippers were crunching
over the gravel of the formal gardens.

She slowed her steps and blew her breath out through
puffed cheeks. She would sit down on one of the
benches here and try to sort out her thoughts. She
would regain control of herself before having to face
everyone at luncheon.

"Miss Fifield," a cheerful voice called, and Sarah
looked up in dismay to find Fanny and Hannah seated
on a wrought-iron seat not far distant, Winston between them. Fanny was the one who had called. She
was waving and smiling.

Sarah smiled too. "How sensible of you all to be
outside," she said. "The weather is beautiful."

Winston stood up and held out a hand for hers.
"Have you escaped too, my love?" he asked. "I must
confess that gazing at art treasures all morning when
one might be gazing at living beauty instead is not
entirely to my liking." He kissed her hand and turned
a smiling face to include the other two girls in his
compliment.

He motioned to Sarah to sit between the two girls
and stood before them, his hands clasped behind his
back.

"Either I am unusually fortunate," he said, "or the
other gentlemen of this party are incredible slowtops.
How comes it that I have the exclusive company of
three such lovely ladies?"

Fanny was clearly enjoying herself. "The others are all being very good and listening to George's history and art lecture," she said. "Not everyone is such a shameless truant as you, Lord Laing."

"Shameless, indeed!" he said. "I am feeling very proud of myself." His grin drew answering smiles from the two girls who flanked Sarah.

"My only regret," Winston continued, "is that there is room on the seat for only three. I must stand here. Now, which of you ladies can I prevail upon to walk with me to the bridge? Lady Fanny?"

She smiled up at him but shook her head. "I have had no chance at all to talk to Miss Fifield since she arrived yesterday," she said. "Do you go, Hannah. But beware, Lord Laing. Both your fiancée and I will be watching."

His eyes widened. "I am all fear and trembling, ma'am," he said. "Lady Hannah?"

The girl blushed and looked inquiringly at Sarah. Then she got to her feet and timidly linked her arm through Winston's. Sarah and Fanny watched them go until they were out of earshot.

"I am so pleased that you were able to come, Miss Fifield," Fanny said. "I really did not have a chance to get to know you in Bath as I would have wished."

Sarah smiled. "Both Lady Murdoch and Winston were eager that I come," she said. "And I am glad I did. The house is lovely."

"You are very different from what I expected," Fanny said, looking directly into the face of the guest.

Sarah flushed. So the girl had decided to come out into the open with her knowledge, had she? It was easier to pretend. She did not really wish to pursue any frank conversation, least of all at the present.

"What did you expect?" she asked reluctantly.

"Oh, I don't know," Fanny said. "I do not know exactly what happened in the past, you know. George always used to tell me that I was too young to know, and now he says that it is past history and not worth resurrecting. But I suppose I imagined someone vulgar and quite heartless. Though why I should have expected that, I do not know. George would never have fallen in love with someone like that. And he was in love. He suffered dreadfully for a long time. And I do not believe he has ever recovered his spirits completely."

Sarah turned and found that the girl was still looking directly into her face. "Did he?" she asked. "And has he not? I am sorry."

"I would guess that you suffered just as much and have recovered just as little," Fanny continued relentlessly. "I can tell. It is true, is it not?"

Sarah hesitated. "It was inevitable that we both suffer," she said. "Divorce is so very rare in our society. And to be separated so completely from someone with whom one has been so intimately connected is bound to be painful. But I think your brother is right, Fanny. It is ancient history and best forgotten about. We both have other lives now and bright futures."

"What did happen?" Fanny asked, leaning forward slightly. "And please do not tell me that I am too young to know. You were only two years older than I am now, were you not, when you married George?"

Sarah glanced at her in distress and away again. "Please," she said, "I do not mean to be uncommunicative, but I cannot talk about it. I will say only that the fault was entirely mine. I did something very bad. Your brother was not at all to blame. Please believe that."

"I cannot believe that you did anything so very bad," Fanny said. "You are a very sensible and kind person, Miss Fifield. I do admire your patience with Lady Murdoch. I mean no disrespect, but I think I should be driven insane if I had to spend one hour in close contact with her. I think I should have liked to have you as a sister."

Sarah looked at her in agony. "Please," she said. "You must not think that way. Geor . . . your brother has chosen your new sister, and I am sure you and she will deal famously together. And I shall soon be married to someone else too."

"Lord Laing," Fanny said. "He is very handsome. Far more handsome than George. And very charming. George does not go to great pains to ingratiate himself with other people. Do you love him, Miss Fifield?"

"Love him? I . . ." Sarah floundered in her embarrassment. "I loved him once, of course. When I married him I loved him. I have no right to love him now or to have any feelings for him beyond respect. I do respect him."

"I meant Lord Laing," Fanny said quietly, her eyes riveted to Sarah's face.

"Oh!" Sarah could have died of mortification. "Win? Well, of course. He is to be my husband. As you say, he is very handsome and very charming. What woman would not wish to be his wife?" Her laugh sounded unconvincing to her own ears.

Fanny did not smile. "Shall we go into the house?" she said. "I think it must be close to luncheon time, and even George is scared of the chef when his concoctions are ruined by our tardiness."

Sarah gulped with relief, but Fanny did not immediately rise from the seat.

"You must dislike me intensely," she said. "I know I have embarrassed and distressed you. But please try to understand. I have no parents. George has been like a father to me for most of my life. And I do so want to understand the most important event in his life. Now more than ever. I can no longer picture some sort of witch and think him well out of the marriage. I like you very much. I can understand why he loved you. I think the two of you suit perfectly."

Sarah got to her feet and pulled her shawl closer around her shoulders. "Yes, I am embarrassed," she said. "But I know I shall look back on this conversation with gratitude. I have not had many votes of confidence in my life. It feels good to be liked by someone who was my sister for a brief time. I do not resent you, Fanny. I admire your concern for your brother."

She hurried along the gravel walk ahead of Fanny.

As soon as they had passed through the doorway into
the hall, she mumbled something about getting tidied
up for luncheon and hurried up the stairs without
looking back. She almost ran into her room, where
finally she could shut the door and be alone. She
closed her eyes and sagged back against the door.

Why, oh why, had she come? It would have been
better far to have stayed away, to have let Win come
on his own, even. She had been here less than twenty-
four hours and already she had gone from one embarrassment to another. She would have to get away. But
how? Could she persuade Win to leave after all? Promise him anything? Only one argument might work with
him. If she could persuade him that she was desperate
to sleep with him but was too afraid to do so with so
many people around them, he might agree to take her
away to an inn. And once away, she could lure him on
to some other place and finally back home for their
wedding.

Sarah shuddered and put one hand over her mouth.
Could she do it? And should she? She was already
well aware of just how shaky was their betrothal. Win
had agreed to marry her because of the money. He
had the money. What was to stop him now from
turning his attention to Fanny after all and adding her
fortune to what Sarah had given him? He would do it,
too, if he thought he could get away with it.

Oh, would Win always, always have his own way?
she asked herself. She had thought herself free of him
after Graham died. When she had moved away to her
cottage, she had thought she need never have anything
more to do with her past.

And indeed, the first time Win came, she had succeeded in sending him packing with relative ease. She
had felt very satisfied with herself. But he had come
back again when her new life was already more than
three years old and seemed secure. He needed money,
was quite desperate for some, in fact. And he knew,
of course, that Cranwell had given her some, though
he must have been aware that it was no fortune.

He had used all the arguments she expected: it would be merely a loan; he was her cousin and had treated her like a sister when she was newly orphaned; his father was desperately sick and must not be troubled with financial problems. She had resisted it all, though that last argument had pained her. She was proud of her new strength of character. She would not give in again, whatever the threats or blandishments. Let him do his worst!

And then, a mere two weeks later, Uncle Randolph had finally succumbed to his consumption. She had realized immediately that now Win would take over the management of her money, and she had written for it. She would ask the Reverend Clarence what to do with it to keep it safe. Winston had written back to say there would be some delay. His father had borrowed the money to repay some debt, he wrote. Sarah had understood what that meant. Win himself had used the money to pay some gaming debts or merely to gamble with. She had also realized that she would never see the money again. She was destitute. Perhaps it had been Win's way of trying to force her to return to the home that was now his. Instead, she had applied for a position.

Now Win appeared to be maneuvering after all to attach Fanny's affections. And he would marry her, too, if he had the chance. He would do it in the cheerful belief that he could still win Sarah for his mistress. Win seemed quite firm in the belief that she desired him more than anything else in life.

And she knew that he desired her. Their long-dead affair seemed only to have whetted his appetite. And this desire was her only hold over him, the only fact that might make him continue with his plans to marry her. If she gave herself to him now before their wedding, he would have no need to marry her at all. He would take her, have his fill of pleasure for a few days, and probably return to court Fanny. Sarah was sure that she had not imagined that his attentions had been quite marked to the girl since their arrival the day before.

She could not lure him away, then. She must wait quietly and live through this week of torture. Then she must return home, marry Win, and face a lifetime of misery so that George and Fanny would be free from the man who had ruined her own life. But she must watch Win. She did not trust him not to cheat her. She must make an effort to be alluring to him, so that his appetite would be aroused and his mercurial instinct dulled. She must focus his attention on herself, however much pain it caused her to do so.

Sarah crossed the room to the wardrobe where her shawl was kept. She folded it and put it neatly away. She crossed to the washstand and began to splash cold water over her face.

Oh God, she was aching with love for him. For George. She pressed her hands over her wet face and concentrated on not giving in to the instinct to cry. What was it about him that could make her forget herself so easily? It had always been so. At the Saxtons' house party she had been determined not to become involved with any of the guests. Yet before many days had passed she was drawn into an easy yet deep friendship with George. It had happened entirely against her plans. And the same thing had happened the following year when he came to her uncle's house day after day to court her. She had been so determined to resist, for his sake. Yet before she knew it, she had forgotten her resolve and relaxed into the warmth of his friendship and his love again.

But to have allowed it to happen again today! After all that had happened between them. Despite the embarrassment of her predicament in finding herself the houseguest of her former husband. It was true, though. While they had looked at those two paintings together, the years had rolled away without trace. She had once again been with her closest friend, the man with whom she felt so relaxed that he hardly seemed a separate being. She had shown enthusiasm for some of his most treasured possessions. And worse, she had reminisced about the past, just as if those memories could bring only pleasure to them both.

Still with her hands over her face, Sarah shook her head violently from side to side, as if by doing so she could shake away what had happened earlier. How utterly mortifying. What must he think of her?

She removed one hand and groped around for a towel. She patted at her face, hoping that no telltale red marks would be visible when she went downstairs. The fact was, though, the puzzling fact, that the same thing had happened to him. She was sure of it. The years had rolled back for both of them. He had taken her to show her his favorite painting, telling her that only she would appreciate it. And she knew that it really was his favorite. He had told her so years ago. And he had looked at it with her, his head bent close to hers. They had laughed together.

"Oh, George," she said aloud. If only the years really could be taken away. If only she had a second chance. Would the outcome have been different if she had gathered the courage to tell him the full truth before their wedding? If she had told him everything— about Win and Graham and the fact that she had never consented willingly to their couplings, would he have forgiven her? Would he have married her, and would they be together now? She might be in this very house now, its mistress. George's wife. His lover.

No, she must not think such things. If she did, she would surely start to cry. And how would she explain red eyes downstairs?

The meeting with Fanny had been disturbing. It was true that she felt an unwilling sort of warmth about the heart to know that she was liked by George's sister, that the girl thought well of her and thought she suited her brother. She knew that for the rest of her life she would hug to herself the girl's opinion that George must have loved her very much and had never fully recovered from her loss.

But it was not right to allow George's sister to

develop an affection for her. What she really ought to do was go back to Fanny and tell her exactly what had happened. Everything. All the sordid details. Then the girl would turn from her with horror and disgust as she should. Sarah herself would then find it easy to do what she knew she should do: stay away from those two young and impressionable girls, the women in George's life.

That was what she should do. But she knew that she would not do so, perhaps for much the same reason that she had not told George before their wedding. It is a dreadful thing deliberately to destroy the esteem that another feels for one. It is too tempting to bask in that person's love or admiration, even when one knows oneself wholly unworthy of those feelings. No, she would not tell. She must just continue to avoid Fanny as much as she possibly could.

Sarah drew a few steadying breaths. It was becoming harder and harder to leave her own sanctuary and face other people. Finally she opened her door and descended the staircase, a determined spring in her step. She went in search of Winston, intent on flirting with him over luncheon.

16

"SARAH, LET us not join this ride, shall we?" Winston asked, drawing her to one side as they drank tea in the drawing room after luncheon. "I should much prefer a stroll in the hills with you. One disadvantage of a house party like this is that it makes a *tête-à-tête* very difficult to achieve." He smiled his most beguiling smile.

Sarah smiled back into his eyes. "How glad I am that you have suggested it, Win," she said. "I really am not in the mood for viewing farmlands this afternoon."

His eyes strayed to her lips. "A whole afternoon to ourselves," he said. "I can hardly conceive of a greater pleasure."

"Perhaps we are not the only ones to be reluctant to ride," Sarah said, looking brightly around. "Perhaps some of Lady Hannah's cousins would like to accompany us." She smiled at young Christine Tenby, who happened to be looking her way.

"A *tête-à-tête* does not lend itself to an activity involving more than two people," Winston said quietly. "I want you to myself, Sarah. And don't pretend you do not wish to be alone with me, too."

Sarah looked into his eyes. "You know I did not even want the delay of the week here," she said, and watched his eyes stray to her lips again and down to her breasts.

"Sarah, dear," Lady Murdoch called from halfway across the room, "what are you planning to do this afternoon? Bertha and I are going to have a rest and a stroll in the garden. So you really need not feel obliged

to stay to keep me company, you know. Not but what
I should dislike your company. You know I always
enjoy having you near, you being my cousin and all
and reminding me of my own youth. But it really
would be much better for you to take some exercise.
Why do you and Lord Laing not go riding with his
grace and the others? I know you do not ride a great
deal, but I am sure his grace has some quiet horses in
his stables."

"Winston and I are going walking, Cousin Adelaide," Sarah said, looking hopefully around at the
gathered group. "We have been told that the view
from the hills is well worth seeing."

"What a wonderful idea," Fanny said. "George, the
weather is really too good to be riding around looking
at fields. Let us walk instead. I for one am determined
to, even if no one else will join me."

Captain Penny, Joshua Stonewall, and Samuel Tenby
immediately expressed their intention of joining the
walk, and Faith Wright and Barbara Tenby quickly
joined their voices to the notion.

Cranwell laughed. "I seem to be outnumbered," he
said. "But so be it. The farmlands can wait until
another day, when the weather may be a little duller.
And you have heard quite rightly, Miss Fifield. I may
be partial, of course, but I believe the view from the
hills to be one of the loveliest in England."

Sarah felt jolted by the unexpected attention and
turned away under the pretense of leaving the room to
fetch her bonnet. Winston followed her.

"Curses!" he muttered for Sarah's ears only. "Did
that tabby have to choose that moment to ask you so
publicly what you planned? And does no one have the
imagination to realize that a man sometimes wishes to
be alone with his betrothed?"

Sarah smiled sympathetically at him and ran up the
stairs to her room. Her own powers of seduction sometimes frightened her. All she had had to do was deliberately sit next to Win at luncheon, smile warmly at
him, touch his hand briefly when asking him to pass a

dish to her, and let her shoulder touch his ever so briefly as he did so. He had been instantly her slave. She had aroused his appetite for her with alarming ease so that now he could scarcely wait to be alone with her.

It was the effect she had set out to achieve, but now she had a panicked sensation of having lit a fire that had spread quickly out of her control. It was all very well to have focused Win's attention on herself and away from Fanny, but it was equally important to her to keep him in suspense, to allow him no gratification of his desires. A solitary walk in the hills with him would be fatal. She would not be able to avoid ravishment. And indeed, it would not even be ravishment. She would be forced by the part she played to affect enthusiasm. Yet once he had had her, he would quite possibly think no more about marriage, despite the formality of their betrothal. She knew rather well how Win's mind worked.

It had been a stroke of good fortune that Lady Murdoch had spoken up when she did and that some of the other guests preferred a walk to the ride that George had suggested.

Almost all the young people gathered in the main hallway within the next twenty minutes. Sarah was surprised to find that Cranwell was there too with Hannah. The latter smiled at her.

"I was looking forward to the ride," she said, "but really I think I would prefer the walk because his grace has said that I may take Argus. A groom is to bring him around to the courtyard."

A rather noisy group set off across the Palladian bridge and over the gently sloping ground that led to the hills. The collie, bursting with unleashed energy, raced around them in circles and made frequent rushes on ahead and back again. Sarah, her arm linked through Winston's, soon discovered to her consternation that they were walking with Cranwell and Hannah. He certainly seemed to have recovered from the embarrassment of the morning. He entertained them all with a description of how the landscape had been constructed deliberately to look picturesque.

"It seems so artless," he said, "as if nature has had the good sense to arrange itself to perfection. In fact, every tree and bush on the lower slopes was placed there deliberately."

"Oh, Argus," Hannah cried suddenly. "Do look. The foolish dog has run into the woods and will surely get lost."

She drew her arm free of Cranwell's and ran to the edge of the trees, calling for her dog. He came bounding out and jumped up to put his forepaws on her shoulders and lick her face enthusiastically. She laughed and proceeded to play with the dog, apparently forgetting her companions.

"Lord Laing," Fanny said, abandoning Captain Penny, with whom she had been walking, and laying a hand on Winston's arm, "my favorite view of the house is just above here. It looks just too lovely to be real. Do come and see." She dragged him off, the captain trailing along with them.

Sarah had a feeling of *déjà vu*. This had happened before, she could swear. And then she remembered Beechen Cliff in Bath. Just thus she had been left alone with George. She turned away. There were plenty of other people with whom to walk.

"Have we spoiled your afternoon?" he asked quietly. Sarah looked across at him in astonishment. His voice was pleasant and polite.

"Spoiled it?" she asked, frowning. "By no means. I wished to walk."

"But I believe you planned to be with your fiancé?" he said inquiringly. "I am afraid that the rest of us imposed our company on you quite shamelessly."

"It really does not matter," she said. "It is better to have company, I think."

He looked at her levelly. "I am glad that you are going to be happy," he said.

Sarah turned fully to him, her arched eyebrows showing her surprise. "Happy?" she repeated.

"Yes," he said. "I am glad that you are to marry your cousin. He seems a sensitive and good-natured man. He will make you a good husband."

Sarah felt the insane desire to laugh. Did he know? Was he taunting her with her own shame? But no. That could not be possible. George was incapable of such biting sarcasm. He was serious. He thought she was fortunate to have found a man willing to overlook her past and offer her respectability. She looked over to the small knoll on which Win stood with Fanny and saw him through George's eyes. Handsome. Always sunny-natured. Friendly. Always willing to talk to anyone and humor everyone. Charming. A good catch for any single lady, even one of unblemished reputation.

"Yes," she said, "I am very fortunate."

Winston turned toward her at that point and waved. He began to walk back to her. Captain Penny bore Fanny on up the slope in the wake of a noisy group of people all walking together.

"Lady Fanny is quite right," Winston said to Cranwell as he came up to them. "The landscaper certainly knew what he was doing here. Are you ready to walk on, Sarah?"

Cranwell touched his hat to her and turned toward Hannah, who was on her knees hugging the panting collie.

"Enough of this," Winston said, looking ahead to the others and back briefly to the two who were still behind. "I have no intention of sharing you any longer, my love. This seems to be a splendid opportunity to lose ourselves."

He turned sharply toward the dense cluster of trees to their right and drew Sarah after him into the cool shade that the thick branches offered. Almost instantly they were enclosed, and outside noises seemed to be hushed.

"I really do not think we ought, Win," Sarah said, looking nervously back over her shoulder. "The others will think we are lost and worry about us."

"Nonsense," he said. "This is not exactly a forest,

Sarah. I don't think it would be possible to get lost here even if we tried. Besides, love, it might be enjoyable to lose our sense of direction for a little while at least."

"What will the others think?" she said. "I think we should go back and join them."

"What will they think?" he said, and grinned as he twined an arm around her shoulders. "They will probably think that I want to be alone with my fiancée for a while and be horribly jealous."

"Just for a few minutes, then," she said uneasily "It is not very proper for us to be alone like this." She was uncomfortably aware of his hip and his thigh moving against hers as they walked.

He stopped entirely and turned her to face him. He was laughing. "Sarah," he said, "you are talking like a prim virgin. Have you forgotten so soon? There was a time when you did not spare a thought for the proprieties. You knew exactly what I wanted and gave it to me. Very sweetly too, I must add. It is not wrong to admit that you want it too, you know. I will not think the less of you. Maybe there are some men who would be repulsed to find that their women were as eager as they, but I am not one of them. I like my women hot and willing."

The arm that had been around her shoulders was now twined about her waist and held her fast against him. The other hand pulled loose the strings of her bonnet, tossed it to the ground, and twined into the coils of her hair. He tilted her head to one side and lowered his mouth to hers.

Sarah felt as if she were suffocating. His hands held her completely his prisoner. His open mouth was wet and warm over her own. His quickened breath was hot on her cheek and loud in her ear. His body was pressed to hers, his arousal painfully obvious. She felt the old familiar waves of nausea rising into her nostrils. She fought panic. She started slowly to recite the multiplication tables to herself. She relaxed her body against his. And she became aware of the full horror of what she had deliberately stepped into. She could not struggle. She had freely betrothed herself to him. She was mad! In Bath her plan had seemed so sensible and so noble.

"Ah, Sarah," he said at last, raising his head to look down at her, "you are the hottest little woman that I have ever handled. Let's walk a little farther among the trees and find a soft place to lie down. It is going to be good to have you again after so long."

She shook her head and forced herself to smile. "No, Win," she said. "Please humor me on this. I want our wedding night to be very special. Let us wait. Just one week. Please, Win?" She twined her arms around his neck.

"It *will* be very special," he said thickly, "I promise you, love. But a good experience in bed does not come from abstinence, you know. It comes from practice. This afternoon we will teach each other again what is pleasing, and on our wedding night everything will be perfect."

She did not have a chance to reply. His lips had found hers again and his tongue was urgently pressing against her teeth and forcing an entrance to her mouth. His hands moved to cup her breasts and to push impatiently first at her shawl, which fell to the ground, and then at the fabric of her dress, which he dragged free of her shoulders. His mouth moved away from hers and trailed kisses along her throat.

Sarah was losing her battle against panic. The multiplication tables were failing her. The product of nine and six would not form itself in her mind. She started to squirm against him, desperate to be free.

"Win," she moaned. "Please, Win."

Her eyes were open. In her effort to get away she turned her head and found herself looking at the Duke of Cranwell, who was standing perhaps twenty feet away. This time her frantic shove at Winston's chest pushed them apart and he too saw Cranwell.

"Your grace," Sarah said foolishly, and realized almost as she said it that both her shoulders were exposed and a good part of her bosom too. She pulled at her dress with frantic fingers.

Cranwell suddenly came to life again. Hannah had appeared behind him. "Get out of here, Hannah," he said sharply. "Go and see if Argus has found his way out."

"Oh," Hannah said, her eyes growing round at the sight of Sarah and Winston, and she turned and disappeared from view.

"My apologies," Cranwell said stiffly, and turned to follow Hannah. "We were in search of that infernal dog."

"No harm done," Winston said cheerfully. "Sarah and I were merely enjoying a moment alone."

Cranwell disappeared without another word while Sarah was still pulling at her dress and brushing leaves and grass from her shawl and bonnet.

"Well," Winston said, "I came closer to committing murder then than I have ever come. What damnable timing. And just when I had you coming hot all over me, Sarah. I have to agree that it would not be at all seemly to absent ourselves any longer. I am sorry, my love. It seems we will have to wait for another time."

He smiled ruefully at her and reached out to take her hand. Sarah managed somehow to smile back, even to look mildly regretful, she believed. In truth, she did not know how she was to walk back out of the woods. Her legs were trembling so badly that she was afraid they would not support her weight. She had come so close to being taken again. She did not think she could have borne it. Something in her mind would surely have snapped. She would have gone insane.

And yet, she thought, as she placed her hand in Winston's and found that she could just walk after all, she had freely committed herself to giving him the legal and moral right to possess her whenever he pleased. They were to be married within a week. There would be no more excuses then, no more miraculous rescues.

It was only then, as they emerged into the sunlight

again and she was beginning to breathe deep gulps of air in her relief, that Sarah realized the full import of what had just happened. George had seen them there, had seen her disheveled and struggling. Surely he would realize now that Win was not quite the paragon he had thought. And surely he would realize that she really was different now, that she did not encourage advances even from the man she had chosen to marry.

But what did it matter anyway? she thought. It was far too late now to be cultivating his good opinion. It did not matter if he still considered her a loose woman.

And oh, the embarrassment. To have been seen thus by him! By George Montagu, always so correct, so much the gentleman. Even if the scene had proved to him that she was no longer a woman of low morals, she would have preferred him not to see it. And Hannah, too. She would give anything in the world to slip away from Montagu Hall and never see either of them ever again.

"It looks as if the crowd has grown tired of climbing," Winston said. "They are on their way back already. We might as well turn around and head back to the house. Another time perhaps we will have better fortune." He linked her arm through his and squeezed her hand.

Sarah kept her eyes on the ground. She did not look around for Cranwell or Hannah. She hoped they were not close. She allowed Winston to lead her back down the hill toward the bridge and the house.

The Duke of Cranwell was having trouble with his neckcloth again. He was not even trying to create some lavish style of knot and folds, he thought irritably. Why was it that he could not produce even a simple, tidy effect without ruining every starched neckcloth he laid his hands on? His eyes met those of Peters in the mirror. The valet was brushing an already immaculate velvet evening coat, a pained look on his face.

"All right," Cranwell said, smiling reluctantly, "you

need not say anything, or look anything, Peters. You may have your heart's desire and come and help me."

He turned away from the mirror and stood still, chin up, while Peters worked one of his miracles with what Cranwell considered to be almost insolent speed. He turned to examine the effect in the mirror.

"Hm!" he said. "It is a pity I am not on my way to court or at least to a formal ball. It is a masterpiece. Come. Help me on with my coat or you will never be satisfied that my shirt is not wrinkled beneath it."

Finally he was ready to go down for dinner. Peters had been dismissed. But he was early. There was no need to put in an appearance just yet. He wandered to the long window across which the brocaded curtains had not yet been drawn. It was only early dusk. He loved the view from his window, across the sloping lawn to the south of the house and eventually to trees and fields stretching to the distance. But his eyes did not really see the view this evening.

It had been a busy day. He felt a little guilty about the morning. He never had finished the guided tour of the state rooms that he had promised. Not that anyone had complained. They all seemed to have enjoyed looking at the bedrooms, the dining room, and the library without his guidance. Then there had been the afternoon walk, after which his attention had been claimed first of all by Lady Cavendish and Lady Murdoch, who had wished merely to talk with him. Then he had been summoned by his bailiff, who had come to the house on some emergency business. He had been escaping to his room when Uncle Justin, Cousin Herbert, and Allan Wright had invited him to play billiards.

He had had no time to himself until now, though he should not complain. His houseguests appeared to be enjoying themselves and finding a variety of activities with which to amuse themselves. It was just that he was so unused to company, he supposed. He normally spent so much time alone, no one but himself to please, that he found it difficult to be constantly sociable and constantly called upon to entertain or be entertained.

Of course, it was not just that which was making him feel unusually weary and depressed. He just could not shake from his mind the events of the afternoon. He had finally decided only that morning that he must put past impressions of Sarah behind him and treat her with a greater respect. He had been convinced at last that she was not as she used to be. He had been not at all reluctant to change his plans for the afternoon and join the others with her and Bowen on their walk. He had even looked forward to seeing her reaction to the view from the hills. And he had made an effort to walk with her and her fiancé in order to try to show both of them that he bore no grudges, that he did not resent their presence as guests in his house. When he had been unexpectedly left alone with Sarah for a few minutes, he had tried to speak pleasantly to her.

For the space of a few minutes he had felt pleased with himself. He could put behind him the embarrassment he had felt in her presence ever since he had first set eyes on her again in the Pump Room at Bath. He could even forgive her for not keeping her promise to take herself out of his life with his money.

God, if he had just not gone chasing into the woods after that infernal dog! It was pointless anyway. The collie never disappeared from Hannah's side for long. All they had needed to do was to stroll on slowly and wait for it to come dashing out from among the trees again.

He did not know quite what had come over him when he saw them there. They had apparently not heard him approach. He could quite easily have turned and left. Instead, he had stood there stupidly watching until Sarah had spotted him. And then there had been all the embarrassment of knowing himself discovered, of witnessing their confusion.

His mind just had not worked rationally for the space of a few minutes. His first reaction, he remembered now, when he saw them together, was to rush across the distance that lay between him and them, tear them apart, and pound Bowen to a pulp. How dared the man maul his wife in such a manner! had been his thought. He had wanted to kill.

Yet that had been only his first flash reaction. Almost as soon he was feeling a blinding rage against her. She was standing pressed against Bowen, arched backward, her head thrown back in an ecstasy of desire. Her dress was off both shoulders and halfway down her breasts, and she was writhing against her lover, begging him with every movement of her body to lay her down and possess her. And she was begging him in words, too, calling his name and pleading with him.

She had been behaving like a whore!

If he had arrived even one minute later, how would he have found them? The thought did not bear contemplating. And not just he. Hannah had been not far behind him. She had not seen them actually embrace, but it must have been glaringly obvious to her what had been going on. Both were still looking flushed and disheveled. Neither of them had talked about it after he had rejoined her on the open hillside. He had not even apologized for the harsh way in which he had told her to get away from there.

Sarah. Cranwell turned away from the window and crossed the room to the empty fireplace. He leaned one arm on the high mantelpiece and gazed into the empty grate. He had loved her once. He wanted so much to believe her changed. Yet she had not changed at all. It was true that Bowen was her fiancé. He supposed that made some difference. But it argued a dreadful lack of restraint in her to embrace him with such abandon just a scant few feet from the path along which several of her fellow guests were walking. They could at least have waited until they were quite alone together.

He did not think he blamed Bowen in any way. Sarah was an extremely lovely and desirable woman. He doubted if any man could resist her for long if she set out deliberately to seduce him. And who could have resisted the performance she was putting on among the trees? Her fiancé would have had to be made of stone.

He was not quite sure how he should act. It had been a private moment he had broken in upon, after all, even if the choice of location was indiscreet. He supposed he must continue to treat her with the courtesy due to a guest. He must, though, be very careful to guard his heart against her. She had been insinuating herself into his good graces again, and he had not realized what was happening. He must never forget what she was. Perhaps her life for the previous four years had been exemplary. Yet it seemed that once back in society again she was unable to resist the temptation to enslave every male with whom she came in contact. Stonewall was almost making a fool of himself over her, and one or two of the younger cousins were eyeing her appreciatively.

Sarah was sitting on a wooden chest at the foot of Lady Murdoch's bed. Lady Murdoch was standing in front of her, a hand on her shoulder. Sarah was crying.

"So there," she said between painful sobs. "Now you know everything, and I cannot say I am sorry. I am so tired of lies and deceit."

"There, there, dear," Lady Murdoch said soothingly, patting the shoulder beneath her hand.

"I shall leave immediately," Sarah said, "as soon as I have pulled myself together. I shall leave the house tomorrow and you need never see me again. I shall trust you to explain to his grace."

"There, there," Lady Murdoch repeated. "Dry your eyes now, dear, or you will be in no fit state to appear downstairs. There is some water on the washstand. Come and splash some on your face. It is cold and will take your breath away and will not feel at all comfortable. But it will be worth the discomfort, dear, just to take the redness from your eyes. You would not wish anyone to know that you have been weeping, for then there would be any number of awkward questions."

"Oh, please, ma'am," Sarah said, "do not be kind to me. Indeed I shall go to my room and send word that I shall not be down to dinner. I shall pack my bags."

"Sarah, dear," said Lady Murdoch, an unusual firmness in her tone, "you must go and wash your face immediately and then come and sit down at the fire. We will talk. There is a little time yet before we must go downstairs, and I see that you are dressed already."

"Yes," Sarah said, "I dressed for dinner, and it was only then that I knew that I could go on like this no longer. I am sorry, indeed I am, for deceiving you so."

"Pooh!" Lady Murdoch said, crossing heavily to one of the chairs set close to the fire and gesturing Sarah yet again toward the washstand. "I am not so easily deceived, my dear. Of course I knew about your marriage and divorce. Stories like that do not miss many ears, you know, and I discovered who you were too. I thought your uncle's name was Bowen and I remembered that yours was Sarah. It did not take me long to find out that you were the abandoned bride."

"You knew all the time?" Sarah asked, aghast.

"When I saw your advertisement in the newspaper under your own name," Lady Murdoch continued, "I am afraid an old woman's curiosity got the better of me, dear. I had to go and see what you were like. And I loved you after only five minutes in that little cottage of yours. I knew right then that you could not possibly be the girl that gossip had made you out to be. Sometimes I sense these things. I started to blame your former husband, though I had never met him."

"Oh, no," Sarah said, her voice muffled by the towel with which she was dabbing at her dripping face. "No, George was never to blame for anything. He was the one who was wronged."

"Oh yes, I know," Lady Murdoch said. "Soon after I was presented to him in Bath I knew that he was neither an untruthful man nor a vindictive one. I must confess the mystery intrigued me, dear. I have watched you both ever since and have grown only more and more puzzled. If you were to ask me, I should say that you must have suited admirably. Now, of course, I understand perfectly."

She glared severely as Sarah came and sat in the chair opposite hers.

"But why, Sarah dear, did you not tell me sooner about Lord Laing? That part of your story I still find hard to believe. I have never been so taken in in my life. I thought him the most charming man I had met in a long time, and he is nothing but a blackmailer, a seducer, and a rake. I never would have suspected. And how you could have come to engage yourself to him, dear, I cannot understand."

"I was trying to explain when I lost control a few minutes ago," Sarah said. "It was the only way I could think of to take him away and keep him from other innocent girls. I was mortally afraid that he was going to pay his addresses to Lady Fanny, and I had reason to believe that she would look on him favorably. I know that he is very handsome and very attractive to most women. I tried and tried to think of another solution, but nothing would serve. I was counting on some other solution to occur to me before the wedding day."

"But, dear," Lady Murdoch said, "there is a very obvious way of avoiding what you set yourself to do. All you have to do is tell his grace the truth. Indeed, I cannot for the life of me understand why you did not do so when you were married to him. Why would you wish to protect such a scoundrel and make the whole of your life a misery as a result?"

"Is that what I have been doing?" Sarah asked, frowning. "Yes, I suppose I have been protecting Win. I think originally I did it because his disgrace would have hurt my aunt and uncle dreadfully. They were very kind to me after Papa died, and I could not repay their love by getting Win into trouble. They doted on him so. And Uncle Randolph was so sick for years.

And I hated the thought of the truth about Graham coming out, even though he was dead already."

"Yes, Sarah," Lady Murdoch said, "it is just like you to behave so selflessly. Though as to that, I don't know, dear. It seems to me that you have made his grace suffer greatly by your silence."

"Oh, have I?" Sarah asked, stricken. "But I did not mean to. I felt so guilty for having married him under false pretenses that I could think only of releasing him so that he might forget me and be happy again. Did I do wrong?"

Lady Murdoch shook her head and smiled reassuringly. "No, dear," she said, "but I really think the truth must come out now. You cannot sacrifice the whole of your life for the sake of some notion of honor. I would never allow it."

"Oh, I know," Sarah wailed. "I realized that this afternoon, Cousin Adelaide. I could not do it. I just could not." She shuddered. "It was horrible. Horrible! I would rather die than have him touch me again. I did not know what to do. And then when I was ready for dinner, yet it seemed far too early to go downstairs, I knew that I had to confide in someone. I thought of you."

"And glad I am of it," Lady Murdoch said, and Sarah was surprised to see that there were tears in her eyes. "That means that you really do think of me as some sort of mother to you. That has been my dearest wish."

"What am I to do?" Sarah asked.

Lady Murdoch thought a minute. "I think his grace must know," she said. "However, perhaps it would not be the best idea to tell him immediately. He would be burdened with a nasty situation, and this is after all a special week for him, with his dear Hannah here and many of their relatives. I think we must wait, dear, until the last day. We must tell him then so that he will know how to act in the event that that viper comes after his sister. In the meantime, we must see to it that you are not alone with Lord Laing. I shall be a rigorous chaperone."

"It really is time to go down for dinner," Sarah said. "Do my eyes look very red?"

"You look pretty as a picture—as always," Lady Murdoch said. "Oh, I shall find it extremely difficult to be civil to that young man."

"Cousin Adelaide," Sarah said as that lady hoisted herself to her feet with one hand splayed firmly on each arm of the chair, "how can I ever thank you? I never knew my mother, but I am sure I could not have loved her more than I do you."

Lady Murdoch hid emotion in gruffness. She caught Sarah's arm and leaned heavily on it. "Come along, Sarah," she said. "We are going to make that man sorry he was ever born."

17

Winston's smile was looking somewhat forced. "Of course, ma'am," he said. "I would have suggested it myself, but I seem to have become accustomed to you and Lady Cavendish being inseparable, and I heard her at breakfast say that she means to spend the morning in the library writing letters."

"I hate writing letters," Lady Murdoch said amiably. "I would prefer to travel halfway across England to pay my friends a visit than to write one page to them."

"Quite so, ma'am," Winston said with a bow. "And I am sure that they are infinitely more gratified."

Lady Murdoch gestured for his arm to help hoist her to her feet. "So you see, young man," she said with a grunt when the mission had been accomplished, "you know what to expect when you and dear Sarah are married. You will never know when to expect me on your doorstep. And I usually make my visits extended ones. Otherwise, the journey seems hardly to have been worthwhile. Would you not agree?"

"Quite so," Winston muttered again.

Sarah could not quite suppress a gleam of enjoyment. It was so rare to see Win discomfited. But he was clearly rattled now. It had all started the evening before when the party had been about to go into the dining room. Win had been moving confidently toward her to lead her in when Lady Murdoch had yoo-hooed from across the room and indicated a rather red-faced Benjamin Fairlie.

"Oh, Sarah," she called, "do allow Mr. Fairlie to

take you in to dinner. He wishes to ask you himself but is afraid that you will reject him."

While Benjamin squirmed with visible mortification, Lady Murdoch smiled coquettishly at Win and announced that he would be granted the honor of leading her in. And once inside the dining room, she steered her unwilling escort to the opposite end of the table from that occupied by Sarah.

Later, in the drawing room, Winston crossed to Sarah's side while they both drank tea and suggested that they take a turn in the garden while the air still retained some of the heat of the day. But Lady Murdoch seemed to have ears everywhere.

"Oh, Lord Laing," she called, "you are never thinking of taking dear Sarah outside, are you? The evenings at this time of the year are much too chill, my dear sir. I really cannot allow it for all that I am not Sarah's mother and therefore do not have a maternal right to forbid her to do anything. But I am just a foolish old woman, you see, and dear Sarah has come to indulge my whims. Anyway, I really must beg your partnership in a hand of cards. Lord Fairlie has been trying this quarter of an hour to make up a table, and he lacks one player."

Winston looked incredulous for one unguarded moment, but his smile of great charm instantly took its place. "I should be delighted, ma'am," he said. "I perceive you are treating me as a son already. What greater honor could I wish for?"

When the game was over, much later in the evening, Lady Murdoch immediately called Sarah to her. Winston stayed for a while, but when it became obvious to him that he was not to have Sarah to himself that evening, he wandered off. For the half-hour before bedtime he sat on the window seat *tête-à-tête* with Hannah.

And now this morning it had started again. Cranwell and several of the gathered guests had decided to ride out to view the farms, the expedition that had been canceled the previous afternoon. Those who had de-

cided not to go seemed to have something with which
to occupy themselves. Sarah had no particular plan
and felt helpless before Win's suggestion that they go
walking. She knew beyond a doubt what he had in
mind. The events of the previous afternoon had merely
whetted his appetite.

But again Lady Murdoch overheard the invitation
and had chosen to assume that she was included in it.

They walked as far as the bridge, Lady Murdoch
leaning on Sarah's arm and moving at a snail's pace.
Sarah was convinced that they moved even more slowly
than usual. And she talked constantly. They stood on
the bridge for all of half an hour, spaced between the
graceful Grecian columns that supported the high roof,
leaning on the stone parapet. And even Sarah began
to feel boredom as her elderly cousin prosed on about
the house, the gardens, the hills, and the wonderful
hospitality of his grace. Sarah's eyes met those of Win
over the head of Lady Murdoch at one point, and he
pulled a face. But she refused to participate in the
silent communication. She smiled only slightly and
turned away to look down into the slow-moving water
beneath.

They made their slow way back to the house when it
must have already been long past the middle of the
morning. As they entered the hallway, Lady Murdoch
patted Sarah's arm and released it.

"Now you run along, dear," she said, not looking at
Winston to note the brightening look on his face, "and
fetch that green bonnet of yours to my room. You
know, the one that you have been talking about alter-
ing? I believe I have the very thing with which to trim
it. I found it last night and, 'Bless me,' I thought, 'if
that is not perfectly made for dear Sarah's bonnet.'
We just have time to make the alteration before
luncheon.''

Sarah turned to Winston and smiled. "You will excuse me?" she asked.

He took her hand and raised it to his lips. "I shall

look forward to seeing you in the transformed bonnet, my love," he said.

"Thank you so kindly for escorting us on that walk, Lord Laing," Lady Murdoch said graciously. "So stimulating. And it is so generous in you to think of inviting a slow old woman like me. Not but what I was once as slim and as spry as Sarah. But age slows one down, alas."

"You may have lost your youthful looks, ma'am," Winston said gallantly, "but they have been replaced by the handsomeness and character that develop with wisdom."

Lady Murdoch tittered.

"Now, my love," Lady Murdoch said ten minutes later when Sarah appeared in her room dutifully carrying the green bonnet, "I have been obliged to search my belongings for something with which we might trim that bonnet. Do you think these cherries from the bosom of my black satin dress will look anything like if we sew them beneath the brim over your ear like this?"

She pinned the bunch of bright red cherries in the chosen spot and watched while Sarah tried the bonnet on. "Indeed," she said in some surprise, "they look most charming, my love, though I never would have thought of them if I had not been forced to find something. Take it off. I shall find a needle and thread and have them sewn on in no time. I must write a letter before luncheon, too. Would you like to run back to your room, dear, and fetch some work or a book? I shall be poor company for the next hour, yet it must seem that we are busy together."

Sarah grinned at Lady Murdoch, whose face was bent over her workbox. She went toward her impulsively and hugged her. "Thank you, Mother dear," she said. "I love you so much I could squeeze the life out of you."

"There!" Lady Murdoch said. "Now look what you have made me do. I almost had this needle threaded.

Now I shall have to start all over again." She kept her head bent low over the needle as Sarah left the room.

Cranwell was apologetic at luncheon. He must use at least a few hours of the afternoon, he said, to visit his bailiff on business. His guests did not seem unduly perturbed. The Earl and Countess of Cavendish and Lord and Lady Fairlie were to pay a return visit to some neighbors who had called on them the afternoon before. The dowager Lady Cavendish and Lady Murdoch announced their intention of resting before tea. Most of the younger people, led by Fanny, decided to ride into the village a few miles distant. There was a Norman church there to look at and a graveyard full of ancient and interesting tombstones. And there was a cook shop where they could indulge themselves with cakes and pastries before riding home again.

Fanny invited Winston almost before anyone. She was sitting next to him at luncheon. And she smiled at him most engagingly, Sarah noticed from across the table. In fact, Fanny's general behavior since their arrival had shown a preference for Win. Poor Captain Penny, whose silent admiration she appeared to take much for granted, was not offered near as much of her attention. Sarah was once again almost glad of the betrothal between her and Win. Even though she did not now intend to honor it, its existence would still perhaps prevent Fanny from falling in love with him.

Fanny turned to Sarah at last and smiled warmly at her. "I know you do not enjoy riding, Miss Fifield," she said, "and there will be six miles of it altogether. Would you prefer to stay at home? I do know that you enjoy reading, and George has a splendid library. I do not believe you have seen it yet?"

"How rag-mannered you are, Fanny," Cranwell said sharply from the head of the table. "Perhaps Miss Fifield would like to ride rather than be doomed to a solitary afternoon in the library."

Fanny flushed and looked stricken as she turned back to Sarah, but Sarah was the first to speak.

"On the contrary, your grace," she said. "I am delighted to find that I will not offend anyone by remaining behind. Indeed, I should prefer to stay here."

She smiled at Fanny and turned back to the conversation she was having with Mr. Stonewall. He was disappointed that she would not be one of the riding party, but she laughed off his regrets and turned to a different topic. Inside, she was feeling a certain elation. Unexpectedly, she had been granted a whole afternoon to herself. It was a rare luxury these days. She frequently found herself looking back almost with nostalgia to those quiet days in her cottage when sometimes she saw no one but Dorothy for days at a time.

After everyone had left about his own business, Sarah planned her afternoon. She could go to the library and read, as Fanny had suggested. But it seemed such a waste of beautiful weather and lovely scenery. She could take a book and sit in the ornamental gardens. Yet she knew that she would not be able to concentrate on reading. There was just too much turmoil in her mind these days. She thought of the walk they had taken the previous day. Despite all the emotional events that had happened then, she could yet remember just how beautiful the valley and the house had looked and how lovely the hills and the trees themselves had been. She would walk up there again and see if she could draw some peace from the loneliness of her surroundings.

A half-hour later, Sarah stood on the little knoll where Fanny had taken Winston the day before. The view indeed looked like an artist's picture. Carefully placed trees on the slopes below framed the house and the bridge, emphasizing the classical symmetry of their lines. How wonderful it must be to look from here and know that the house was one's own home and all the land within sight too. She was glad it all belonged to George. It suited him so well, and she knew that it was not a possession he took for granted. He put a great deal of both work and love into his home. One could almost tell. There was a beauty about the place that had nothing to do with the merely picturesque. That building seemed more home than stately mansion. How could Hannah possibly feel otherwise?

Sarah strolled on upward until she was walking along the crest of the hill, looking down to the house on one side and rolling farmland on the other. Could this be all his too? But yes, it must be. Fanny had said that their nearest neighbors were five miles away. The nearest landowners, that was. The duke had numerous tenants, Sarah knew.

She turned eventually downward again, following a different path from the one by which she had ascended. This one led soon through a copse of trees, but she did not turn back. The path looked well worn, and the trees on the hillside did not form woods dense enough for anyone to get lost. She turned her face up to the early autumn sun, which shed warmth despite the coolness of the air. She took deep breaths. She felt relaxed for the first time in days. It was a great burden off her mind to have told Lady Murdoch. She could not now understand why she had not done so a long time before. And it was wonderful to know that she was alone yet safe here. Everyone was accounted for and far away.

It was as she was smiling over this last thought that Sarah suddenly became aware of the sound of hoofbeats behind her. She looked hastily back, but the horse was still hidden over the brow of the hill. She felt instant panic turn her insides to jelly. Win! Of course, he would have guessed what she would do. He knew she liked to walk when alone. He had caught her at it numerous times in the past. He had left the others on some pretext and was coming for her.

And she was completely alone, far from the house, far from Lady Murdoch. If she screamed as loudly as she could, no one would hear her. If she could not reach the cover of the trees before he came over the hill, she was lost. She would be ravished again.

Sarah began to run, the trees suddenly seeming a long way distant. But the uneven ground caused her to stumble. She began to sob and hurry onward, quite beside herself with terror. The sounds of the approaching horse were getting louder. She did not look back, but she knew finally that she was not going to reach safety. Win must be over the top of the hill already. He must have spotted her. He was even now riding down to catch her. She stumbled on, though she knew that to do so was pointless. She was sobbing with terror. She was almost at the first tree.

"Sarah," the rider called, "why are you running? What is it?"

"No," she wailed. "Please, no. Please."

"Sarah!" Cranwell flung himself from his saddle and let his horse go free. "What has happened? You are terrified. What is it?"

Sarah looked over her shoulder at last and saw who the rider was. "Oh," she said, pressing her closed fists against her mouth. But she was still distraught, unable to bring herself under control. Her eyes were wild, her cheeks tear-streaked.

Cranwell caught her by one arm. "What is it?" he asked again. "Were you frightened of footpads? You are on my land, Sarah. You need not fear that anyone will harm you here. You see, it is only me."

His free hand went to her other arm and he pulled her against him. Then he impatiently lifted the same hand to her chin, pulled loose the ribbon there, and tossed her bonnet to the ground. He cupped the back of her head and held it against his shoulder. He held her close and rocked her as she continued to sob wildly against him.

"Don't cry," he said, his mouth against her hair. "You are quite safe, Sarah. You are with me. There is nothing to fear. Can you not feel my arms about you? Do you think I would let anyone harm you?"

The sobs were beginning to hurt her chest. Sarah clutched the lapels of Cranwell's coat and buried her head more deeply against him. "I thought," she said. "I thought . . ." But she could get no farther.

"You thought what?" he asked gently against her ear.

But she could not reply. Her hands were trembling on his lapels, and indeed her whole body shook against his.

"There is nothing to fear now, my love," he said. "I have you and I shall see that you are safe. I shall hold you until you realize that you need not be afraid."

"George," she said. "Oh, George, I thought—"

"Hush," he said. "It does not matter. Hush. You do not have to explain yourself to me."

He held her while her sobs gradually subsided and her body stopped shaking. He stroked his fingers through her hair, which had come free of its knot, and kissed first the top of her head, then her ear, her wet cheek, and her eyes.

"I must dry my eyes," she said shakily, feeling around in the pocket of her pelisse, her eyes lowered.

"Here, use mine," he said, and he lifted her chin and dried her eyes and cheeks himself with a large linen handkerchief. "You never have one when you need one, do you, Sarah?"

She laughed shakily and took the handkerchief to blow her nose. She stuffed it into her pocket and then felt all the utter impossibility of looking back up into his face. They still stood almost touching each other. Her heart began to pound so heavily that she could feel it in her throat. They both stood very still, unnaturally still.

"Sarah," he said very quietly. One hand reached out to touch her hair again, and the other hand went beneath her chin to lift it.

She looked up into his searching blue eyes so close to her own. "George." Her lips formed his name, though she was unaware of any sound coming from her mouth.

And then it was impossible for either of them to say anything. Their arms went around each other and their mouths met, searching, urgent, demanding. Their bodies, pressed together, caught fire. Their hands explored, caressed, excited. Sarah's heart was beating wildly against his chest. She ached and ached to be closer, closer. She wanted him, wanted him now, inside her. She opened her mouth to his questing tongue, moaned against its welcome, tantalizing invasion. Not just this. More than this. Oh, please, more than this.

"Please, George. Oh, please, my love. More than this. More than this."

His mouth was against the pulse at her throat. His hands had undone the buttons of her pelisse and thrown it to the ground. Now they were at her breasts, molding their fullness, caressing them, bringing an almost painful tautness to them.

"My love," he was saying against the side of her face, into her ear. "Oh, my love, I cannot live any longer without you. I need you. I need you, Sarah. I want you, my love."

He reached down suddenly and scooped her up into his arms. He strode toward the trees and amongst them, away from the path. He knelt before releasing her, and laid her down on the longish coarse grass. They gazed into each other's eyes, passion eliminating any embarrassment as he stripped off his coat and lifted her head to set it beneath.

And then he was kissing her again, the upper part of his body across hers, his hands tangled in her hair, his breath warm against her cheek. He eased his weight aside so that he might caress her breast again, and then he groaned and reached down to pull up her dress and remove her undergarments. Sarah lifted her hips to aid him and looked through the haze of her desire into his face above her.

She lay still and watched him as his hand caressed her: her thighs, her stomach, up under her dress to her breasts, down between her legs. She felt desire grow in her until the ache of wanting him grew unbearable. Her breasts were painful beneath the occasional touch of his hand. Her womb throbbed with unfulfilled emptiness. His hand, the touch of his body, the look in his eyes could no longer satisfy. She closed her eyes and arched toward his hand, which was close, close. But not close enough. She turned her face into his shoulder and moaned.

A lifetime seemed to pass while he fumbled with his own clothing, a lifetime of longing, which was nevertheless not unpleasurable. He was going to take away the emptiness. He was going to stop the ache. Soon he would satisfy her. Soon. Now!

Cranwell had covered her body with his own, first placing his hands beneath her to cushion her against the hard ground. She parted her legs to accommodate him. And he pushed inward, meeting immediately that throbbing ache, making it many times more acute so that she had to lift herself against him, twist against him, urging him with frenzied hands and hips to thrust into her with ever deeper and faster strokes. It was becoming unbearable. Oh, dear God, she would not be able to endure it much longer. It was getting beyond her. It was—

"George!"

All her passion shattered against him. She jerked convulsively and clutched him to her, terrified by the power of her own release, opening her eyes wide in the shock of discovering that such ecstasy was possible. And she pressed her head against his shoulder, closing her eyes tightly again as she realized afresh who had opened this world of wonders for her, with whom she lay and loved.

Cranwell wrapped his arms tightly around her as his body relaxed in the aftermath of its own passion. He did not move out of her or away from her until her trembling had stopped. Then he carefully disengaged himself and lifted himself away. He lay on his back on the ground beside her, not touching her. He was soon aware from the sound of her breathing that she slept.

He clasped his hands behind his head and stared up through the branches of the tree above him to the sky. He could easily sleep too. He felt relaxed and drowsy. But he did not want to sleep. He wanted to feel. He turned his head and looked at Sarah. She lay on her back still, her lips slightly parted in sleep. Her face was flushed, her bright hair in wild disarray around her face and over her shoulders. One arm lay across her waist. The other was flung out toward him but did not quite touch him. She looked beautiful. He had never before seen her asleep.

He tried to feel guilt, disgust with himself, anger with her, shame at his own lack of restraint. Surely he would feel all these emotions soon. He was betrothed to one woman and had just made love to another. A guest in his home. A woman who had been terrified not long before that someone was about to do her harm. His former wife. A woman whom he had divorced for fornication and adultery. A woman now herself betrothed to someone else. He recited the list slowly and deliberately to himself.

Soon enough surely he would feel satisfyingly guilty. But now he could not. Now his body knew that it had achieved perfect fulfillment. He was physically contented as he had not been for a long time. He had not had a woman, in fact, since Sarah. He had even felt uneasy about the fact that he had not desired another in all that time. Now he knew that there was nothing at all wrong with him. It was merely that, having once had Sarah, he could never possibly desire another woman in the same way. Now he had had her again and he was content. Happy, even.

He turned his head away from her and looked upward again. There was no point at all in trying to deny the truth. At the moment he did not even wish to do so. He loved Sarah, with all the passion and tenderness he had felt before he knew the truth about her. And it was not a renewal of that love; it was a continuation. He had never stopped loving her. One might be disappointed in a loved one, disgusted perhaps, horrified even, but one could not stop loving. "Love is not love which alters when it alteration finds." Now, where had he heard that before? It sounded like something Shakespeare might have written. It did not matter.

He loved Sarah. He verbalized the words very deliberately in his mind, savored them, repeated them. He waited for the denials to come, the protests. Nothing. His mind could not deny the truth. This was a strange, mad moment. It could not be true, of course. Soon—this evening—he would return to his senses. But for now it was the truth. He loved her. And he would revel in this temporary truth. It is very sweet to love, to be able to turn one's head and see one's loved one asleep and flushed from a recently satisfied passion.

One's wife. That was why he did not feel guilty, was it? She was his wife. One did not feel guilty making love to one's wife. It was natural. Right. He had just had marital relations with Sarah for the first time in four years. He was not going to feel guilty about that. She was not his wife, of course. He had divorced her. In a few months' time they would both be married to others. But in one way, in the way of the heart, she was his wife, his friend, his lover, and always would be. But he would never be sorry for this afternoon. He steeled himself against the return of rational thought. He would not allow himself to regret it.

It had been good for her too. He must never look back and doubt that, wonder perhaps if he had taken advantage of her when she had been in an emotional state. She had wanted him with every bit as much passion as he had felt. She had urged him on with both her body and her voice. She had even called him her love, he remembered. And there had been no misinterpreting her intense pleasure at the end of it all. She could not have faked that.

Perhaps many men had possessed her. He did not care to explore that thought at the moment. But there was no doubt of the fact that she had been wholly with him that afternoon. It was he she had made love to, not just any man. It was his name she had cried at the end. She had some feeling for him after all. Sometimes he wondered if she had ever felt anything for him beyond contempt. But she had loved him that afternoon, with her body even if not with her soul.

Cranwell turned his head to watch his sleeping wife. Her head had fallen over to the side, facing him. It was as if she felt his eyes on her. Her own opened almost immediately, looking into his vacantly for a few seconds and then with a returning awareness. She did not move or say anything for a while. They lay side by side, not touching, gazing into each other's eyes.

She spoke finally, very distinctly and unhurriedly. She did not look away from his eyes. "I am not sorry," she said, "and I am not ashamed. Perhaps you are. Without a doubt you soon will be. But I do not care. I am not and I will not be. I shall set the memory of this beside the memory of our wedding night. And that is precious little happiness on which to live for a lifetime. But I shall do it. Only don't ask me to feel ashamed, George. I have done with shame. I am who I am, and I make apology for the fact no longer."

She sat up and looked around her. She gathered up her discarded garments, got to her feet, and walked away in the direction from which they had come. She did not look back.

Cranwell stayed where he was. He had not moved at all. He still lay with his hands clasped behind his head. He considered going after her to protect her from whatever it was that had caused her terror. But no. She was over it now, and really there was nothing on his own property that she need fear. She must have been merely startled and had given in to an irrational panic.

He was still in the grip of the massive lassitude that had succeeded their lovemaking. He did not wish to move. If he did so, he might shake off forever this dream he was experiencing. She loved him. It must be so. She had described this afternoon's coupling and their wedding night as "precious little happiness" in her life. Even then she had loved him. Physically, at least. That night had not been such a mockery as he had always feared. She must love him. Despite every-thing, despite her behavior before and after their marriage, despite her behavior of the afternoon before with Bowen, she loved him.

The situation could not possibly be that simple, of course. There were thousands of unanswered questions, hundreds of obstacles in the way of their love flourishing again, numerous facts which made a reunion totally impossible. He could not recall a single one of these things at the moment, but he was quite aware that they existed to throw cold water on his joy. Soon. Probably very soon. But not quite yet. For now he could lie here and dream. He could close his eyes and see Sarah again, that bright titian hair loose over her shoulders, silky to the touch, her green eyes heavy with desire, her lips soft and parted for his kiss. He could feel her softness, the curve of her waist and hips, the fullness of her breasts. And he could feel the soft, hot depths of her. His lover! His only love. His wife.

The Duke of Cranwell slept.

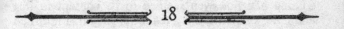

18

THE NEIGHBORS and their two young adult daughters returned to Montagu House with the Earl and Countess of Cavendish, on invitation from Cranwell. They were to stay for dinner and the evening. Fanny suggested that they celebrate the extra company with a dance in the drawing room. Hannah's aunt, Lady Phyllis Wright, would play for them on the pianoforte, she was sure.

Lady Wright was applied to anxiously by several of the young people. She readily agreed to play. She was quite used to doing so, she said, coming as she did from a neighborhood where there were many lively young people who were forever wanting to dance.

Sarah had sat at dinner with Joshua Stonewall and unconsciously charmed him with her glowing beauty, her shining eyes, and her sprightly conversation. He had always thought her uncommonly lovely, but tonight she was quite breathtakingly beautiful. Was it that fiancé who had put that glow there? he wondered jealously. It was hardly surprising. Laing was easily as handsome as she was lovely. But it did not somehow seem fair. Why should the beautiful always win the beautiful? What did they leave for the very ordinary, like himself?

He was not even sure that Laing quite deserved Miss Fifield. Joshua suspected him of having a roving eye. He had spent much of the afternoon with Lady Fanny, and it was hard to say which of the two had been more intent on flirting with the other. That young lady, in fact, quite deserved a good spanking for seemingly trying to come between another lady and

295

her betrothed. But how could Laing behave so? Lady Fanny was pretty and vivacious, but she could not come close to Miss Fifield in either looks or breeding.

Laing had not even seemed to be content to flirt with Cran's sister. During tea, after they had returned from their ride, he had sat in the window seat with Lady Hannah, somewhat apart from the rest of the group. And they had seemed to be deep in earnest conversation. Cran had not come in until much later. Miss Fifield had come in halfway through tea and seated herself beside that elderly cousin who seemed to be so fond of her. Laing had not moved even then, and she had not seemed perturbed. She had hardly seemed to notice him, in fact. But she had looked wildly happy.

Well, Joshua thought with a silent sigh, perhaps their love for each other was so deep that they did not need to live in each other's pockets all the time. He just wished he had the chance to bring that glow to her face. He would not leave her to her elderly companion while he went off and flirted with other young ladies.

Fanny, too, had noticed the change in Sarah. She had eyed her surreptitiously in the drawing room at teatime while apparently entertaining Captain Penny, Barbara Tenby, and Allan Wright. She had watched her during dinner along the length of the table. She approached her in the blue salon after dinner, where they took tea while the carpet in the drawing room was being rolled back and the furniture moved out of the way.

"Hello, Miss Fifield," she said. "Did you like the library? I must admit it is not my favorite room, but I have been told that it has an unusually excellent collection of books. And George spends a great deal of time there."

"I am afraid I did not go there," Sarah said, "though I greatly look forward to seeing it. I went walking."

Fanny looked a little nonplussed for a moment. "Oh, did you?" she said. "Where did you go?"

"I walked up into the hills again," Sarah said. "The air was so lovely that I could not bear to stay indoors. And the view is glorious."

"You went alone?" Fanny asked.

"Yes." Sarah flushed suddenly. "I have always enjoyed walking alone. Sometimes when one is with someone else, one is so busy talking that one forgets the beauty of the surroundings."

Fanny looked closely at her companion, at her shining eyes, the flush that was still visible on her cheekbones. "George usually rides over the hills when he goes to the bailiff's house," she said. "Did you see him?"

Sarah's flush deepened. "Er, no," she said. "No. I did not see anyone."

"How silly of me to ask," Fanny said. "George did not arrive home until almost an hour after you."

She watched Sarah swallow rather painfully and concentrate her attention on her teacup. Then Fanny's eyes strayed across the room to her brother, who had just entered the room with the gentlemen and was talking to Hannah's mother. He was his usual immaculate, grave self. To a sister who knew him well, though, there was perhaps something about his eyes. A half-smile flitted across Fanny's face for one moment.

"Did you enjoy the ride to the village?" Sarah asked.

"Oh, immensely," Fanny said. "When the vicar saw such a large party disappear inside his church, he came to conduct us himself, and he told us all about the graves. There were so many interesting stories, half of which I had never heard before."

"A Norman church! It must have been interesting," Sarah said.

"I do hope I did not offend you by suggesting that you stay at home to read," Fanny said in a rush. "I did not mean that you would not be welcome to come. I merely thought you would not enjoy so long a ride."

Sarah reached out and touched the girl's hand. "Don't feel guilty," she said, "just because Geor . . . your brother reprimanded you. You were quite right. And I would not have missed my walk for worlds." She flushed again and looked away.

Winston was walking toward them, a cup of tea in his hand. He was looking particularly handsome, Sarah thought dispassionately, in gold satin knee breeches and coat, sequined white waistcoat and matching stockings and linen. He succeeded in making all the other men look very ordinary.

"How could I resist joining the two most lovely ladies in the room?" he said with his customary charming smile as he approached them. "May I?" He pulled up a chair without waiting for an answer and seated himself facing them both.

Fanny smiled dazzlingly. "Are you not tired after our ride, sir?" she asked.

His eyebrows rose. "When the company was so charming?" he said. "Lady Fanny, I swear the miles seemed like so many yards."

Fanny giggled.

"May I be permitted to say that that particular shade of pink suits you to perfection?" he said. "And you, my love." He turned to Sarah. "What can I say? You look more dazzling tonight than I have seen you, I believe. May I hope that my presence has something to do with your good looks?" He smiled confidently at her.

"Thank you, Win," she said. "You are always so complimentary."

She was feeling alarmed. There seemed to be a very definite attraction between Win and Fanny. On Fanny's part, anyway. One could never be sure of Win's feelings, if indeed he had any. Should she have forced herself to go on that ride this afternoon? She had not worried because the party was to be a fairly large one. But she knew from experience that Win could often maneuver one into semiprivacy. Had she given him a whole afternoon's opportunity to win his way into Fanny's affections? She was just a young and innocent girl. She would be no match for his practiced dalliance.

It was her concern for Fanny that made her accept Win's suggestion that they stroll in the garden for a few minutes before the dancing started.

"You look rather flushed, love," he said. "It will be cool outside."

Sarah smiled fleetingly at Lady Murdoch as she passed her on the way from the room, but she did not stop. She ran up the stairs to fetch a warm woolen shawl.

"At last!" Winston said on a sigh of relief when they had stepped out into the courtyard and the door closed behind them. "What on earth has happened to that old tabby, Sarah? One would swear you were a sixteen-year-old virgin all of a sudden. It is as much as I can do to be civil to her."

"Cousin Adelaide?" she said with a smile. "She has grown very fond of me, Win. She never had children of her own, you see, and she has begun to see herself as my mama. She wishes to see me properly chaperoned until my marriage."

"Heaven help us if she keeps up the illusion and starts to visit us every few months when we are married," Winston said. "I doubt if I shall be able to stand it, Sarah."

"You know, Win," she said, "I never really knew my mother, either. I can sympathize with her. I have begun to think of her, too, almost as if she were my mama."

"Sarah!" he said incredulously, and laughed. "You are bamming me. I don't believe I have ever met anyone quite so excessively vulgar."

Sarah said nothing.

Winston laughed again. "We could tell her a thing or two, couldn't we, Sarah?" he said. "Playing the careful chaperone now is rather like closing the stable door after the horse has bolted, is it not?"

Sarah did not smile. She merely held lightly to his arm and continued their slow progress across the lawn that stretched around two sides of the house.

"I am still smarting from the frustration of yesterday

afternoon," Winston said, bending his head close to hers and covering her hand with his own. "Cranwell's timing could not have been worse. Though perhaps it could have, at that. It would have been hopelessly embarrassing had he turned up five minutes later, would it not?"

Sarah bit her lip.

"Let's walk across the bridge," he said. "I think we must have a clear half-hour before the old tabby raises the alarm. We can satisfy ourselves in that time, can we not?"

"Oh no, Win," she said, pulling back on his arm. "Not now. We are both all dressed up for the evening. I have had my hair dressed. We really could not return all disheveled."

"How delightfully prudish you are, Sarah," he said, squeezing her hand and grinning down into her earnest face. "Did you imagine I meant a tumble on the ground? There are other ways of doing what we want to do without emerging looking all rumpled, you know. Come, let me show you."

"No, Win," she said firmly, "you know it is not part of our agreement. I want to wait until our wedding night."

He stopped walking and pulled her into his arms. Sarah's flesh cringed from contact with his chest and his thighs. Her head was bent back so that she was forced to look up into his face.

"Ah, Sarah," he said. "Always the tease. I see that you want to be persuaded. Well, my love, as you know well, I am always willing to oblige. Take as long as you like to admit that you want to come across the bridge with me."

He grinned, and Sarah felt the old nausea intensified as his head bent toward hers. She supposed she would have to submit to his kiss, at least, and probably to some wandering of his hands. There were still four days of their visit left, and she must keep his attention away from Fanny as much as possible and avoid any public unpleasantness that might spoil the house party for George.

"Blast!" Winston said when his lips were a mere breath away from her own. He looked over her head, swung her to his side again, and smiled. "I see that we have set a trend," he called pleasantly across the lawn.

When Sarah looked, she could see Faith Wright and Samuel Tenby, Fanny and Captain Penny walking toward them. There was another couple also approaching at some distance.

Faith giggled. "Naughty, Lord Laing," she called gaily.

Fanny was laughing too. "Would you believe that Lady Murdoch just about shooed us out-of-doors like a crowd of chickens?" she said. "She insisted that the air would add color to our cheeks and give us energy for the dancing."

"And just last night," Samuel added, "I seem to remember her saying that Miss Fifield should not go out-of-doors in the evening air at this time of year. It is deuced chilly tonight."

"Sarah and I were just going to stroll to the bridge and back before going indoors again," Winston said. "Would anyone care to join us?"

It seemed that everyone cared to join them. Sarah could almost have laughed. She and Win walked a little ahead of the others, but she could relax now. Those chattering young people behind them would ensure that he did no more than talk.

"Win," she said when she was sure they were out of earshot of the others, "you have not forgotten our agreement, have you?"

"You mean about not lying with you until our wedding night?" he asked. "It seems to me that it does not matter whether I remember or not, Sarah. The whole world seems to be in conspiracy against us."

"No, I did not mean just that," she said. "I mean the money and our going away together and staying away from the duke for the rest of our lives."

He grinned. "That was your agreement, not mine,

love," he said. "It was you and Cranwell who worked that out, I believe."

"But of course you are involved, Win," she said. "You have the money, after all."

"Safely in my keeping," he said. "Given unconditionally, I believe, Sarah, as a token of your love?"

"Win," she said sharply, "you are not planning to cheat me, are you?"

"What a little worrier you are, Sarah," he said. "Whatever do you mean by that?"

"I don't like the way you have been flirting with Fanny," she said bluntly. "You are not thinking of maybe offering for her after all, are you, Win?"

He grinned down at her. "Your green eyes suit you, love," he said. "You are frantic with jealousy, are you not? What if I did marry her, Sarah? We would have double the money or more. And you would know that you are the one I will always love. What does it matter whether you are wife or mistress? They are both only labels, after all. And let's face it, love. Your reputation is already in shreds."

"Oh!" Sarah said. She was almost bursting with fury but was aware—as he undoubtedly was—that there were six people not very far behind them. "You *are* planning to cheat me. You are planning to marry her."

He laughed outright. "Sarah," he said, "a lifetime is not going to be long enough to appreciate you. You are quite impossibly adorable when you are angry. I really cannot resist provoking you. I shall say this, love, and I think I am safe in making it a solemn promise. I will never marry Lady Fanny Montagu or even make her an offer. Will that satisfy you, you little termagant?"

Sarah brought her fury under control with effort. "I am not sure I trust you, Win," she said. "Leave her alone. She is too young and impressionable to deal with someone like you."

"And you are old enough and experienced enough to handle me to perfection?" he said. "You know just how to excite a man's desires, my love, do you not? Damnation! Look at those inviting trees just the other side of the river. And we have to be trailed by an escort of six!"

This time Sarah could not restrain her own laughter.

Back inside the house everyone had moved to the drawing room, where a large space had been cleared for dancing, and Lady Wright was practicing on the pianoforte. Sarah sat beside Lady Murdoch and smiled at her.

"Thank you," she said.

"For what, dear?" Lady Murdoch asked. "All the young people were looking like wilting flowers. It was clear that all they needed was a breath of fresh air. I merely pointed out to them how sensible you and Lord Laing had been."

"I thank you on their behalf, then," Sarah said.

Lady Murdoch leaned slightly toward her, not a smile on her face. "Are we driving him crazy?" she asked.

"I think," Sarah said with equal seriousness, "that he is in fear and trembling that you mean it when you say that you like to make frequent and lengthy visits to your friends."

"Ah," said her elderly cousin, "then I shall have to assure Lord Laing whenever I may that I consider him my particular friend."

The evening began with a minuet. Sarah could remember learning the steps when she was a girl, but she had been told that the dance was old-fashioned. It was lovely, though, she thought now, and suited very well the grace of Montagu Hall. She could just imagine the state ballroom filled with ladies and gentlemen in the fashions of a few decades before—wideskirted gowns and tall wigs, frock-coats and buckled shoes. Even today, with modern fashions, she felt, it would be like a dream to be at a ball in that apartment.

She danced with Lord Justin Tenby, George's uncle, and found his stately manner and polished conversation delightful. One could tell easily that he was closely related to George. He might have been her uncle too, she thought with something of a pang. But she refused to dwell on the thought. She intended to enjoy the evening, and did so, dancing every dance with a different partner.

Joshua Stonewall insisted on having some waltzes played, although several of those present protested that they had never learned the steps. There was almost nothing to learn, Joshua said, and proceeded to demonstrate with Sarah as a partner. She was laughing after a couple of minutes. Indeed, he was right; the dance was easy to learn. But there was something very embarrassing about whirling around a room with a man's hand at one's waist and his other hand in one's own.

"I knew it, ma'am," he said to her after the short demonstration while everyone else chose partners and took to the dance floor to try out the new steps. "You have a natural grace. I would scarcely have known that I had anyone in my arms if my eyes had not constantly beheld your beauty."

Sarah laughed. "It was little short of miraculous, sir," she said, "that I did not tread on your feet. Then you would have known that you had a partner."

She was enjoying the evening as she had not enjoyed any event since that morning in Bath when Lady Murdoch had discovered her long-lost friend. It seemed perfectly natural when Cranwell came up to her before the third waltz to ask her to dance with him. He bowed formally and looked grave, but Sarah placed her hand in his without hesitation and even smiled.

He felt very right as a waltzing partner. Since he was not much taller than she, her hand did not have to reach very high to rest on his shoulder, solid beneath her touch though he looked so slender. His hand was spread firmly behind her waist so that she could lean back against it, confident that he would guide her safely through the steps. She looked up into his face. He was looking back, his expression quite unreadable. But she did not think it was hostile. Surely he would not have asked her to dance had that been so. They looked at each other quite openly for fully half a minute before Sarah smiled slightly, felt herself blush, and looked down. But she did not feel uncomfortable. She refused to do so. This was her magical day, and she was not going to allow her own feelings to spoil it.

"You waltz well, Sarah," he said.

"Yes," she agreed, "Mr. Stonewall told me the same thing, and he is something of an expert, I think." She grinned.

"What were you afraid of?" he asked very quietly a minute or so later.

Sarah shook her head. "Nothing, really," she said, and blushed hotly at this reference to the afternoon. "I was merely startled."

"You do not have to be afraid on my land," he said. "There is no one here to harm you."

Sarah said nothing. She kept her eyes on the buttons of his silver waistcoat.

"Unless you see me as a threat," he said. "Did I harm you, Sarah?"

"Oh, no," she said quickly, looking up earnestly into his blue eyes. "No. You did not harm me."

He nodded, and they continued to stare into each other's eyes, unaware for a while of their surroundings.

That one dance was all she saw of him for the rest of the evening. She saw almost as little of Winston. He danced with all the cousins and with Fanny twice. And he danced with Hannah once and sat talking with her during three of the other dances. Sarah, noticing this, was very thankful that Hannah at least was safely betrothed. Otherwise, she would have been as worried about her as she was about Fanny. Perhaps not, though. There was nothing flirtatious in Hannah's manner with Win—nor in his with her, for that matter. But they seemed to find a great deal to say to each other.

Winston made sure that he had the last dance of the evening with Sarah, yet another waltz. Most of the young people, having learned the steps, decided that they enjoyed the dance greatly and demanded more and more of the indefatigable Lady Wright.

"You look as fresh now as you did at the start of the evening, my love," Winston said, "and quite lovely. What is it about you tonight? Is your hair different? Is that a new gown?"

"It is probably just the country air that is agreeing with me, Win," Sarah said.

Winston grinned. "I noticed old Cranwell dancing with you earlier," he said. "Was he giving you a scold, Sarah, suggesting that you leave early, perhaps?"

"He would never be so discourteous to a guest," Sarah said, flushing.

"Ah, no. Cranwell the cold fish, always meticulously correct," he said. "He would probably like to consign you to Hades but feels obliged to ask you to waltz instead."

Sarah did not answer his grin.

"Since you do not seem at all tired, Sarah," he continued, bending his head closer to hers, "shall we put your energy to some use?"

"Whatever do you mean, Win?" she asked, looking up sharply at him.

"I shall come to your room when everyone is safely settled for the night," he said. "It seems to be the only way we can ensure that no one will interrupt us at the last moment."

"You most certainly will not!" Sarah said. "We will not repay hospitality by behaving like that, Win."

"Nonsense!" he said. "We are betrothed, love. Whom are we like to offend by spending the night in the same bed? And I must have you soon, Sarah. I really cannot wait until next week. Be ready for me."

Sarah was frantically trying to remember whether there was a lock on her door.

"I want to see you without all the trappings," Winston whispered into her ear. "And I want to touch you, Sarah, all over. I think you have been too long without me. You seem almost as nervous as you were that first time, when you were a virgin." He chuckled.

"Do you remember, love? You were so nervous I almost had to hold you down. You soon learned what delights you had been so afraid of, though, did you not?"

"Not tonight, Win," Sarah said. "I will not allow it. Don't come to me. There is a lock on my door, and I shall be using it." It was a bluff. She really did not know if she told the truth or not. Was there a lock?

For once the veneer of his charm slipped. "You know, Sarah," he said, "when you decide to be coy with me, you have to remember that there are limits beyond which it is not wise to push me. If you are not willing to grant me your favors, there are any number of women who would be only too delighted to do so. I could name one or two in this house right now. Remember that after we are married, my love. Deny me your bed then, and you may find that I shall be reluctant to climb into it at all."

He was speaking very quietly, but even so Sarah gripped his shoulder more tightly. "Don't let us quarrel here, Win," she said. "Someone will notice soon."

His manner changed immediately. He smiled full into her eyes, his own crinkling at the corners. "You are a tease, Sarah," he said. "You see your power over me? Be warned, though. I am not made of iron, you know."

There *was* a lock on the door. Sarah was very thankful to find the heavy bolt. Had it not been there she would have gone along to Lady Murdoch's room and slept on the daybed there. But she did not really want to do that. Ever since the afternoon she had been looking forward to this part of the day. She had been longing to be alone at last so that she could let her mind go back to the events of the afternoon and assess fully what had happened.

She undressed without the assistance of a maid and brushed out her hair. Then she sat on top of the bed, her knees drawn up under her chin, and let her eyes wander over the green hangings of her bed and the bright foliage and birds on the Chinese wallpaper. She would always remember these few days and this room. Surely it was the most attractive bedchamber in the house, as Fanny had told her. She liked to think that George had deliberately assigned it to her, though more likely he had left the distribution of rooms to his housekeeper.

But he did have some feelings for her. He did not hate her, despite what she had done to him in the past, despite what she had done to him in the last week, taking his money and failing to honor her promise to take herself out of his life forever.

He had shown real concern for her that afternoon when she had been so beside herself fearing that he was Win. He had held her, soothed her, wiped away her tears.

He had made love to her! Sarah hugged her knees closer and rested her forehead aginst them. Just so many hours ago she and George had made love to each other. She relived the experience moment by moment. It had been perfect, beautiful. Right. Yes, it had been right. There had been nothing ugly or sordid about it, though it should have been both, happening as it had among the trees on top of the hill, each of them betrothed to someone else. But it had been beautiful.

If she had ever doubted the fact, she had only had to feel his lips on hers again to know that it was with him that she belonged. He was her only love, her lover, her husband. Yes, he was her husband. She had married him, vowed to love, honor, and obey him until death. And they were both still alive. She had never broken those vows. She was still married to him. No divorce could ever cancel those vows. Not for her, anyway.

Nothing would ever make her believe that what they had done that afternoon was wrong. It had been very right. She knew he must hate her in many ways. She knew he would regret what had happened, perhaps come to hate her even more for causing him to behave

that way. She knew, at least, that what had happened
would change nothing essential in their relationship.
He would marry Hannah before Christmas, and at the
end of this week she would warn him about Win,
break off her engagement, and honor her agreement
never to see him again. She would honor her vows in
that last, final way. But none of what they had done
had been wrong.

For the space of a few minutes they had loved each
other totally. She knew her own feelings; and she
would not doubt his. It had not been just lust on his
part. It had not been. It was not just a woman he had
been lying with up on the hill. It was she, Sarah. He
had used her name more than once. And he had made
love to her, worshiped her with his hands and his
body. He had not just taken her for his own satisfaction. She had felt worshiped. She had felt loved. And
with him she had reached a world of sensual delight
that she had not even dreamed of. And he had shared
it. She knew that. She had been in a world of ecstasy,
but it had not been a private world. He had been there
with her. They had known each other both physically
and in the way that only the heart can understand.
Words could not express it, or even thoughts.

George had loved her. It was a relative emotion, of
course. There was a great deal in her that he must
dislike, despise, hate. But there, at the core of being,
where meanings had their root, he loved her. He
always had and always would. Just as she would always love him, though in her case there was nothing to
sully the feeling.

She had meant those words she spoke to him after
she woke to find him beside her and looking at her.
She would never regret what had happened, and she
would never feel ashamed. She would treasure the
memory for the rest of her life. And somehow that life
was no longer a dreadful thing to look forward to. It
was true that it would contain a great deal of loneliness and heartache. A great emptiness yawned somewhere in the pit of her stomach already when she let

her mind touch on the knowledge that after this week she must never see George again. And soon she would have the added pain of knowing that he had another wife, the vows he had made her past history, no longer existent.

But it would not be a dreadful life. It would have dignity. She had meant it, too, when she told him that she was done with shame. She had done dreadful things in the past. She had made him share in her sin. But somehow she had atoned for that past. She had suffered. She was going to see to it that George's family did not suffer from the fiendishness of Win. And she was going to make it possible for him to forget her existence. He had made love to her that afternoon, almost in recognition of the fact that she was no longer soiled, untouchable. In some intangible way he had cleansed her, restored her self-respect, her confidence in her own basic goodness.

And for that, more than anything else, she would love him for the rest of her days. His courtesy, his gentleness during the evening had been like one extra bouquet. She refused to feel sad or lonely or depressed. Not yet. For tonight, perhaps for a few more days even, she was going to revel in the glow of knowing herself loved. She felt clean again, whole.

Sarah smiled and clasped her knees even tighter. She would not go to sleep. Not all night. It would be such a waste to sleep.

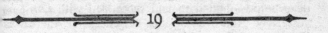

19

CRANWELL WAS riding back to the house from the south. It was still early; he doubted that many of his guests had yet breakfasted, though he had been up for several hours. The harvest had started today, and he had gone to watch his laborers going to the fields to begin. It was always his favorite time of the year. He had itched to throw off his coat, roll up his sleeves, and join them. Instead, he had merely stood at the gate greeting each worker by name, listening good-naturedly to the teasing over his elegant attire. He was on good enough terms with his men that they felt at liberty occasionally to tease.

It was certainly not the right time to have houseguests. If he had been wise, he would have thought of this party as soon as the Bath scheme was suggested. By now, he would be free again to follow his own inclination. But then, he thought, if he had not gone to Bath, he would not have seen Sarah again.

And would that have mattered? Would it not be a thousand times better if he had never set eyes on her again? A few days before he would have answered without hesitation in the affirmative. Had things changed so much since? He was still waiting for the onslaught of guilt feelings over what had happened the afternoon before.

With his mind he could feel guilty. He had divorced Sarah four years before for behavior that could never be tolerated by any decent man. Even if she had changed, there were still basically those facts against her. And much of the evidence of the last couple of weeks suggested that she had not changed a great

deal. She had defrauded him of a large sum of money
and failed miserably to keep her side of the bargain.
She had been attempting to seduce her betrothed two
days before—and then had succeeded with *him* just
yesterday. And even besides her character, there was
the fact that she was betrothed, to be married within
the next week or so.

And he was betrothed to a young girl who did not
deserve to be deceived. She was here at his home with
her parents and several of her relatives. And he had
spent part of the previous afternoon up on the hill
making love to another of his guests.

Yes, it was very easy to list all the facts that should
make him feel guilty. The trouble was, he could not
feel shame. Last evening he had not been able to
withdraw his attention from Sarah. He had been consumed by jealousy when she had gone outside with
Bowen, had sighed with relief when Lady Murdoch
had suggested that more of the young people go outside too. He had been constantly aware of her all
evening and had not been able to resist asking her to
waltz with him once. And just to touch her again had
been sweet agony.

He had expected the reaction to come sometime
during the night. Then, surely, he would realize the
enormity of what he had done. Instead, he had lain
awake for half the night thinking about her, reliving
their lovemaking of the afternoon. And he could not
find anything ugly about what had happened. It should
repulse him that he had slept with a woman who gave
herself willingly to any man she fancied—or who had
used to do so, anyway. But he could only remember
how she had clung to him, surrendered herself to him,
urged him on to the climax, and called his name as she
reached what could not have been a feigned release.

He had spent so many years feeling humiliated by
his memories of her. He had always persuaded himself
that she had despised him from the start. There was
nothing in his person, he had felt, to attract someone
of Sarah's extraordinary beauty. She must have laughed

at his devotion and passion. His pride had been restored yesterday. She clearly had been attracted by him. There was something about him, after all, that could arouse a very powerful passion in her.

And it had not been purely physical. He still could not quite explain it to himself, but he knew that there had been more than a meeting of their bodies. Perhaps the best way he could explain it to himself was to say that their lovemaking had been a marriage act. They had become one for the space of a few minutes.

He could not feel ashamed. And now he was riding homeward with an eagerness to see her again. How would she look at him this morning? Would she look with that bright-eyed expression she had had last night, the flushed cheeks? Would she look with the aloofness with which she had treated him for most of the last couple of weeks? Would she look with hostility, distaste? Would she avoid his eyes altogether?

Cranwell slowed the pace of his horse. He must think about this matter. He must not behave like an infatuated schoolboy. And he must definitely not act in a manner that would arouse anyone's suspicions. And he certainly owed Hannah more of his time than he had granted her in the last few days. He must force his attention away from Sarah.

It was going to be difficult to do. He wanted Sarah. He wanted to talk to her. He wanted to show her more of his house. He wanted to be with her this afternoon during the trip into Salisbury that had been planned the previous evening. He would love to see her reaction to the cathedral, which must surely be the most magnificent in all England. He wanted to look at her, to watch the lights in her hair, her eyebrows which always seemed to suggest surprise, her green eyes and sensitive mouth. He wanted to make love to her again.

Damnation! Cranwell drew his horse to a halt so suddenly that the animal reared up and nearly threw him. He had not been mistaken the previous afternoon. He was in love with Sarah again. There was no denying it, was there? It was not just that he desired her. He wanted her again as his friend, his companion. He wanted her in his home, his life.

Had he completely taken leave of his senses? He was wanting to share his life with a woman who had been a whore just a few years before, a woman to whom money meant more than honor, a woman who had tricked him into marriage and then cuckolded him almost immediately afterward. What power she had! She could almost make one consider her an angel even when one knew perfectly well that she was more akin to the devil.

Dammit! He loved her.

Even as he admitted the thought to his conscious mind he saw her. She was sitting on the lawn south of the house, beneath a tree, her yellow dress spread around her like a ray of sunshine, her uncovered hair shining in the morning light. He felt his heart turn over and then noticed with some guilt that Hannah was there too, her arms clasped around the neck of her collie. He had not even seen her at first, though she sat right beside Sarah.

He rode toward them, intent on greeting them in an appropriate manner. He doffed his hat and smiled at them, Hannah first and then Sarah.

"Good morning, my love," he said. "Good morning, Miss Fifield."

Hannah looked up briefly, then lowered her head to her dog again. "Good morning, your grace," she said.

"Good morning," Sarah said. "You are out early, your grace. The harvest must have started. Are you not sorry that you cannot be out in the fields working yourself?"

He smiled. "There will still be plenty left to do next week when I shall be alone again," he said.

Hannah looked up, startled. "You do not work in the fields, your grace?" she asked.

"Yes, indeed," he assured her. "There is nothing more invigorating."

"But why?" she asked. "You have sufficient laborers, do you not?"

"Oh yes," he agreed. "It is entirely a personal whim, as you will discover for yourself."

He nodded to both of them, replaced his hat, and rode on to the stables. Well, he had discovered how she would look at him this morning. With wide-open eyes, flushed cheeks, and the whole of the sun behind her eyes.

Damnation!

"Do you think he noticed?" Hannah asked anxiously. "I shall die if he did, though he did not say anything, did he?"

"You are sitting in the shade," Sarah said reassuringly, "and the brim of your bonnet hides your eyes even more. I don't think his grace knew you have been crying, Hannah. He would have said something."

"I feel so stupid anyway," Hannah said. "It is just that out here with Argus it all came over me somehow. I know it is stupid, Miss Fifield. I have had a long time already to get used to the idea. And there is nothing I can do about it. I must just learn to be brave."

Sarah hesitated. Hannah's affairs were really none of her business, but the girl had been so obviously distressed a half-hour earlier when she had found her in this very spot, her arms around her dog's neck, sobbing her heart out. Somehow it was hard to keep oneself from interfering when another person seemed so helpless and so alone.

"Do your mama and papa know how you feel about Mr. Ferris?" she asked.

Hannah looked at her with startled eyes. "Oh no!" she said. "We never said anything. Donald wished to wait until I was eighteen before speaking to Papa. We were both foolish enough to imagine that there would be no objection to our marrying. But when his grace came to pay his addresses, Papa was so obviously set on the match that I knew there would be no use at all in telling him that I love Donald."

"And Mr. Ferris said nothing?" Sarah asked.

"No," said Hannah. "He is very aware that he is not a wealthy man. Even when his father dies—and he by no means wishes that event to be soon—he will have only a modest fortune. He felt that he would be standing in the way of my advancement if he tried to stop this marriage."

"I see," Sarah said. "And there is no chance, Hannah, that your feelings for Mr. Ferris are just youthful infatuation? You are very young, you know."

"Oh no," the girl said earnestly. "Donald and I have always loved each other dearly. We decided when I was twelve and he fifteen that we would marry when I was eighteen. Oh, Miss Fifield, I cannot bear the thought of never seeing him again. I still cannot believe that all this is happening."

"His grace is a kind and considerate man," Sarah said gently. "Is there no chance, Hannah, that you will grow to be contented with him even if you cannot love him as you do Mr. Ferris?"

"Oh," Hannah wailed, "I know he is kind, Miss Fifield. He is a good man. I can respect him. I think I could even like him if I did not know that I will have to spend my life with him. I do not know how I shall do it. I just cannot feel close to him. I think I am somewhat afraid of him."

"Hannah," Sarah said. "Why do you not have a talk with your mama? Perhaps it will not change matters at all, but perhaps too she will be sympathetic. After all, if she and your father do not even know the true state of your feelings, you cannot entirely blame them for urging this marriage on you."

Hannah was quiet for a moment. She scratched the stomach of her dog, who was lying on his back, legs waving in the air, in an ecstasy of sensual bliss. "I know it would not help at all," she said. "I must just force myself to get used to the idea." She laughed. "I am foolish, am I not? Most females would give a great deal to have my chance to be the Duchess of Cranwell."

Sarah watched the girl's bowed head for a minute. How incredible were human preferences. How could any woman have the opportunity to marry George and not be blissfully happy? How could any woman possibly prefer another man to him? Her own feelings were quite confused. Part of her felt elated. This was not a love match, clearly. If Hannah claimed that she hardly knew George, the chances were that they had spent very little time together. In all probability, then, he had chosen her because he felt the need of a wife and not because he loved her. Why that thought should be comforting, she was not quite sure. Did it follow that if George did not love Hannah, he did love her?

On the other hand, she felt unutterably sad. In just a few months' time George would be married to a girl who did not love him and who pined for her childhood sweetheart. He would never know love in his home. He would surely be lonely and ultimately unhappy. And she had so much love to give. She was just brimming over with it, so much so that she had not even been able to look at him a few minutes before without having to restrain the desire to get to her feet and rush to him. If only circumstances had been different!

"Perhaps we should go inside," Sarah suggested. "The plan is to start for Salisbury before luncheon, is it not? We should begin to get ready."

"Yes, you are right," Hannah said. "I had almost forgotten that mad scheme. I wonder what put it into Grandmama's and Lady Murdoch's heads last night. Salisbury is all of eight miles away."

"His grace suggested it when they asked where one might go on an excursion," Sarah said. "There is the cathedral to see. I have heard it is quite magnificent."

"Yes, I suppose so," Hannah said. "I just cannot get too excited about old buildings. Can you, Miss Fifield?"

They got to their feet and brushed grass from their

skirts before returning to the house via the stables, where Argus had a noisy reunion with Cranwell's dogs.

All the members of the Duke of Cranwell's house party were to join the expedition and picnic to Salisbury. A veritable cavalcade of carriages and horses left Montagu Hall late in the morning, the duke's own carriage laden with food and drink for their luncheon. Sarah rode with Winston, Lady Cavendish, and Lady Murdoch in Lady Cavendish's traveling coach. Cranwell, Joshua Stonewall, and Captain Penny rode their horses.

Sarah was awed by her first sight of the cathedral. Its tall tower and spire dwarfed the city around it. The intricately carved stonework was breathtaking even at a distance. She sat with her face pressed to the window during all the time it took to wind through the narrow streets, while her companions continued to chat as they had during the whole journey. The ladies, that was. Winston, apart from a charming smile at the start and a comment about how fortunate he was to be traveling with three ladies, had been unusually quiet.

Sarah was delighted by the size of the grounds that surrounded the cathedral. The flat lawns and trees enabled one to have a good view of the massive building from some distance. It was truly a wonder. How could mere men have possibly built such a structure and decorated it with so much skill?

Most members of the party were happy to descend from carriages and horses to stretch their legs. Most of them thought immediately of the picnic baskets and discovered that they were ravenously hungry. Blankets were spread under the shade of some trees quite a distance from the cathedral, and the picnic baskets were lifted down from Cranwell's coach. Lord Tenby took charge of the wine bottles.

Sarah wandered off by herself. She wanted to see the main doors at the front of the cathedral. She was sure they would be suitably magnificent.

"Do you admire old buildings, Miss Fifield?" a man's voice asked from behind her.

Sarah turned to find that Joshua Stonewall had followed her. "Yes, indeed," she said. "I have not done a great deal of traveling in my life. I take full advantage of every opportunity like this."

"You would enjoy traveling around Europe," he said. "There is so much to see."

"Have you traveled there much?" she asked wistfully. "I would give a great deal to see Italy and Greece in particular."

"Yes," he said with a smile. "You would appreciate them, Miss Fifield. But perhaps you will do so very soon. Will Laing take you on a wedding trip, do you think?"

"Win?" she said, raising her eyebrows. "I very much doubt it, sir. He is not at all interested in art or architecture or books or anything else that I love." It was only after the words were out of her mouth that she realized how dreadful they sounded.

He walked beside her, his hands clasped behind his back. "I see," he said. "And what is the attraction, then, if I may make so bold?"

Sarah blushed. "Oh," she said evasively, "we grew up together, sir. We have grown fond of each other over the years."

"And is that enough?" he asked. "Fondness, I mean. Are you enough alike to be happy together for a lifetime?"

Sarah stiffened. "Really, sir," she said, "I think that is a matter that concerns only Win and me."

He looked suitably contrite. "I do beg your pardon, Miss Fifield," he said. "I am afraid I have been driven on by jealousy."

"Jealousy?" she said, looking at him, startled.

"I admire you greatly, ma'am," he said, flushing under her scrutiny. "And I cannot help feeling that you are wasted on someone like Laing."

"And what is he like?" Sarah asked quietly.

He smiled ruefully. "Pardon me," he said. "I am already biased against him because the lucky dog is betrothed to you. And I must admit that he is a handsome devil. But I think him a little shallow for you, Miss Fifield. Charming, yes, but I suspect there is very little character beneath the charm."

Sarah looked away from him and said nothing.

"And now I have really spoken out of turn," he said. "Most impertinent of me. Please forget everything I have said, ma'am."

Sarah smiled briefly at him. "I did ask your opinion," she said.

"May I escort you back to the others?" Joshua asked, offering Sarah his arm.

When they returned, everyone was sitting down eating, except Cranwell, who was standing against one of the trees, his arms folded, gazing at the cathedral—and at them. Winston and Fanny were in animated conversation. Instead of joining them, Sarah took the glass of wine offered by Lord Tenby, allowed Mr. Stonewall to heap a plate with food, and sat down with him on the only unoccupied corner of one of the blankets. Cranwell finally helped himself to some food too and joined Hannah and her parents.

The older ladies, although they had been the ones to urge the expedition, decided that they were well content to see the outside of the cathedral only. They would stay where they were and rest for a while. Several others decided that they would prefer to walk closer to Mompesson House that bordered the cathedral grounds than to see the cathedral itself. The house was reputed to have extensive gardens. Perhaps they would be allowed to walk in these even if they were not permitted to enter the house itself.

A few of the young people were contented to stroll in the grounds. Winston and Hannah made two of this number. Winston had made straight for her, in fact, when the meal was over, Sarah noticed. He had bent over her, smiled, and led her off a few moments later. They were walking now, quite apart from any other group, apparently quite engrossed in conversation. Sarah could make nothing at all of that particular friendship, but she would not worry about it. They were in a public place, and Win could really do no harm to Hannah. She was betrothed to George and in love with her Donald Ferris. She must surely be beyond the dangers of Win's charm.

Only Lord and Lady Fairlie, Joshua Stonewall, Fanny, Captain Penny, Cranwell, and Sarah wished to go inside the cathedral. Fanny took Sarah's arm as they walked across the grass toward the main doors, which Sarah had still not seen.

"I want to see what you think of the nave of the church when we get inside," Fanny said. "I do not know much about architecture, and usually I do not much care. But even I love this cathedral. It is the perfect setting for a wedding, Miss Fifield. Can you not imagine all the guests standing around on the lawns? And the inside is perfect. I have always been determined that this is where I shall marry. Would you not like to marry here too?"

Sarah smiled. "I really do not think the setting is of great importance if one's partner is the right man," she said. "One could be just as happy in the smallest of country churches." She was thinking of a certain church with only a vicar, her aunt and uncle present. And herself, of course. And George.

"I am surprised Hannah does not want to marry here," Fanny chattered on. "But the earl seems to have his heart set on holding the wedding at their own home."

"That is only natural," Sarah said.

"Of course," Fanny added in a rush, "I do not think Hannah really wishes to get married anywhere. Not to George, anyway."

Sarah did not immediately answer. "What makes you think that?" she asked.

Fanny shrugged. "I can tell," she said. "I have known right from the start. Perhaps it is because George is my brother. I love him dearly, you know, even though we are so different from each other and he is so much older than I am. I am sensitive to such things. Hannah does not love him or wish to marry him. And he does not love her, of course. I think Hannah probably loves what's-his-name—that neighbor she is always talking about. And I think George should wait until he can marry for love. He will not be happy without it, you see, though he does not realize it himself."

Fanny was considerably flushed, though Sarah did not turn her head to see. "It is so easy to criticize," she said. "Even if what you say is true, I do not suppose Lady Hannah has any choice in the matter. I suppose her father has pressed for this match because your brother can offer her position and wealth."

Fanny laughed briefly. "Position, perhaps," she said, "but hardly wealth. The Earl of Cavendish is easily as rich as George, and most of his fortune will pass to Hannah, as she is his only child."

Sarah said no more. But her mind had received a jolt. Did Win know? she wondered, and immediately hoped that the thought was irrelevant. Why was it that she had always assumed that the Earl of Cavendish was impoverished, that he had arranged this marriage for his daughter for that reason? She glanced hastily around her, but Win and Hannah were nowhere in sight. She and Fanny were approaching the cathedral by a circuitous route. The others had disappeared inside already.

Fanny was talking again. "Perhaps you think my concern for my brother unnatural," she said, "or perhaps you understand. You had a brother, did you not?"

"Yes," Sarah said. "He died."

"Poor boy," Fanny said. "I met him once."

"Did you?" Sarah asked, looking up in some surprise.

"Yes," Fanny said. "It was the dreadful day when that other boy was killed. What was his name?"

Sarah's arm had stiffened beneath Fanny's. "Albert Stanfield?" she said.

"Of course," Fanny said. "How could I have forgotten? For years I felt guilty about feeling hostile toward someone who was dead. I am sure he did not deserve to die, but at the time I felt that he almost deserved it."

"You were there?" Sarah was breathless.

"He was so horrid to your brother," Fanny said. "The poor little boy was sobbing and hugging a tree when I came riding by and decided to come to his defense. I called that boy some names in return for the ones he was calling your brother. When he started to back away, jeering at both of us, I saw his danger almost immediately. He was very close to the edge of the quarry. But I suppose he thought my screams all part of my fury." She shuddered. "I shall never forget the sound of . . . But I am sorry, Miss Fifield. I had not intended to speak of it. It must be painful to you to be reminded of that episode."

"Not at all," Sarah said faintly.

"For months I was convinced I had killed him," Fanny said. "I did not even tell anyone until we went home a few days later. George was very upset with me when I finally told him. I believe he wrote to the authorities immediately, though the case had already been closed. It was a dreadful time. George comforted me after his first anger was over and convinced me that I was in no way to blame. We always have the right and the duty to defend the weak against the bullies of this world, he said."

They were at the doors of the cathedral, and Fanny fell silent as they passed out of the sunshine between the massive stone doorways.

It was immediately apparent to Sarah when she and her companion had walked through the great doors what Fanny had meant about getting married in this cathedral. The nave stretching before her was entirely Gothic. Everything—high-arched ceiling, massive columns, richly decorated stained-glass windows—reached toward heaven. A mere mortal standing on the hard stone floor felt tiny and insignificant. But oh yes, a bride would feel very special indeed here.

Sarah sat on one of the wooden chairs. Fanny continued on down the nave to join Lady Fairlie and the

men, who were down by the quire already. Sarah was
not feeling anything yet. She was too utterly stunned
to feel. She must sit here until what she had just heard
had penetrated into her conscious mind.

Graham had not killed Albert Stanfield. Fanny had
been there and witnessed what had happened. Win,
presumably, had not. Her brother was innocent. Win's
blackmail had been all bluff. All. Her virtue had been
lost, her marriage destroyed, her life ruined, all because she had not seen through his bluff. And Win,
whom she had for many years considered devilish, was
worse than that. Far worse. Worse than the devil.
What could be worse than the devil? Winston Bowen.

Her brother was innocent. Graham had not been a
murderer. Sarah's head dropped into her hands, and
she sank to her knees on the hard stone of the cathedral floor. She raised her head and gazed at the distant
altar.

Later, Sarah began her own tour of the cathedral. It
was cold and silent, heavy with an other-worldly atmosphere that she could not explain to herself. Was it
possible that just beyond the windows and the stone
walls were the lawns, the trees, their carriages and
blankets? Here she felt totally cut off from everyday
life. She sat again in Trinity Chapel, behind the great
altar, gazing at the triple-arched stained-glass window.
How insignificant one's own wishes and problems
seemed in such a setting. She felt something like peace
soothing her soul.

"I can remember being similarly awed during my
first visit here," Cranwell said from behind her, "although I was only thirteen years old at the time. And I
must confess, I am amazed anew each time I come
here. It is always more magnificent than I remembered."

"One can almost feel the presence of God here,"
Sarah replied, her voice hushed. She did not turn her
head.

Cranwell came and sat two seats away from her. "I
have seen many cathedrals in Europe," he said, "but I
do not believe there is one to match this. Milan Cathe-

dral perhaps comes close. Of course," he laughed, "I am partial."

Sarah smiled at him and was immediately sorry for her involuntary movement. She felt as if a giant hand had grabbed her by the throat and was squeezing the breath from her body.

"If you have seen enough inside the church," he said, "perhaps I can take you out to the cloisters? They are lovely too. Not quite as awe-inspiring as the church itself, maybe. But there is too much in here to absorb all in one visit, is there not? You will have to see it many times before you will feel that you really know it. Or that you partly know it."

Sarah rose to her feet and he placed a hand at the small of her back to guide her along the side aisle, past the vestry, to the arched doorway that led out to the cloisters.

It was a different world again, as quiet, as beautiful, but more peaceful somehow. They strolled around the stone cloisters, looking out through the open archways at the grass and old gnarled trees that formed a quadrangle at the center. They did not talk. They did not touch.

"It is lovely," Sarah said at last. "Thank you. I think I would have missed this, left to myself. Where is everyone else?"

"Outside walking or sitting on the blankets," Cranwell said. "Most people are not as sensitive to atmosphere as you are, Sarah. A quick look at beauty and they are satisfied."

"I am sorry," she said, self-conscious again. "Did you wish to leave?"

"No," he said, "not at all."

He offered Sarah his arm and she took it hesitantly. They strolled on, silent again for a few minutes.

"Sarah," he said at last quietly, "do I owe you an apology for yesterday?"

She blushed painfully. "No," she said, "please do not say you are sorry."

"If I did," he said, "it would be only for having offended you."

"I was not offended," she almost whispered.

Cranwell was waging an internal battle as they lapsed into silence again. One part of him felt almost drugged, to the extent that he no longer cared what she was or had been. The whole of their divorce and the lonely years since had been a terrible mistake. He should have persevered four years before in his efforts to patch up their differences. He should not have taken her confessions so much to heart. The future was what should have mattered to him, not the past. He should have fought for her, fought with her if by so doing he might have turned her away from her craving for other men.

He might have succeeded. Certainly he could not believe her as depraved as he had once thought. It was true that she was beautiful and therefore attractive to many men. She must have been sorely tempted by their admiration. And perhaps it was not surprising that she had given in to that temptation to indulge her power over men. She had been left alone with a mentally handicapped brother at a very early age. Although she had loving relatives with whom to live, it must have seemed to a twelve-year-old that the security had dropped out of her world. She must have needed to reassure herself that she could hold other people's love by using her sexual attractions.

It was not a very pretty explanation of what she had done, but it was at least understandable. She had been very young, barely nineteen when he had married her. She had matured since. She had probably learned that no lasting satisfaction could be achieved by such casual relationships. If he had waited a little longer, he could have been there for her when she finally learned the truth. They might have put the past behind them and started again.

Perhaps. Certainly now he was feeling for her again that powerful attraction that had drawn him when he first knew her. He could easily allow himself to walk with her now, pretending that she was still his wife, that there was nothing but love and harmony between them. He could turn to her now so easily and kiss her lips. Not with passion. The setting was not conducive to such emotion. But with tenderness.

But beneath these feelings ran the thought that he was being a fool. He had been completely taken in by her once before, had he not? He would have wagered his fortune, his life even, on her innocence and sweetness at that time. He could not have been more deceived. He could recall now with terrible clarity his shock on discovering that she was not a virgin, and then in hearing her admit quite openly that she had performed the act more times than she could count.

Had he not had ample evidence in the past weeks that she had not entirely changed? There was the money first and foremost. Not that the sum mattered to him greatly. He had enough, and his estates brought in enough that the loss was almost insignificant. But she had asked him for it, demanded it really as a condition for removing herself from his life. And what had happened? The fact that he was walking with her here more than a week later was answer enough.

She apparently lived a respectable life now. At least she seemed to have done so for the past four years. But she had betrothed herself to a man of some charm and was apparently quite eager to give herself to him before the wedding night. She had made a slave of Josh. The two of them had been wandering around before luncheon, arm in arm, apparently quite oblivious of the presence of anyone else. Was she trying to ensnare him into her bed too?

And of course, she had succeeded with him. Despite everything, he had come under her spell again. He had kissed her when they were still in Bath. He had thought of little else except her since then. Yesterday he had actually made love to her. And since then his thoughts had been obsessed by her. Here he was, strolling with her as if they were still husband and wife. She had just admitted that she was not sorry for

the day before. Yet she was to marry Bowen the
following week. Was she walking beside him now,
apparently so meek and contented, laughing at him, at
her power to make such a fool of him?

"Do you give your favors as freely to Bowen?" this
more negative side of his mood asked her.

"I beg your pardon?" Sarah looked full into his
face, those eyebrows arched high above startled eyes.

"Do you sleep with him too, Sarah, and tell him
that you are not sorry?" he asked. "Do you still need
more than one man to make you happy?"

She was still looking at him. Her face was very
white. They had stopped walking. "Don't," she said.
"Please don't do this."

"Why not?" he asked. His voice was cold, the side
of his nature that loved her noted almost dispassionately. "Never say that you have a conscience that can
be bothered."

She shook her head slowly, her eyes wide and bright,
though he could see no tears there. "Don't, George,"
she said. "Oh, please don't. This is all we will ever
have."

"Nonsense!" he said, his voice a sneer. "You will be
my guest for three more days, Sarah. I can arrange to
be alone in the hills each afternoon of those days if
you wish. Would that satisfy you?"

Her face had calmed, though it was still deathly
pale. "And do you make love to Hannah and offer to
apologize each time afterward?" she said, only a slight
tremor in her voice.

Cranwell's face flushed with anger. "Only you could
think of such a thing," he said. "You have only to
look at Hannah to know that she is pure and innocent.
That is a filthy suggestion, Sarah."

She nodded, her face hard. "Of course," she said.
"I did not think of that. But then, you cannot expect
me to, can you, your grace? We whores become so
hardened in our depravity that we forget that such
qualities as purity and innocence exist."

Cranwell blanched. He reached out a hand to her.

"Don't touch me!" she said. "You may become contaminated, your grace. In fact, it may already be too late for you. Who knows what dread disease I may have passed along to you yesterday? It would have been wiser to wait for your pure bride than to pick up a whore, would it not? One never knows where she may have been. Or with whom."

"Sarah," he said, "listen to me. I am sorry. I don't know why I spoke as I did. I did not mean—"

"Oh yes, you did," she said. "And I know why you said what you did. You are like most men. You impose one standard on your own behavior and quite another on that of all women. On our wedding night you knew that you were not my first lover. How did you know, your grace? If I was your first woman, how did you know? There was a time when I believed that I had wronged you as much as it is possible for a woman to wrong a man. And I still know that what I did was very wrong. But was my past so much more immoral than yours? With how many women had you slept, George, and how many times? How would you have reacted that night had I asked you those questions?"

"Sarah," he said, reaching his hand out to her again.

"I have not finished," she said. "Yes, what I did yesterday with you was wrong. We are each betrothed to someone else and we wronged them by making love with each other, even if they never know about it. But we sinned equally, George. You did not sin the less just because you are a man. Why are men merely satisfying a need when they make love to women who are not their wives, while women are whores? Do you think I like that label? I do not, and I never did. And what is more, George, I have never—never!—done anything to deserve that name."

They stared at each other wordlessly when her tirade came to an end. She was shaking and almost panting with shortness of breath, Cranwell noticed.

He nodded. "You are quite right," he said. "I am sorry." He had not meant his voice to sound so curt.

She laughed harshly. "And that makes everything

all right again," she said bitterly. "His Grace of Cranwell has just done the noble thing and apologized to a whore."

"Don't call yourself that, Sarah," he said wearily.

"I shall leave Montagu Hall in the morning," she said. "I should not have come here in the first place. I shall try to persuade Lady Murdoch and Win to come with me. I must talk to you about Win before I leave. But not now. And it will not take long." Her voice was flat. She no longer looked at him, but at the buttons of his coat.

He could think of nothing to say. His interior war was raging again. Part of him wanted to grab her, drag her against him, kiss her, plead with her not to leave him, now or ever. Part of him acknowledged that what she planned was the only sensible thing to be done. Once she was gone, he could put her out of his mind and his heart again and devote his energies to getting to know his bride.

He said nothing as she turned away and walked to the arched doorway that led back into the cathedral. He followed her with his eyes. He swallowed against a lump in his throat.

20

SARAH WISHED that Lady Cavendish was not with them in the carriage on the way back to Montagu Hall. She would have liked to speak to Win and Cousin Adelaide right then about leaving the next day. As it was, she was forced to enter into the conversation as much as good manners dictated, showing enthusiasm over the picturesque setting of Salisbury Cathedral and agreeing that the excellence of his grace's chef had demonstrated itself more in the picnic fare than in all the formal meals they had taken at the house.

Winston had recovered from whatever had made him quiet during the morning. He was his most charming self, complimenting all three ladies on their appearance and their opinions, praising Cranwell for having suggested such an agreeable outing and for having gathered around him such a refined and interesting group of guests. With a smile at Sarah and a hand laid lightly over one of hers, he complimented himself on his decision to join the house party and postpone his wedding for one week.

"Would you not agree with me, my love?" he asked. "I know you were deeply disappointed last week. But will you not admit now that I was right?"

Sarah smiled back. "Yes, Win," she said. "You were perfectly right. I am very glad we postponed our wedding. This week has made all the difference."

He squeezed her hand and turned his charm back to the older ladies again.

Sarah cringed with inward horror at having to sit with Winston's hand covering hers on her knee. But she would not push it away. The situation was bad

331

enough as it was. She certainly did not wish to provoke a quarrel with him today. And she would have to
endure his attentions for only a little while longer.
Tomorrow, once she had talked to George and got Win
safely away from Montagu Hall, she could stop pretending, break her engagement, and tell him all that
was within her heart to say. He could keep George's
money. Being free of him would be cheap at the price.

Tomorrow. She felt slightly sick at the thought. She
could be rid of Win for ever and that fact must make
the day an occasion for rejoicing. But she would never
see George again either. Never. And she had to try to
blank the thought from her mind. She would panic if
she faced the naked truth.

That had been a dreadful quarrel and a totally unexpected one. She had felt so close to George since the
day before and had been convinced that he felt the
same way. There had seemed to be no hostility in his
manner when he had joined her in Trinity Chapel. In
fact, he seemed to have gone out of his way to find her
and make conversation with her. She had felt a marvelous uplifting of the heart at the sound of his voice,
a total awareness of him as both a person and a man.

She had let him guide her to the cloisters and had
walked with him there quite consciously happy. It was
not that she had formed any unreasonable expecta-
tions or hopes for the future. She had known that
nothing could develop from that moment. There were
far too many obstacles in the way. But that had not
mattered. She had been prepared to take the moment
for what it was worth. If she could only spend the
remaining three days of the visit thus, in quiet harmony with him, she would be content, she had convinced herself. If they could part from each other at
the end of the week without resentment or hatred, she
could find the strength to face the bleak future.

And it had been so lovely there at first. The surroundings were beautiful and peaceful. They had been
alone and had shared the mood of the place. For one

moment she had been afraid that he was going to tell
her he regretted their lovemaking. But he had not. He
had merely been concerned that she regretted it. They
had walked on in silent harmony, she had thought.
She had been holding to his arm, the warm glow of
her love for him growing until she felt she could not
walk another step without telling him. It would not be
so wrong, would it? she had asked herself. It was not
as if she were trying to lay any obligation on him. But
she had wanted him to know that she loved him, that
she always had.

But he had started to speak to her first. And it was
as if someone had taken a pitcher of cold water and
flung its contents in her face. She had assumed that his
thoughts were moving along the same lines as her
own. Instead, his face was cold and set, his voice
quickly matching it. And he had made those terrible
suggestions about her again, assuming that she was
promiscuous. Why had he always assumed that? Why
had he never thought that perhaps she had sinned with
only one partner before him?

She had been hurt beyond endurance. She had been
on the verge of throwing herself at him to cling and
plead and cry. Finally, far too late, she had wanted to
tell him the whole truth. She could not bear to have
him think all those hurtful things about her. She craved
his good opinion, his admiration, his love.

But pride had come to her defense. For once in her
life she had seen the Duke of Cranwell as a less-than-
perfect human being. Perhaps it was a result of her
newfound belief in herself—a belief, ironically, that he
had helped her to on the previous afternoon. For once
his words seemed more cruel than just, his attitude
more hypocritical than moral.

And so she had lashed out at him, caused a bitter
and irreparable rift between them. They had parted
with mutual anger and hatred. He had not looked at
her or come anywhere near her when he had finally
rejoined the group. And this was the way they would

part forever the next day. She would warn him as briefly as she could about Win and his possible designs on Fanny. And that would be the end. He would hate her for the rest of his life as he had for the last four years. And she would have that quarrel to remember, drowning out the memory of his tenderness and passion on the hillside.

Sarah finally succeeded in drawing her hand free of Winston's by pretending that the ribbons of her bonnet needed retying. She felt more and more sick with every turn of the wheels beneath them.

"And so you see," Lady Murdoch was saying when Sarah's attention returned to the conversation again, "it is just possible that these two young Murdoch brothers may be long-lost nephews of my dear late husband. I shall certainly have to investigate the matter. And if that is so, they will have a very large claim on my fortune. It would be most provoking just when I was on the verge of changing my will in dear Sarah's favor. And of course, I should much prefer to leave everything to her, for I have come to think of her as my very own daughter. However, I suppose the claims of the male line of the family have to be considered first." She sighed loudly.

"But when did you hear all this, Adelaide?" Lady Cavendish asked. "You have not mentioned it before."

"No," Lady Murdoch admitted, "I have kept it all to myself, Bertha, for a whole week. But the subject has been nagging at my mind so much that I just had to let it all out this afternoon. It is a gratifying thought, Lord Laing, to know that you love my Sarah so dearly. If you were a mercenary man, sir, this news might well tempt you to cry off." She tittered.

Winston bowed and smiled. For once he seemed to have nothing to say. Sarah looked at Lady Murdoch with a new respect. One could almost swear that the woman was telling the truth. If only she were not feeling quite so wretched, she might be having difficulty containing her amusement. Poor Win!

*   *   *

"You did not believe that cock-and-bull story, did you, dear?" Lady Murdoch asked Sarah an hour later when the latter had followed her to her room in Montagu Hall. "I really did not wish to distress you, dear. But I thought you would realize that I made up the story entirely for Lord Laing's benefit. I wonder if he is off on his own somewhere at this very moment wondering how he can most honorably withdraw from his betrothal. Or does honor mean nothing whatsoever to that young man, Sarah? We shall see."

"No," Sarah said, "I did not believe your story, Cousin Adelaide. But even if I had, I would not have been distressed, you know. I do not covet your money. I love you for yourself and because you have been very kind to me."

"Bless you," Lady Murdoch said. "You had better not delay here too long, dear. There is only an hour until dinnertime and you will wish to wash and change, I am sure."

"I wished to talk with you," Sarah said. "I am planning to leave here tomorrow. I hope to persuade Win to leave too. I do not know what your wishes will be."

"Tomorrow?" Lady Murdoch echoed. "Whatever has happened, my love? Has Lord Laing been unendurable again? Do I need to whisper in his ear that you are suffering from a mild attack of the smallpox?"

Sarah laughed despite herself. "No," she said, "but I learned something so disturbing about him this afternoon that I really cannot keep up the pretense for one day more. I must leave." She proceeded to tell Lady Murdoch the story that Fanny had told her earlier that afternoon.

"Bless my soul!" Lady Murdoch exclaimed. For once she was at a loss for words. "Well, bless my soul!"

"Besides," said Sarah in a rush of agitation, "I should not have come here in the first place. I told his grace this afternoon that I would be leaving. I can hardly go back on that decision now."

Lady Murdoch was very still for a moment. "I was very blind, was I not?" she said. "You must blame my age, Sarah dear. I am old and somewhat senile, no doubt. Years ago I would never have been so insensitive to other people's feelings. Until we had our little talk a few days ago, I had not noticed at all. But I have seen quite clearly since. You still love the dear duke."

"Oh," Sarah said, "it is not that, Cousin Adelaide. It is just that the situation is extremely awkward and embarrassing."

"And of course he feels the same way too," Lady Murdoch said, just as if she had not heard a word of what Sarah said. "I can always tell these things. When my eyes have been finally opened, that is."

"Oh, no," Sarah said, "it is not true, ma'am, believe me. He can feel nothing but resentment for me after what I made him endure in the past. He has shown remarkable restraint in putting up with my presence since we met again in Bath."

"His betrothal is as much of a mistake as yours, of course," Lady Murdoch continued, "though for vastly different reasons. Lady Hannah is not the right wife for him. He needs someone of far more character. Someone like you, dear. And she needs someone with more gaiety." Her brow was furrowed in concentration.

"Will you leave with me tomorrow?" Sarah asked timidly. "Or will you stay?"

"I shall do whatever you do, without a doubt, my dear," Lady Murdoch said, "especially if Lord Laing decides to leave with you, though I would by no means count on that if I were you. But you must not leave him here without saying something to his grace, Sarah dear."

"I have already told him that I wish to speak with him in the morning," Sarah said with lowered eyes.

"Oh dear," Lady Murdoch said, more to herself than to Sarah, "this is a very difficult situation. We need a plan."

"I shall go and get ready for dinner," Sarah said, "and call for a maid to pack my bags."

Winston was surprisingly easy to persuade. Sarah did not have a chance to talk to him until after dinner, though she realized that the dinner table would not have been the right place to discuss such a subject anyway. When she entered the drawing room prior to the meal, it was to find Fanny, flushed and bright-eyed, in close conversation with Win. He was looking equally pleased with life. When dinner was announced and Winston, without a glance in her direction, offered his arm to the girl, Sarah found Joshua Stonewall at her elbow, bowing and offering his escort. He did not say anything, but Sarah could guess his feelings from the tight set to his lips and the meaningful glance he cast in Win's direction.

She took the initiative when the gentlemen joined the ladies after their port. The drawing room was crowded, as a musical evening had been arranged. Lady Wright had spent a couple of days finding out the musical talents of all the guests, with the result that there were to be enough pianoforte recitals and vocal solos and duets to last for an hour or more. Fanny was even to play on the violin, though she protested that she occasionally sounded little better than a cat in pain.

Sarah touched Winston on the arm as he was taking a cup of tea from Lady Cavendish. He smiled broadly when he saw who it was.

"Could I talk to you, Win?" she asked.

"It would be my pleasure, my love," he said. "But if it is a private matter, I am afraid we will be hard pressed in here."

"Yes," she said, "you are right. Shall we walk in the cloister, Win?"

His smile broadened to a grin. "That is a suggestion after my own heart," he said. "Might we leave before Lady Murdoch takes her attention away from that

Tenby chit? If she sees us, we will very soon have a large escort."

He put down his cup, and Sarah led the way from the room. Only one side of the lower cloisters was frequently used. The other three sides led to the library, Cranwell's study, some offices, and other rooms not in daily use. Sarah and Winston had the dimly lit corridor to themselves. Their footsteps echoed on the bare flagstones.

"What is on your mind, love?" Winston asked, drawing her arm through his and lowering his head until it was intimately close to her own.

"I want to leave here tomorrow, Win," she said. "I do not wish to stay until the end of the week."

"Are you not enjoying yoursef?" he asked. "I must confess that I find the company quite congenial."

"I do not belong here, Win," she said. "I came to please you and Lady Murdoch. But I cannot stay any longer." She prepared to do battle.

"If that is how you feel, love," he said, covering her hand with his own, "then by all means we shall leave."

"Do you mean it, Win?" she asked, brightening.

"But of course," he said. "Anything to please you, you know."

Sarah was smiling. "May we leave in the morning?" she asked. "I hate to delay once I have decided something."

"Whenever you like," he said indulgently. He smiled down into her face, his teeth very white in the semi-darkness. Only a few candles burned in the wall sconces. "Now, what do I get as a reward, Sarah?"

"Oh, don't be absurd, Win," she said, keeping her tone light. "We will be married soon."

"Somehow," he said, standing still and turning to her, "that thought does not offer too much comfort at the moment. What about tonight, love?" He was still smiling. He backed her slowly against the inner wall of the cloister.

Sarah did not feel frightened. There were numerous

people fairly close at hand. But she did feel revulsion. She would feel that old nausea, she knew, if he came one inch closer. But she must not antagonize him. It would be better for everyone if she could draw him away from the house tomorrow without fuss.

He came several inches closer and put one hand against the wall beside her head. "Come to bed with me now, Sarah," he said. "No one will know. They are all too busily occupied in the drawing room. I want you, and I don't think I can wait any longer."

She smiled and deliberately spread her hands over his chest. "No, Win," she said, "not bed, please. Just one kiss?"

His eyes burned into hers. He leaned against her so that his full weight pressed her to the wall. His mouth, hot and open, came down against her neck where it joined her shoulder, and his hands moved to cup her breasts and squeeze them painfully. She gritted her teeth as she felt a sharp pain against her neck. He had bitten her!

She forced herself to stand there and endure, though she was very close to panic. She concentrated on keeping her breathing even. His mouth moved up to cover hers, open still and wet against her closed lips. She could feel her stomach muscles tense. How long must she endure this before she could decently push him away from her and smile fondly at him? His knee was pushing persistently between hers so that she had to move her feet apart to keep her balance. She found herself straddling his leg, which was pushing slowly upward against her.

Now, Sarah thought, trying to hold on to her control. Now I may tell him that this is far enough.

"Blast!" Winston hissed against her mouth. He raised his head and lowered his leg before she had begun any resistance.

She saw why immediately. Cranwell was quite close to them. He had clearly just drawn to a halt and looked quite startled for the moment.

"I beg your pardon," he said. "I am on my way to the library. I had no idea there was anyone out here."

Winston smiled lazily. He had not moved away from her at all, Sarah noticed. His body still pressed her to the wall; his knee was still pushed between hers. "You have damnable timing, Cranwell," he said. "Is there nowhere private in your home or on your estate where a man might take his lady?"

Cranwell appeared to have recovered from his shock. "I shall be inside the library within thirty seconds, Bowen," he said, "and I do not expect anyone to follow me. Please feel free to carry on your . . . er . . . conversation."

He walked past them without another glance. His footsteps echoed on the stones until he turned and left the cloisters through an archway. Sarah could not understand why she had not heard his footsteps coming.

Winston was gazing down into her eyes. His own had lost their customary charm. They looked almost cold, although he was smiling.

"I hope he got the message this time," he said. "I think he can have hardly missed it. Do you?"

"What message, Win?" she asked. Her heart felt like lead inside her.

"The message that you belong to me, love, body and soul," he said very distinctly. "I think sometimes that you have forgotten that, Sarah. I don't know quite what game you are playing, but you cannot win it, you know. You will always be mine, no matter what. You gave me your body years ago, and it belongs to me for all time. Don't forget that. Cranwell won't, you know. Have you really hoped that he will take you back? The man has far too much pride to take someone else's leavings. And that is all you are, after all, Sarah. My leavings. Sometimes you act as if you think you have the upper hand. You enjoy teasing. But I can have you whenever I want you, my love. Body and soul. Of course, you are welcome to your soul. I shall be quite contented with your body."

Sarah's lips had compressed into a thin line. Her

eyes had hardened. She glared into his unflinchingly. "Oh, there you are wrong, Win," she said quietly but very deliberately. "There you are wrong. I do not belong to you. Once my body did. But you gained possession of that through lies and threats and force. You have never possessed even one corner of my heart or even of my liking or respect. All you ever told me to gain power over me was untrue. You are a liar and a cheat, Winston Bowen, a cruel, heartless fiend. But you have lost your power over me. It is only my respect for my former husband that keeps me civil to you. We will leave here tomorrow, and I shall be free. Free never to set eyes on you again."

He looked at her measuringly for a long moment, his face serious. Then he grinned. "Well, well," he said, "the cat has claws. I don't think I like you any the less for the fact, Sarah. I shall enjoy the taming of you. A little violence always adds excitement to love-making, I have found from experience. But tame you I shall, my girl. I dare you right now to scream and summon the attention of all those respectable people in the drawing room and of your stuffy lover in the library. Let me hear you, Sarah."

He put his palms flat against the bare flesh above the rather low décolletage of her gown, fingers outward, and swiveled his hands until his fingers were down inside her dress, curved beneath her breasts. His touch was quite ungentle. His eyes did not look away from her own.

"I am sure you have more packing to do, Sarah," he said. "Go and do it. I am no longer in the mood to enjoy your body tonight. But the time will come. Soon. And whenever I wish it. Is that clear, my love?"

Sarah swallowed. She held his eyes, refusing to flinch.

He stood looking down at her for a long while, his knee still holding her immobile against the wall, his hands still clasping her naked breasts.

He smiled finally, the full force of his charm in his dancing eyes, crinkled at the corners, and the curve of his lips. "Good night, my love," he said, and he kissed her warmly and lingeringly on the lips. When he lifted his head, he also withdrew his hands slowly and one at a time from inside her gown. And he put those hands against the wall on either side of her head and slowly eased his weight away from her.

She said nothing. She continued to look directly at him, her face expressionless. Finally she turned and walked back the way they had come. She forced herself not to run, but all the time her back bristled, almost as if she expected to feel a knife blade against her spine at any moment.

The Duke of Cranwell was sitting in his library, behind the large leather-covered desk. He was methodically dipping his quill pen into the inkwell and doodling with it on the blotter before him. The ink spread out into satisfying blobs on the pink surface of the blotter. He had been sitting in the library for most of the time since last evening.

He had left a few times, of course. He had gone back to the drawing room the night before, feeling the obligation to appear at least to say good night to his guests. And he had gone to bed at some time during the night, though he might as well have stayed, for the amount of sleep he had had. But he had been back here early. He had not even ridden out this morning. The harvest could proceed quite effectively without his supervision.

He had seen her leave the drawing room the evening before and had assumed that she was going walking in the garden with her fiancé again. He had certainly not expected to come upon them in the cloisters. He had left in order to steal an hour alone in the library, his favorite retreat. He had wanted to sort out his thoughts and feelings, which had been in a whirl since the afternoon.

Afterward, he had wished that he had stayed in the drawing room and listened to the music. He had been justly punished for abandoning his guests. Of course, he had already been imagining what they were doing together out in the garden. But it is one thing to imagine and quite another to witness for oneself, he had found.

He was upon them before he had even realized they were there. And Bowen must have heard him at about the same moment. Certainly he had been treated to a full display of a very intimate embrace. They had been all but making love there against the wall. Bowen's hands had been all over her breasts, his leg thrust between hers.

It was only afterward, when he was inside the library, his back pressed against the closed door, his eyes closed, that Cranwell had realized that they had not even broken their embrace while he stood there. It was almost as if they were proud to be caught thus. Their behavior had been quite indecorous. The least they could have done was to break apart when they saw him. For the first time he had felt some disgust with Bowen.

And for Sarah? Could she not at least have taken her lover to her bedroom, where other people did not stand in danger of coming upon them? What if Hannah had been with him? Or Fanny?

Finally he had pushed himself away from the door and sat in the chair before the fire. He had felt vicious with self-loathing. He had allowed his life to be turned upside down again by Sarah Fifield. He had fallen in love with her again. He had lost interest in his marriage plans. He had even come almost to believe in her, despite all the opposing evidence. Even this afternoon, after she had left him, he had been filled with contrition. She had almost convinced him with her talk about his dual morality. He had almost believed her when she said that she had never deserved that ugly label he had put on her.

He had certainly suffered agonies of misery and remorse during the return journey to Montagu Hall. He had been torn between the sensible course of allowing her to go the next day and the irrational one of begging her to stay.

And then this!

And now, the morning after, he was still sitting here inactive, furious and disgusted with Sarah, longing to be told that she was ready to go so that he might at last be rid of her . . . desperate with panic at the knowledge that within a few minutes, an hour at the most, he would be saying good-bye to her forever.

There was not an inch of room left on the blotter. It was totally saturated with ink. He flung the pen down, not even bothering to pick it up again when it landed on the bare leather of the desktop. He put one hand across his eyes and massaged his temples.

There was a knock at the door. Cranwell looked up sharply. "Come in," he called.

There was a pause before the door opened hesitantly and Sarah appeared there. She was dressed for traveling in a plain woolen dress and half-boots, though she had not yet put on a cloak or bonnet.

"I told your butler not to announce me," she said timidly. "May I speak with you for a minute, your grace?"

Cranwell had risen to his feet. He came around the desk now and crossed the room to her. She stood aside as he reached out to close the door.

"Come and sit by the fire," he said. "It is a cold day."

"Yes," she said, and meekly took the chair that he indicated. He took the one across from her. His face looked pale and set, she noticed as she glanced at him.

"Lady Murdoch and I are ready to leave," she said. "I have not seen Win yet, but he said he would be ready to leave this morning. I expect him down at any minute."

Cranwell merely looked at her.

"I want to thank you for your hospitality," she said. "You have been very kind—"

"Sarah," he interrupted, "I think we can dispense with such meaningless small talk, don't you? You said you wished to talk to me. About your betrothed, I believe?"

"Yes," she said. Her voice was shaking. She felt as if she had been running for several miles.

"Well?" he prompted after she had stared at him silently for a while.

"I wanted to tell you . . ." she said. "That is, I think you ought to know . . . and Lady Murdoch has urged me to tell you too." She stopped.

"Tell me what?" he prompted.

"I . . . I don't know if there is really any need," she said. "That is, perhaps my fears are groundless, and—"

Cranwell jumped impatiently to his feet. "Sarah," he said, "will you please just tell me— What now?"

These last words were spoken irritably as there was a hasty knock at the door. Whoever was outside did not wait for an answer but swung the door inward without a pause. Joshua Stonewall's head appeared around it.

"Ah, Cranwell," he said, coming right inside the room. "Sorry to interrupt you, old boy, but this can't wait."

Sarah rose hastily to her feet, but Joshua held up a restraining hand.

"No, Miss Fifield, don't leave," he said. "Normally I would speak privately to Cran, but this seems to concern you as well."

Sarah sat down again and looked at him with a puzzled frown.

Joshua looked hastily from one to the other of them. "Cran," he asked, "do you have any idea why Lady Hannah would have been driving off with Winston Bowen in a hired carriage?"

There was silence for a moment. Then Cranwell moved.

"I suppose there could be any number of reasons, Josh," he said. "Perhaps Hannah has some purchases to make in the village and Bowen has been kind enough to convey her there."

"She had a large valise with her," Joshua said.

"And they did not drive away from the house, Cran. They were walking when I saw them, beyond the river and behind the trees. I was about to hail them when they turned off the path and scrambled up to the road. I thought it extremely peculiar. Then I saw that there was a carriage waiting there. They climbed inside, and it drove off."

The other two occupants of the library stared at him. He looked at them apologetically.

"I am sorry, Miss Fifield," he said. "I hope the explanation is as simple as Cran suggests."

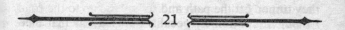

21

SARAH'S EYES met Cranwell's. Both looked blank.

"But Win is leaving here with me this morning," Sarah said. Even as she said it, her heart plummeted.

"Have you asked Cavendish about this?" Cranwell asked. "There surely has to be some simple explanation." But he did not sound convinced.

"No," Joshua said. "I didn't want to alert her father, Cran, until I had talked with you. I don't like it, y'know."

"It seems most unlike Hannah," Cranwell said, "to go off like that unchaperoned. It doesn't seem like Bowen's type of behavior either. Does it, Sarah?"

Sarah looked back at him, but she said nothing. Her cheeks flamed.

"Would anyone else know about this?" she asked at last to fill an uncomfortable pause. "Lady Hannah's maid? Lady Fanny, perhaps?"

Cranwell crossed to the bell rope and pulled it. There was an awkward silence in the room until the butler answered the bell. He was sent in search of both Hannah's maid and Fanny.

They arrived almost at the same moment. Cranwell tackled the maid first.

"Is your mistress at home?" he asked her.

The girl curtsied. "I'm not sure, your grace," she said.

"Did she say anything about going riding or walking this morning?"

"No, sir," the girl said.

"What was she wearing, girl?" Joshua asked.

The girl turned to him, her eyebrows raised.

"Was she dressed for the outdoors, Mattie?" Sarah asked more gently. "I wished to say good-bye to her and cannot find her anywhere."

"She went down to breakfast, ma'am," the girl said, "but I have not seen her since. She told me she would not need me until she rang."

"That will be all, girl," Cranwell said, his eyes on the heightened color in Fanny's cheeks.

When the maid had left the room, he turned to his sister and looked levelly at her.

"You must have realized that Hannah has disappeared, Fanny," he said. "Tell us what you know about the matter."

"Disappeared?" Fanny asked brightly. "Nonsense, George. I am sure she is somewhere."

"Yes, I would imagine she is," her brother said dryly. "The question is, where, Fan?"

Fanny shrugged. "Have you tried the stables?" she asked. "She is probably with that dog of hers. Or perhaps she has taken him walking. She was saying but yesterday that he was in need of some strenuous exercise. I am sure she will be back in time for luncheon."

"Fan," Cranwell said, "you will grant, I think, that you and I understand each other unusually well. I know when you are acting, my dear. You know something about Hannah's whereabouts. Now please tell us. Time may well be important here."

Fanny glanced nervously at Sarah. "Perhaps I should talk to you, George," she said.

"No," he said firmly. "I can see that you know Lord Laing has disappeared too. Miss Fifield has a perfect right to hear your explanation. And as for Josh, he is the one who alerted us to the situation a few minutes ago. Now, speak, Fan."

"It really is nothing so very dreadful," Fanny said. "At least, it might seem to be so at first, George, but I do not believe you will think so when you have had time to think about it properly."

"Fan!"

"She does not love you, George," Fanny said in a rush. "And she does love her neighbor, Mr. Ferris. She has been dreadfully unhappy. I believe that at first she thought she might get used to the idea of marrying you, but I have seen that she has only become increasingly miserable. She was reluctant to confide in me, of course, because I am your sister, but occasionally I have had parts of the truth from her. And then last night she told me everything."

"Last night?" Cranwell prompted.

"She came to me," Fanny said. "She was dreadfully upset and did not know what to do. Lord Laing has become her particular friend in the last few days. She has found him to be extremely kind and sympathetic. He had persuaded her that it would be wrong to marry you if she truly did not love you. He told her that she should go back to Mr. Ferris and persuade him to marry her. To elope even, if necessary."

Sarah had risen to her feet, her hand over her mouth. Fanny glanced at her nervously.

"You must not be angry at Lord Laing," Fanny said. "He really has been a true friend to Hannah. He offered to take her to Mr. Ferris' house today. They will be there before nightfall, and Lord Laing will be back here sometime during the night. He will be ready to accompany you tomorrow morning, Miss Fifield, if you still wish to leave before everyone else."

Cranwell moved finally. "Fan, are you mad?" he said. "You lent your support to such a wild scheme?"

"It is not so wild," Fanny said with some indignation. "It would be wrong for you and Hannah to marry, George. She loves another, and you . . . Well, you do not love her, and I do not believe you would be happy with her. It is best this way."

"And Hannah," Cranwell said, incredulous. "How could she have agreed to do anything so totally indecorous? What are her parents to be told? What will this Ferris fellow have to say when she turns up quite unexpectedly on his doorstep?"

"True love will triumph," Fanny said, sounding far from convinced suddenly.

Cranwell raked his fingers through his hair. "She will be putting him in an impossible situation," he said. "The man will be almost forced to elope with her. What sort of a start will that be to a marriage?"

Joshua cleared his throat. "I would guess that Laing is largely to blame, Cran," he said. "Lady Hannah is very young and impressionable, y'know. He obviously talked her into it. A madman, pure and simple, if you will pardon me for saying so, Miss Fifield. He has given her most improper advice. At least he could have taken her maid with them."

"He persuaded Hannah to leave even without her dog," Fanny said. "He said the journey would take less time if just the two of them went. But you need not be concerned, George. Lord Laing will protect her from harm. He is her friend."

"Well, what do we do, Josh?" Cranwell said. "Let them go and hope that everything will somehow sort itself out? And who is to tell Cavendish and his wife? You, Fan?"

"I was not to tell anyone until at least teatime," Fanny said miserably. "The main reason Hannah confided in me, I believe, was that she felt someone should know the truth so that you could all be told eventually. She was afraid that you would worry if you did not know her whereabouts."

Cranwell passed a hand over his eyes. "I never dreamed I had such featherbrains for a sister and a fiancée," he said. "Really, Fan."

"I suppose you should call Cavendish in here and let him decide what is to be done," Joshua suggested. "After all, Cran, he is the one mainly concerned, y'know."

"Yes," Cranwell said, "I suppose you are right." He turned back to the bell rope.

"No, don't," Sarah said, taking her hand away from her mouth at last and stretching it toward Cranwell. "It is not as simple as you think, George. He won't be taking her to Mr. Ferris. He will be eloping with her himself."

"What?"

"Oh, no, really, Miss Fifield."

"My fear exactly."

All three of her listeners reacted to her words at the same moment.

"You don't know Win," Sarah said. "He has never performed a selfless deed in his life. His own interest is the only thing that ever matters to him. He has undoubtedly found out that Lady Hannah is wealthy. He will be determined to marry her himself."

"Miss Fifield," Fanny cried, "you cannot know what you are saying. There is no one more concerned for others than Lord Laing. He is taking Hannah to Mr. Ferris. Then he is coming back here. All within a day."

Cranwell was ashen-faced.

"No," Sarah said, her voice shaking now. "I know him. I have known him for many years. Believe me, George, please."

"But she will not agree to marry him," Fanny said with some scorn. "She does not love him."

"That will not matter to Win," Sarah said. She had not taken her eyes from Cranwell.

"You think they will be going to Gretna?" he asked, his eyes locked with hers.

Her hand crept back to her mouth. She stared at him silently for several moments. "No," she said. "That would not work, would it? There would be every danger that the earl would cut Lady Hannah out of his will if she did such a thing."

"Then you have changed your mind?" he asked with a frown.

"No," she said, "no. Let me think. He must make it seem as if he is acting nobly and honorably. Will he hope that Mr. Ferris will reject her? No, of course, that would be far too risky. He will have to make sure that she is forced to marry him—that will be it. He will make sure that they do not reach their destination today. Then she will be compromised and he will be honor-bound to marry her. Even the earl will not be able to argue, whether he likes the match or not."

Cranwell looked long and levelly into her eyes before turning abruptly away. "I understand you are upset by the turn of events, Sarah," he said, "but I cannot help thinking that you are overreacting. The man could not be so conniving. You have painted a picture of a devilish kind of fiend. We are all acquainted with Bowen. And you have freely engaged yourself to marry him. Let us waste no more time. I shall send for Cavendish."

"George, please!" Sarah moved forward a step and held out a hand to him again. She glanced hastily at the other two. "Let me talk to you alone for a minute?"

Cranwell stared at her.

"Lady Fanny," Joshua Stonewall said, opening the door and bowing in her direction, "shall we take a turn along the cloister? We will be within calling distance if you need us, Cran."

Fanny preceded him from the room.

"Well?" Cranwell said when the door closed behind them. "What is it, Sarah? There really is no time to lose, you know."

"I do know," she said, "better than you, George. You must go after them, and without Lord and Lady Cavendish's knowing, if possible. There will be a dreadful scandal. Perhaps it can be averted if you hurry."

"I understand that you are less than pleased about the part your betrothed has played in this mess," Cranwell said. "But really, Sarah, this whole affair is beyond my concern now. It is her father you should be speaking to."

"George!" she said. "Listen to me. It was Win . . ." She stopped and took a shuddering breath. "It was Win who ravished me when I was no older than Hannah is now. And he showed no mercy on me though I begged him and begged him to stop. Not then or the times after. He will force her to marry him if you do not stop him. Win always gets what he wants."

She really thought for one moment that he was going to collapse. He turned even paler than before, if that were possible, and swayed noticeably on his feet. Then he turned and ran for the door and yanked it open.

"Josh, come in here!" he called. "Fan, go and give orders at once that I want my curricle and my grays ready before the door in no more than ten minutes."

Fanny hesitated for only a moment, but something in her brother's face appeared to alarm her. She hurried off without a word. Joshua was equally prompt in coming back inside the library and closing the door behind him.

"Josh," Cranwell said, "I am leaving immediately to pursue those two. Pray that Sarah is right and they are headed in the direction of Ferris' home. With luck I should be able to overtake them sometime this afternoon and bring her back here before her parents can become too alarmed. You and Sarah must make up some story to explain our absence for the whole day. Whatever it is, I shall be in for a thundering attack when I bring her back. It will not look good for me to have her from home all day without chaperonage. Put your heads together. I must get ready."

He made for the doorway again, until Sarah's voice stopped him.

"I am coming with you, George," she said. "No, don't say no. I cannot remain here inactive. And it will be better if I can be there when you find Hannah. Mr. Stonewall's task will be easier, too, if it seems that the four of us have gone somewhere together. Our disappearance will seem only bad-mannered rather than improper."

"You would not be safe, love," Cranwell said. "I shall not be driving with a lady's comfort in mind."

"Please, George," she said, crossing the room to him and placing a hand on his sleeve. "I need to be with you."

A fascinated Joshua Stonewall watched Cranwell hesitate and nod his head. They both hurried toward

the door. But before they could reach it, there was a
light tap on the other side and it opened.

"Yoo-hoo!" Lady Murdoch called. "I heard that
Sarah was in here saying good-bye to you, your grace,
and thought it would be a good opportunity to say my
own farewells too. Oh, good morning, Mr. Stonewall." She smiled.

"Oh, Cousin Adelaide," Sarah said, "a dreadful
thing. Win has run off with Lady Hannah, and his
grace and I are going to go after them."

Lady Murdoch did not even seem unduly shocked,
Cranwell noticed. She clasped her hands to her large
bosom.

"Well, bless my soul," she said, "that poor little
lamb. Do you know where they have gone, dear?"

"Back toward her home," Sarah said. "But I am
sure he will try to delay her on the road."

"Come then, my love," Lady Murdoch said decisively. "Let us go and get your bonnet and a warm
cloak. While you are gone, I shall see if Lord Laing's
belongings have been packed. I shall have them sent
on to Gretna Green."

She was already urging Sarah through the doorway.
Joshua Stonewall, following behind them and Cranwell,
said, "But it seems improbable, ma'am, that they have
gone to Gretna."

"Eh?" Lady Murdoch said, looking up at Sarah.
"Did someone say something, dear? I seem to be
rather deaf these days. I used to be quite sharp of
hearing in my younger days."

The first part of the journey was relatively simple. It
involved merely driving as fast as the horses could be
made to go. There was no need to stop until it was
time to change the horses, and no need to look at
anything but the road ahead. If Bowen had indeed
planned events as Sarah guessed, Cranwell was quite
sure that he would not have attempted to stop on the
road until they were too far from Montagu Hall to

make it possible to return, yet far enough from Ferris' to make it impossible to keep going.

The only matter that need concern him, then, Cranwell decided with a sideways glance at his companion, was Sarah's safety. She sat on the high seat beside him, clinging to the armrest on the far side, staring straight ahead, her face expressionless. He would not have worried about the danger to himself. Driving his curricle fast had always been his one indulgence in reckless living, and he had never had an accident. But he found himself slowing down slightly at the larger bends in the road, more cautious than usual.

They spoke not at all during the first half-hour of the journey. Cranwell tried to think only of the task ahead of him. If Sarah was wrong, of course, they would drive on until they came to Ferris' home or until they met Bowen on his way back to Montagu Hall. He supposed that that would be the best outcome. His responsibility to Hannah would end there. It would be up to Cavendish, Ferris, and Hannah among them to work out a satisfactory solution. His own betrothal would be effectively at an end. He would be free again.

Would it matter to him? He would have to begin all over again selecting a suitable bride, offering for her, planning a wedding. Would he do it? He very much doubted it. It just seemed as if he were not destined for marriage. In fact, he found, he was almost relieved to think that there might be a way out of this betrothal. Fanny was right. It was doubtful that marriage to Hannah would bring him much happiness. Not that he had been looking for such an outcome, of course. It was his succession that had been his main concern. Well, the title would have to pass out of his direct line after his time, that was all. It would not be the end of the world. And he would not live to see the day, anyway.

There would, of course, be the embarrassment of being jilted. He had a houseful of guests at home, gathered to celebrate his betrothal. He found, though, when he tested the thought in his mind, that he really did not care. He had lived through much worse scandal. He would live through this. When the guests had all left, he would still have his home and his lands and his work. He had learned how to live alone.

But what if Sarah was right, and they came across Bowen and Hannah at some inn along the road? What would he do about her? Offer to take her on to Ferris himself and leave the two of them to take the matter from there? Or take her back to Montagu Hall? He supposed that the decision would have to be hers. And if she chose to go back with him, what then? Would she tell her parents the truth and break off the betrothal? Or would she wish to keep quiet about the whole matter? Would he be willing to continue with the wedding plans under the circumstances?

Why had she not told him that she did not wish to marry him? He did not think he had even heard of this Ferris before Fanny had mentioned him earlier. Did he appear to be such a tyrant to her that she could not tell him the truth? Of course, he must be fair to her. She was only seventeen years old, a mere child. And Cavendish was quite an overbearing character. If he had decided that she must marry Cranwell, then probably she had had little choice.

Poor Hannah! Poor, foolish little girl. He did not love her and never had. But he worried for her safety. Unconsciously he took the next bend without slowing at all, and Sarah swayed against him before gripping the armrest more tightly and pulling herself upright.

God, but he could not keep his mind off Sarah's words any longer. But he must if he was to keep anything like concentration on the road ahead. Think of Hannah. Think of Ferris. Wonder what he looked like, how old he was, what he would do if Hannah should arrive unexpectedly at his door. Think about Lady Cavendish and how she would treat her granddaughter's foolhardy behavior if she found out. Think of Salisbury Cathedral and that stained-glass window

Sarah had been looking at yesterday afternoon. Think of the harvest, proceeding without him.

It was Win who ravished me.

Think of the horses. It was time they were changed for fresher ones. Look out for a good inn that will be likely to care for them well until I can pick them up on the way home again.

He showed no mercy on me, though I begged him and begged him to stop.

Start looking. Was that a village up ahead? Or just a farmhouse? He could not see now. There were trees in the way.

Not then or the times after.

"Why are you betrothed to him?" he asked almost viciously. "Why are you going to marry him?"

Sarah turned her head jerkily to look at him and then turned to face the road again. "I am not," she said. "I was merely waiting until we left Montagu Hall to break off the betrothal."

"And that is why you were permitting such intimacies last night?" he asked.

"I . . . I did not want to cause a scene," she said.

He laughed. "Come," he said, "you can think of something better than that, surely. And you might have chosen a cloak that would cover you to the chin. That purple mark on your neck could have been caused by nothing other than a man's teeth."

He saw her swallow as he watched. She said nothing. He turned his attention back to the road. Yes, it was a village. Should he stop, or were the horses fresh enough for a few more miles? He did not slow down as they approached and passed the cluster of buildings. Soon they were in open countryside again.

It was Win who ravished me.

She sat silent beside him, her posture more rigid than it had been before. Her eyes were fastened to the road ahead as if she were directly responsible for their staying on its surface. Why, in heaven's name, was she going to marry the man?

"How would you define 'ravishment,' Sarah?" he

asked. He was surprised to hear his voice sound quite
conversational.

"What?" She turned to him, startled.

"I would like to hear how you were ravished," he
said. "Did you lead him on as you did in the woods a
few afternoons ago and as you were doing last night?
And did his control snap? And were you annoyed
afterward that you had been unable to stop him? Is
that how it happened?"

"No!" she whispered.

"Did I ravish you the other day?" he asked. "I did
not stop to ask your permission either, did I?"

"No," she said. "You know that I gave myself willingly, George."

"Ah," he said. "I was to be fully indulged, was I?
For old times' sake? While poor Bowen was to be
merely teased. But you might have known, Sarah, that
he is a red-blooded male. I would imagine it would be
playing with raging fire to try to tease him. So he lost
control, and you were ravished. Perhaps you should
choose your next victim with more care, my love."

"Don't," she said. He had never heard her voice
sound more miserable. "Don't, George. Ignore me if
you will. I know I was not invited on this journey. But
please do not abuse me like this. Please!"

Her voice disappeared on a high note, and when he
looked across at her, it was to find that she had turned
her face away at a sharp angle so that he could see no
part of it around the brim of her bonnet.

Oh God, he thought, why was he doing this? Did he
not believe her? She had been no older than Hannah
was now, she had said. No older than Fanny! And that
must be true. She had been scarcely nineteen when
they married. She had been living with her uncle and
aunt—and her cousin—since she was twelve. She was
a remarkably pretty girl. Was it not conceivable—highly
probable, in fact—that her cousin had looked on her
with lust? They were not even blood relations. Bowen
was a large and strong man and probably had been so
even at that time. He was a few years older than

Sarah. It would have been easy for him to force her. And the opportunity would not have been hard to find.

I begged him and begged him to stop.

Cranwell clamped his teeth together and tightened his grip on the ribbons.

"Why did you not tell anyone?" he asked abruptly. "If he ravished you when you were seventeen, why did you not tell your aunt and uncle? Why did you not tell me before we were married? Or after we were married? You had ample opportunity, and that story would have set you in a better light than the one you told. Why have you said nothing until now?"

Her head was still turned away. She turned back to face the road again after a few seconds and he could see that her eyes were red and her cheeks stained with tears. She was searching in her reticule.

"I was seventeen," she said, "a mere child. I did not know how to fight someone like Win. I tried to avoid him, and I begged him not to touch me. I would have told, but he threatened, or seemed to—"

"Threatened what?" Cranwell asked sharply. He pulled a handkerchief impatiently from his pocket and put it into her hand.

"He told me that Graham—my brother—had killed a boy in a rage a few years before by pushing him over a cliff," she said. "He said he would tell and Gray would be hanged."

"Absurd!" he said. "That was the child who fell into a quarry? But Fanny was there. The child was not pushed. I wrote to the magistrate to explain the facts after Fanny finally told me."

"I discovered that only yesterday," Sarah said, staring fixedly ahead. "But I believed Win at the time. He physically forced me. I had to give in to him. And then I was ashamed and even more afraid to say anything. I thought Aunt Myrtle and Uncle Randolph would drive me away in disgust if they knew. And when it happened again I felt even more depraved. I thought I must somehow be consenting to what was happening."

"But you never did?"

"No! It was loathsome," she said, her voice shaking with revulsion. "Loathsome! I think hell must be like being touched by Win."

"And did your aunt and uncle never suspect what was going on under their very noses?" he asked.

"No," she said. "They always doted on Win. And he has a gift for making other people like him and trust him. And I did my best to keep it from them. Uncle Randolph was very sick for years and Aunt Myrtle very worried about him. I could not add that to their worries."

There was another village ahead. Cranwell, looking critically at his horses, knew that they must stop there for a change.

"Why is it that he never got you with child?" Cranwell asked.

Sarah turned to stare at him. "He said he knew a way," she said abruptly.

He laughed shortly. "How fortunate for you," he said. "We will stop at the next inn. It is just half a mile ahead. You may get down to stretch your legs and have some refreshments. But only for a few minutes. We must keep going."

"Oh yes," she agreed. "Let us not be long, George. I cannot help feeling responsible for Hannah. If I had told you about Win sooner instead of waiting until I was leaving, this might not have happened."

"Is that what you wished to talk to me about this morning?" he asked, looking across at her in surprise.

"Oh yes," she said. "Cousin Adelaide and I had decided that you must know. I was afraid he was aiming for Fanny."

"Fanny?"

"Yes," she said, "I knew he would think it huge enjoyment to win himself a rich wife and hurt you at the same time. That is why I asked you for the money and persuaded Win to become betrothed to me. I hoped that I could lure him away and marry him before he had a chance to do you any harm."

"Me?" Cranwell said, glancing at her with a frown and maneuvering the curricle into a small cobbled innyard. "Why would he wish to hurt me?"

"I don't think he has forgiven you for trying to take me away from him," Sarah said.

They traveled almost in silence after that first stop. Cranwell drove on again at the same breakneck speed as before until after they had changed horses for the second time. After that, he slowed down at each town and village and even at each farmhouse that was close to the road. He looked into every innyard and questioned grooms and ostlers. In only one place did he have news that might have been promising. A young man and young lady in a hired chaise had changed horses there about an hour back and, yes, they had continued along the road. The descriptions fit quite well, too, except that the ostler being questioned insisted that the young man had had jet-black hair.

Sarah became more and more filled with anxiety. What if she was wrong? She could not be wrong on the main point, of that she was convinced. Win was not taking Hannah anywhere out of the goodness of his heart. She was quite convinced that he meant somehow to marry the girl. But what if her theory was incorrect? What if he had not even come by this road? He might be heading north for Scotland, though she very much doubted that he would do so. But were there not other alternatives that would bring Hannah as much under his power as the scheme she had guessed at?

Her own suggestion seemed the most obvious course for Win to have taken. It would be so easy for him to stop somewhere along this road and convince Hannah that they must stop for the night. Lame horses, a broken conveyance: Win would think of some cause of delay with no effort at all. Hannah was such an innocent that she would probably agree to the delay without even realizing until it was too late that her honor had been compromised to such an extent that she must marry Win. She would probably never even realize that he had brought about that effect deliberately.

But what if she was wrong? What if they drove all the way to the Earl of Cavendish's property, found their way to the neighbor, and then discovered that Hannah was not there? Would they immediately drive north? They would surely be too late to intercept the travelers on their way to Gretna even if they were headed there. And where else would they look? She had to be right. If she was not, there was no way of saving Hannah. She could tell her story to the earl, of course, and hope that he would prevent a marriage. But Hannah would be permanently disgraced, her life ruined. Just as her own had been. And both by Win.

Sarah was beginning to feel despair. Could she do nothing right? In the last few days she had been beginning to feel a new hope, a new confidence in herself. She had hoped that even if there was nothing too bright in her future, at least she could learn to like herself again. She had finally accepted what the Reverend Clarence had tried to tell her many times, that she need not feel guilty about her past, that she had been more sinned against than sinning. And she had gathered for herself more tender memories of George to last her through the lonely years ahead.

But what had she done in the process of rebuilding her own life? She had forgotten her responsibility to others. She knew from her own experience that Win was dangerous even when one seemed to have ringed oneself around with security. Look at last night, for example. If he had chosen to carry her off to his bedchamber or hers when he became angry, she would have found it hard to stop him. She would have been reluctant to scream, she thought. And she had known that there were at least two young and wealthy girls in the house who might be in danger from him. She had owed it to them to offer all the protection she was able to offer. She should have spoken to George and even perhaps the Earl of Cavendish much earlier in the week. In fact, she should have spoken to George when they were still in Bath.

By her silence she had brought all this about. And it might be too late.

And George did not believe her. Finally, after all these years, she had told her secret. And he did not believe her. He still believed that she had been the seductress and Win the victim. He still despised her.

She had fantasized a great deal over the years, and even as recently as that morning, when she had finally plucked up the courage to go down to the library. She had dreamed of telling him the truth. And always in the dreams he had believed her instantly and held out his arms to her. That one confession had always broken down all the barriers between them. She had always been well aware that it was fantasy, of course. She had never expected reality to be the same. But it had been a pleasant fantasy, the ultimate comfort for all her misery. If only he knew, she had always been able to tell herself.

And now he did know, and the fantasy was permanently dead. For the rest of her life she would have to face the truth. George had been told that she had never given herself willingly to any man, that she had been ravished at the age of seventeen. He had been told, and he had chosen to disbelieve. He had no trust in her at all. No love left. What had happened two afternoons before had been only a result of desire on his part. Nothing more.

Sarah gazed ahead along the road to a bleak and loveless future.

years before. He had run the trail from her. To Win-
 throp Cavendish's elegant charges. Who would leave
her innocence as she was little more than a child,
and then...

He clenched his teeth on a flood of guilt. Such an
understanding of her was his fault. With her innocence
— ——— ——— ——— ——— ——— ——

22

THEY HAD been traveling for a little more
than four hours. From his previous journeys to Cavendish's home, Cranwell guessed that there were about
two hours yet to travel. If Sarah was correct in her
guess, this would be about the place Bowen would
choose to stop. If he had gambled on the alarm not
being raised until at least teatime, he would guess that
no one would catch up with them that day. Yet he
would not wish to journey much closer to Hannah's
home for fear that she would know some people with
whom to stay or from whom to procure help to com-
plete the journey. It would have to be soon, if at all.

There was a village ahead. He had seen the church
spire a couple of minutes before. He was feeling very
tired from the hours of sitting and concentrating on
controlling several different sets of horses. Sarah must
be exhausted. He understood that she was not accustomed to traveling, and certainly she would not be
used to riding on the high seat of a gentleman's curricle.

He glanced at her and noted that she was staring
quietly ahead along the road. He did not think they
had exchanged a word since the last stop to change
horses and partake of some quick refreshments an
hour before.

He felt the nagging of guilt at the edges of his mind
again. For the last few hours he had tried to put from
his mind everything except the pursuit and the constant inquiries at every inn and farmhouse. How could
he have been so brutal to her earlier in the journey?
He did not feel brutal. Not to her, anyway. To himself, perhaps, for not having taken more pains four

years before to find out the truth from her. To Winston Bowen, the smiling charmer, who had taken away her innocence when she was little more than a child and who had ruined her life. But not to Sarah.

He could not even apologize. He should do so. He wanted to do so. But in three hours he had not been able to form the words in his mind. What to apologize for? For doubting her word? He had not really doubted it at all since that appalling moment in the library earlier that morning when she had told him that it was Bowen who had ravished her before her marriage to him. Apologize for ever having doubted her basic innocence? For having divorced her and made her a pariah in all of England?

An apology was so inadequate that it was ludicrous even to think of making one. How could one apologize for having called a suffering young girl a whore? For having sentenced her to four years of solitary living during the very years when she should have been experiencing the joys of youth and life? For having doomed her to a lifetime away from the people of her own social class if her identity were known? If the truth were to be faced, he was far more guilty than Bowen. Bowen had degraded her body. He had destroyed her whole life.

"If there is a decent inn in this village, we will rest, Sarah," he said. "You must be exhausted." As if a little kindness were going to atone for four years of injustice.

"I can keep going if you can, George," she said. "We must find them. Oh, please, God, let me be right."

From her voice he could tell she was very close to tears. Impulsively he reached out with his gloved hand and squeezed one of her hands tightly.

"If you are not," he said, "it is not your fault, Sarah. None of this is your fault. You have done your best."

It was the wrong thing to have done. Her hands flew

to her face, and she sat with her shoulders hunched and her hands tightly covering her eyes.

Cranwell drew the horses to a halt and looked help-lessly across at her. He wanted to put his arms around her, to cradle her head on his shoulder, to tell her that everything would be all right, that he would make everything all right. But he could do none of those things. He did not have the right to offer comfort to this woman whom he had destroyed. He could not assure her of anything. He did not know that they would be able to save Hannah's honor. And he could not assure her that everything would be well with her life. How could it be? He could not reverse the harm he had done her in the past.

"Don't cry, Sarah," he said. "We will find them if they are on this road. You are very tired. We will stop at the village. You must have some tea and warm up before a fire. You will feel better afterward."

"Oh yes," she said shakily, not removing her hands from her face. "I shall be all right. I am sorry, George. I am being a horrid watering pot. And this time I do have a handkerchief." She reached down for her reti-cule, which she had set behind her feet, and pulled out the large and crumpled piece of linen that he had given her earlier.

She smiled determinedly at him after drying her eyes. "You may drive on," she said. "I am not going to have hysterics or the vapors or anything like that."

She kept the smile on her face until he had turned away again and given the horses the signal to start. There was no point in tears, she thought. No point at all. She must teach herself all over again, as she had four years before, not to cry, not to give in to emo-tion. All emotion in her life must be put to death, and there was no time like the present for starting. His voice had been kind and the touch of his hand reassur-ing. That was what had started the tears, in fact. But she must not mistake a natural kindliness of manner for real feeling toward her. He had offered no real comfort, although every muscle in her body was sore, and she had ached and ached to feel his arms around her, just to rest her head on his shoulder for a few minutes.

She was still smiling as they drove into the village and along a narrow street to a small inn on the far side of it.

Winston was standing outside the door into the taproom, in conversation with a portly older man.

He saw them at almost the same moment they saw him. If Sarah had expected him to look horrified, or surprised even, she was to be disappointed. He raised his eyebrows, smiled slightly, turned to say something to the man with whom he was standing, and strode over to the curricle, which Cranwell had pulled into the yard. But of course, Sarah thought in the few seconds granted them before he came up with them, she might have known Win well enough by now to have learned that he was not easily flustered.

"I wondered if you would come in pursuit, Cranwell," he said with an apologetic smile. "And I cannot say I blame you. I can only say that I have acted in what seemed to be the best interests of everyone concerned. Perhaps we can discuss the matter inside, like civilized beings? Sarah, my love? Have you thought it necessary to make this long journey too? There was no need, you know. I was returning to you tonight. But it is a delightful surprise to see you. May I help you down?"

Winston did not wait for her answer. He caught her around the waist as she rose to her feet and lifted her to the ground. He was smiling warmly down at her when she looked up at him, her feet safely on the ground.

"Where is Lady Hannah, Bowen?" Cranwell asked curtly, nodding to a groom who had emerged from the inn stables and handing him the ribbons of his curricle.

"Quite comfortable in a private parlor inside," Winston said. "You may come and see for yourself,

Cranwell, though I would guess that she will be none too pleased to see you."

Cranwell strode into the inn without another word, Sarah close at his heels. A flustered innkeeper indicated the door of the parlor, and Cranwell knocked on it.

"Come in," a timid female voice answered after a slight pause.

Hannah had clearly just risen from the table, on which were spread tea and cakes. Her eyes grew huge with terror when she saw Cranwell in the doorway.

"Your grace!" she said, scrambling farther around the table so that it lay between her and him.

"Hannah," he said, striding into the room, "are you all right? Has Bowen harmed you?"

Sarah came quietly into the room and closed the door after Winston had come inside too.

"Oh, Miss Fifield," Hannah said, a shaking hand going to her mouth, "I am so sorry. Really I am. I knew that Lord Laing should have told you that he was bringing me, but he said that you might try to stop me and . . . But I am truly sorry if you have been in distress. He meant to return later today, truly he did."

"Has Bowen harmed you?" Cranwell repeated, and the terror returned to Hannah's eyes as she looked back at him.

"N-no, your grace," she said. "He has been most kind."

"He has not tried to delay your journey?" he asked.

"To delay it?" She looked mystified. "He has been taking me as fast as possible to . . . to . . ."

"Yes," Cranwell said, "I know where you are going. And Bowen has been taking you directly there with no delays?"

Winston laughed. "That is the general idea when one is running away, is it not, Cranwell?" he said. "Why would one delay under the circumstances? Of course, we have obviously not been as fast as you and Sarah, but then you had the advantage of us. We merely had a hired carriage, no match for a curricle."

He sounded as if he were making polite conversation on the most ordinary occasion, Sarah thought incredulously. He smiled his old charming smile even as she looked up at him.

"Why do we not all sit down?" he asked, gesturing at the empty chairs around the table. "I shall order more tea for the ladies. I am sure we could all do with refreshments. What will you have, Cranwell?"

Cranwell ignored him. "Do you realize what a mad scheme this is, Hannah?" he asked. "Does this Ferris know you are coming?"

"N-no, your grace," she said, "but he loves me."

"And that makes everything acceptable?" he asked. "Has he ever offered for you?"

"No," she said. "We were planning to wait until I was eighteen."

"And did he do anything when you became betrothed to me?" he asked. "Did he speak to your father?"

"He did not wish to stand in the way of my advancement," Hannah said miserably, looking down at her hands.

"And what is he going to say when you arrive this afternoon?" Cranwell asked none too gently. "Have you realized that you will be almost forcing him to elope with you?"

Hannah said nothing for a moment. "He loves me," she said eventually.

"Will you be sure of that when he will have no choice?" Cranwell said. "Will you wonder for the rest of your life if he married you of his own free will?"

Hannah said nothing.

"Lady Hannah is a very young lady, Cranwell," Winston said, moving around the table and laying a hand reassuringly on her shoulder. "I think you and her father have spent long enough bullying her. It is time she was allowed to think for herself and make up her own mind what she wants."

"Precisely!" Cranwell agreed. "And I would suggest

that you too give her that opportunity, Bowen. Left to herself, I know that Lady Hannah is far too sensible and well-bred to behave in such a shockingly improper fashion."

"I do not wish to marry you, your grace," Hannah said with a short burst of spirit. But she hung her head again after looking him briefly in the eye.

"And I shall do nothing to force you, Hannah," Cranwell said, his voice more gentle at last. "It was never my intention to coerce you. I did not know your feelings until today, my dear. But that is not the point at issue here. The point is that you have run away without your parents' knowledge and with no proper chaperonage to a young man who does not even know that you are planning such a move. You are placing several people in a very awkward and embarrassing situation."

"I would advise you not to listen to him, Lady Hannah," Winston said in the warm, sincere voice that usually melted female hearts. "If you do not go on now, Cranwell will take you back and you will be forced to marry him. And I imagine he will not let you forget easily what you have done today. Don't allow yourself to be bullied any longer."

"Will Donald feel that I am forcing his hand?" Hannah asked. Then she looked at Sarah, her eyes huge with fright and indecision. "Will he blame me, Miss Fifield, and even come to hate me?"

"You must go back, Hannah," Sarah said. "No one can force you to marry against your will, and I am certain that his grace will not even try. Perhaps your father will not allow you to marry Mr. Ferris even if he offers for you. But maybe it would be better not to marry him at all than to force him into matrimony and wonder all your life if he really wished to marry you."

"Oh," Hannah said, "but Lord Laing said . . . Oh, Miss Fifield, what shall I do?"

"You must come back with us," Sarah said. "It will be well into the evening by the time we reach Montagu Hall again, but I believe scandal can be averted. Your parents may be angry that you have been gone so long, but Lady Fanny and Mr. Stonewall have agreed to say that the four of us went out together for the day. His grace is prepared to suffer the ill opinion of anyone who will think that he has kept us from home for too long."

"Oh," Hannah said, her eyes straying to Cranwell. She flushed. "You would do that for me, your grace?"

"You are my betrothed," he said. "I owe you all the protection I have to offer. If you wish to end the engagement, I would suggest that you talk with your father tomorrow or the next day. You will find that I shall not make the matter awkward for you at all."

"And if she does not speak with her father, I suppose you will be prepared to do the noble thing and marry her, eh, Cranwell?" Winston said. For once his charm had slipped. His tone was heavy with sarcasm.

Cranwell looked at him levelly. "Lady Hannah is my betrothed, Bowen," he said. "Until I am informed differently, I plan to marry her in December."

Hannah looked around her and sank into the nearest chair. "I am so confused," she said, "and so ashamed."

"Well, Bowen," Cranwell said, "there is no time to be wasted, I think, if we are to return to Montagu Hall before much of the night is wasted. Do you plan to return with the rest of us?"

Winston smiled and made Cranwell a half-bow. There was no trace left of his sarcasm. "But there never was any question of my returning," he said. "I was merely serving the wishes of Lady Hannah. If she has now decided that she wishes to return to the bosom of her family after all, I am, as always, her servant."

Hannah looked up at him. "I am so sorry, sir," she said, "for the inconvenience I have caused you. I shall always be grateful for your concern."

Winston bowed.

"Sarah," Cranwell said, "I shall have fresh tea sent

in for you. Rest yourself as much as you can in the next few minutes. We shall start back as soon as we may. You have a hired carriage, Bowen?" Winston bowed again. "You and Lady Hannah must ride in the carriage, Sarah. Your return journey will be more comfortable, at least."

He turned and left the parlor without another word. Winston stayed with the ladies.

"I think we have one angry man there," he said easily. "I do hope you have not had too unpleasant a journey of it, my love. Lady Hannah? Now that he has gone, you must tell me what your wishes really are. If you wish to continue your journey, I shall see that Cranwell is defied. He cannot order you back, you know. I feel quite competent to stand up to him."

Hannah smiled bleakly up at him. "No," she said, "he and Miss Fifield are right. I should not have come in the first place. I thank you for your support, sir, but I must go back and try to sort out my problem in a more proper manner."

Winston smiled first at her and then at Sarah. He looked long and hard at Sarah, the smile steady on his face the whole while. He nodded at last, turned abruptly, and left the room.

"How mortifying all this is," Hannah said, stealing a glance at Sarah.

"Unfortunately," Sarah said gently, "we all do foolish things in life, Hannah. We just have to learn to live them down. But believe me, you have made the right decision now."

They both stopped talking as a little maid backed into the room carrying an enormous tray laden with meat pasties, cakes, and a large pot of tea.

"Hannah," Sarah said when they were alone again, "was Win taking you directly to Mr. Ferris? Had he made any suggestion that you delay your journey until tomorrow?"

Hannah looked at her with a little frown. "Why would he do that?" she said. "It was important that we reach Donald's before nightfall. Lord Laing was anxious to return to you before you could become too upset."

"Shall I pour?" Sarah asked brightly, picking up the teapot. "Do tackle one of those pasties, Hannah. We have a long journey ahead of us. I am sure we should eat."

It certainly was a long journey. The return distance seemed twice as far as the outward one, despite the fact that Sarah was sitting in much greater warmth and comfort. Not that the carriage was very well-sprung or well-upholstered. It was an ancient, ponderous conveyance, driven by a coachman who grumbled at having so few opportunities to rest and fill his belly with some warm ale. Cranwell, with Winston beside him, drove his curricle behind the carriage, holding it to a much slower pace than before.

It was not a comfortable journey for either group. Hannah became increasingly nervous with each returning mile. Sarah, relieved that a terrible catastrophe had been averted, nevertheless found that relief did not bring happiness. She remembered suddenly that the next morning she would be leaving Montagu Hall and George forever. And she would carry with her the knowledge that he would always despise her, never believe the story of her past. Cranwell was uncomfortable with his companion. The high road during a long journey was certainly not the right setting for the sort of conversation he wanted with Bowen. He refused to make small talk. They sat in near-silence the whole way. Winston, for his part, made no attempt to converse. He sat, apparently relaxed, a half-smile on his face.

As they traveled closer to home, Cranwell began to think of the scene ahead. It was still only early evening, but at this time of year darkness came soon enough to make the hour seem later than it was. It was going to be deuced awkward to explain his absence from his home and his guests for a whole day. Such behavior would seem bad manners at the very least. Cavendish would be none too pleased, either, at his taking Hannah away for a whole day without his permission.

Then there was the problem of the conveyances. With luck, no one would see their return. But if luck was not with them, it was going to be difficult to explain why they had needed both a carriage and a curricle to take four of them on an outing. And a hired carriage at that!

And what in heaven's name was Hannah going to do? She was such a confused young girl and apparently so in awe of her father that it was quite possible that she would do nothing. And where would that leave him? He could certainly make no move to end the betrothal. But it was quite unthinkable now to go ahead with the marriage plans. She had told him straight out that she did not wish to marry him. She had been running away to a man whom she did love. And the events of this day had proved to him beyond any doubt that he really did not wish to marry her. He had no particular objection to Hannah. He even felt a sort of paternal affection for her, much as he did for Fanny. But he did not wish to marry her.

Then there was Sarah. There would not be much of the evening left by the time they reached home, and the next day she would doubtless be planning to leave again. Could he let her go? He really did not have any choice. She was a free woman. He was certainly not a free man. But damnation, he fumed inwardly, she was his wife! He could not let her go.

Only Bowen posed no problem. Cranwell knew quite definitely what he planned to do about the man who sat silently relaxed in the seat beside him.

Much later that night Cranwell stood at the door of the drawing room bidding his guests good night. Most of them seemed to be in good spirits after a lively evening of charades.

He was feeling some relief. The main crisis of the evening had passed off surprisingly well. They had, in fact, arrived home in time for dinner, though they had had to rush through the process of dressing. And they had escaped notice as they drove up to the house. The hired carriage had set down its occupants and driven away and the curricle had been returned to the stables without a sign of any guest at windows or doors.

Bowen had been their chief rescuer, surprisingly enough. Or perhaps it was not so surprising when one had come to know that character. He had directed his attention immediately to Hannah's mother and to Lady Murdoch, both of whom had already come down for dinner. He had bowed over their hands with fervent apologies for having convinced his grace to take them far afield, though of course they had meant to be home by midafternoon. But alas, one should always allow for the unexpected. Who could have foreseen that one of the horses would throw a shoe and that when they finally led the poor creature to a smithy the smith should be found to be in a drunken stupor? He and Cranwell had been almost mad with anxiety lest the ladies should fret for the safety of their charges.

Cranwell had watched the performance with fascination. Lady Cavendish had melted immediately under Bowen's charm, and Lady Murdoch had declared very loudly that she had never had any doubt that the four of them would return to the house safe and sound before the evening was over. She had smiled with as much charm as Bowen had ever shown. Cranwell was beginning to admire that lady more than a little.

And now the evening was apparently over. At least the bulk of his guests were off to bed. It was not over for him, though. The Earl of Cavendish had just requested a word with him before he went to bed, and he had his own errand to attend to as well. And one more thing.

Sarah was leaving the drawing room, looking anywhere but at him. She had avoided him all evening, in

fact. He moved closer to the door so that she was
forced to stop to speak to him.

She raised her eyes unwillingly to his. "We will be
leaving in the morning, your grace," she said. "I shall
say good-bye now. There will be no need to disturb
you again in the morning." She held out her right
hand.

He took the hand in both his own and held it. There
was no one else close by. "Will you promise me that
you will see me in the morning before you go, nevertheless?" he asked.

She hesitated.

"Please, Sarah?"

"All right," she said.

"And I would not count on Bowen's going with you
tomorrow," he said. "Will you mind?"

"He is staying?" Sarah asked in surprise.

"Don't worry about him," he said. "I take it that
you are still planning to end your betrothal?"

She nodded but said nothing.

"Good night, Sarah," he said, letting go of her hand
at last.

"I am sorry," she said in a rush. "Perhaps you wish
that we had not gone in pursuit after all. I was wrong.
Win was intending to take her to Mr. Ferris'. Maybe
you would have preferred it so."

"Oh no," he said, looking directly into her eyes,
"you were exactly right, Sarah. Bowen had just paid
the coachman to damage his own carriage so that it
would be unusable for the rest of the day. He had
ascertained that there was no other carriage for hire in
the village."

Sarah gazed back at him, round-eyed. "How do you
know?" she asked.

He smiled fleetingly. "I paid the coachman twice as
much," he said.

Little more than a half-hour later Cranwell was knocking on the door of Winston's room. He was a free man
again, though he had not yet had time to digest the

fact fully. Hannah had not been as timid as he had thought, it seemed. She had spoken to both her parents immediately after dinner and had told them the whole truth. Cavendish had not gone into detail. He had merely wished to thank Cranwell for his part in saving his daughter from a great scandal and to beg that Hannah be released from the betrothal.

Cranwell did not know how the girl was to be treated or what punishment, if any, was to be meted out for her attempted elopement. He had no idea if an offer from her Donald Ferris would ever be received favorably. He could only hope that her life would turn out well. He must believe that it would. For all his gruffness, Cavendish appeared to love his daughter. And she was very young. There was plenty of time yet for an agreeable future to be secured for her. In fact, he had been very wrong even to have suggested marrying a child from the schoolroom. He should have allowed her to see something of life first.

The door of Winston's room opened and he stood there in his breeches and a shirt open at the neck.

"Ah, Cranwell," he said, "come inside. I perceive that you are about to challenge me to a duel for trying to spirit away your fiancée." He smiled. His tone was light.

"Not for that reason," Cranwell said.

"Eh?" Winston said with a grin. "You really have come to challenge me? You are mad, Cranwell."

"Perhaps," Cranwell agreed, "but the provocation has been great."

Winston grinned and leaned one elbow on the mantelpiece. "Do you hate being so exposed to the world as a man who cannot inspire love in a female?" he asked insolently.

"I intend to fight you for two reasons," Cranwell said steadily and quietly. "First, for attempting to gain possession of a young girl's fortune by compromising her honor and forcing her unwillingly into marriage."

"Ha!" Winston said, seemingly quite unperturbed.

"I see you have been bribing that infernal coachman. The man made a veritable fortune out of the two of us, Cranwell. However, you can hardly blame a man for trying, you know. We are not all as wealthy as you, my friend."

"You should know," Cranwell said. "I believe you are already in possession of a small chunk of my fortune, Bowen?"

Winston regarded him coolly before bowing slightly. "And your second reason for wishing to remove me from this life, Cranwell?" he asked.

"For having ruined the virtue, the happiness, and the very life of my former wife, Bowen," Cranwell said.

Winston was very still. "She has always been mine, Cranwell," he said. "And I knew how to make her happy far better than you did, apparently."

"A woman who is blackmailed and repeatedly raped at the age of seventeen does not know much happiness," Cranwell said very quietly, "or much faith in either herself or the other people around her. For this more than anything, Bowen, I plan to beat you to within an inch of your life."

Winston laughed and pushed himself away from the mantel. "I am in fear and trembling, Cranwell," he said. "Your words are sheer bravado, as you must realize. You have only to consider the contrast in our sizes and physiques to understand why I shall politely decline your request. It would be a massacre, my friend, and I really have no wish to do you any such harm."

"Of course," Cranwell said, "if you refuse to do this the honorable way, I shall feel quite justified in taking a horsewhip to your hide. In fact, you do not deserve the courtesy of a formal challenge. You are vermin, Bowen." He walked coolly over to the fireplace, picked up a half-full glass of brandy that Winston had set on the mantel when he came into the room, turned, and very deliberately threw its contents into the startled face of his companion.

Cold hatred replaced the sneer on Winston's face.

"Very well, Cranwell," he said, wiping his face with his sleeve, "this gives me the choice of weapons, I believe. I almost hate to do this to you under the circumstances, but it will be fists. I think you will be very sorry for this little display of self-righteousness. I assume you have a second in mind. I shall find some-one before I go to bed. You wish to settle this matter in the morning? Early?"

"You might try Penny," Cranwell said curtly. "He may meet Stonewall in the library at six tomorrow morning."

He turned and strode from the room.

23

SARAH HAD slept a sleep of exhaustion after the very busy day and a long talk with Lady Murdoch before going to bed. They had decided to keep to their plan to leave Montagu Hall the next morning. They would go to her Aunt Myrtle's, Sarah had decided, where she would break off her engagement to Win. She hoped that could be done without causing unnecessary unpleasantness. She and Lady Murdoch would then go home to Devonshire.

It was in many ways a welcome thought. There she would be able to relax and forget all the emotional upheaval of the last few weeks. It seemed like months since she had known any peace of mind. The years ahead were likely to be dull ones, but she blanked her mind to the prospect. She would think of something to make life meaningful. The years of her early adulthood had been largely wasted in heartache and self-recrimination. But she was young yet. It was far too soon to give up on life.

She had slept deeply. But she awoke very early and could not get back to sleep. It would be hours before she could hope to begin the journey into her unknown future, she thought. It was daylight outside, but she could hear no noises either outside or inside the house. Lady Murdoch was not an early riser, and neither was Win. Also she had promised to see George before she left, and sometimes he was from home until after breakfasttime.

She felt too restless to stay in bed. She pushed the bedclothes back impatiently and crossed to the window. It was a beautiful morning again with all the promise of a glowing early autumn day. The hills looked very inviting. She would get dressed and walk up into them once more. Perhaps she would find the spot where George had made love to her, though she must, of course, train herself soon to forget all such memories. They would do no good to her peace of mind in the life ahead.

Ten minutes later Sarah was walking briskly across the lawn to the bridge, a heavy gray cloak wrapping her warmly against the chill of the morning. It was not even seven o'clock, she had noticed in some surprise when she came downstairs. But she was not sorry she had come. The air was crisp, the grass wet with dew. And she needed this short time to herself, time in which to say her mental good-byes to Montagu Hall, to George, and to love.

It was a pity that she would also have to say a physical good-bye to George before leaving. It would be far easier not to have to face that ordeal, knowing as she looked at him, touched his hand maybe, that it would be the very last time. She felt panic quicken her breathing at the mere thought.

She stopped climbing when she reached the knoll from which there was such a picturesque view of the house. She stood there for many minutes looking down, committing the whole scene carefully to memory, while at the same time telling herself that tomorrow, later today even, she must begin to forget. George Montagu, she thought very deliberately, I love you, but tomorrow I shall start living without you again. She tried to will happiness into his home and his life as she stood there.

And then she saw him, and her heart turned over. He was walking south of the house in the direction of a large grain field and a small pasture. There was another man with him. Mr. Stonewall, Sarah guessed. They must be going to inspect the harvest, though it seemed strange that they were on foot. She had understood that the harvesters were working in a distant field.

It did not matter. She let her eyes rest on the unmistakable figure of George, slender and considerably smaller than his companion. There was an ache of pain in her throat. Under different circumstances she might have been watching him leave from their bedroom window, a familiar but beloved figure after four years of marriage. Instead she stood apart, drinking in this almost final view of the man from whom she had been estranged since their wedding day and who was no longer her husband or her companion and friend. She allowed herself the full luxury of self-pity.

Then her eye was caught by two other figures leaving the house and moving off in the same direction. One of them could be no other than Win. Even at this distance his very handsome physique set him apart from anyone else who was staying at the house. The upright bearing of the other man led her to believe that he was Captain Penny, though she could not be sure.

Sarah frowned. Win? Up at seven o'clock in the morning? And where was he going? The two men seemed to be heading in exactly the same direction as George and Mr. Stonewall.

As she stumbled and ran down the hill a minute later, Sarah did not know where the idea had come from. No, it was more than an idea. It was a conviction. "You must not count on Bowen's going with you tomorrow," George had said last night, or words to that effect. Win had run off with George's fiancée the day before and had intended to trap her into marriage with himself. Of course George would not be able to overlook such an insult to his pride. They were going to duel!

She did not know quite what she was going to do. Stop the fight, of course. But how could she do that? If the challenge had been given and accepted, it would be impossible to persuade two gentlemen to back down. And George would never allow the insult to his honor to pass. There was nothing she could do to stop it. But she sped on, intent on doing just that.

He would be killed. Oh, dear God, he would be killed. She loved him dearly, and there was no doubt in her mind that George was one hundred times the man that Win was. But even an imbecile could see that George was no match for Win physically. He was at least four inches shorter and did not have nearly Win's breadth of chest and shoulder. He spent his life here at Montagu Hall. He surely would have had no practice at all with pistols or swords. Win traveled around. He was probably adept at manly sports.

George would be killed, and then she would kill Win, she swore she would. She would find a gun somewhere, and she would kill him without any warning at all. She would doubtless hang for the offense, but it would be worth hanging to know that Win was no longer on this earth. And there would be no point in living anyway if she knew that George was dead.

Sarah was panting and deliberately planning murder by the time she was on the house side of the bridge again and running in hot pursuit of the four men, who she now knew were headed in the direction of the pasture. It was out of sight of the house, but the sound of the shots would be heard there, she thought in panic. They would all come running when they heard the report of two pistols, but it would be too late by then. He would be dead.

The pasture was quite open. There was no shelter once one was beyond a thicket of trees that stood between it and the house. Mr. Stonewall and Captain Penny were standing together when Sarah emerged from the trees. Cranwell and Winston were standing apart from each other. Both had removed their coats. Cranwell was already in his shirt sleeves.

Winston spotted her first. "Go back, Sarah," he called. "I appreciate your concern, my love, but this is no place for a lady." His tone was quite cheerful, careless almost.

The other three men looked up sharply. Cranwell paused in his task of rolling back his sleeves and

strode over to where she now stood at the open gate
to the pasture.

"Sarah," he said, looking at her with frowning concern, "what are you doing here? Bowen is quite right,
you know. This is no place for ladies. Go back to the
house now."

"You are going to fight," she accused. Her voice
was shaking.

"As you see," he said, his eyes looking directly into
hers.

"Don't," she said. "Please don't. I know that you
feel you must defend Hannah's honor. But I am sure
that she would not wish you to fight for her. And I
don't think her father would either. And no real harm
was done, George. It is not worth dying for."

"No one is going to die here, Sarah," he said,
coming closer to her and half-smiling down into her
eyes.

"He will shoot you," she said, "and you will be
dead before a surgeon can be summoned. I don't want
you to die, George."

"Don't you?" he said gently. "But we will not be
using weapons, Sarah. Only our fists."

Her eyes grew round with horror. "Fists?" she said.
"George, he will kill you for sure. He is twice as
strong as you."

He smiled outright. "You may be right," he said,
"but I think not. I do a great deal of physical work,
Sarah, and am perhaps stronger than I seem. A righteous cause gives one added strength too, I believe. I
am eager to begin this fight. Go back to the house,
love. And don't worry. No one is going to die."

"I don't want you to be hurt," she almost whispered.

"Perhaps you would like to come and mop my brow
too, Sarah," Winston called with a gay laugh. "Or
perhaps you are too busy telling your champion there
that he does not need to fight for your honor."

Sarah turned her head to look at him and then
jerked it back to face Cranwell. "You are not fighting
over me?" she asked incredulously.

"Go back now, Sarah," he said. He reached out one hand to touch her arm and try to turn her in the direction of the house again.

"But you did not believe me," she said wildly, pulling her arm away. "Why would you fight over me?"

"I believed you, Sarah," Cranwell said quietly and gently. "Go now."

"I don't want you to fight," she said, close to panic.

"Allow me to escort you part of the way, ma'am." Joshua Stonewall had taken her elbow in a firm grip and was turning her away from the pasture. "Indeed, you must leave, Miss Fifield," he said as she walked with him in some bewilderment. "Cran won't want you here. Penny don't have any more eagerness for this type of thing than I do. We will stop it before any great harm is done. You have my word on it, ma'am. Now, do I have yours that you will go all the way back to the house without stopping?"

Sarah hesitated. "I will give you my word not to try to interrupt the fight anymore," she said dully.

"Not quite what I asked," he said. "But there really is not enough time to take you all the way back m'self. You really ought to go, though, ma'am. It won't be a pretty sight for a lady. You go back. I'll bring him back safely to you."

He left her when they reached the clump of trees and bushes. Sarah turned to watch him go back to the pasture. Both George and Win were now in their shirtsleeves. She felt a knot of panic clench her insides. Now, how had Mr. Stonewall known that it was George she wanted brought back safely? She was still officially betrothed to Win. Or had he meant Win?

She turned around again and half-ran along the path through the trees. She dreaded to hear the sound of fighting behind her. She must get back to the house and up to her room, where she could wait without the distraction of other people around her. They would all still be in bed anyway. But she stopped as abruptly as she had started. How could she go back to the house? How could she wait there, not knowing the outcome, not knowing if George was hurt, perhaps bleeding and unconscious on the ground?

Almost against her will, dreading to look back and watch the violence, Sarah made her way off the path and into the densest of the bushes, pushing her way forward until she could again see the pasture without being seen.

It had already begun. They were circling each other, hands clenched into fists before them. It was such an unequal-looking contest that Sarah had to bite her top lip painfully in a determined effort not to go crashing through the undergrowth in another effort to stop them.

But soon she was clinging to a slim tree trunk, her fingernails digging into the bark, all thought of moving or making a sound or even keeping herself hidden forgotten. Win had thrown the first punch, and it had caught George squarely in the mouth, snapping his head back and making him stagger backward. But he did not fall and no longer circled cautiously. Both men were soon hitting, weaving, and dancing out of the other's range, fighting their way inside the other's guard, landing bruising blows.

To Sarah it seemed that it went on forever. George went down on one knee once, and she tasted blood from her upper lip. Captain Penny was forced to step in to prevent Win from pursuing him to the ground. She thought the fight was all over, but George picked himself up again and fought doggedly on.

Surely neither of them could stand the punishment for much longer, she thought finally. Why did Mr. Stonewall and Captain Penny not put an end to it? What was happening was cruelty. George surely must be half-dead already. He had been pummeled by Win's powerful fists for all of ten minutes, surely. He must go down soon. She prayed it would be very soon. She could not stand seeing him suffer any longer. Oh, dear God, she begged, let it just be over with. Let him go down and stay down before he is killed.

But it was Win who staggered a moment later, his

head turning sharply as a blow from Cranwell's fist caught him on the jaw. He did not go down, but he shook his head and appeared not quite steady on his legs. Cranwell followed up his advantage. Winston's guard was no longer effective. His fists were held loosely in front of his body, but there was visibly no strength left in them. He took three more powerful punches to the head before his legs finally buckled under him and he went down.

Sarah held her breath. Splinters of wood lodged beneath her fingernails as she grasped the tree trunk even more tightly. Win did not get up. Soon he would. In a moment he would be up again, his strength renewed. But he did not get up. Captain Penny was bending over his inert form. Mr. Stonewall was shaking George's hand and throwing a loose cloak around his shoulders. They were walking away to the place where George's garments were lying on the grass. And Win did not get up.

Sarah realized suddenly that she was crying. She fumbled around in the pocket of her dress for a handkerchief but found none. She rubbed at her eyes with the backs of her hands and sniffed wetly. Then she laughed shakily. "Oh, George," she said aloud, "I never have a handkerchief when I need one."

She turned and pushed her way back through the bushes. She was feeling panic-stricken again. She had to get across the open land between the bushes and the house before the men came up from the pasture. They must not know that she had watched.

Flying feet were soon carrying her across the lawn to the main doors. The eyes of the wooden-faced footman who opened the door for her looked unusually startled for a moment when Sarah flashed him a radiant smile and whisked her considerably disheveled person up the staircase to her room. He won, her mind was singing over and over again. He won! And he fought for me!

Fanny found Sarah in her room a half-hour later.

She knocked at the door and opened it timidly when Sarah called her to come in.

"Oh," she said, looking around the room, "you are still planning to leave today? Your bags are all packed."

Sarah was sitting at the window. "Yes," she said. "Lady Murdoch is only now breakfasting. When she has finished, we will order the carriage and be on our way."

"Without even saying good-bye to anyone?" Fanny asked.

"I said good-bye to almost everyone last night," Sarah replied. "I was hoping to see you this morning. And I have promised to see your brother before I leave."

Fanny's face brightened. "Mr. Stonewall sent me up to you," she said, "though I was already looking for an excuse to come. He said I was to tell you that George is all right and that he won the fight."

"I am very glad," Sarah said carefully.

"Did you know that he has been fighting Lord Laing?" Fanny asked, her eyes growing wide. "I was down early this morning or I might never have known. Though I suppose the news cannot be kept quiet. Mr. Stonewall and Captain Penny had only just finished carrying Lord Laing to his room when I ran into them. And I expect George has a black eye or some injury."

"Yes," Sarah agreed, "I suppose the truth will be generally known soon."

"I have never known George to fight or do anything violent," Fanny said, "beyond spanking me a few times when I was still a child. He will not even hunt. But I suppose a man feels honorbound to challenge someone who runs off with his fiancée. Do you think?"

"It seems so," Sarah agreed.

Fanny was looking at her closely. "Or someone who engages himself to his former wife."

Sarah rose to her feet with a smile. "The word 'former' is an important one, Fanny," she said. "Your brother and I have been divorced for four years. It is a long time. And he is betrothed to someone else now."

"Did you not know?" Fanny asked. "The engagement no longer exists. Hannah's papa spoke to George last night."

Sarah looked quickly at the girl and blushed. "No, I had not heard," she said.

Fanny threw herself down in the chair that Sarah had just vacated. "I really have botched the whole matter rather badly," she said forlornly.

"What do you mean?" Sarah asked, frowning. She had picked up the pelisse that she was to wear for the journey and was smoothing out its folds.

"I have tried so hard to bring you and George back together again," Fanny said. "But I have failed. You are leaving after all. And I was so sure that you were meant for each other."

"Fanny, whatever are you talking about?" Sarah had dropped the pelisse into a heap on the bed.

"I thought perhaps if you were both free again, you would realize that you love each other," Fanny said. "I knew almost as soon as I met you, Miss Fifield, that George had chosen well all those years ago. You are right for him. I suspected that Hannah did not really love George, and it was not difficult to get her to confide some of her unhappiness. And then you became betrothed to Lord Laing, and the problem was complicated."

Sarah sat on the bed next to the forgotten pelisse and stared at the young girl.

"I liked him," Fanny said, "and thought him a very attractive man. I thought that perhaps I could lure him away from you even though you are so beautiful and all. I did not feel very guilty, for I did not believe you loved him. I did not love him myself; I have no wish to fix my choice yet. I am too young. But I thought that if it would bring you and George together, I would be willing to marry Lord Laing. I thought him amiable."

"Fanny!" Sarah said. She was feeling stunned. She had suspected none of this.

"Then he grew friendly with Hannah," Fanny said, "and wished to help her to win the man she loves. I did not like the scheme, but I must confess I encouraged it. It seemed the perfect opportunity to remove Hannah from George's life and make her happy at the same time. And I hoped that when Lord Laing came back, I could make him love me. I even thought I might have to persuade him to elope with me, for I did not think he would be willing to break his betrothal to you unless you asked for your freedom."

"Oh, my dear," Sarah said, "you have had a narrow and most fortunate escape."

"Yes," Fanny agreed, her voice expressionless. "If he was willing to trick Hannah into matrimony, he cannot be a very honorable man. And he must like money a great deal, for he does not love Hannah, I think. And he certainly knows that she does not love him. I do not believe I would have been happy with him. I am glad that George knocked him senseless this morning. Though I do not know how he did it. I would have thought Lord Laing to be much stronger than he."

"George is very strong," Sarah said proudly. "He fought magnificently. He did not give up even when Win knocked him down."

"You were there!" Fanny accused. Then she laughed with sudden merriment. "Oh, you do love him, Miss Fifield. I know you do. I shall go and tell George so, for I am quite sure he loves you. I know these things. George and I always understand each other."

"No, you will not!" Sarah said in alarm, jumping to her feet again. "You will say nothing, Fanny. And I am reminded that I should go and find his grace to say my good-byes. Do you suppose he is downstairs? Or is he in his room?" She suddenly had distressing mental visions of George stretched out on his bed suffering some deadly reaction to the pummeling he had received earlier.

"I really do not know," Fanny said. She was looking forlorn again.

"I shall go down and see," Sarah said. She held out her hand to Fanny. "If I do not see you again, good-bye, Fanny. I have been very happy to make your acquaintance. And thank you for what you tried to do, though it was wrong of you, of course, to try." Impulsively she withdrew her hand and hugged the girl hard.

Fanny was still in her room when Sarah left. She was standing in the middle of the floor looking utterly dejected. There were tears trickling down her face.

Cranwell was standing at the library window looking out. He ached all over. He felt as if every rib in his body must be broken. Every breath was painful. His knuckles were stiff and sore. And his face stung worse than if he had been lying out in the summer sun for several hours. His jaw ached. His upper lip was cut and swollen. Every facial movement brought sharp pain. He was trying to hold his face immobile. He had given up trying to eat breakfast after a few mouthfuls. He had come to the library to avoid having to talk to anyone.

But he was feeling exultant. He had believed that he had a good chance of winning the fight. But he had had some doubts. Bowen's size and physique gave him an obvious advantage even if he had not had any vigorous exercise in the recent past. But Cranwell had wanted so badly to give the villain a thorough drubbing. He deserved worse. He deserved to die. But at least he must not escape without knowing that he had been severely punished.

And Cranwell had done his best. He had pounded his adversary with all the strength in his body until he had fallen and it was no longer the honorable thing to hit him. And he had the satisfaction of knowing that Bowen was unconscious for several minutes and indeed so groggy afterward that he had had to be half-carried back to the house by both Josh and Penny. He would know for a long time that he had been in a fight. He had a black eye and a split lip, to mention only his facial injuries. And if Cranwell was not mistaken, he believed that Bowen's nose was broken too.

Cranwell had allowed him into the house, but only until noon. By then he was to remove himself.

He thought of Sarah. She had been so alarmed when she came upon them earlier. And she had looked so lovely, her titian hair catching the light of the morning sun beneath the brim of her green bonnet, her eyebrows arched in that look of surprise that had always intrigued him. She had been anxious for his safety. Yes, for *his* safety. She had not seemed to think of Bowen. Well, he had tried to redeem her honor in some small way by punishing her seducer. It was not much, of course. What was a thorough beating in comparison to what Bowen had done to her?

Cranwell sighed and turned away from the window at the same moment as a gentle knock sounded at the door.

"Come in," he called, wincing at the pain the two words caused to his lip. He held his breath.

She came into the room and closed the door behind her. She stood against it and looked across at him.

"I have come because you made me promise to see you before I left," she said breathlessly. And then she came a few steps into the room. "Oh, George, your face!" she said.

"I am sorry," he said. "It is rather a mess, is it not? Will it help to say that Bowen's looks a good deal worse?"

"But I did not want you to get hurt," she said. "George, is it true that you fought because of me?"

He nodded. "Yes, Sarah," he said, "four years too late."

"But why?" she asked. "It was all a long time ago."

"And you have suffered the consequences ever since," he said. "I would have preferred to kill him, Sarah."

"I am glad you believed me," she said. "I am glad of that, at least."

"I deserve no less punishment than he," Cranwell said. "I escaped lightly with these cuts and bruises."

"No," she said in amazement, advancing a few steps

farther into the room. "Why would you say that, George?"

"In some ways I am more to blame than Bowen," he said. "You must have needed so much at that time, Sarah, to be loved, to be made to feel good about yourself again. You were still so very young. And oh, my dear, how you must have suffered in the years previous to our marriage. And how lonely and bewildered you must have been to have no one in whom to confide. I do not wonder that you did not tell me the truth before our wedding day. You must have needed that marriage very badly."

"Don't blame yourself, George," she said. "Not telling you is one of the worst things I have ever done in my life. It was in remorse for that that I knew I must set you free again as soon as possible."

"That is why you behaved as you did, then, when I came to see you?" he asked.

She nodded. "And there was no one after you," she said. "I must tell you that now, George. There has not been anyone since. Only you."

"I should have dragged the truth from you," he said almost viciously. "I was older than you. I had seen more of life. I thought myself wise enough. I cannot forgive myself for having condemned you so hastily and for having humiliated you so publicly. I loved you but did not trust you. And I ended up destroying you far more effectively than Bowen ever did."

"Oh no, George," she said. "You do not know what you say. Do you think the scandal, the shame, was anything compared to . . . to . . . ? Oh no, George. Nothing on this earth could ever be as ugly, as degrading, as utterly hellish as that."

"Oh, my dear," he said, frowning and wincing simultaneously.

"I am glad you gave Win a good beating," Sarah said. "I shall remember that for the rest of my life. Thank you, George. I must see him before I leave and tell him that our betrothal is at an end, though I believe I made myself clear on that point two evenings ago."

"There will be no need," Cranwell said. "I went to his room before coming down here and told him myself."

Sarah's eyebrows shot upward. "You told him that I was not going to marry him?" she said.

He smiled and immediately fingered his swollen lip. "I am afraid I took a great liberty, Sarah," he said apologetically. "I told him that I could not permit him to marry my former and future duchess."

Sarah went very still.

"I am sure you will not have me," he said. "Why should you? I let you down badly at the time when you most needed someone to stand by you. But I can think of no other way to try to atone for what I have done. I cannot amend the past, Sarah, but I can offer you my protection for the rest of your life. The scandal will not end, of course. In fact, it will be renewed and redoubled for a time, I am sure. But I will be at your side to help you face it down. If you will let me, Sarah, I shall see that you never have to face an unpleasantness alone for as long as I live."

Sarah was shaking her head, her face ashen. "No, George," she said, "no. You must not do this. You do not have to atone for the past. There is nothing to atone for. Oh, thank you for being so kind. But no, there is no need. Really there is not."

"My God," he said, striding across the room to her and catching her by the arms. "Have I explained myself so poorly? Have I given the impression that I am offering only out of a sense of obligation? Sarah, do you not know that you are my life? I want you as my wife again because I love you. I always have, though I have spent four years ruthlessly denying the fact to myself."

"No," she said. "You cannot do this, George. Perhaps now you feel that you want me. You have just found out the truth and feel sympathy for me. But I am still a fallen woman. I have been possessed by another man and can never be only yours. You would not be able to forget that."

He gripped her arms more tightly. His face was only

inches from hers. "Sarah," he said, "tell me the truth. Regardless of what the outcome of this meeting will be, do you love me?"

"I have always loved you," she said. "I have never even pretended to myself that I did not."

"I had possessed other women before you," he said deliberately, looking directly into her eyes. "Three, to be exact. One for six months. I slept with them voluntarily. There was no force involved. I enjoyed the experiences. I even fancied myself in love with the one, though there was never any question of marriage. Do you find it impossible to love me, or do you find your love diminished, knowing this?"

"No, of course not," she said.

"Why not?" he asked.

"Because I love you for yourself," she said. "The past is of no concern to me. What you have done makes no difference to the way I feel."

"And why should our attitudes be different just because we are of different gender?" he asked. "I love you, Sarah. It does not matter who possessed you before me. I do not need the assurance that my bride is an untouched vessel."

Sarah swallowed painfully. "I did not fight as much as I might have," she said.

He pulled her roughly against him, gritting his teeth only briefly against the pain. "Oh, my love," he said, "you must leave this. You have tortured your mind with guilt for far too long. Perhaps you need to talk to someone about it all. At some other time, if you wish, you must tell me all about it, put into words all the dark memories that have haunted you for years. But not now, Sarah. I want to hear you tell me again that you love me. I want to hear you say you forgive me enough to marry me. Will you marry me, love?"

She pulled her head away from his shoulder and looked up into his eyes. "Are you very sure, George?" she asked wistfully.

He sighed audibly. "I am not at all sure that I have finished doing violence for this morning," he said. "I have a strong urge to put my hands around your throat, my love, and squeeze very slightly." He looked deeply into her eyes and smiled. He seemed not even to notice the effect on his swollen lip. "Yes, Sarah," he said, "I am very sure. We have lost four years. Let us start to make up for them today. Shall we?"

He bent his head and touched his lips to hers. She responded instantly, putting her arms up around his neck and pressing closer to him. Heat flared instantly. He wrapped his arms around her and opened his mouth over hers. He did not need to coax her lips apart. Her tongue came to meet his and to entice it into the warm softness of her own mouth.

But she pulled away from him before the embrace could advance to any more interesting phase. "Oh, your poor mouth, George," she said. "It must be hurting so. It is all cut inside."

"It hurts to have it away from yours," he said, risking excruciating agony by grinning at her. "I think there must be remarkable healing powers in your lips, love, and even more in your tongue." He moved toward her again.

"Damnation!" he said as someone knocked on the door.

It opened at his bidding and Fanny and Lady Murdoch stood in the doorway.

"Oh, George," Fanny said, her eyes wide with anxiety, "the most provoking thing. When Lady Murdoch sent for her carriage, it was discovered that the axle is completely broken. It will take all day to mend. And we cannot lend our traveling carriage because I promised it yesterday while you were away to Lady Cavendish to go visiting this afternoon. And when we sent into the village to hire the carriage there, we were told that the coachman is dreadfully ill and there is no other. It looks very much as if Lady Murdoch and Miss Fifield will have to stay until tomorrow."

"And if the carriage being broken were not enough, Sarah, my love," Lady Murdoch added, "the groom swears that one of the horses is looking rather lame.

Will you mind very much staying another day, dear? I know you have your heart set on leaving this morning, but really one more day will be neither here nor there. And indeed, my digestion is not all that it should be again. I must need more of those Bath waters. I shall not be sorry for an extra day of rest."

Sarah repressed a smile. They looked an unlikely pair of conspirators.

"I could not agree with you more, ma'am," Cranwell said, moving one step back from Sarah. "One day is really of little importance when I have got Sarah almost to agree to delay here for the rest of her life."

"Almost?" Fanny squealed. "What do you mean by 'almost,' George?"

"I talk too much," Lady Murdoch said. "It is an old woman's infirmity. Not but what I could always talk twice as much as almost anyone else I have ever known. My dear late husband once said that he should have a trumpet to blow when he wished to add a word to the conversation. I perceive, my dear Lady Fanny, that we have interrupted a marriage proposal and that dear Sarah has not yet had a chance to say yes. I think we should run to the stables—that is, that you should run to the stables, for I am just a slow old woman, though the time was when I could have given you or any young lady you could name a good run for your money. What I am trying to say, dear, is that we should notify the groom that perhaps he does not have to do anything drastic to the coach after all. If we are not too late, that is."

"Oh, Miss Fifield . . . Sarah," Fanny said in an agony, "you are going to say yes, are you not? Please, please. I want you so much as a sister."

"You can go and get better acquainted with Lady Murdoch, my girl," Cranwell said, "without further delay. If I have my way, we shall be seeing a great deal of her in the future."

He pointed firmly to the door when Fanny opened her mouth again, and the two ladies left the room in a state of suppressed excitement.

Cranwell reached out for Sarah and pulled her against him again. He rested his forehead against hers. "Perhaps you would be wise to say no," he said. "I have the feeling that those two will be trying their best to rule our lives in the future."

"I have grown to love them both very dearly," Sarah said.

"Heaven help us if they ever find out," Cranwell said fervently. "They are probably out there now with their heads together planning our first child."

"Oh, George," Sarah whispered.

He pulled her closer to him, his cheek against hers. "I want to give you children, Sarah," he said. "I want to fill your life with love. I want to make the past like only a bad dream. Let me love you. Marry me."

"Oh, I do love you, George," she said.

He lifted his head and smiled down at her. "I have never met anyone more reluctant to say yes," he said. "Do you need more persuasion, love? I have a whole arsenal of arguments if I need to use them."

He moved his hands around to cover her breasts and touched his lips lightly to hers again.

"Oh, my answer is yes," she said, pulling back from him a mere two inches. "Of course it is, George. Yes, yes, yes."

He tried to close the gap between their mouths again.

"Of course," she added, putting up a hand and touching his lips lightly with her fingertips, "I would still love to know what all those arguments are."

"Would you, love?" he said tenderly, his mouth smiling, his eyes on her lips. "Would you really? It might take some time. We had better lock the door."

"And throw away the key?" she asked hopefully.

"What a very tempting idea!" he said. "I can tell you of one key you may certainly throw away, Sarah. You already have the key to my heart and have had it for a long time. You may do what you will with it. I shall not want it ever again."

His mouth covered hers in a kiss that contained all

the affection and tenderness and love that had been missing from their lives for four years. The loneliness, the pain, the bitterness were forgotten for the moment. The healing had begun.

They both drew back to smile into each other's eyes.

"Sarah," Cranwell said, "I am the most fortunate man in the world. When I think of the odds against this happening!"

"I know," she said. "I still cannot believe it. George, I do love you so."

They continued to smile for a moment longer before he caught her to him again in a bruising hug. His injuries were forgotten. He sought her mouth once more, and soon everything outside the circle of their arms receded.

It was fortunate that Fanny and Lady Murdoch had put the library strictly out of bounds to all guests and servants for the rest of the morning, for its two occupants completely forgot to lock the door.

About the Author

Raised and educated in Wales, Mary Balogh now lives in Kipling, Saskatchewan, Canada, with her husband, Robert, and her children, Jacqueline, Christopher, and Sian. She is a high school English teacher.

MARY BALOGH

was born and raised in Swansea, South Wales.
She moved to Saskatchewan, Canada, after
graduating from college and taught high school
English for twenty years before retiring
to write full-time. She currently enjoys a stress-free
life at home with her husband and the
youngest of her three children, and with
the family dog and her computer. She has won
the Romantic Times Award for Best New Regency
Writer in 1985, four Waldenbook Awards and a
B. Dalton Award for Bestselling Regencies,
and a *Romantic Times*
Lifetime Achievement Award in 1989.

PASSION BEFORE PRIDE

Theirs should have been the perfect marriage. Sarah was as wildly in love with the Duke of Cranwell as he was with her…until, on their wedding night, Sarah was forced to reveal the secret of her past. And that, amidst great public scandal, ended their marriage almost before it began.

Then in fashionable Bath their paths crossed again. The stunningly beautiful Sarah knew it was folly to think this dashing and sought-after lord would ever get over her shocking betrayal. His fury made it painfully clear that they should separate again, this time forever.

Sarah could find a thousand arguments against the wisdom—or likelihood—of so miserable an edict. For one the duke's ridiculous masculine pride was no match for the sensuous power of her affection for him…as she counted on love to melt the last shred of his resistance to her passionate surrender….

SECRETS OF THE HEART

"One of the Regency genre's brightest stars turns her hand to a longer-length novel and comes up with a winner….When love finally does conquer all, there will be more than one tear in your eye."
—*Romantic Times*

15289

0 71162 00450 2

ISBN 0-451-15289-1